Advanced Praise for T

Peter Donahue has produced a rare anin.... .... as separate novels and also succeed as a single book. He deftly details a brooding, primitive coastline, a juvenile detention center, and the modern I-5 corridor. In these landscapes are genuine souls—strange, hopeful, sometimes tragic—rendered with a remarkable honesty and care, who struggle for nobility in thoroughly compelling narratives.

—Bruce Holbert, author of *Lonesome Animals*, *The Hour of Lead* (winner of the Washington State Book Award), and *Whiskey*

There is much to admire [in Three Sides Water], much to see, and much to experience. Donahue takes us from wild, rocky beaches to deep, dark woods and back again as his varied characters try to get along with their lives in a countryside as beautifully described as it is physically challenging. Like a trip around the peninsula, Three Sides Water is consistently surprising and always engaging, because you never know what you might experience next or what form it might take.

—Lance Weller, author of *Wilderness* (2014 Washington State Book Award finalist)

Praise for *Madison House*

The historical detail is compelling and effectively interlaced with the action. Those interested in the history of the Northwest will find much to savor here.

—*Booklist*

An ambitious novel...Donahue's story is a paean to a significant part of the city's history.

—*The Seattle Times*

Praise for *Clara and Merritt*

For those interested in the history of the Pacific Northwest, author Peter Donahue has an approach akin to that of E.L. Doctorow in meshing prominent historical figures into fictional narrative...Donahue knows Seattle inside and out...There are encounters with real-life players in mid-20th century Seattle: painter Guy Anderson, for example, and union leaders Dave Beck and Harry Bridges. But it is the fictional characters that are utterly engaging—reticent Merritt, spirited Clara, her odd-couple parents, their singular friends.

—*The Seattle Times*

Like the best historical fiction, Donahue's well-paced novel provides a strong sense of place and well-drawn characters to convey its time. Each character tries in his or her own way to make sense of an increasingly confusing world by putting faith in a higher force—the power of art, faith and, of course, the unions that at one time seemed omniscient and omnipotent enough to give working men a sense of solidarity... This is a good summer read that will draw you in with its portraits and leave you knowing more about a fascinating stretch of Northwest history.

—*The Willamette Week*

Three Sides Water

Short Novels

Three Sides Water

Short Novels

Peter Donahue

Ooligan Press
Portland, Oregon

Three Sides Water: Short Novels
© 2018 Peter Donahue

ISBN13: 978-1-932010-98-5

Ooligan Press
Portland State University
Post Office Box 751, Portland, Oregon 97207
503.725.9748
ooligan@ooliganpress.pdx.edu
http://ooligan.pdx.edu

Library of Congress Cataloging-in-Publication Data
Names: Donahue, Peter, author.
Title: Three sides water : short novels / Peter Donahue.
Description: Portland, Oregon : Ooligan Press, 2018.
Identifiers: LCCN 2017050905 | ISBN 9781932010985 (pbk.)
Subjects: LCSH: Novellas, American. | Self-realization—Fiction. | Olympic
    Peninsula (Wash.)—Fiction. | Bildungsromans.
Classification: LCC PS3604.O533 A6 2018 | DDC 813/.6—dc23
LC record available at https://lccn.loc.gov/2017050905

Cover design by Michele Ford
Interior design by Andrea McDonald
Map illustration by Andrea McDonald

Text and image permissions granted. For full list of permissions, see pages 328–329.

References to website URLs were accurate at the time of writing. Neither the author nor Ooligan Press is responsible for URLs that have changed or expired since the manuscript was prepared.

Printed in the United States of America

For Philip Heldrich (1965–2010),
Poet, Writer, Teacher, Friend,
In Memoriam

Knowist thou the joys of pensive thought?
Joys of the free and lonesome heart, the tender, gloomy heart?
Joys of the solitary walk, the spirit bow'd yet proud, the suffering and
the struggle?
 —Walt Whitman, "A Song of Joys"

your true path
like water flows,
dissolves, dances,
falls, rises,
is one with everything
 —Lao Tzu, *Tao Te Ching*

There are those who hate the peninsula on sight and consider it a great
wet thicket, and others who covet it as a secret garden.
 —Murray Morgan, *The Last Wilderness*

Contents

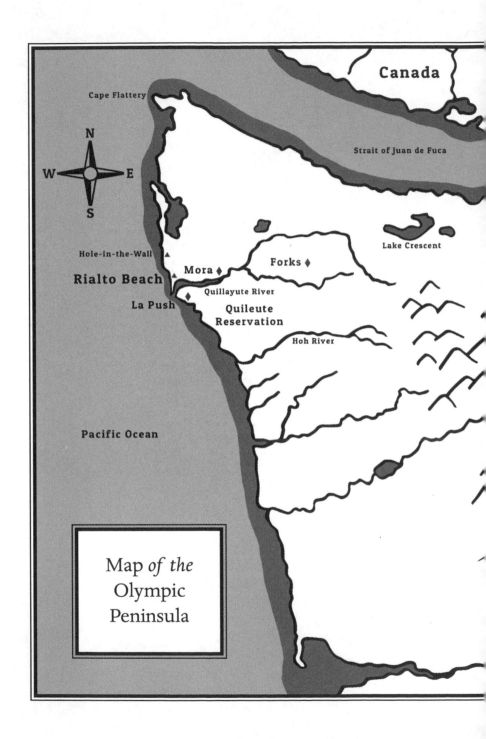

Map *of the* Olympic Peninsula

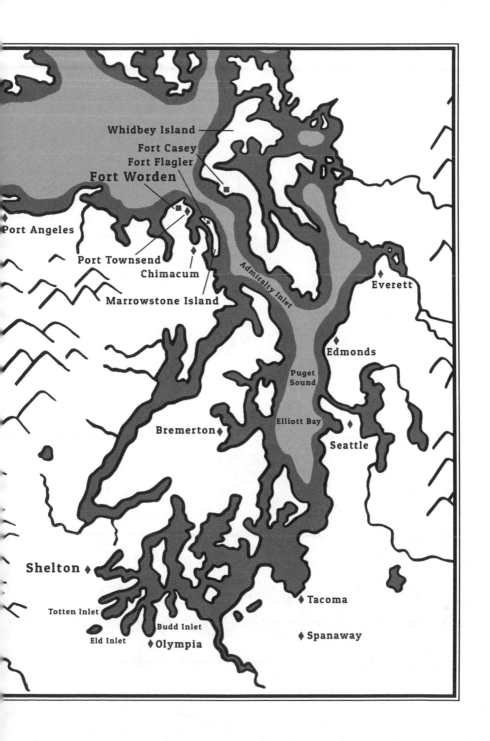

Whidbey Island

Fort Casey
Fort Flagler
Fort Worden

Port Angeles

Port Townsend
Chimacum

Marrowstone Island

Admiralty Inlet

Everett

Edmonds

Puget
Sound

Bremerton

Elliott Bay

Seattle

Shelton

Totten Inlet

Budd Inlet

Eld Inlet

Olympia

Tacoma

Spanaway

ON RIALTO BEACH

Gusts of briny spray off the breakers met me as I climbed over the bone-white drift logs and clambered onto the beach. The sand at Rialto Beach hardly qualified as such, especially given the silky, tan-hued, warm-to-the-toes sand Marie and I were accustomed to from our childhood on Redondo Beach in California. Here the sand was a strip of dark granules that gradually grew larger as the beach sloped upward, becoming tiny pebbles, then marble-size stones, and lastly perfectly spherical rocks the size of a fist. It was the indisputable power of erosion on full display on this swath of beach. The first thing I did was scoop up a handful of the wet granules and gaze at them, their umber, black, viridian, and blue-gray with specks of opaque white mixed in, all arrayed across the skin of my palm and fingers.

It was 1925, the second week of our annual summer stay at the compound Mr. C had built on this remote corner of the continent. I had gotten an early start on my morning outing. It was not yet 7:00 a.m., and the tide was still receding. I had never ventured up the beach alone before because of the fear of the surf and tides that Mr. James, a friend of C's, and so many other locals had instilled in me and my twin sister, Marie. In our five years of coming to Rialto Beach we'd been told horrific tales of rogue waves snatching solitary walkers off the beach and pulling them into the icy cold ocean with its fierce under-tow, of mammoth logs being tossed ashore on the surf and crushing unsuspecting campers, of someone being trapped on an outcropping as the tide rapidly rose, stranding the helpless soul and eventually shredding his tender flesh on the abrasive sea rocks before drowning him. Despite my caution in checking the weather forecast and tide tables and keeping a close eye on my wristwatch, these stories held steady in the back of my mind as I walked up the beach toward the sea stacks that rose ahead like colossal sentries in the foggy distance.

At a rivulet that poured down from the hillside and zigzagged across the beach, the dark sand became finer. The water carved a small canyon into it, and the sand looked firm enough to step on. Yet when I leapt across the rivulet, my foot sank straight up to my ankle. My quick dancer reflexes saved me, though, and I was able to bound forward another step and extract my foot before my shoe filled with water. The incident made me pause and look back at how far I'd come. The house and cabins situated at the bend in the bluff, near the mouth of the river, were no longer visible through the ocean haze. I looked around and realized how alone I was on this remote beach. It was beautiful—*In a bleak sort of way,* I could hear Marie in my head say in her most sarcastic voice—but it was also a little unsettling to be out there. Above the drift logs piled high on the beach, the wind-twisted trees along the hillside appeared deformed and menacing. Beyond these the dark woods seemed impenetrable and foreboding, like something out of the Brothers Grimm. In the other direction, out past the breakers, a foursome of brown pelicans glided past, skimming the ocean's surface. Other than this, the only movement on the beach came from the tireless waves crashing onto the sand and the steady wind rustling the treetops. I told myself not to be a nervous ninny, that there was nothing to be afraid of. I reminded myself I'd been walking only thirty minutes or so and was not very far from the compound. And with this bit of reassurance, I continued up the beach.

I was elated when I reached the Hole-in-the-Wall rock that Tucker, Mr. James's hired hand, had described to me a couple of days earlier. The jagged opening in the enormous sea stack was twenty feet high and just as wide, and since I reached it at optimum low tide I had no trouble walking through as if it were an enormous portal opened just for my entry. At this point along the shoreline, there was in fact a row of three sea stacks that had once formed the headland and now created a kind of demarcation between Rialto Beach and the length of beach extending up the coast of the peninsula to Cape Flattery.

On the other side of the wall, I sat on a dry rock, took the thermos from my rucksack, and poured myself a cup of tea, which smelled especially fragrant in this isolated setting. I alternated sips of the steamy tan liquid with deep gulps of ocean air and took in the rugged splendor that surrounded me. The sea stacks served as a windbreak, cutting down on the chill and mist from the surf. Due to the low tide, the interceding rocks of the headland stretched far out, well above the waterline. Seeing the countless tidal pools among the rocks, I finished my tea and headed off to explore. In some places the uneven rocks were slick with greenish sea slime, elsewhere encrusted with vast colonies of barnacles or covered in jagged beds of mussels no larger than a thumb but numbering in the thousands. As I combed the nooks and crannies among the rocks, my curiosity my only guide, I was glad I didn't have Marie along to distract me—or anyone else for that matter. I was an explorer, adventuresome and independent, on a natural history expedition from Captain Vancouver's ship, which lay at anchor in a nearby cove. My discoveries were all my own.

The rocks were strewn with purple and orange starfish. Sometimes a score or more crowded a section of porous rock, many with arms that stretched several feet across from tip to tip. A few had a whole ganglia of tendril-like arms. The field guide booklet I'd brought with me called these peculiar creatures basket fish because they could be dried in such a way as to make their arms form a basket. The most wondrous creatures, though, were the large sea anemones with their turquoise strands magnified by the clear shallow pools, and then the smaller ones that were fewer in number yet more startling in their violet and pink clusters. Limpets and whelks—which I would have mistook for scallops and snails without the field guide—were abundant as well. There were also a number of prickly sea urchins, including a vibrant red variety. Tucker had told me that the Indians liked to crack open their egg-like center and eat the viscous yellow substance inside. Along the sides of the tidal pools, the rocks were often draped in kelp and seaweed. Twice I slipped and grasped the nearest rock surface to balance myself, each time giving my hand a mild abrasion that left my palm and fingers smarting. Yet, determined to investigate as many tidal pools as I could, I carried on.

I was out on the rocks for an hour or more, planning how I would return to this spot again and explore even farther up the shoreline. After all, our summerlong residence at the compound had only just begun. So as I made my way back to the beach I rehearsed the words I'd choose to describe my outing to a skeptical Marie when I returned to the house, how I would tantalize her with my adventures. I retrieved my rucksack and walked toward the logs, eager to eat my sandwich, drink another cup of tea, and make a few drawings in my sketchbook. At this point I had been drawing for several years, but only recently had people around me, including Mr. C and Lillian, begun to remark on the quality of my sketches. I hoped to do a lot of drawing during our stay at Rialto Beach.

Since the morning air was no longer so bracingly cold, I took off my hat and coat and pushed up the sleeves of my sweater before sitting on a dry log high up on the beach. I could not have been more contented as I sat there quietly and enjoyed my modest repast. After neatly folding the wax paper in which Cook had wrapped my sandwich and emptying the last of the tea from the thermos into my cup, I placed everything back in the rucksack and took out my sketchbook and pencil. I paused with my pencil over the blank page while gazing out upon the expansive ocean.

I can't say when exactly my gaze was broken. I may have heard something, perhaps the soft sound of a foot pressing down into the smooth beach rocks. But before I could form the intention of turning about to look, someone's arms were clutching me and I was being hoisted off my log. My first thought was that a bear had seized me, but I could hear grunting—a man's grunting—as he carried me back toward the trees. I thrashed and kicked, trying to free myself from his hold, but he was twice my size and squeezed me like a Raggedy Ann doll. I might have been screaming; I can't remember. But it wouldn't have mattered. My screams would have disappeared amidst the whirl of the wind and drone of the surf. Moreover, no one was nearby to hear. I do remember jabbing at his forearm and the back of his hand with my pencil until he yelped and knocked it from my grip.

Only when he threw me on the ground at the edge of the woods and stood over me did I see who it was.

"Lou," I said, relieved to see his familiar face and believing for an instant he was only engaging in a little playful roughhousing with me, that if I glanced about I would see Charlie and Mel—the other two members of the road crew who had accompanied us to the Olympic Peninsula—standing there and sharing a good laugh over the scare they'd just given me.

"Just shut up," he growled and reached down, grabbed two fistfuls of my sweater, and ripped it off me, snapping my head forward and nearly yanking my arms from their sockets. I fell back onto the ground and knew that Charlie and Mel weren't there. They couldn't tell Lou that was enough and then offer their apologies for frightening me so.

"Don't, Lou," I said. "Please."

WHEN WE INTUIT THE demesne that lies beyond the opacity of our dim senses, it's like a glimpse of unexpected light in the dark. There, then gone. And while I don't pretend to be an occultist or spiritualist, mystic or clairvoyant, I believe the world is brimming with phenomena both seen and unseen. Whether Mr. Claude Alexander Conlin, the man who had brought us to Rialto Beach that summer—and who hired the brute who attacked me—ever subscribed to such fancies, I could not say definitively. He did, however, exploit those fancies in others.

In the years that Marie and I spent as his stage assistants—1920 to 1926—he claimed to be the world's greatest mentalist, billing himself variously as The Man Who Knows, The Crystal Seer, The Telepathic One, He Who Foresees, and Alexander the Great. Privately, he acknowledged his feats of psychic fluency were predicated on mechanical deceit and the unflagging gullibility of the public. "And little else," he would add. Yet, it was this *little else*, this unidentifiable element, that always left me wondering. Indeed, he liked to keep me and Marie guessing, as when he foretold that our mother would remarry and one month later she did.

"She told you," we protested.

"Ridiculous," he replied. "Your mother would never entrust such knowledge to me. And besides"—here he lowered his chin to peer at us with his swami's gaze—"you should know better than to doubt the mystic undercurrents that swirl beneath the world's sham appearances."

It was true that our mother tended to be a secretive person, unlikely to divulge such details from her private life to Mr. C or anyone else. It was also true that even after handing us over at the tender age of seventeen to the care of Mr. C and his wife, Lillian, for the purpose of advancing our stage careers, our mother was never particularly fond of him. It wasn't that she suspected his motives, but more that she had always been wary of people in general, especially men. As for the "mystic undercurrents," Marie scoffed at such pompous talk. I, on the other hand, preferred to keep an open mind.

Regrettably, no notions of either this world or its nether corollaries—as alluring as these may be—can adequately account for what happened that particular summer. Lou Morton was new to Mr. C's road crew. Charlie, who had been Mr. C's road manager for eight years, recommended him, saying he knew Lou's brother in Los Angeles, and so Mr. C had hired him. But he'd only been with the crew three weeks before this latest trip to Rialto Beach, the spot at the mouth of the Quillayute River where Mr. C had built his summer compound. No one knew him very well, not even Charlie. During the six shows we did in Nevada, Arizona, and Utah prior to the long trek north, no one had even introduced us. He drove the equipment truck and hauled trunks in and out of the theaters. Otherwise I rarely saw him. He was a big, hulking fellow, well over six feet tall, with thinning yellow hair, though he couldn't have been more than thirty years old. He was also moody. He always seemed to be brooding about something or another, almost to the point of being rude when you crossed paths with him. A person could barely get a "Hello" out of him, much less a proper "Good morning." Marie said that he once opened a backstage door for her, which she thought gentlemanly of him, but in the next instant he reached out and touched her hair. When she jumped back and demanded to know what he was doing, he said he'd spotted a bug and was going to pluck it out. He didn't apologize for startling her, and from then on every time she saw him, his face burned red and he rushed out of her presence. I joshed and said he had a crush on her, but really, he gave us both the willies, and that's why we tried our best to steer clear of him.

I have no idea why Mr. C brought him along to Rialto Beach except that was just Mr. C's way. He liked having his entourage close at hand, road crew and all. Even when he took time off from performing, he wanted his hirelings attending to him—which was why Marie and I always had to travel to his preposterous outpost on the Northwest coast. He said he enjoyed our companionship too much to abandon us to the dusty summer heat and noise of Los Angeles.

And yet, it was no easy journey from Los Angeles to Rialto Beach. It took nearly a week. For the first two years we would ride the train to Seattle, then board a boat to Port Angeles, take a car to the end of Lake Crescent, board a small steam ferry the length of the lake, take another car to the township of Forks, and finally ride a horse-drawn wagon the rest of the way through the woods to the settlement of Mora, where we would stay at the hotel owned and operated by Mr. James, one of Mr. C's longtime friends. Meanwhile, during these first years, Mr. C oversaw the construction of his compound a short distance away on Rialto Beach, so named after the many Rialto Theaters he performed in across the country. Shortly after the main house and adjacent cabins were constructed at Rialto Beach, the road around Lake Crescent was completed and the road to Mora properly graded for automobile passage, and we could then drive all the way from Port Angeles.

Once our arduous travel was behind us and we arrived at Rialto Beach, I was quite content. I could do all the drawing I wanted. But poor Marie, she would have preferred to stay in Los Angeles. Unfortunately, Mr. C never liked being with just one of us. It had to be both or neither—and he preferred both. We were, after all, "The Nartell Twins," Marie and Marguerite, his "tender young ferns," as he began to call us shortly after making our acquaintance in the Los Angeles hotel room where he, Lillian, and our mother arranged for us to join his act. He officially changed our last name to Nartell, which he felt suited the exotic dance routine we would be performing as part of his show better than Johnson, our real last name. There were plenty of times, right from the start, when we wanted to drop the phony stage name, forget we were twins, and simply be ourselves—Marie Johnson and Marguerite Johnson. It was Marie, though, who made the mistake, prior to our last trip to Rialto Beach, of suggesting to Mr. C that she might stay in Los Angeles to oversee the cleaning and mending of the outfits, et cetera, et cetera. Mr. C would have none of it.

"That won't do," he said. "Roy will see to all that." Roy Heinman was Mr. C's business manager. He oversaw all the business and operational details for Claude Alexander Conlin, who by 1925 made more money than Harry Houdini, Douglass Fairbanks, or Babe Ruth. Indeed, Roy was also one of the few from Mr. C's entourage who was excused from accompanying him to the Olympic Peninsula. "Besides," he added, "Marguerite would be lonesome without you."

This wasn't necessarily true, but I didn't say anything. In point of fact, a short sisterly separation would have done us both good, and we knew it. Since birth—seven minutes apart: Marie at 3:57 a.m. and me at 4:04 a.m., October 3, 1902—Marie and I had rarely been out of one another's company for longer than an hour or two. Such were simply the circumstances fate handed us, as it does most twins. From those early childhood years with our parents, to our boarding with the nuns at St. Anne's at age twelve after our father's disappearance, to our joining Mr. C's stage show five years later, the contiguity of our twinship was rarely broken. The truth was we were both highly independent spirits, as twins often are, and we would readily have welcomed the summerlong separation, had Mr. C allowed it. We knew our lifelong union, our mirroring bond—she right-handed, I left-handed—extended far beyond mere nearness to one another. We were synchronized in an almost preternatural way. Yet, as we continued to slide into adulthood, this synchronicity grew somewhat tiresome for both of us. We each felt the need to exercise our independence one from the other—our autonomy, if you will—and to this end we increasingly made efforts to stay out of one another's business. Plus, Marie found herself more and more preoccupied by her interest in Charlie (and his in her), which was probably the only reason she gave in to Mr. C's insistence on dragging her to the Olympic Peninsula for the fifth year in a row. That and the fact that we both knew a person did not argue with Claude Alexander Conlin—period.

And hence we and the rest of his train of underlings arrived at Rialto Beach in mid-June. Our first evening back was quite celebratory, though Lou withdrew early from the festivities and wasn't seen for the rest of the night. Right after dinner several locals from Forks and Mora dropped in to visit, people Mr. C had befriended over the years, folks who enjoyed his generous hospitality and bonhomie. There was whiskey smuggled from Canada and ale brewed in the backwoods shed of a Clallam County commissioner—a high-potency concoction worthy of the commissioner's Scottish heritage. Meanwhile, a short man with a white beard and a fisherman's cap played the mandolin accompanied by his son, a stout-faced lad squeezing the concertina. When a fiddler showed up and started sawing away at his strings, Charlie took Marie by the hand and led her through a schottische dance. When they were done, he planted a kiss on her cheek and they bowed as everyone applauded.

As usual, there were requests for Mr. C to perform magic tricks and read someone's fortune, which he politely declined to do, saying he needed to rest his powers and perhaps in a few days he would invite everyone back for a small demonstration.

"Furthermore," he told the assembled guests as he turned to Marie and me, "my beautiful assistants are tired as well. The long trek has made my little ferns droop."

Everyone laughed, and taking our cue, Marie and I blushed.

"I'm sure the region's moisture will replenish us," I tossed out, contributing to the general amusement.

Unamused, Marie leaned into me and whispered, "If it doesn't drown us first."

As stated, she wasn't fond of Rialto Beach. And who could blame her? Was any place more remote in all the forty-eight states? Until

Mr. C showed it to us on the map four years ago, neither of us had ever heard of the Olympic Peninsula. And once we arrived that first time, the frighteningly jagged mountains, the towering trees, the bears and wolves prowling the impenetrable forest, the icy streams racing down every hillside, the turbulent ocean storms, the incessant rain…all these elements exacerbated our already foreboding sense of removal from the civilized world. At times it seemed as if Rialto Beach were the loneliest place on the planet. In addition, Marie and I knew it would be impossible to leave on our own, that once there we were effectually held captive by the dense forest, torrential tributaries, and pounding ocean surf that penned us in.

Nevertheless, a good deal of activity took place in the vicinity. There was Forks, of course—a logging town, but a bona fide town nonetheless—yet because it was a dozen miles inland, going there required a car, and Mr. C kept only one at the compound, his Franklin sedan, and refused to let Marie or me (or Lillian for that matter) learn how to drive it. Only a mile from Rialto Beach, however, was Mora, where the Dickey River flowed into the Quillayute River. In addition to the motel owned by Mr. James, Mora had a post office, saloon, dry goods store, and several houses. Within a two- or three-mile radius of Mora, several fishing camps clung to the silted banks of the two rivers, and a handful of farmsteads had taken hold in the small prairies situated throughout the forest. There was also La Push, just across the mouth of the Quillayute, where the Quileute Indians had their reservation. It had several streets lined with clapboard houses, a mercantile store, a schoolhouse, a smokehouse, two church buildings, and several piers with shacks at the end of them. Because it was tribal land and going there seemed like trespassing to us, Marie and I had never ventured across the river to visit.

Then, finally, there was Rialto Beach. Mr. C's compound was built into the bend in the bluff so that to the left it overlooked the mouth of the river and to the right the beach and open ocean. It included the two-story main house with its wraparound sitting porch, three sizeable cabins, a carriage house that held the Franklin and a disused buckboard wagon, and a treehouse constructed among the sturdy limbs of a big-leaf maple tree located a dozen yards up the slope. Among all the structures, including an apartment above the carriage house, there were fourteen beds, and nearly all were occupied while Mr. C was in residence at Rialto Beach. My favorite part of the compound, though, was unquestionably the treehouse, where I would often go with my sketchbook and pencil to draw.

In addition to his usual entourage, Mr. C had let drop at dinner that his good friend the comedic actor Harold Lloyd would be travelling from Los Angeles in just a few weeks to visit. Marie and I had seen his most recent picture, *Safety Last!*, at the Granada Theater in Los Angeles the year before and had laughed ourselves senseless at his adorable antics—so we were excited by the news of his visit. How Mr. C had ever convinced him to come all the way up to the Olympic Peninsula, I couldn't imagine. Perhaps Harold Lloyd, like Mr. C, was an avid sportsman and the two would go hunting and fishing the whole while. That's all I could figure.

Before the Hollywood star's visit to Rialto Beach, though, Mr. C had various projects to keep him occupied, one of which was photography, in particular taking photographs of Marie and me. He liked to say we were ideal models for what he termed his pictorialist aesthetic. So on the second evening following our arrival, he told us to be ready first thing the next morning for a photographic session—"While the dew is still wet on the grass," as he put it—and though Marie and I objected to having to rise so early—"Please can't we sleep in one more day?" we pleaded—he would have none of it.

SO MARIE AND I were up early the next morning, still in our nightshirts, sitting across from one another at the large wooden table in the kitchen, sipping the coffee that Cook made and eating our usual toast and orange marmalade, when Mr. C entered and declared it a most glorious day for taking pictures.

Marie yawned and said, "So what?"

Mr. C ignored her.

He was already a tall man, yet in his knickers and calf-high boots he looked as if he were standing on stilts. He also wore a felt campaign hat and a thigh-length canvas jacket trimmed in leather along the collar and side pockets. His grooming never took a vacation and, as ever, he was clean shaven and walked in the olfactory aura of his favorite fragrance, "Eau de Lausanne"—which, because he purchased it at a swank menswear shop on Rodeo Drive, Lillian called "Eau de L.A." But that was just Lillian. Though several years younger than Mr. C, she had his number, as the saying goes. And even as she put up with his personal affectations and various shenanigans—and, I believe, genuinely loved him—little about her husband escaped her attention.

"What, pray tell, shall be today's theme?" I asked Mr. C in what for me was a rare display of sarcasm.

Before each photo session, he would declare a theme he wished us to adopt and we would try to dress accordingly. It might be Indian maidens, Arabian concubines, Mayan slave-girls, London waifs, Eskimo nuk-nuks, Celtic sprites, or Russian princesses, but really all that mattered was that we donned something sheer and revealing and for effect maybe added a few feathers or a fur hand muff.

"Woodland nymphs," he said. "So get ready."

A half hour later the three of us were trudging off into the woods while everyone else in the house and cabins still slept soundly. The sun had risen by then and the woods, though wet and misty, were illuminated by shafts of yellow sunlight. We walked along a puncheon trail that had been built the year before by Charlie and his crew. Mr. C carried his camera box in his right hand and the tripod over his left shoulder while Marie and I lagged behind, hugging our matching wool mackinaws about our bodies. Then, right where the wood planks ended and turned into a narrow dirt trail snaking into the forest, I glimpsed a figure up the slope to our right, perhaps a hundred feet away.

"Who's that?" I said to Marie, who was walking several steps ahead of me. She stopped and looked to where I pointed.

"Where?" she asked. "I don't see anyone."

I had already lost sight of the figure. That part of the woods was thick with alder trees and the drooping boughs of young hemlock. A thick undergrowth covered the forest floor. In addition, the morning sunlight created all manner of deceptive shadows. I peered a few moments longer at the spot where I thought I saw the figure and decided it must have been one of the men from the crew relieving himself or a trick of the light.

"Maybe you saw a bear," Marie said, trying to frighten me.

"That's quite possible," chimed in Mr. C, who stopped several yards up the trail to see what was keeping us. "*Ursus americanus* is all through these woods. But he's typically very shy."

Mr. C handed the camera to Marie and the tripod to me and walked ahead to scout out sites where he could pose us in one of his tableaus. We eventually found him standing before an enormous fir tree, studying its trunk.

"Here," he said and took the equipment from us. As he went about setting up the tripod and securing the camera to it, I scanned the woods for bears. They didn't worry me. I just wanted to see one. Meanwhile, Marie took her slim cigarette case from her coat pocket, removed a cigarette, and lit it with a small silver lighter. No one spoke until Mr. C instructed us to remove our coats and for each of us to stand on one side of the tree trunk with hands and forehead pressed against it.

Marie stomped out her cigarette and gave me an exasperated glance as we removed our mackinaws and approached the tree.

"Shoes off too," he said as he screwed a lens onto the camera.

We removed our shoes, and when Marie tossed one of hers at Mr. C, he didn't even glance up, but just said, "That'll do."

The forest floor was soft and almost ticklish, but very cold. In our white chiffon-and-lace nightgowns—negligees really—Marie and I leaned into the tree. The bark was coarse, and an amber-colored pitch stained its thick grooves here and there. Marie and I could not even see one another from our opposite sides of the trunk. It would have taken The Nartell Quadruplets to reach all the way around its circumference.

"How old is this tree?" I asked, looking up through the lower branches to its crown. "Older than America?"

"Much older," Mr. C said and looked up at us from the camera. "Are you ready?"

We pressed our palms and foreheads against the trunk as instructed and he took several shots of us. He then had us sit at the base of the trunk, facing each other and leaning forward to grasp one another's arms. By now, without our coats or shoes, the morning chill had made us both, well, *attentive*, and with this advantage in mind, Mr. C next had us pose with our backs against the trunk and—as Marie rolled her eyes at me—drape our arms languorously over our heads.

From the fir tree we moved on to a marshy bed of skunk cabbage where we crouched in among the bunchy green leaves, which, low to the ground, gave off a faintly sweet civet odor. Mr. C had us hold the center stem of the plant in one hand and with the other cup the yellowish sheath at the end of the stem while gazing with woodland amorousness at the knobby red stamen within.

"*Really*, Mr. Conlin," Marie said as he snapped his photographs. "Does Lillian know what a naughty man you are?"

"She knows," he said bluntly.

Most everyone knew of Mr. C's photographic predilections, and although he assured us that the photos remained in his private collection, we knew he occasionally bestowed them upon male friends and associates as gifts, including photos far racier than those he took in the woods that day. Yet, when he hinted once at holding a private exhibition at his home in Los Angeles, Marie and I threatened never to pose for him again if he dared do such a thing. That said, we enjoyed indulging him. The sessions were usually playful outings, a chance to poke fun at Mr. C, and young as we were, we felt flattered by the attention. We also liked to speculate that the photographs might help us get into the movies someday.

We spent another two hours in the woods. He had us straddle the trunk of a spruce tree that had fallen beside the trail. We put red columbine in our hair, hung long stringy Methuselah's beard over our arms and shoulders, and pirouetted through the salal and sword ferns. We even removed our gowns and covered ourselves with cedar boughs as if they were large fans.

Mr. C was delighted with how the session was going when we came upon a sprawling big-leaf maple, an old, solitary tree with limbs that stretched out and away from its massive trunk, making a small clearing at its base.

"Come on, girls," he called. "Up you go."

Mr. C, as I've said, was a tall man. Six feet and a half, Lillian once told us, adding, "It's the half you need to watch out for."

Marie and I, on the other hand, just cleared five feet and barely weighed a hundred pounds each.

"That's awfully high," said Marie. She had her wool mackinaw back on and pulled it tightly about herself as she looked worriedly at the old maple tree.

This was how it was with her. She was generally the more cautious and I the more daring. I was the first to attempt anything, whether it was trying a backflip, riding a bicycle, or plunging into the surf at Santa Monica beach. Identical twins are funny that way. They might match one another in appearance down to the daintiest detail, yet temperamentally they can be true opposites. Our own mother had difficulty telling us apart, and it was downright impossible for the nuns at Saint Anne's to do so, but all anyone ever had to do to distinguish one from the other—me from Marie and vice versa—was to genuinely come to know us.

"I'll go," I said, eliciting a predictable scowl from Marie. There was a crook in the trunk of the tree where I could get a handhold. I hoisted myself up to the lowest limb and from there climbed up to the next.

"It's easy," I called down.

Now Marie had no choice but to follow and she knew it, given that Mr. C refused to photograph us separately. So she doffed her mackinaw and stood on Mr. C's shoulders while I reached down and pulled her by the hands. With only minor whimpering, she let me guide her up the tree before she sat herself down on one of the sturdier branches and announced she would not go an inch farther.

Mr. C proceeded to take a number of photographs with Marie staying right where she was while I clambered about from limb to limb. It was liberating to find one perch after another and gaze out through the leafy branches. I could even see the ocean in the distance.

"Okay, girls, that's enough," Mr. C shouted finally.

Marie, however, who'd been content to sit perfectly still in the tree, was suddenly stricken with fear at the prospect of climbing down. I had to coax her, inch by inch, back the way she'd come until she was able to reach one leg down and step onto Mr. C's shoulders. Just as she extended her second foot down, though, she took hold of a particularly mossy branch, lost her grip, and fell right on top of Mr. C, knocking him down before tumbling onto the wet ground.

"*Owwwww*," she screamed and reached for her ankle as I dropped from the tree and Mr. C crouched at her side. When I asked if she was hurt, she just glared at me and moaned.

Mr. C took her calf and foot in his hand and ran his fingers around the circumference of her ankle. "I don't believe it's broken," he said. "It's probably just twisted."

"Why'd you make me climb that stupid tree?" she screeched at us, grimacing. "If I can't dance ever again, it'll be your fault."

Then Mr. C turned so baleful and apologetic, begging his little woodland nymph to forgive him, that I became furious and wanted to pounce on his back and bite both his ears off just to make him stop.

"Valeska can take your place," I shot right back at Marie, standing over the two of them defiantly. Valeska was one of Mr. C's other stage assistants. She was several years older than Marie and me, and married, which exempted her from having to travel to Rialto Beach.

"You let go of my hand," Marie accused.

"How dare you," I answered and almost began to cry.

"Now, now girls," said Mr. C. He then turned to Marie. "I'll carry you, dear, and Marguerite will have to carry the camera and tripod."

Marie gave me a self-satisfied scowl as Mr. C scooped her into his arms, and after I gathered up the equipment, we set off.

We had walked a good ways into the woods, and yet every time I asked to stop for a rest she complained that her ankle was throbbing and couldn't we hurry. Finally I said that she and Mr. C should go on ahead without me. "If a bear comes along I'll just take his picture," I told them.

"Thank you," Mr. C said without so much as a glance back at me, and he proceeded down the trail with Marie grasping his neck.

I took a short rest, enjoying the stillness of the forest after they disappeared from view, and then picked up the equipment and slogged on. I was about ready for another rest when I reached the puncheon trail and found Lou Morton sitting atop a tree stump, smoking a cigarette. His sudden appearance gave me a start, yet I caught myself and smiled as if happy to see him. From where we were, I couldn't make out the house and cabins through the trees, but I knew they were not far off. How long had he been sitting there, I wondered, and did he see me coming down the trail toward him? And also—why was he there at all?

"Hi, Lou."

"Hey," he said gruffly. Seated on the stump, he was maybe four feet off the ground, reminding me of the hookah-smoking caterpillar in *Alice's Adventures in Wonderland*. And just as bewildered little Alice had with the Caterpillar, I found him rather off-putting. He seemed to squint at me as he took a drag from his cigarette.

"Wha'cha doin'?" I asked in as friendly a manner as I could muster.

He shrugged and exhaled smoke through the corner of his mouth, causing his face to distort momentarily.

"Did you see my sister and Mr. Conlin walk by?"

"Marguerite?" he muttered. "Uh-un. I didn't see her or Mr. Conlin. Neither one."

How was that possible? I thought. They weren't more than a few minutes ahead of me on the trail. Then I realized that he'd mistaken me for Marie. But I simply wanted away from him as fast as I could politely manage, so I didn't bother to tell him I was Marguerite, not Marie.

"Where's Charlie?" he asked. There was something snide in the way he asked this, which I didn't appreciate. Also, I realized, he figured I would know where Charlie was because he believed I was Marie, and she and Charlie seemed to be keeping more regular company with each passing day.

"I have no idea," I said, and then, changing my mind suddenly about straightening him out about who was who, I added, "*Marie* hurt her ankle, and Mr. Conlin said he was going to send someone to Forks to get the doctor since the telephone wire was down this morning from last night's wind." It was true that the wind had brought a tree down across the wire along the road, but as for Mr. C sending someone to Forks to fetch the doctor, I made that part up just to have something to say. "Maybe you should go see," I said for extra measure.

He looked at me for an instant, as if trying to figure out who I was, then rubbed his cigarette out on the stump. The next moment he hopped down onto the puncheons with such a thud that the boards shook and I nearly lost my balance. I thought for a moment he might be a gentleman and offer to unburden me of the photography equipment, but he didn't. All he said was, "Okay," and stomped down the trail back toward the compound. Even with my having to lug the camera equipment the rest of the way by myself, I felt relieved he was gone.

MARIE SPENT THE ENTIRE next week lying in bed in our room or on the divan in front of the fireplace downstairs. Mr. C had brought Epi, his Mexican houseboy in Los Angeles, with him to Rialto Beach for the first time, and now Epi (short for Epifanio) spent most of his time fetching for Marie whatever her little heart desired—tea, cookies, magazines, an extra blanket, an extra pillow, a hot water bottle, whatever she wanted. She acted as if she were a total invalid when in fact all that was wrong with her, according to the doctor dragged in from

Forks that morning after all, was a sprained ankle. At some point I told her about my encounter with Lou in the woods, but she was still in a pout with me and didn't show any interest, so I didn't mention how he'd confused me with her and asked if I knew where Charlie was. I understood good and well she was behaving so spoiled simply in protest for being made to come to Rialto Beach in the first place.

"This is your lay-down strike, isn't it?" I said after three days of watching her being pampered.

"What of it?" she replied, and I just had to smile at her brazenness. Try as I might to hold a grudge against my sister, I never could. Her self-assurance, often bordering on impudence, always amused me.

Her whole act gave me the chance, furthermore, to get out and about on my own, unaccompanied and unattended, free to do as I pleased. In the days following our photo sessions in the woods, Mr. C went off fishing with his friend and drinking buddy Mr. James. As owner of the Mora Hotel, Mr. James was essentially the mayor of the unincorporated hamlet since everything there revolved around the hotel. In many ways, I preferred it to the compound. Mr. C would not bring as many of his entourage when we'd stayed there, which meant we would mingle more with the locals from Mora and Forks. Of course, Marie didn't like the smaller quarters of the hotel and preferred having Mr. C's people around, including Charlie, with whom her flirtations had become increasingly overt. I could never comprehend why Mr. C wanted so many people along, except to have a ready audience whenever he wished to hold forth as master of his realm, or perhaps simply to ensure he always had ready companions for his fishing or hunting excursions. As for myself (and even more so Marie), fishing and hunting held no appeal. I went one time during our second summer on the peninsula just for the experience, and then only because Tealie Taylor, the postmistress in Mora, was also going and was someone I'd begun to have a friendly acquaintance with. I realized the first night out, though, that no matter how capable a woman was—and many local women like Tealie were quite skilled at fishing and hunting—she was still expected to assume her customary role when it came time for setting up camp for the night. Which is to say, she was expected to wait hand and foot on the men.

There was also the problem of Tucker, a local boy hired by Mr. James each year to tend to the equipment when the men went on one of their adventures. I say *boy*, but really he was about my age, in his early twenties. Despite his rough manners, he was terribly good looking. He was slim and fit and had a thatch of dark hair on his head as thick as a Malamute's mane. He bragged that he worked as a timber cruiser most of the year, riding horseback up and down the length of the peninsula scouting the best plats for logging. He lived in Forks. The lower management types that worked for the true timber barons, who themselves resided in Port Townsend and Seattle, tried their best to establish a township there. Some brought their families. And for the most part, given the town was literally at the end of the road—the terminus of the turnpike from Port Angeles, which had yet to be extended beyond Forks on that side of the peninsula—they didn't do too badly. Forks had become a full-fledged town while Mora was just an outpost of sorts, the site for what Mr. James imagined would one day be a resort for outdoorsmen. Forks had a mayor and a marshal, a two-story school, a drug store with a soda fountain, a hardware store, three restaurants, two hotels, half a dozen taverns, and a railroad station. A grid of streets where the management men and local merchants had built their houses was laid out on either side of Main Street, and the half dozen mills that encircled the town employed a good many men. There was occasionally union strife in the woods and mills, but for the most part the town seemed relatively peaceful and generally prosperous.

Tucker came to Forks seeking work when he was fifteen and immediately found a job shoveling sawdust into silos in the mill yards. "And all these years later I'm still here," he said when we first met the year before. "But now I'm cruising timber, which is about the most plum job a guy like me can have."

"What do you mean a *guy like you*?" I said, looking askance at him. We were on the porch of the recently completed house at Rialto Beach, and I was standing watching him as he sat on the top step tying red and black pieces of knitting yarn onto fishing hooks, preparing for the next day's steelhead fishing trip with Mr. C and Mr. James.

"A guy without any family or schooling," he answered with a quick glance up at me.

I then felt like a heel for making him account for himself like that and resolved not to question him further. Yet, I must have mistook his reaction because without any prompting he went on to explain how he'd lost his mother and father when he was just a kid and learned early on how to take care of himself. He told me he wanted eventually to quit the timber business and team up with Mr. James to run his resort in Mora. I felt bad for his having had such a rough upbringing, but at the same time he had a boisterousness I didn't quite appreciate. Sure, he'd had to make his own way, but did he have to always be so cocksure of himself and what he wanted?

"You see, fellas like your Mr. Conlin will come up here from California and from all over. They'll drop their families off at the hot springs at Sol Duc and then come out to Mora to hunt and fish."

I had to admit, it was a sensible plan. Resort lodges were being built all over this area. In fact, on our second trip to the Olympic Peninsula, Mr. C had rented out the entire lodge at the Sol Duc Hot Springs. It was a new three-story lodge half a city block long and set deep in the big timber just past Lake Crescent on the north side of the peninsula. It was famous, of course, for its hot springs—the stinky, sulfurous holes in the ground that had been lined with cement and turned into oversized bathtubs. The waters purportedly had healing properties. After reserving the springs for his twenty-two guests, Mr. C proposed that we all go into the water *au naturel*. He said this was how the Finns and Russians did it, people without our Puritan inhibitions. He himself laid claim to a hybrid lineage of French (Claude), Greek (Alexander), and Irish (Conlin), a combination that, he asserted, accounted for any number of his quirks and unusual habits. Marie refused to go in without a bathing suit, but I consented, thinking we were so far from anywhere or anyone, what difference would it make? But when he failed to cajole Marie into joining us, Mr. C called the whole thing off. The next morning, however, I awoke before anyone else and tiptoed out to the steaming pool in my robe, slipped bare naked into the bracingly hot water, and concluded that Mr. C was absolutely right: au naturel was the superior method.

Now Tucker was back for another season, this time preparing to accompany Mr. C and Mr. James elk hunting, and again I encountered him on the front porch of the house, where he was cleaning and oiling the rifles.

"I thought I might see you," he said. I didn't like the mischievous curl of his half smile. "Where's your sister?"

Apparently he had no difficulty telling us apart. I mentioned Marie's sprained ankle and looked out across the mouth of the Quillayute

River. A couple of Indians from La Push were paddling a canoe, the kind made from a cedar trunk, upriver to Mora, probably to do some trading. Closer to the beach a cormorant, black atop the colorless beached log on which it perched, dried its outstretched wings, looking more like the phoenix rising from the ashes than the simple shore bird it was.

"Mr. Conlin likes bringing you girls with him, doesn't he?" Tucker squeezed oil from a tin into a rag and rubbed down the wood stock of the rifle he held.

I picked up on the drift of his question and wasn't going to allow it. "We like it here," I replied. "We want to come."

He paused, nodded, said only, "It's good country," and resumed his task.

I turned my attention from the river to the ocean. A heavy wind pushed the surf hard onto the beach and, it being high tide, nearly to the bluff. "Does anyone ever go out to those?" I asked, pointing to the wide sea stacks that rose out of the ocean just offshore.

"Haven't you ever walked out there?" he asked in return. "You get a good low tide and it's just a hop and a skip. Not all of them, but the closer-in ones, sure."

I felt the fool for having to admit I'd never walked out to them. In past years, though I might have been willing to do something mildly adventuresome like that, I'd always relented to Marie, who just wasn't the type. Even if she did agree to take a long walk on the wild beach, she wouldn't get more than three feet from the house before she complained about the wind giving her an earache or some such and insisted on going back to the house and have Cook bring her a cup of hot cocoa.

"They say the Indians used to climb that big one when the Haidas would come down to raid their village for women and slaves. They'd haul all their valuables to the top and pull up the rope ladders after them, and if the Haidas tried to climb up our Indians here would pour boiling seal oil on them and bean them with rocks."

I laughed at that and looked at the largest of the sea stacks. It rose just beyond the cluster of shacks that made up La Push across the river. It had a good stand of trees on its flat top, and I could well imagine the Quileute taking refuge from the marauding Haidas up there.

"I'll look up the tide table when I get back," Tucker said, "and if there's a good low tide I'll take you up the beach to the Hole-in-the-Wall. That's a really good one."

I had to think on this before answering. I wanted to explore the sea stacks, yes, but I wasn't sure I wanted Tucker as my guide. I already felt he was too forward and didn't want to encourage him. I don't think I could have put up with his self-sure manner any longer than I already had to. And I didn't want him thinking I was available. It wasn't that I'd vaulted my heart or taken a vow of chastity or any such thing. It just seemed that with things warming up between Marie and Charlie, there was enough sparking going on already. Plus, I didn't want the distraction from my drawing. On the other hand, I thought as I stood on the porch, Tucker was certainly knowledgeable about things like wildlife and sea stacks and tides, and I could probably learn something from him. So I told him maybe, and added as a precaution, "That is, if I'm not busy," and this seemed to satisfy him.

THE NEXT MORNING MR. C left on a hunting trip with Mr. James and Tucker to track the elk that, according to Mr. James, were heading into the high country after wintering in the lowlands. Things quieted down around the compound once they departed and those of us left behind occupied ourselves each in our own way. Lillian responded to the scores of requests for psychic readings that Mr. C received each week by mail. Epi, who mostly kept house while Mr. C was around, entered the kitchen and cooked his favorite Mexican dishes—chicken in mole sauce, beef tamales, and *siete mares* with clams, mussels, and octopus—which we all ate happily. Cook sent the two Indian kitchen girls home to La Push and went into Forks to drink beer in the taverns. Meanwhile, Charlie and the other two road crew members, Mel and Lou, worked on building another treehouse on the property and afterward went fishing. Marie, on the other hand, kept to her bed and the sitting room couch, reading old copies of *Variety* and *Munsey's Magazine* and eating Turkish delight from Zanzabelle's in Hollywood.

This left me on my own to do as I pleased. I drove with Cook into Forks and had a piece of chocolate cake and an ice cream soda at the drug store fountain and then caught a ride back with Charlie, who'd come into town for a bag of nails from the hardware store. Later that evening I started reading *Miranda* by Antoni Lange—a Pole, despite the Italian first name. It was a novel Mr. C had recommended Marie and I both read. It was all about free love and mediumism and was full of Polish and Hindi names I couldn't pronounce. Mr. C was a big reader and recommended books to us all the time. Though Marie never read any of them, I tried to, even though my literary tastes ran counter to Mr. C's. He liked foreign novels that explored phantasmagorical and salacious (some might say "vulgar") topics, books such as *The Haunted Woman* or *The Constant Nymph*, both of which he obtained in England and gave gift-wrapped to me and Marie. I, meanwhile, preferred good American adventure stories of the sort Rex Beach and Zane Grey wrote: books that when you're on the road touring with Alexander the Great, the Crystal Seer, the Man Who Knows—riding the interminable train to the next podunk Midwest town, holed up in another sweltering hotel in Jackson, Mississippi, or Mobile, Alabama, or sitting backstage at another theatre house in some East Coast city—will set you down in the rugged Sierra mountains or ice-cold Alaska and make you forget where (and who) you are. So I read maybe fifty pages of *Miranda*, right to where the main character, Jon Podobłoczny, is administered the drug Nivridium by the Ministry of Love, and then put the book down and fell asleep.

The next morning I began to grow restless, as sometimes happened way out there with so few neighbors, no stores, no movie house, no nothing except the endless woods in one direction and the endless ocean in the other. Even my sketchbook bored me, and so I offered to help Lillian with the mail-order psychic readings. She explained that it was paramount to keep the responses uniform, and since she had honed a method that worked exceedingly well, she answered all the requests herself. She allowed me to lend her secretarial assistance, however, opening the letters and addressing and sealing the return envelopes with her typed and signed responses inside. Each response was composed on "Alexander, The Man Who Knows" letterhead that included his logo with the words "Av Yaga Bombay" (made-up gibberish) and an etching of Mr. C in his turban peering at a crystal ball held by a skeleton hand. Each missive was personally signed *C. Alexander* with an ebony fountain pen in Lillian's own hand.

These mail-order psychic readings were just one of Mr. C's lucrative ventures in his ever-expanding monopoly on the mentalist market. The requests were generated through two sources: his stage performances, at the conclusion of which audience members could obtain in the lobby a version of the question cards used during the show and mail them in, and advertisements for psychic readings that ran in the leading ladies' magazines and included a facsimile of the same question card. And since a single dollar bill was enclosed in each envelope—to cover the cost of shipping and handling, according to the small-print instructions on the back of the card, which also included a disclaimer attesting to the subjective and idiosyncratic nature of each psychic reading, and hence exemption from liability in guaranteeing its accuracy—the mail-order readings were a profitable sideline for Lillian, who managed them entirely on her own with no intervention from Mr. C other than to give his blessing when she'd launched the venture two years earlier.

The question card included spaces for the requester to provide name, address, date and place of birth, sex, height, weight, color of hair and eyes, marital status, number of children, and occupation—all of which, in conjunction with the nature of the petitioner's question, typically told Lillian all she needed to know to respond in some ersatz meaningful way. Many of the requests were of the common variety, the sort Mr. C fielded during his stage show, and mostly posed by women: *Will Sam Linklater ever propose to me? Will I ever have children? Will mother ever change her behavior? Will Billy find work?* But some of the requests sent in by mail were not so basic, and some could be quite intimate: *Is my husband cheating on me? Is my Everett going to die a drunkard? Is the pain in my belly the cancer?* And the one that spooked me the most that day: *Will my crime against my family be discovered and if so when?* I asked Lillian if we shouldn't forward this one to the local law enforcement—the return address said Bensenville, Missouri—but she said no, it wasn't our place to intervene in people's private lives (at least not to that extent), and reminded me of the promise of confidentiality printed across the front of the card. I let it drop, a bit perplexed by Lillian's response but deferring to her better judgment.

Given that the majority of requests came from women, it seemed only right that Lillian should respond to them instead of Mr. C. She was a sympathetic and reassuring soul. She also drew a line at behavior that crossed the standards of conduct she set for herself and those around her—not least of all her libertine husband, who was a considerable challenge in this respect. Her response to the Bensenville, Missouri questioner was as follows:

In the world beyond our powers to reckon, your crime, such as it is, has always been known. The spirits of those past, and those to come, do not deign to judge you, though they shall guide your conscience, and you should respectfully listen to them. They trust in you to take measure of your own offense and act in the best interest of those you love, and thereby put your worried heart at rest.

At the rate of about twenty-five requests per hour, by mid-afternoon Lillian and I had answered half the requests that filled the canvas mail bag she'd brought with her from Los Angeles, and we had a stack of nearly a hundred single dollar bills in front of us.

THAT EVENING WHEN I asked Marie if she would like to join me the next morning on a nature walk up the beach, she told me her ankle was not nearly strong enough for such exertion.

"Especially on the beach where it can be so difficult to walk," she said from the settee in the front sitting room. "I could reinjure it."

I rolled my eyes at her—rolled eyes being our favorite gesture with one another.

"I swear, Marie, if sometimes you don't think you're Clara Bow or Vilma Banky, a regular Hollywood starlet, to sit there and primp and pamper yourself to no end," I said.

Indeed, if not for the fact that we were the spitting image of one another, that for most of our lives we dressed identically and as toddlers even shared our own secret language, I would have sworn we weren't sisters at all, much less identical twins. Maybe it was a phase all twins went through, especially as their synergist childhood fell further away, but lately it seemed Marie and I couldn't have been more *unlike*. I never doubted the strength of our sororal love. It was just that instead of seeing myself in my sister as I always had, I now saw someone else—someone whose duplication of my understanding of who I was, and the makeup of the world around me, I could no longer take for granted.

"You can think what you like," she replied and licked the powdered cocoa off her fingertips after popping a bon-bon into her mouth.

So I asked Lillian if she would like to go, but she was busy, having already moved onto her next task of preparing for publication of the *Book of Mystery*, which was to be sold in the lobby of every theater where Alexander the Great performed. The book contained bits of philosophical wisdom from Alexander the Great, testimonials from famous persons as to his "psychomestic powers," astrological readings, dream interpretations, character readings, prognostications and visions, and quotes from ancient Zoroastrian and Sanskrit texts, most of which he and Lillian composed themselves. I next asked Charlie, but he just smiled patiently at me and said he couldn't, that he and the boys had to finish the treehouse before Mr. Conlin returned. I knew, though, what the real reason was—he didn't want to leave Marie behind and thereby give her any excuse to be jealous of me. Once Marie laid claim to something or someone, as she appeared to have Charlie, no one had better go near that person or thing. When we were children it was usually share-and-share-alike, but whenever Marie took an especially strong attachment to a doll or there was not enough of her favorite treat to divide among us, the sharing went out the window.

I figured I could postpone my walk and wait for Tucker to return with Mr. C and Mr. James, but that might take days. So I resolved to go by myself. That evening I consulted the local almanac for the tide tables and found that the lowest of the two low tides would occur at 7:45 a.m. I found *The Guide to Pacific Northwest Flora and Fauna*, the field guide booklet that Mr. James gave to Marie and me as a gift when we first came to the peninsula, thinking we might enjoy becoming amateur naturalists, and I began studying the chapter on "Coastal Life." I also retrieved my sketchbook, placed several sharpened pencils in my tin pencil case, and then put all of these items in a canvas rucksack that Mr. C said had belonged to a childhood friend of his who had perished in the Great War.

The next morning I rose well before the rest of the house—except for Cook, of course, always an early riser no matter how much beer he drank the day before. When I found him in the kitchen, he offered to make me a thermos of tea and a liverwurst-and-onion sandwich for my walk. As he prepared my lunch, I stepped out onto the porch and, to no great surprise, discovered the air exceedingly damp and the sky exclusively gray. Rather than cancel my outing, as I knew Marie would expect me to do, I returned to our room and, while she remained burrowed beneath her bedcovers, changed from my nightgown into a khaki skirt and heavy knit stockings, pulled a wool sweater over my plain white shirtwaist, and donned my mackinaw coat. On my way back to the kitchen, I borrowed a knit skull cap that I found on the coat tree in the front foyer. I then collected the thermos and sandwich Cook prepared for me, grabbed my rucksack, and marched out the front door and down the steps of the porch.

I couldn't believe that in the four previous summers that Marie and I had accompanied Mr. C to the Olympic Peninsula, neither of us had ever walked more than a couple hundred yards up the beach. We were too accustomed to the warm, sunny beaches of Southern California to do anything but scoff at the rough, wind-battered, surf-tossed beaches of the north coast. Indeed, Marie always complained that she had just as well leave her bathing suit at home in Los Angeles because she would never need it up here. And she was right. This was not a beach for sun bathing, playing in the sand, or frolicking in the waves.

It was a much more elemental beach, closer to the origins of the world. It was full of powerful forces, with ever-shifting conditions that made it a dangerous place. It was also a beach filled with life and all of life's attendant mysteries. These were aspects of the place I'd been taking in all morning—and coming to recognize inside myself as well—when I was attacked.

"Lou, no," I continued to beg as he stood over me there among the trees in the margin between the beach and the deep woods farther up the hillside. But he ignored my pleas and bent down again and tore my shirtwaist open. I was not wearing a brassiere and he leaned his large frame over me and stared at my small bosom, his angry face turning almost docile. When I tried to cover myself with my hands, he slapped them aside.

Then he pushed me onto my back and stepped on my wrists with his large boots. Dread supplanted fright, and I could feel myself whimpering as he began to unbuckle his belt. When he lowered his pants and underpants, I closed my eyes and turned my head. I remember smelling the forest's mildewy loam beneath me and hearing the creak of a tree branch rubbing with complaint against another branch above. Then I felt his urine hit my face, almost burning. I closed my mouth and held my breath, but it entered my nose and ears, and I gasped. I squeezed my eyes shut and whipped my head from side to side. His stream went through my hair, down my neck, and onto my chest.

"That's what you get for ignoring me," he said.

When it ceased, I stopped my straining, went limp, and tried to breathe. He lifted one boot and then another from my wrists, numb now from the pressure of his weight, and commanded me to stay. Then, with my eyes still closed, I felt him throw my skirt up to my waist and pull my bloomers down below my knees. I no longer had the strength to resist and waited for him to do what he would. But as I resigned myself to the worst, I sensed that he had moved away, and I opened my eyes to see him a few yards off searching about the ground for something. I watched as he picked up a large stick and with great deliberation snapped the twigs off it…and that's when I yanked up my bloomers, jumped to my feet, and began to run.

I reached the beach logs and scrambled over them before I looked back and spotted him coming after me, the stick in his hand, yet also fumbling with his pants. Mother always said a gal with her skirts up could outrun a fellow with his pants down every time, and I was able to clear the logs and begin sprinting down the beach. Ahead I saw the Hole-in-the-Wall and knew if I could get through it I could outrun him on the other side and reach the house. But as soon as I made it to the exposed rocks, I slipped and fell hard, scraping my knees and elbows badly, and in an instant he was standing over me, beating me about the shoulders and backside with the stick. When he finally picked me up, hefting me over his shoulder like a gunnysack of feed and carrying me out onto the rocks toward the water, I knew his only intention now was to kill me.

I kept imploring him—"Lou, no. Please stop."—but he didn't respond. All I could hear was his labored breathing and grunts as, top heavy with me over his shoulder, he worked to keep his balance. The farther out over the rough rocks he trudged, the larger and craggier they became, and he had to use his free hand to steady himself as he maneuvered from one formation to another. The rocks also became more encrusted with barnacles and mussels as well as more coated with seaweed and kelp the farther out he went. I could only see back toward the beach but knew we were reaching the point where, I fore-saw, he would throw me down, crush my head in with the stick, and heave my body into the waves. In desperation, I began twisting and writhing about, reaching back for his eyes, and as I did so he stepped across a wide crevice between two rock mounds and his foot slipped on the opposite side. His whole body, and my backside, slammed forward into the facing rock. He fell backward into the gap as I, squirming up and sidewise to avoid being crushed between him and the rock, dropped down on top of him.

As I lifted myself off him, he didn't move. He was on his side in the crevice between the rocks, lying in a tidal pool, his torso at a strange angle to the lower half of his body. I stepped onto his hip, pushing down on him, and clawed my way to the top of the rocks, expecting at any moment for him to grab my ankle and tug me back down. Then, as I cleared his reach and made it to the top of the rock, I looked back down at him and saw he was finally stirring. There was blood on his forehead where it had smacked against the rock when he initially slipped. I could also see that his left leg, at the knee, was terribly crooked—likely broken.

I knew I should have fled, but I couldn't bring myself to do so. My back hurt and my knees were bleeding and all I could do was sit down on top of the rock and watch as he opened his eyes, looked about, and grasped his situation. He tried to straighten himself out, yet I found the stick he'd beaten me with, which he'd dropped when he fell, and as he reached out for a handhold on the face of the rock to pull himself up, I leaned over and whacked his knuckles with it. He grimaced, pulled his hand away, and collapsed back into the crevice between the rocks. He turned his head toward me and I looked him straight in the eye. He didn't say anything. He closed his eyes and kept them closed until the first wave hit the rocks and splashed through the crevice. When the cold, frothy water washed over his head and soaked the rest of his body, he came to with a jolt, eyes blinking wildly. The tide was coming in. He knew it too. He tried to move, but his thick body was wedged between the rocks, and each time he tried to free his left leg he groaned in pain. When he reached out again with the same hand I'd cracked with the stick, it wasn't to grab ahold of the rock. He was reaching toward me for help.

I sat on top of the rock and looked down at him. I waited a moment and said, "No"—as simple as that. I knew if I extended my hand to him he would pull me back down. He closed his eyes again, and from that point on I'm not sure how much time passed or how many waves came through the rocks as I remained sitting there. I stared at the surf in the distance, the silver-blue line of the watery horizon, the flat grey sky above it. As if lapsing into a deep meditation—forgetting what had happened, forgetting that he still lay there in the seam of the rocks—I remained very still. A strange peacefulness came over me.

"Please," I heard him murmur and came out of my trance. I looked down at him and he was struggling again to free himself. I peered down the beach and the thought came to me that I could run to the house and find one or two of the men and they could rush back up the beach and pull Lou from the rocks before the tide came in. It would be close, but I could probably do it. Yet, I couldn't make myself move. Why had he attacked me? I looked down at him again as if I might actually ask him. Had he followed me all the way from the house? Had he been stalking me, two weeks earlier, that day in the woods? He seemed to have thought I was Marie at that time. Did he think I was her now? The notion—that he would hurt my sister!—made me furious.

"Help," he begged as I glared down at him.

In my torn shirtwaist, wet skirt, socks, and boots, my hair soaked with his urine and seawater, I braced myself against my own shivering.

"I hate you," I muttered, but not loud enough for him to hear, and watched as another wave pushed into the crevice and poured over him. He spat and sputtered, his eyes closed tight. The cold water washed the blood from his forehead, and when he opened his eyes again he seemed confused, as if no longer sure where he was.

"Go for—" he tried to say as another wave pounded through the rocks. He coughed out water and looked up at me this time with the taut, vacant look of genuine terror.

The next wave came over the rocks rather than through them and splashed onto my boots and skirt. It occurred to me then that the rising water might float Lou enough for him to escape. Yet, as the next wave poured over him and he strained to un-wedge himself, pushing and pulling desperately against the rocks with both hands, his mangled leg becoming more twisted with his efforts, I could see that he would never succeed.

The waves grew fuller and breached the rocks more regularly, and suddenly I became alert to my own risk—as if believing up to that instant that I was invulnerable to the surging waves. As I glanced toward the beach, I realized the flood tide could take me just as well. I spied a line of rocks that I could scramble across if I hurried, and then looked down into the crevice one last time and saw strands of kelp floating in the water above Lou's submerged body, obscuring his face while his lifeless hand floated just below the surface.

I WAS GLAD HE was dead. I could no more regret his drowning than I could regret my walking off the beach alive that day. I retrieved my hat and coat, then my sweater, and made my way back to the house. My body was shaking with cold. I was crying one moment and laughing the next as the full recognition of what happened settled over me. Several times I became startled and turned around sharply to peer down the empty beach, thinking he might be behind me. But he wasn't, and the compound was now just ahead, heat smoke rising from the flue of the coal-burning stove in the kitchen. By this time the incoming tide would have fully submerged the rocks as well as cut off access through the Hole-in-the-Wall. I again wondered if Lou's body would float to the surface. Would he be washed ashore like the flotsam of a shipwreck or pulled out to the ocean depths and fed upon by fish and crabs until no trace of his carcass remained? I paused at the rivulet to cup water through my hair and splash my face. I also arranged my clothes as best I could to look as tidy as they did when I left the house. I knew I could never speak a word of what had happened to anyone. Already the shame of it all was overwhelming me. People would not understand. They might blame me and say it was my fault. I remembered what had happened to a girl at St. Anne's in Los Angeles who'd become pregnant. When she said the baby was Brother Daniel's, Sister Margaret, the mother superior, and Father Albert, the head priest, rallied to the brother's defense and condemned the girl, humiliating her and expelling her from the school.

Of course, Marie was not severe like this. I knew I could trust her to keep my confidence, to show me her deepest love and sympathy, yet I didn't want to burden her with what had happened—especially if, as I suspected, Lou had thought I was her. For whatever reason, though twisted persons like him need no real reason, he seemed to have been obsessed with her. Nothing Marie did deserved that sickening, unwarranted attention. Nor did she deserve to be burdened with the incident that came of it and the attendant worry. There was no way to know for certain what had been in his mind, and furthermore, it no longer mattered. I knew I must keep what had happened to myself. I must carry on, I told myself, the same Marguerite as ever.

As I resolved to keep the attack a secret, I also thought about how I would face Lillian and Mr. C. Nothing seemed to escape their notice. Could I still be who they thought I was, one half of the adorable Nartell Twins, cheerful and charming? The man back there had befouled me, and would have done worse had I not stopped him. I wouldn't bow my head for being that person, the one who fought back. Neither would I allow myself to suffer the scrutiny of anyone who might doubt me, who might question why, once I'd escaped his grasp, I remained crouched on the rock above the crevice, hitting his hand with the stick, watching his panic, then terror, and ignoring his pleas for help as the water rose around him. I watched a man drown—I let him drown—and I had done so with purpose and intent. And pleasure. Indeed, as I approached the compound, a trace of gleefulness came over me in remembering my poise in the moment of his utter helplessness.

I decided to slip into the house, take a hot bath, and try to think no further on the matter. Mr. C wasn't expected back for another day or two. It was early afternoon and everyone was up and about. Charlie and Mel stood on ladders propped against the maple tree in which they were building the second treehouse. I tried to evade their notice by pulling the cap down low on my brow, hunching my shoulders in my coat, and hurrying past them. But as I climbed the stone stairs to the house, Charlie called out to me.

"Have you seen Lou?"

"No," I shouted back, and knew that with this simple lie I had committed myself to full and permanent concealment of what had happened. The first tinge of guilt rippled through my heart.

"Well, if you do," Charlie went on, "tell him to get his lazy behind over here."

I nodded and hurried up the porch, where I adjusted my hat and coat again. My skirt was mostly dry. Then I realized I didn't have my rucksack with me, that it remained on the beach by the log where he first grabbed me. Why I hadn't picked it up when I retrieved my hat and coat from the same spot confused me. Was I too numb with fear and cold and just didn't see it? Perhaps all I could do in that moment was cover myself for warmth and flee. I hadn't given it a single thought until this very instant.

It doesn't matter, I told myself and opened the front door.

Lillian was in the parlor working at the table as I entered the house. I could just glimpse her seated before a pile of papers. "Is that you, Marguerite?"

"Yes," I answered and scurried past her line of vision.

"Marie is upstairs," she said.

I went up the staircase and at the top could see that the door to the bedroom Marie and I shared was closed, which probably meant she was taking a nap and didn't want to be disturbed. So I went straight to the bathroom and locked the door. I turned the faucet on in the tub and as the hot water filled it, I undressed, dropping all my clothes into a heap on the floor. Then, standing naked before the mirror, I saw the abrasions on my knees and elbows and the bruises along my forearms. Turning about, I could see more bruises on my shoulders and back. My hair was a tangle of knots. I sat on the rim of the tub, watching the steam rise from the water, and couldn't constrain myself any longer. I lowered my head into my hands and began whimpering, and as I lowered myself into the scalding water, the tears kept coming and I was weeping uncontrollably.

I eventually settled down enough to scour my skin with the brush and soap and then wash and rinse my hair several times. I drained the tub, filled it again, and this time slid down into the clean hot water and closed my eyes. I lowered myself farther and let the water cover my ears, my cheeks, and finally my eyes and nose, and as I did so I pictured him out there—his body beneath the roiling seawater of the flood tide—and bolted upright and climbed out of the tub.

There came a knock on the bathroom door, and over the thudding of my heart in my chest I could hear Marie in her groggy voice say, "How much longer are you going to be in there? I need to piddle."

"Marie?"

"You've been in there a year and a day."

"Okay," I said. I asked if she could bring me my robe, and as she went for it I toweled myself down.

"Here," she said from the other side of the door.

I turned the lock and opened the door just enough to take the robe from her. I didn't want her to see my bruises and abrasions.

"Come on," she whined, growing frustrated. "Let me in."

Once I had wrapped myself in the robe and opened the door again, she shoved past me with a huff. "What's the matter with you?" she said as I picked up my soiled clothes from the tile floor.

As I straightened up and her eyes met mine, I knew that if I was going to do so, now was the time to tell her what had happened. But I didn't, I couldn't. I was too afraid—for her and for me. She looked at me with concern, but when I didn't answer, she became flustered.

"Sometimes!" was all she said, and pushed me into the hall and closed the bathroom door behind me.

I KEPT TO MY bed the rest of the afternoon, tucked protectively beneath the covers, sometimes sleeping, sometimes just curled up, holding myself against the tremors that shook my body whenever some fragment of the scene that took place on the beach flashed before me. I also prayed—which I'd not done for some time, at least not so solemnly. I prayed for forgiveness, and for grace, and for understanding and mercy. I murmured Our Fathers and Hail Marys until I was no longer aware of even doing so. I said the Apostle's Creed, and I repeated the Litany of the Blessed Virgin Mary, counting off on my fingers since I no longer owned Rosary beads. I no longer owned Rosary beads because I wasn't Catholic, never was. But that didn't matter now as I tried to remember all the prayers I'd learned in my time as a pretend Catholic. It didn't matter now just as it didn't matter then, when Marie and I were twelve and our mother lied to the Mother Superior to get us into St. Anne's, assuring her we'd been baptized in the church, taught our catechism in Sunday school, and given our first Holy Communion just months before. In addition to the mainstay prayers, our mother had us memorize the Glory for the Catholic Church and Intentions of the Holy Father and even some Bible Latin—*De profundis clamavi ad te, Domine!*—and because Marie and I recited them to such perfection that afternoon in the Mother Superior's office, we spent the next five years being schooled, reprimanded, and prayed over by the dozen or so nuns at St. Anne's. As I lay in my bed that afternoon, reciting all the prayers I knew by heart, saying novenas to St. Anne, mother of Mary, grandmother of Jesus, I also recalled Sister Bernadette's daily warning to her classroom full of pubescent girls, quoting from the New Testament: "The virgin thinketh on the things of the Lord; that she may be holy both in body and spirit."

All this helped me eventually to sleep, and when I woke again, to further divert my thought from what had happened, I set about trying to remember the many Mother Goose nursery rhymes that our mother used to recite nightly to Marie and me before putting us to bed. I sang them to myself beneath my breath and cried when I came to:

Up, little baby, stand up clear;
Mother will hold you, do not fear;
Dimple and smile, and chuckle and crow!
There, little baby, now you know!

I kept crying—softly so as not to be heard—wishing I were home so my mommy could comfort me. Despite her many troubles in life, our mother could be tender and caring, not so unlike the mother in the nursery rhymes. Marie and I knew she loved us, even though that love was not always apparent, mainly because she worked so hard. For most of our childhood she cleaned houses during the day and waitressed at night. Only after we'd been admitted to St. Anne's—on charity scholarships—did she receive what seemed to be a break. After a three-month secretarial course, she landed a job with an insurance company on Mignonette Street. If school was out, Marie and I would take the trolley and meet her downtown for lunch. She seemed happy, but we could also tell she was lonely. Then, after about a year at her new job, she took up with one of the salesmen from the insurance company—a traveling salesman at that—who took her on some of his road trips and eventually introduced her to cocaine. The drug was just finding its way around Los Angeles, especially among the picture show people. She fell in love with the man and soon everything came undone. She was fired from her job with the insurance company for absenteeism and went back to waitressing. Then she lost the house in Pasadena, the only possession left to her by our father before he himself went wandering. Eventually the man who started all of her troubles, the salesman, was arrested in Mexico, and even though she traveled down to Tijuana to try to help him, ultimately there was nothing she could do. After she returned she never heard from him again. By that time, when Marie and I were not at St. Anne's, where we were boarding, the three of us lived in a two-room flat near Pershing Square, which was when Mr. C came into our lives and helped my mother buy back the house in Pasadena.

During the remainder of the afternoon, I heard Marie return to the bedroom twice but leave almost immediately. Each time she entered, my back was to the door, my face to the wall, and the blankets nearly covering my head. The third time she came in, she paused beside my bed—I could feel her there—and asked, "Did you have fun on the beach?" sounding mildly solicitous. I grumbled as if to let her know I was still sleeping, and she took the cue and left me to myself again. But as soon as she left, I felt bad for turning her away like that, for rejecting her sisterly concern. Thinking about our mother had made me reflect on how much Marie and I meant to each other, how we'd essentially raised one another. We'd always confided in one another about everything. At the same time, I knew she would react too strongly if I told her what had happened down on the beach, and it might then leak out to the others, beginning with Charlie, and then surely an uproar would ensue. So I renewed my resolve not to tell anyone, even Marie. I could maybe tell her eventually—maybe—but not while we were still at Rialto Beach.

It was an hour or so later that, hearing a male voice give a shout outside, I started to in my bed, fearing Lou had escaped from the rocks and returned to the house looking for me. I jumped to my feet and peered out the window thinking I might see him below, but there was only Charlie and Mel. I was upset at myself for being so alarmed. To dispel the idea that somehow he'd survived—and refocus my anger on him—I forced my mind's eye to see his lifeless body beneath the water, his pale hand suspended just below the surface, the bull kelp swirling over his face.

I put on fresh clothes and snuck out of the house and up the short path to the treehouse, situated just an easy stone's throw from the corner of the house porch. The treehouse had been built two years earlier—part of some boyhood fancy of Mr. C's, no doubt, the very impulse for so many of his endeavors. It was suspended ten or twelve feet off the ground, attached to the stout trunk and thick lower limbs of a large maple tree and reached by a sturdy ladder. About half the size of our bedroom, it had a reading chair and area rug in it, a cot with a blanket and pillow, and a small side table with a desk lamp connected to a power cord that ran all the way to the main house. Whenever Mr. C held a séance at Rialto Beach for the benefit of the wives and daughters of area timber barons, which he did once or twice each visit, he would send one of the ladies to the treehouse for a special communion with the dead, which would be effected through transmitters and speakers wired into the walls. Mostly, though, no one used the treehouse, which is why I'd gradually claimed it as my own special retreat over the course of our last two visits. I liked to go there to draw, take naps, and just escape the others when their company became too much for me.

As I climbed the ladder, I knew I would be safe in my solitude there. Once inside I laid down on the cot and closed my eyes. I wasn't even aware I'd dozed off when I heard an automobile rumbling down the gravel road to the house. I thought it might be Mr. C returning from his hunting trip already—dearly hoping so, believing his calm, steady presence would make everything right again—and waited to hear his booming voice. But when the car door slammed closed and I heard Cook order Epi to retrieve the box of food stuffs from the trunk, my hope collapsed. I remembered the lyrics from another of our mother's nursery rhymes—*Bye, baby bunting, / Father's gone a-hunting*—and began sobbing all over again.

I stayed in the treehouse into the early evening hours. When Lillian came out of the main house at one point and walked up to the base of the tree to ask if I wanted afternoon tea, I stuck my head out the treehouse window and told her no, I was working on drawings from my beach walk. She looked at me a moment, said, "Okay," and then walked back to the house. I then settled onto the cot and began thinking back over the years Marie and I had been with Mr. C and Lillian. There was our professional association, of course, since we were official employees of Conlin Enchantments Inc., the company he and Lillian had founded. From the start, though, there was also something more between us—a trust we shared, a friendship and affinity. Indeed, without a real father in our midst, Mr. C had taken on a paternal role for Marie and me. In the five years since our mother had brought us to the room at the Palisade Hotel in downtown Los Angeles where we were introduced to him and Lillian, he had become our protector and guardian.

It was such an odd encounter that day we first met them. As with everything concerning her twin daughters, our mother exaggerated the extent of our training in ballet and modern dance. We had taken maybe half a dozen dance lessons. We didn't even own tights, much less dance shoes. All the same, the Conlins seemed impressed when, after the hotel furniture was pushed aside, Marie and I did several pliés and jetés and struck a final arabesque. They clapped and said *"Brava!"* Of course, our dancing skills were secondary in regard to their act. What mattered was that we were young and pretty and, above all else, identical twins. Later we learned that Mr. C had only recently married Lillian (three months after divorcing his first wife), and together they had set about remaking his stage show, aiming to do away with routine magic tricks and develop the mentalist portion of the act, giving it several new elements, including exotic dance and foreign instruments, and couching it in the mysticism of the Near East and Orient. It was Lillian's idea furthermore to incorporate the whole enterprise, stage act and associated products, and call it Conlin Enchantments.

Several weeks later, after rehearsing every day in a small abandoned theater in Torrance, Marie and I were thoroughly integrated into the stage show of Alexander the Crystal Seer. Before we knew it, we headed out on the road for a three-month tour up the Central Valley, hitting Bakersfield, Fresno, Modesto, Sacramento, Chico, and Redding, and then working our way through the backroads of Oregon and Washington to places like Salem and Bakersville, Yakima and Wenatchee, before swinging around to hit the coastal cities of Seattle, Tacoma, Portland, Oakland, and San Jose as we wended our way back down the coast performing two or three shows at each stop.

On this inaugural trip, Mr. C mostly had me and Marie do the classic switcheroo—again and again and again. Marie would climb into the front compartment of a wooden crate on stage, and then Mr. C would drape a red silk sheet over it, spin it about several times, and on his cue (some Arabic-sounding gibberish he would intone), I would run down the center aisle from the back of the theatre waving my arms and shouting, "Here I am! Here I am!" and everyone in the audience would look at me in astonishment as I climbed up the stairs to the stage and Mr. C opened the back compartment of the crate to reveal that it was now empty. In another trick, Marie and I used a trap door in the stage floor (all theaters have them) to alternately pop up one after the other in a new costume each time Mr. C waved his silk sheet in front of whichever one of us was on stage so that it seemed the new clothes magically appeared on us with just a wave of the sheet.

These were just the sort of cheap magic tricks that Mr. C and Lillian were already planning to drop from the act. So for the next tour, which would take us through the Rocky Mountains and Great Plains states, Marie and I began to rehearse what would become our new role in the act, including a series of exotic dances. In addition, we were now officially called The Nartell Twins. The advance publicity billed us as "The premier dancers of the Bengali subcontinent, girls born into the subtly seductive mesosphere of India, the foremost exponents of terpsichorean creations in the ancient tradition, who come by their ability to mystically interpret the same most naturally." When Marie and I asked Mr. C what "terpsichorean" meant, he explained that Terpsichore was the Greek muse of dancing and choral singing.

"The term comes from the conjoined root words *terpein*, to delight, and *khoros*, to dance," he said, always willing to demonstrate the breadth and depth of his knowledge of such esoterica.

Additional publicity for the new stage show told how The Nartell Twins were born in Bombay, our father an English army officer and our mother a high-caste Brahmin beauty, hence our pride in preserving not only our native dances but proper English decorum as well.

"We were born in Pasadena," Marie protested when she first saw this statement, which Lillian had likely composed. We were both wearing harem pants and crepe lehengas that exposed the midriff. But since decency laws in most states prohibited exhibition of the midriff, we draped a sheer satin scarf over our shoulders that flowed down over our torsos and past our knees. We also wore embroidered headbands with long ostrich feathers flaring back from them like wings sprung from our ears.

"And Pasadena is next to Alhambra, the revered palace of the Moorish rulers of Spain," replied Mr. C expertly. "So there you are."

We quickly learned that none of it made any sense—geographically, religiously, historically. The important thing was that the aura of the exotic was maintained. Our signature dance became the Dance of the Abbai Radhi Myrai, dubbed "the crystal dance of India," which, according again to the publicity put out by Conlin Enchantments, enabled "The Nartell Twins to share their understanding of the arcane theosophy of motion with their Occidental admirers." This notice even came with the warning to male audience members to look away from our fluid dance periodically or else risk falling into a trance via our hypnotically seductive movements. Neither Marie nor I knew what the name of the dance meant, and it didn't matter since we made up the dance ourselves, twirling and bounding about barefoot, bending and twisting, waving our scarves through the air and about our bodies, while vapors from the dry ice containers in the wings were fanned onto the stage and two company musicians, each dressed in a long white thawb and a red fez with dangly gold tassels atop it, played an eerie sound on the harmonium and tabla.

This was how we prepared the audience for the introduction of Alexander the Crystal Seer, who—assisted by Mademoiselle Valeska, herself a descendant of Russian mystics—would amaze the audience with the Spirit Slate writing, the Metal Ball reading, the Spirit Painting, and conclude with his crystal-gazing finale, known as the Imla Séance, each bit of the act successfully executed with the aid of Valeska's elaborate Slavic-accented explanations, several plants in the audience, an array of hidden microphones and wires, two backstage accomplices, and, of course, the masterful onstage misdirection of the sensuously supple Nartell Twins.

It never troubled me terribly that the act was a big sham. People believe what they want to believe, and we were giving them what they wanted. Mr. C restored wonder and amazement to people's otherwise drab lives. He also gave them reassurance and encouragement. He was a maestro of psychology, the Sigmund Freud of the theater circuit, able to size up total strangers based on a handful of cues and compose his divinations accordingly. Yet, there was always something more to Mr. C's act that was difficult to account for. While there was the sophisticated trickery—which, combined with the public's gullibility, ensured a full house every night—there was, too, Mr. C's undeniable charisma. His words and suave manner not only charmed audience members but lent an air of authenticity to the entire act. There was also, it must be said, a perceptiveness and foresight which he possessed that truly seemed uncanny. Sometimes these qualities expressed themselves in mild ways, such as his ability to articulate an audience member's thoughts before she even uttered a word. At other times his perspicacity proved quite startling, as when he foretold President Wilson's sudden passing or Mary Pickford's surprise marriage to Douglas Fairbanks. Even more mystifying was the time he told our mother items about her departed parents (my and Marie's grandparents) that only she knew, commenting on the cameo brooch that her mother (our grandmother) had given her when she was a little girl and how her father had owned a horse named Bucket because of the buckets of beer it was made to carry from the tavern to home and back again. He also told our mother how, in the afterlife, her mother and father were very proud of the way she'd raised Marie and me. At the same time, oddly enough, Mr. C routinely rejected the idea of supernatural perception and claimed that any mind, properly trained and willing, could glean far more of the universe than our dulled senses currently allowed us to apprehend.

I wondered then why he'd failed to perceive the kind of monster Lou Morton was, why he would allow such a menace to insinuate itself into his entourage. As I hid myself in the treehouse, I began to blame him for not protecting me. If he'd been more *perceptive*, I thought mockingly, he would have seen the danger he was putting Marie and me in by hiring Lou. If he hadn't gone on another of his ridiculous hunting expeditions, he would have made sure Lou was occupied with some project or another. I imagined myself punishing Mr. C once he returned, making snide comments to him in front of company or giving him the cold shoulder when we were alone. Ultimately, though, I knew to treat him in such a manner would be unfair. No one can foresee every threat to the safety and well-being of those around them, those they love. Mostly, I wanted him to return from his hunting trip, to come back to Rialto Beach and through his mere presence help calm the anxiousness that now made every fiber in my body tremble. To this purpose, I considered staying in the treehouse until he did return, however many days and nights that might be.

As it was, I stayed up there until I heard Lillian again calling me from the front porch, like a mother summoning her child to come in from playing outside. It was dinnertime, she said. I composed myself enough to climb down the ladder and walk back to the main house.

When I reached the porch, she was waiting for me. She held the ruck-sack I'd brought up the beach with me that morning.

"Is this yours, Marguerite?" she asked. Her voice had a note of admonishment in it, but also concern.

I was startled by the rucksack's appearance, and for a moment wasn't certain it was even mine. Seeing it dangling from Lillian's hands brought the morning's events back in an alarming way. My heart thud-ded, and I could feel blood rushing to my face. Fear again paralyzed me. Had Lou returned it, given it to Lillian to give back to me?

"An Indian man found it on the beach," she said.

"Oh," I said, fumbling to say something. "I set it down and went walking and then I couldn't find it. I was going to go back and have the men help me look."

Lillian studied me. Did she know I was lying? She was a kind, con-siderate woman, but an alert, sharp-minded woman as well, someone who knew what was what. She wasn't likely to be hoodwinked by a twenty-one-year-old's dissembling.

"You should be more careful," she said matter-of-factly and handed back the rucksack. "Your sketchbook and pencil case are in there as well."

As soon as she said this I remembered that I had been about to draw when Lou seized me, though I couldn't remember what. Maybe the sea stacks, maybe a piece of driftwood. I might have gotten a few marks down, but couldn't really remember. If I had, did Lillian look at my drawing, interrupted and incomplete, and wonder why it was like that? And what of my having told her a little earlier that I was going to the treehouse to work on the drawings from my walk up the beach? Surely she would sense the inconsistencies accruing about my mounting lies. If she did, she didn't comment on them.

"Thank you," I said, taking the rucksack from her and entering the house without another word.

The three of us—Lillian, Marie, and I—were the only ones to eat dinner in the dining room that evening. Sometimes the crew members ate with us, but not tonight, and Cook and Epi always ate their meals in the kitchen.

We said very little as we ate. I asked Lillian how the latest *Book of Mystery* was coming along, and she answered that it was nearly finished. Marie announced that Charlie had asked her to take the ferry with him from Port Angeles to Victoria on Monday. Lillian said she supposed it would be all right as long as Mr. C didn't have chores for the men to do that day, and then Marie said Charlie had already checked before Mr. C left on his hunting trip and he said it would be okay.

"And what will Marguerite do?" Lillian asked. "Is she invited?"

I could almost hear Marie's thoughts aloud—*No, absolutely not! This trip is for me and Charlie and no one else!*—but she didn't dare say this. So I felt bad when she said, "Of course she's invited." She then turned to me and said flatly, "Marguerite, would you like to come to Victoria on Monday with Charlie and me?"

I sat up straight and replied, "No, thank you, Marie. I have things here to do," and with that the matter was dropped.

It was only natural that she would prefer to be alone with Charlie, and this preference in no way felt like a betrayal or breach of our sisterly bond. It was simply one more indication that we were each our own person and must each live our own lives.

Lillian then reminded us that the household would be hosting a séance on Friday evening, and Marie and I would of course be needed to assist with it.

"We've invited twelve ladies and have received replies from all but three. They'll be staying at the hotel."

It was Mr. James who promoted the séances locally and made most of the arrangements for them each time Mr. C came to Rialto Beach. It was he who knew the wives and daughters of the timber barons and their managers, and he who secured transportation for them all to Rialto Beach and reserved rooms for them at the Mora Hotel.

As Epi cleared the dinner plates, I was again seized by the reality that I had killed a man that morning—or, at the very least, had deliberately watched him die. And his body was still out there, not so very far from the warmth and comfort of the dining room where we now waited to be served dessert. Nausea came over me and I laid down my napkin and pushed back from the table.

"Don't you want dessert?" Marie asked.

"Are you all right, dear?" asked Lillian. "You look rather pale."

I stood up, held the back of my chair, and as calmly as I could said, "I'm very tired from my walk. It was longer than I expected."

I could feel Lillian watching me.

"Excuse me," I said, and walked out of the dining room and straight upstairs to my bedroom.

Sometime later in the night, just as the house was being closed up, I could hear Charlie downstairs in the sitting room speaking to Lillian. He was telling her how he hadn't seen Lou all day and neither had Mel and they didn't know where he'd gone.

"He's a big fellow of course and can take care of himself," Charlie said to Lillian. "Even so, he doesn't know his way around these parts."

Lillian said that if Lou didn't appear by morning they should contact the Clallam County sheriff, and Charlie agreed, saying he hoped it wouldn't come to that, and then wished Lillian a good night.

A few moments later Lillian knocked on the bedroom door, opened it partway, and asked how I was doing.

"Better," I said from beneath the covers of my bed. "I just need to rest."

"Of course," she replied. She then repeated the conversation she'd just had with Charlie downstairs and asked me if I'd seen Lou at all that day.

I started to say no, but then stopped, and instead, not knowing why, said that I'd seen him that morning.

"Where?" she asked.

And here suddenly I realized I had two options—confess to what had happened on the beach or again lie. It didn't feel like a genuine choice, though, and why the words that came out of my mouth did so, I'm not sure I can explain.

"I saw him on the road," I said.

"Really?" said Lillian, sounding surprised. "And where was he going?"

"I don't know," I answered. "He asked me how far the town was where we came in on the boat."

"Port Angeles?" she asked.

"That's what I figured, but I told him I didn't know."

Lillian put her hand to her chin and blinked several times as if trying to comprehend this information. Finally she said, "I'll let Charlie know." She looked at me more intently then and said, "I'm worried about you, Marguerite. You get a good night's sleep."

"I'll try," I replied and watched her leave the room to go find Charlie.

Find Marie and you'll find Charlie, I could have told her, since shortly after dinner Marie had come up to the room to thank me for not wanting to go to Victoria with her and Charlie, and then confided that they'd arranged for a late-night tryst in one of the cabins.

I turned out the light and thought about the two of them together, and I was happy for Marie, truly, even as I stared at the dark ceiling, my heart constricting with my own terrible secret.

THE HUNTING PARTY RETURNED two days later on Sunday, and I was never so glad to see Mr. C. I had walked up the road to Mora to stop at the P.O. and chat with Tealie, the postmistress, who was just a few years older than I and had lived in Mora most of her life. I was on the stoop of the P.O. when the Franklin sedan came rumbling into view with Mr. C at the driver's wheel and Mr. James on the seat beside him. He blew the claxon horn several times to announce his return and summon any and all to come share in the triumph of their hunt.

He pulled to a stop in front of the post office and rolled down the driver's side window. "Wait'll you see what we bagged, Marie," he exclaimed. He rarely misidentified us like that, and I was hurt by it. All the same, my heart warmed to see him.

"Hello," I said. A light rain was falling so I stayed on the porch, watching through the rain that dripped steadily off the eaves.

Soon a horse-drawn wagon rattled up behind the car, with Tucker sitting on one side of the buckboard seat and a much older man on the other side holding the reins. Tucker saw me and nodded. He looked tired, yet as full of pride and bluster as Mr. C, especially as he climbed off the wagon seat and swung his rifle over his shoulder. The man driving the wagon wrapped the reins around the wagon's brake stick and hopped down with the agility of someone half his age. He was a short fellow with stocky arms and legs and a chest like a pickle barrel that stretched his red suspenders. He had a dirty gray beard that looked like a tuft of tree lichen and wore a brown felt hat with a brim that extended out to his shoulders.

With all the ruckus, people started to gather round, coming out from the stable and garage across the road, the meeting hall next to the post office, and the dry goods store. I could see children's faces crowding the windows of the small schoolhouse across the road, just wishing they could break loose and join the fun outside.

Mr. C climbed out of the car and waved me forward. I placed my floppy sou'wester on my head and approached the wagon like everyone else. The back of the wagon was piled with a menagerie of dead game animals, their eyes open and glazed, their carcasses forming a patchwork of hides.

"We took one of each," Tucker said from the other side of the buckboard as I gazed at the slaughter. Laid out side by side were an elk with an enormous rack of antlers, a black-tailed deer with a much smaller rack, a wooly black bear with gigantic padded paws, and a lean, muscular mountain lion with a tan coat and jagged white teeth flashing from its pink mouth.

The mountain lion was just below where I rested my hand on the wagon's sideboard, and as I reached out to stroke its sleek coat, Tucker shouted, "Don't!" and then laughed as I yanked my hand back. "It might still have some life in it!"

"That's quite a display all right," bellowed Mr. James, standing beside Tucker now. "You'd think we'd gone to the zoo and shot 'em in their cages. Not so. That elk took a full day to track. And the cougar, that's all John's work." Mr. James pointed to the old man in the loose-brimmed hat who rested his thick forearms on the opposite sideboard and stolidly looked at his kill.

"Mr. Conlin bagged blackie here," Tucker said and poked at the snout of the black bear with the butt of his rifle, "and that bull elk too."

Mr. C stood tall and proud at the back gate of the wagon, smiling down at his work. He wore the same belted Norfolk jacket he wore on all his hunting trips, along with a pair of thick wool pants, calf-length gaiters, and high-laced boots, the whole ensemble making him look like a true country squire.

"Who killed the deer?" I asked.

"That would be our boy Tucker here," said Mr. James and slapped Tucker on the back.

Tucker kept his eyes down and seemed abashed by the acknowledgment. The deer obviously didn't have the trophy status of the other animals. He then raised a thumb and index finger to his lips, gave out a piercing whistle, and waved two Indian men over to help him unload the wagon.

I told Mr. C it was good to have him back and he nodded.

"Everything going well at the house?" he asked.

"Yes," I answered and tried to blink back the tears I could feel welling up. I hated lying to him. I wanted my answer to be truthful. I wanted everything to be going well. And maybe at the house, it was. Maybe everything was going just fine. As for me, I wanted to collapse into his arms and start sobbing.

"Good," he said and turned away.

I returned to the post office and found Tealie. She agreed to make me a blue serge skirt like the one she was wearing, which I'd complimented her on, if I agreed to introduce her to Harold Lloyd when he arrived from Hollywood.

When I came out again, the elk and deer were strung up with ropes by the neck to a tree next to the stable. They'd already been bled out in the field, and now Tucker, holding a large knife, inspected the elk carcass, considering how best to skin it. Three dogs crouched at a distance whining in anticipation of any scraps that might be thrown their way. Since the bear and cougar carcasses were nowhere in sight, I figured they'd been brought to the stable or garage for skinning.

I thought about walking over to the hotel and treating myself to an ice cream when I saw Mr. C come out of the garage with a bloody apron on. He walked over to the spigot and concrete basin between the garage and stable and washed the blood off his hands and hung the apron on a nail on the garage wall. I hardly recognized him as the man on stage who wore a turban with a ruby pin stuck in the center of it, donned a flowing silk robe from which hung a silver naja necklace, sat supremely upon an ornately carved canapé, waved his hands over a crystal ball, then peered into it with a transfixed gaze and fooled people into believing he could actually speak to their dead relations and foretell their futures.

He saw me watching and came over to speak to me. He didn't address me by name, and I could see he still wasn't sure whether I was Marie or Marguerite.

"Go tell Lillian that Mr. James and Mr. Huelsdonk will be dining with us this evening," he instructed me. "And tell Cook we'll be having elk steak and bear stew."

Mr. Huelsdonk, I took it, was the old man responsible for shooting the cougar. A few hours later, back at the house, Tucker informed me that he was a legend in those parts of the Olympic Peninsula, known in local lore as the Iron Man of the Hoh. He lived on the upper Hoh River, where he'd made his homestead back in the 1880's, one of the area's first settlers.

"Long before the Forest Service boys came around," was how Tucker put it, and then admitted he'd only ever heard tell of Mr. Huelsdonk and wasn't even sure he was real until Mr. James enlisted him for this trip as their guide in the mountains above the Hoh River. Tucker recounted some of the stories about him that circulated, how Mr. Huelsdonk wrestled a bear to the ground and snapped its neck like a dried twig, shot more than a hundred of the elusive cougars that stalked his grazing sheep, single-handedly cleared more than twenty acres of the biggest timber known to man, hand-milled a three-hundred-foot spruce that he used to build the sturdiest barn on the peninsula, and hauled not one but two cast-iron stoves on his back to his cabin in the woods so his wife would no longer have to cook in the hearth. Local Indians called him *Barth Ar-Kell*, The White Bear. So wondrous were the tales about him that it was little surprise he was more like a Paul Bunyan or John Henry figure to Tucker than real flesh and blood.

Yet here he was, the Iron Man of the Hoh, now sitting on the front porch of the main house at Rialto Beach along with the rest of us, watching the tide push up the Quillayute and chewing on the elk jerky he carried with him wherever he went. He offered some to the rest of us, and Marie, who'd come out to the porch using a cane, seizing everyone's attention and sympathy, took one small bite of the jerky and spent the next five minutes spitting the gamey taste out of her mouth. I gnawed away at my own piece, trying to soften it enough to swallow, and sat back against a porch rail to listen to the men recall their hunt. Mr. C and Mr. Huelsdonk were like old chums with one another, and it surprised me how chatty the legendary Iron Man of the Hoh was. All those years in the woods must have made him desirous of social intercourse. He rocked on the rear legs of the straight-back chair in which he sat and mused on the early days of settlement on the peninsula, before the Forest Service pushed so many of the original homesteaders off their land. However, he'd held out against Gifford Pinchot, the strong-headed USFS Chief, and held onto his homestead. Now, as Mr. Huelsdonk explained, there was talk among the government men of turning the great forest up river from his land into a national park, of all things.

"It'll put a crimp in the hunting," he said, and explained how he and his wife still lived mostly on what they could shoot, raise, or grow.

"Sometimes I'll take a salmon from the river," he added. "But there's only so much fish a person can eat before he wants real meat."

I could tell by looking at Mr. C that he was fancying himself in Mr. Huelsdonk's place, residing year-round on the peninsula, fishing and hunting whenever he pleased, living off the land. This was one of his regular flights of fancy, yet we all knew he could never live without the hectic performance schedule that kept him shuttling from city to city, the curtain calls and blazing stage lights, the oohs and aahs of the packed house, the hobnobbing with Hollywood stars, and the devotion of his dedicated entourage, including his beloved Nartell Twins. If given the chance, he couldn't endure a single week of the remote, hard-scrabble life that the Iron Man of the Hoh thrived on.

It turned out, though, that Mr. Huelsdonk was just as intrigued by Mr. C as Mr. C was by him. He peppered Mr. C with questions about his stage act, and Mr. C regaled him with stories of playing San Francisco, Kansas City, Chicago, Boston, Philadelphia, and New York.

"I'll never forget the run we had at the Bronx Opera House," he said. "The New York Yankees baseball club had played a game that afternoon in their new park nearby. They came as a group and sat in the front three rows of the opera house and were about the most raucous bunch I'd ever seen. They especially loved the twins here and hooted up a storm when they did their Interikue Dance."

Here Mr. C looked over at Marie and me, and we both smiled at him, confirming his recollection. Hearing Mr. C tell his tales of our travels was a welcome reprieve from my ever-circling anxiety, my failure to put the attack out of mind for more than a few short segments of time. It was chilly on the front porch and it just so happened that Marie and I were wearing the very mink coats that Mr. C bestowed on us during the trip to New York he was talking about. He had insisted we wear them before we strode down Broadway with him, one of us on each arm, and we were happy to do so. Thinking back on our extravagant visit to big, flashy New York City pushed the dark thoughts of Lou far from my mind, and as I listened to Mr. C go on, I pulled my coat closer about me and nestled my cheek into its smooth collar.

"It was the Great Bambino himself who asked me to reveal the score of the next day's game against Cleveland," Mr. C said. "And so I obliged him…" and here Mr. C cupped his hands in front of him as if holding the metal ball reader he sometimes used in the fortunetelling portion of the act, "and told him in no uncertain terms, '9-2, Cleveland.' And let me tell you when those ballplayers heard that, a riot nearly broke out. But I kept my composure—that's the key to any act. I also knew my boys were in the wings, with their own baseball bats if I needed them."

I remembered the scene well. Alexander the Crystal Seer stood his ground upon the raised stage, straight and stolid, and as the jeers continued, he waited them out, sagacious as ever and emanating calm.

"I raised both hands, commanding them to still themselves," Mr. C went on, holding the attention of everyone gathered there on the porch at Rialto Beach. "I then peered into the future again and revealed that the Bronx Bombers would win the pennant that year in a six-game series against their archrivals, the Giants, and instantly the ballplayers and the rest of the audience broke into wild cheers." Mr. C laughed at the recollection of his easy manipulation of the unruly audience that day. "Later I heard the team's manager, a man named Miller Huggins, wasn't so keen on the prediction, fearing it would jinx the team."

"That was '23," Tucker piped in, wide-eyed at the story. "Two years ago, right? The Yanks beat the Giants four games to two that year!"

Mr. C confirmed this with a nod.

"Man sakes alive," Tucker exclaimed. "A fella could make a pretty penny with that kind of know-how. You care to say who's gonna win this year's pennant, Mr. Conlin?"

Mr. C shook his head solemnly.

"Son," he intoned, "to do so with the intention of pursuing personal lucre would be to violate the spirits' injunction against the venal exercise of the powers of thaumaturgy."

Tucker understood his meaning, if not his words, and immediately settled down.

"I will say this," Mr. C added. "Mr. George Herman Ruth sent me a very kind letter at the end of the season thanking me for my forecast and saying he'd taken it to heart and doubled his World Series earnings in a wager with a player on the opposing team."

With this, Mr. C concluded his story, and Marie and I looked at one another with a sly smile, remembering our double date with two of the Yankee team members after the show—one named Wally, the other Waite—and how we got all dolled up for the two ballplayers, wore our mink coats, and all they did was take us to a Blarney Stone on Times Square to drink mugs of beer. By the end of the night, Marie and I were both so tipsy we couldn't tell the two apart, and kept slurring their names together.

"*Whileyouwait*," I whispered to Marie on the porch, and she snorted out a laugh, eliciting confused looks from the men sitting about us.

The elk and bear were not ready in time for Cook to prepare them for that evening's dinner, so he served pork cutlets and roasted potatoes. This came as a great relief to Marie, who wanted nothing to do with eating wild game.

"It's disgusting," she said to me. "Besides, nothing surpasses Cook's breaded pork cutlets with white gravy."

After dinner, the party of tired hunters retired to the sitting room. Charlie and Mel, who had both eaten earlier, came in and joined them for a cigar, while Marie and I served snifters of French brandy smuggled down from Canada. Meanwhile, Lillian sat to the side, working a piece of needlepoint and simply enjoying the company. Once everyone was comfortable, Mr. Huelsdonk regaled everyone with tales about skoocooms, the half-man, half-ape creatures that stalked people at night in the mountains and ate their still-beating hearts; about Sisiutl, the horned sea serpent that lingered about the mouth of rivers consuming salmon by the hundreds and capsizing boats; and about the Clallam Killer, a madman who cut off the hands and feet of his victims and hung the appendages from trees in the woods.

Marie was utterly horrified by these tales but at the same time too afraid to leave the room and retire to the bedroom unless I went with her. Which I refused to do. In my own mind, I was thinking how I could tell a tale just as scary as any of Mr. Huelsdonk's—a true-life tale—about a vicious man pinned by rocks in a tidal pool and drowned by ice-cold water slowly rising around him. Finally, Mr. Huelsdonk changed the subject, and turning to Mr. C, asked if he might see for himself a demonstration of Mr. C's psychic powers.

"You might say I'm a skeptic," Mr. Huelsdonk said.

"And well you should be," replied Mr. C, and then expressed his reluctance to oblige Mr. Huelsdonk. I knew that he rarely gave spur-of-the-moment demonstrations. He always wanted to know well in advance what he was going to do and for whom. His reputation as a mentalist—which at this point was impeccable, save for the few swipes from self-appointed defrauders—depended on each and every gesture being executed flawlessly. Even when in his cups, as he was this evening, he maintained supreme vigilance in protecting his reputation. All the same, having the Iron Man of the Hoh in his sitting room must have been too great a temptation for him, because in the next breath he consented to giving a demonstration.

"What do you say to an arm-wrestling competition?" he asked.

The men seated about—Mr. Huelsdonk, Mr. James, Tucker, and Mel—all looked at him as if he'd lost his mind. Only Charlie, who was in the know on most of Mr. C's tricks, sat placidly by, observing his boss go about making suckers of his guests.

"Between whom?" Mr. James asked incredulously. "You and John? Don't be absurd, Claude. John's the strongest man on the peninsula. It's an undisputed fact."

"No, no, no," Mr. C returned. "I would never presume to challenge John Huelsdonk to a test of strength. I may be foolhardy, but I'm no fool. Between John and the twins, I mean."

Lillian sat back with a wan smile on her face. She knew better than to interfere with her husband's demonstrations once he had his mind set to one. Marie and I, in turn, had learned over the years to take our cue from her and remain still until Mr. C made his intentions more evident.

"I propose that either one of the twins here, Marie or Marguerite," he went on, acknowledging us with a small bow, "can singly defeat Mr. Huelsdonk in an arm-wrestling contest."

Mr. Huelsdonk remained silent, perhaps asking himself what he'd gotten himself into. With the challenge thrown down, it was hard now to tell whether he still doubted Mr. C's mentalist powers or not. I had difficulty determining the truth of the matter myself. I understood the artifice and deception behind Mr. C's most famous mind-reading tricks—had seen the mechanical devices that were used—but there were times nevertheless when no pedestal prompter, hand box reader, or electrical wire system was employed and yet he still succeeded in making a truthful reading of a random audience member's most closely guarded thoughts or predicting some absolutely unforeseeable outcome, such as the winner of the 1923 World Series. I generally attributed such occurrences to his vigilant perusal of the most current studies in the science of psychology, the ancient texts of the most obscure religious sects, and the reams of first-hand accounts documenting any and all paranormal activity that he made Marie and me cull for him from the public libraries of every city we visited. Whatever the source of his aptitude in this regard, I had to wonder why he hadn't already guessed my secret, or if he had, why he was keeping it to himself and not questioning me about it.

He rose from his chair and assumed his performance persona, which allowed everyone to take note of his full height and angularity. This evening, instead of his turban and silk robe, he wore a red hunting shirt and brown canvas pants.

"Let me be clear," he pronounced. "I would never question or underestimate the strength of my new friend, John Huelsdonk. Not one whit. I've witnessed it for myself when he hauled that elk out of the woods on his back."

I looked at Tucker for confirmation of this, and Tucker murmured, "It's true."

"Nor, I must add," Mr. C continued, the pitch of his voice rising, "should he or anyone else ever question or underestimate the powers of Alexander the Great!"

With this he took a cigarette from the small cedar box on the mantle, struck the head of a match on the hearthstone, lit the cigarette, and began puffing out circles within circles of smoke. "So let us proceed," he said and explained how the challenge would work. First, Mr. Huelsdonk would arm wrestle me and Marie both at the same time to prove his unmatched strength. Then, with Mr. C interceding telepathically, he would take on each of us individually and, as Mr. C proclaimed, be roundly defeated in each instance.

"Are the terms agreed to?" he asked Mr. Huelsdonk, and the Iron Man of the Hoh nodded his consent.

A small table was brought in from the kitchen. Mr. Huelsdonk sat on one side, Marie and I on the other. The first contest had our four arms against his one. His hand formed a massive fist atop his bulging forearm, and Marie and I grabbed ahold of it as best we could. When Mr. James, serving as referee, said *Go*, we both lifted up from our chairs, put our full weight into it, and yet could not so much as budge Mr. Huelsdonk's arm from the straight perpendicular. We groaned and grimaced, putting all our might into the effort, until Mr. Huelsdonk let out a laugh, pushed back in the opposite direction, and pinned our hands to the table.

Everyone laughed as Marie and I shook our arms out to restore the circulation to our fingers.

"That was a good one," exclaimed Tucker.

Mr. C then turned to him and asked, "Do you care to try?"

"No, sir," Tucker swiftly answered. "I don't need a man to whup me if I already know he can."

"Smart lad," said Mr. C. "And now, ladies and gentlemen and other gathered guests from the world beyond..." He paused over this last bit to give everyone the chance to look around the room. "We shall now enlist the psychical persuasion of mind over matter to permit each twin to singly defeat Mr. John Huelsdonk, the legendary Iron Man of the Hoh, in a solitary mano a mano hand-wrestling match."

Mr. C had me sit down across from Mr. Huelsdonk and then stood behind me. Mr. James then instructed me and Mr. Huelsdonk to clasp hands.

"This is ridiculous," Mr. Huelsdonk said, taking my little hand in his giant paw.

"Please, John," said Mr. C. "You mustn't hold back, but use all your strength. I promise, you will not hurt the young miss." Mr. C then raised his hands on either side of me. Though he stood behind me, I could imagine him going into what he called his soothsayer's trance, his eyelids fluttering as his eyeballs rolled back into his head.

I squeezed Mr. Huelsdonk's hand as hard as I could, but he didn't seem to notice. Then, when I glanced over my shoulder, I saw Mr. C give the faintest nod, which signaled Mr. James to start the contest. Mr. James gripped my hand and Mr. Huelsdonk's in both of his, and when he released them said, "Go!"

I pushed as hard as I could against Mr. Huelsdonk's hand and at first thought my effort was pointless. It was like pushing against a fence post. But then I felt it give, just a little at first, but then more as I kept pushing. I glanced up and saw that he was straining. His face had turned red. Veins like large cords of rope rose from his temples, neck, and forearm as he strained to pull his arm straight again. Then in one final thrust—though hardly exerting myself at all, as if I possessed an internal strength I never knew I had—I slammed the back of his hand and wrist to the table.

Tucker hooted, while Mr. James shook his head in disbelief and raised my arm in victory. I was as dumbfounded as everyone else. I knew Mr. Huelsdonk had not thrown the contest. I could feel him straining against my own meek force, and yet, as if all his physical might had been magically transferred to me, I'd won. In his defeat, Mr. Huelsdonk just grinned and rubbed his sore wrist. Only then did Mr. C come out of his trance and look about.

"Marie," he said calmly, turning to my sister, "shall you try now?"

"No thank you," she said abruptly, and looked bored by the whole display. Mr. C appeared a little put out by her unwillingness to play along. It occurred to me that she was beginning to assert her independence not just from me but from him as well.

"We need a neutral party," Mr. James proposed. "Someone who isn't privy to all your tricks, Claude."

"Why sir," Mr. C retorted, sounding offended but also smiling pleasantly at his friend. "Do you doubt my authenticity?"

"I'm just saying," said Mr. James.

"All right then," he said. "Marie, go into the kitchen, will you, and bring in one of the girls."

Whenever we came to the peninsula, Lillian hired two Quileute girls to assist Cook in the kitchen. They were school-age girls, usually in their teens.

"Do come in, Detta," said Mr. C to the girl Marie led into the sitting room from the kitchen. "Don't be afraid. Please, have a seat." Detta was maybe fifteen years old, short and dark-complexioned. She wore a white housedress and her long black hair was braided and hung down her back like a silk cord.

Seeing her take the seat at the table where I had just been seated, Mr. Huelsdonk stood up and rolled down the sleeve on his right arm.

"Thank you for the demonstration," he said, addressing Mr. C. "We'll spare the child the humiliation of giving an elder another horsewhipping." He then reached out and shook Mr. C's hand. "I'm convinced, sir."

"Very well then," Mr. C said, sounding satisfied. "Detta, please tell Cook he can serve the coffee now."

As we made our way back out to the front porch to drink our coffee, Mr. Huelsdonk leaned in toward me and asked me how Mr. C had done it, and I had to answer that in all honesty I didn't know. It was clear that for Mr. Huelsdonk, having his legendary physical strength so readily nullified would require some personal reckoning, as though a fact he'd taken for granted for so long had now been brought into question. I understood—deeply understood—how he felt. And yet, at the same time, for me the arm-wrestling contest had the exact opposite effect. It made me feel as though I might have sources of strength I'd never realized.

After drinking coffee and eating the almond pithiviers that Cook had Detta bring out to the porch, Mr. C bestowed a crate of Valencia oranges on Mr. Huelsdonk, with his compliments to Mrs. Huelsdonk. In return, Mr. Huelsdonk let Mr. C know that he was letting him keep the cougar he'd shot. Mr. C then invited Mr. Huelsdonk to Los Angeles. "Who knows, we might get you in the movies," he said. But Mr. Huelsdonk said he hadn't been off the Olympic Peninsula in forty years. "I'm content just where I am," he added.

The two men were so simpatico with one another that I couldn't help but wonder whether they'd been in cahoots over the arm-wrestling stunt after all, it being something they'd cooked up between them in the woods, with the final touch being Mr. Huelsdonk asking me how Mr. C had done it. Yet that's just how it was with Mr. C's stunts—a nubbin of doubt was forever poking its head out from the periphery of one's utter astonishment.

<hr />

THE NEXT MORNING TUCKER delivered the elk and bear meat and packed it into the icebox in the cellar. As for the bear hide, the tanning process would take longer. The cougar, meanwhile, was sent to Port Angeles to be stuffed and mounted.

When we crossed paths on the front porch, Tucker asked if I was ready to take that walk down the beach that we'd talked about, and I had to tell him it was too late, I'd already gone. The exchange caught me off guard, and I lost the equilibrium I'd begun to feel since Mr. C's return. In that short time I'd managed to settle myself down somewhat, to convince myself the incident would never be found out and life would go on as it always had—before I'd been attacked, before I'd watched a man die.

"You have?" he said with a look of astonishment. Then he caught himself and squinted at me. "How come?"

I could see he thought I'd gone on the walk with someone else. He straightened up against the news of such a slight. I simply didn't want to have this conversation, thinking the longer it lasted, the more my fear would ebb back over me.

"I wanted to," I answered.

"All by yourself?"

"Yes, all by myself."

He didn't say anything, but kept looking at me, trying to figure me out.

"But how come?"

"I wanted to," I said again, and went into the house without another word to him.

After Lillian reported to Charlie what I'd told her in the bedroom, word spread that Lou had gone to Port Angeles and from there, everyone speculated, was probably headed to Seattle. In case he hadn't caught the boat yet, Charlie made the trek to Port Angeles to look for him in the taverns. The assumption was he'd gotten stir crazy at Rialto Beach and went off looking for diversion. When Charlie returned from Port Angeles two days later without Lou, he telephoned Lou's brother in Los Angeles to tell him what had happened and let him know Lou might show up down there at any time. According to Marie, Charlie also told Lou's brother to tell Lou, when he saw him, that he was fired. "Charlie doesn't like guys walking off the job like that," Marie added. Then Charlie had to inform Mr. C about Lou's departure, and Mr. C got mad and chewed Charlie out for recommending "the big lout" in the first place. A perfectionist, Mr. C ran a tight ship—"The show depends on it," he always said—and didn't take lightly to this sort of breach of duty. This standard of conduct held firm with him whether he was touring about the Midwest, rehearsing in Los Angeles, or vacationing at Rialto Beach. In fact, he became so riled by the news about Lou that he told Charlie he couldn't go to Victoria that Monday, that he needed him instead to help prepare for next Friday's séance.

"That makes no sense," Marie complained to me later in our bedroom. "It's not Charlie's fault Lou wandered off like that. Besides, good riddance. The guy was a slink, always watching a person from the corner of his eye. Giving a gal side-eye. So I'm glad he's gone. As for Friday night, what's there to get ready for? Charlie can have everything done in half an hour. Mr. C's just being mean and I have half a mind to tell him so."

I appreciated her disparagement of Lou—and thought, *If she only knew*—but Marie and I both understood she would never speak directly to Mr. C about the Victoria trip. And for good reason. She wouldn't want his anger to turn on her. As for myself, I wondered whether forbidding Charlie to go to Victoria was Mr. C's way of tamping down the romance growing between Charlie and Marie. He openly admitted to having a jealous streak in him when it came to, as he put it, "my twins." It's partly what made him so protective of us. I suspected if he ever found out what happened to me on the beach, he'd fire Charlie right on the spot for recommending Lou, which I knew Charlie didn't deserve.

Marie was right in saying Friday evening's séance needed little preparation. We'd all done dozens of them before and knew the routine. All the same, on Thursday morning, Mr. C called a meeting of everyone involved—Lillian, Charlie, Marie, and myself—to run through our assigned roles. As he did prior to every performance, he'd hired a sleuth from among the many he retained throughout the country to go to Port Townsend and Port Angeles a week in advance of the séance and with a list of names of those invited scour the surrounding communities to learn as much as he could about them. Now, a full day before the séance, Mr. C held a file with the sleuth's detailed account of each person who would attend, including personal habits and peccadilloes, social affiliations and interests, names and profiles of family members, and, of course, recent and prominent deaths in each person's family. Mr. C had studied the file, memorizing every piece of information in it, and had already selected the exact bits he would use. He gave us the highlights and quizzed us on them. Then, along with a sheet that outlined the sequence of "psychic phenomenon" to be revealed during the course of the séance, he let us each know what our cues would be and quizzed us on these. Finally he had Charlie review which mechanical devices would be utilized and double-check that each was functioning properly.

Such painstaking preparations were par for the course with Mr. C. Yet, because of the mystery surrounding Lou's disappearance, Mr. C was more tense than usual about Friday's séance. There was also the fact that none other than Harry Houdini, one of the most famous performers in the country, had recently launched his own crusade to discredit mediums and call for an end to all séances. This came after Houdini himself had enlisted a raft of mediums to summon his own mother's spirit following her death. And even though Mr. C only ever held small private séances, and only about a dozen of those per year, Mr. Houdini had decided to make him a special target of his crusade, condemning Mr. C as a "spurious spiritist" and "hoodwinker extraordinaire" in the New York Herald Tribune two months earlier. The attack had Mr. C fuming for weeks afterward.

"*Spurious*! What does that mean? We're all illusionists and interpolators! As far as I'm concerned, Houdini can go bury himself alive and stay buried. It's professional jealousy, plain and simple."

But Mr. C was not the only one on edge anticipating Friday's séance. The whole notion of communing with the dead unnerved me now as it never had before. Not only had I recently been witness to death, but I had in a manner become an agent of the grim reaper. In five years of performing with Alexander, the Man Who Knows, I never became so cynical as to dismiss out of hand that correspondences exist beyond what our five physical senses can detect.

Indeed, even after retiring from the stage years later, Mr. C himself never fully abandoned the belief that we can glimpse a fuller, more universal truth, one that lies behind the opaque veil of empiricism, if we train our minds properly—hence his reference to the term *interpolation*. Who among us, I sometimes ask myself, hasn't wondered at his own preternatural powers, hasn't felt that he has dreamt, foreseen, or even lived a certain moment before it actually occurred—what the subtle and inquisitive Frenchman calls *déjà vu*—whereby concrete experience and the infinitude of time sync with one another in an instance of simultaneity? Who hasn't, at one time or another, felt the presence of another when knowing full well he was alone? To this day I wonder.

NINE LADIES IN ALL came for the Friday evening séance. They arrived in fur stoles and feathered hats. Their matronly bodies were draped in beaded evening gowns, their hair in neat Marcel waves. One of the ladies brought her two daughters, who seemed to be about the same age as Marie and me. The more homely one wore a long-pleated skirt and buttoned sweater, while the other, the more attractive of the two, looked like a flapper girl straight out of a newsstand magazine. A tulle dress with a dropped waist and calf-length flounces hung down her skinny frame, and a long, knotted string of pearls dangled from her neck. Beneath a felt cloche, her hair was bobbed short. Her eyes were darkened with mascara, her thin lips pronounced with red gloss.

"Does she think she's going to the Cotton Club?" Marie whispered to me when we ducked into the kitchen to bring out the tray of liqueurs for our guests. Mr. C liked to serve his guests a little something prior to commencing the official séance. He also liked to coat the bottom of each glass with a few drops of camphorated tincture of opium, which helped ensure the spiritual receptiveness (and general glad feeling) among the participants.

"Stop that," I said to Marie through my giggles at her remark. "Who knows what Mr. James told those poor girls to get them to come all the way out here? Maybe she thought she was going to audition for Louis Mayer's next picture."

"Why Marguerite," Marie came right back, "it was Mr. C's own natural charisma and psychic wonders that lured them to our wilderness outpost. You know that as well as I do."

"Enough," I said, having reached my fill of her witticisms.

We returned to the sitting room, Marie carrying the tray of liqueurs and I the tray of Belgian crystal. All the ladies, including the two sisters, were seated now. Only Mr. C remained standing, leaning on the mantle of the hearth, where a fire blazed. He was telling the group about his latest trip to Egypt, where he and Lillian visited the Pyramids of Giza and encountered the renowned archaeologist Howard Carter, who gave them a tour of the recently uncovered tomb of the Tutankhamun, the Boy King, in the Valley of the Kings.

"Didn't you fear the infamous curse?" one of the matrons asked.

"It doesn't exist," replied Mr. C. He looked down into the flames of the fire and then about the room. "Instead of fearing the cult of the ancient Egyptians, I prefer to learn from it. Take the god Ptah, for example, one of their oldest and most potent deities, whose temple was in Memphis and who possessed untold creative powers. 'The primal creator,' he was called. The majestic *Egyptian Book of the Dead* cites him as the great architect of the universe."

"You don't say," said the flapper girl, seated on the piano stool and half-swiveling herself about, first one way, then the other.

Mr. C turned his eyes on her and she stopped swiveling. "I see you are a skeptic," he said.

"Pauline," her mother piped in. She was the wife of one of the local mill owners. "Behave yourself."

"That's perfectly all right, Mrs. Eisely," Mr. C said. "Skepticism is a perfectly natural trait. Especially among the young. It's only when it sours, like milk, and contaminates the soul with cynicism that one should worry. It's my hope that this young lady's skepticism will, tonight, be transformed into understanding."

He turned to me and Marie, standing at the threshold to the dining room, and with a nod signaled us to serve the liqueurs. Then, on a lighter note, he asked if any of the present company belonged to the local temperance society.

"Goodness, no," one lady responded. "We would all have to divorce our husbands if that were the case," which prompted titters from everyone in the room.

"That's reassuring," Mr. C went on. "Ergo, I trust no one will turn me in to the authorities for being a proper host and offering you each a glass of my finest cordials from France."

Marie and I passed around the glasses filled with the fruity bootleg liqueurs Mr. C purchased from an orchardist near Los Angeles. Even Pauline accepted a glass, as did her dowdy sister, Bernice, who kept her eyes cast down and her hands firmly in her lap the whole while.

After another half hour of conversation, which allowed Mr. C to further acquaint himself with his guests, Lillian escorted everyone to the dining room. Charlie and Mel had removed the long dining table that morning and replaced it with a large round table with enough chairs to seat everyone, save Marie and me, who would stand at either end of the sideboard behind Mr. C, prepared, as he explained, to assist anyone who might feel a fit of inhalations coming on. To avoid disrupting the spell created by the communal summons, we would either help the person calm herself, perhaps by bringing her another glass of cordial, or escort her from the table and into the sitting room where she could lie down. In place of his robes and turban, Mr. C wore a tailcoat, silk vest, and black bowtie. Lillian, in a simple lavender evening gown, sat directly across from him at the table, evenly dividing the guests on either side of them. In each corner of the room, there stood a candelabra atop a fluted stand. The many lighted candles on these gave the room a luminous glow while casting all manner of faint shadows about the table.

Mr. C's first act was to consecrate the room by having Marie and me each take two small bowls of water—which he explained as "the four primal waters, representing the infinite, the absolute, the eternal, and the unknown"—and with our fingers spritz droplets from the bowls onto the candles on the candelabras so that the flames fluttered and hissed. As we did this, he recited a passage he claimed was drawn from the *Tibetan Book of the Dead*, honoring the spirits of all the dead from time immemorial and asking their indulgence in allowing us to communicate with the ethereal world of the great beyond. From where I stood, I could see the ladies watching Mr. C intently. A few stole excited glances at one another or peeked over their shoulders to see that no spirits were sneaking up on them.

When a cool draft came through the room, released by Charlie from the icebox in the cellar and fanned through the floor vents, Mr. C asked, "Can you feel that?" And as heads nodded about the table, he announced that initial contact had been made. He then instructed Lillian to place the spirit board and planchette upon the table.

"You have each come here," he said, "with a wish to reunite with someone whom you have lost." He looked across the table to the only widow in the group. "Mrs. Bingham, would you like to be first?" The woman he invited to take the first turn with the spirit board had been predetermined, of course, since there was no one more prime for communing with the dead than a lonely, grieving widow.

Lillian placed the spirit mat in front of Mrs. Bingham on hidden marks that would allow her to manipulate the magnets beneath the table. Mrs. Bingham was instructed to lay her fingertips lightly upon the base of the teardrop-shaped planchette and form an image in her heart and mind of the person she wished to summon.

"The rest of those present shall clear their minds of all thoughts and concentrate solely on the spirit board," Mr. C instructed, and as soon as all eyes were upon the board, the planchette skidded across the board beneath Mrs. Bingham's fingers and the dear lady, who still mourned her husband five years after his passing, sucked in her breath.

"I did not do that!" she said.

"With whose being, Mrs. Bingham, do you seek to reunify?"

"My Roland," she said.

"Your son?" Mr. C inquired, even though he knew very well that Roland Bingham was Mrs. Bingham's deceased husband. That fact, along with every imaginable detail about Roland from his suit size to his habits as a philanderer, was part of the file Mr. C had committed to memory prior to the séance.

"Mr. Bingham," the widower answered. "My late husband."

"Keep the image of your husband clear in your mind's eye," Mr. C instructed. "And concentrate, Mrs. Bingham. Concentrate."

The planchette moved again, this time less jerkily—first to the letter I, then A and M before pausing.

"'I am,'" said Mr. C and snapped his fingers, the signal for Marie to hand him a pencil and for me to lay a sheet of paper before him on the table. "Continue, spirit," he intoned.

The planchette moved faster now, S-O-R, then paused on the R, before moving to the letter Y.

"Roland?" Mrs. Bingham muttered, and Mr. C urged her to remain calm and keep concentrating.

The planchette then spelled out M-U-N-C-I-E, and Mrs. Bingham could no longer check her tears and removed her hands from the planchette to dab her eyes with a handkerchief. "That's what he called me," she said. "His 'little Muncie.'" She was sniffling and smiling simultaneously. "We're from Indiana, you see, and Muncie is where I grew up."

"Do you know why he would say he's sorry?" asked Mr. C.

When the question registered with Mrs. Bingham, her posture stiffened and she raised her chin. "I do," she began. "My Roland died in the arms of another woman. And she later had his child, whom I've since taken to sending money to, in Roland's memory." The poor woman then broke down sobbing, at which point Marie and I led her back into the sitting room, had her lie down on the sofa, and brought her another glass of opium-laced cherry cordial.

The next guest to lay her fingertips on the planchette, a Mrs. Thornberry, summoned her deceased mother and received the message F-A-I-T-H, pause, N-O-T, pause, P-U-N-I-S-H. When Mr. C asked Mrs. Thornberry whether this message meant anything to her, she explained that she had recently become angered by her pastor for refusing to sanction a fellow congregant for skimming from the church coffers. "The thief was a dear friend of Mother's," she averred, and then she too began to cry.

After summoning two more spirits from the beyond with the spirit board, Mr. C raised open hands to the air and in a sonorous voice said,

"Thank you, spirits, for your recognition of we who remain burdened with unknowing in this earth-life. Thank you for your understanding and sympathy. We now ask that you communicate still more directly with us…seeing as you now know that we mean no ill will, but seek only your wisdom."

At this point, Lillian removed the spirit board, brought out a slate in a frame, and, with everyone watching, slid a sheet of blank paper into the frame behind the slate. She then laid the slate on the table. Next she fastened a blunt stylus to the end of the planchette and set the planchette on the slate.

"Now, spirits," Mr. C continued, "help us further." He turned to the diminutive woman on his right. "Mrs. McKay, my dear, you told us before we began that you lost a son in the war."

"Yes," Mrs. McKay answered, appearing as tiny as a child next to Mr. C. "He was killed in France and is buried there. I've never been able to visit his grave."

"Would you care to try to contact him?" Mr. C asked in so gentle and soothing a voice that I could not help but be touched by his solicitousness toward her.

Mrs. McKay blinked several times and said softly, "I would like that very much."

Lillian then placed the slate with the planchette on it in front of her. Everyone at the table watched as Mrs. McKay tentatively placed her fingertips on the planchette and then looked to Mr. C for further guidance.

"Speak to him," he told her. "Let him know it's safe to make himself known to us."

Mrs. McKay continued to blink and finally bowed her head and addressed her son. "Alec," she said, "it's okay. I'm here with friends. I miss you. Your father and sister do too. We all do. Please, Alec. Let me know you're—" and before she could finish her sentence the planchette nudged forward and she gave out a short gasp.

"It's all right, Mrs. McKay," Mr. C assured her. "Just picture your son as you knew him in the remembered flesh and now know him in your heart. Trust his spirit to do the rest."

The planchette moved smoothly across the slate in no clear discernible pattern. Mrs. McKay, her mouth open, seemed to hold her breath the entire while and when it finally stopped moving Mr. C had to advise her to wait. "There may be more," he said, and sure enough the planchette made a fast flourish across the bottom of the slate before skittering over the edge of the frame and clattering onto the table. Appearing both fearful and delighted, Mrs. McKay held her hands to her face.

"Thank you, Alec," Mr. C said with a light laugh. "Your son, Mrs. McKay, has an exuberant spirit."

Mrs. McKay laughed. "He always did," she said happily.

Mr. C then signaled Lillian to retrieve the spirit slate and reveal what impression Alec's spirit had left for his mother. Lillian picked up the slate and withdrew the sheet of paper from behind it. She inspected the paper for a moment to build suspense and then, appearing satisfied, she held it up for all to see. On the sheet of paper was a sketch portrait of a young man of eighteen or nineteen years, wearing a military hat and jacket, smiling, and beneath his portrait an inscription that read: *We will meet again. Love, Alec.*

Astonishment lit the faces of the ladies as Lillian carried the portrait about the table for each to see more closely. When she at last handed it to Mrs. McKay, the dear woman was trembling.

"That's him," she exclaimed. "That's my Alec."

As this demonstration confirmed, the spirit slate was one of the more successful elements of Alexander the Great's performance. A photograph of the person was found well in advance, a portrait drawn from the photograph (I had done the honors with Alec), and the drawing concealed beneath the slate with the blank sheet of paper placed over it. The movements of the stylus across the slate, of course, were meaningless.

The séance, however, was just getting started. These ladies, after all, had paid twenty dollars each to commune with the spirits of the netherworld. So, to draw forth the more shy and reluctant spirits, Mr. C signaled for Marie and me to extinguish the candelabras in the corners of the room while Lillian set a single three-arm candlestick in the middle of the table. This adjustment to the lighting commenced the next significant phase of the séance, during which the table lifted from the floor, both strange and familiar voices echoed throughout the room, apparitional illuminations appeared along the walls and across the ceiling, bells and chimes rang out from nowhere, the temperature turned suddenly warm, then cold again, and several participants felt a feathery trace of something across the back of their necks.

These occurrences, which were all part of the plan for the evening, went on for more than an hour until, approaching the end of the séance, Marie and I raised our arms before us in a V-shape, threw back our heads, and began a low, pulsating hum deep in our throats—our best imitation of the strange Tibetan throat singing that Mr. C had acquired a phonograph recording of six months earlier.

Mr. C then asked everyone present to take their neighbor's hand and close their eyes.

"Speak, spirit," Mr. C commanded. "Who are you?"

When Lillian unexpectedly groaned, everyone opened their eyes to see her head rolling about from shoulder to shoulder. "Ulom, Ulom, Ulom," came a yawning bass voice from her mouth as her head came to a stop and her eyes popped open wide. "To the sisters, beware!" the voice intoned.

This odd warning caught even my attention, and suddenly I was scared by Lillian's medium act, thinking how she might be referring to Marie and me—but especially to me. I tilted my head forward ever so slightly to glance at her. Her eyes were like lanterns, and although her mouth moved, the voice was one I didn't recognize her ever using before.

"A tall one strains the sororal bonds," the voice went on. "Secrets prevail, and will out! The heart grows dark in confinement. Take heed that waters rush not between you."

I stopped humming at this point, convinced the spirit oracle that Lillian was channeling was addressing me, letting me know my crime had been discovered and my secret, now almost two weeks old, was being revealed. I grew dismayed. My chest constricted, and I became short of breath. Yet, when Marie nudged me with her foot, I dropped my head back again and resumed my humming.

"Love thy own and sow not the seed of betrayal. Sisters, beware!"

I was about to look up again when Bernice, the dowdy of the two daughters who'd come with their mother, pushed her chair away from the table, stood back, and declared, "I've had all I can take of this nonsense." She glowered at Lillian. "Who told you? Tell me!"

"Told her what?" Mrs. Eisely, the mother of the two young women, asked, looking with alarm from one daughter to the other. "Are you the sisters the spirit is warning?"

"About Henry," Bernice blurted, and bolted from the dining room.

Everyone turned and watched as she raced through the sitting room and out the front door.

"*My* Henry?" the other daughter, Pauline, asked in a bewildered voice.

As this exchange was taking place, Lillian solemnly closed her eyes and lowered her head, and Marie and I, in turn, lowered our arms and stopped humming. No one was holding hands any longer. Pauline got up from the table and left the room whimpering. From where I stood I could see her collapse into an armchair in the sitting room and bury her head in her arms. Her mother hesitated a moment but then went to comfort her. Those who remained seated at the table looked to Mr. C for guidance.

"Help Lillian to her room," he said to Marie and me, and we moved to guide Lillian, who appeared drained, away from the table and into the kitchen, where she winked at us and took a chair at the kitchen table as if sitting down to breakfast.

When Marie and I returned to the dining room, Mr. C was thanking the spirits for indulging us—"We who still inhabit the corporeal world, limited by our senses, bound by our prejudices," and so on and so forth. As the ladies left the table and returned to the sitting room, Mr. C remained seated, his hands folded before him on the table, while Marie and I retrieved coats, stoles, and hats for everyone. Though subdued, the ladies now spoke among themselves in animated whispers. Mrs. Bingham appeared contented, even glad, while Mrs. McKay beamed, gazing at my portrait of her son, which she held in her hands. Meanwhile, out the front window I could see Mr. James and Tucker standing beside the omnibus they'd brought the ladies in, ready to carry them back to the hotel. Before they left the house, though, Mr. C emerged from the dining room, took the hand of each lady in turn and, politely bowing, thanked her for attending. There were many expressions of gratitude and wonder from the ladies—all, that is, except Pauline, who pouted by the door while her sister, Bernice, remained outside on the porch.

It was later, well after the ladies had left and Mr. C and Lillian had retired to their bedroom, while Marie and I were helping Charlie put everything away and return the furniture to its proper place, that I found myself repeating over and over Lillian's phrase—*Ulom, Ulom, Ulom*—puzzled over what it could mean.

WHEN MR. JAMES CAME to the house the next evening, he reported that the two sisters (the ones sharing the same man, identified as Henry) and their mother were made quite upset by the séance, but that, on the whole, the praise for Alexander's extraordinary psychic prowess was resounding. Several ladies expressed the wish to request a private séance if Mr. C ever came to Port Townsend.

"In all," said Mr. James, "I think the evening was a success."

Mr. C concurred and then changed the subject to fishing. "We need to catch a few of those springers," he said to Mr. James. "If they're still running."

My own opinion, though no one asked me for it, was that the evening had ended very disagreeably. I felt sorry for the Eisely sisters having their private affairs revealed before all those biddies, who would undoubtedly gossip it up at their tea parties and Sunshine Club socials. For the first time in a long time, I felt bad for duping those ladies who left believing they had communed with their dearly departed. Yes, they believed what they wanted to believe, and yes, they received a measure of solace in thinking their loved ones were waiting for them on the other side. But wasn't this solace based on a fabulous ruse, one that shamelessly exploited them in their weakened emotional condition? The answer was *Yes*. Unequivocally, *Yes*.

Furthermore, the whole performance left me unnerved. While most of the evening's events had been rehearsed, a portion had not been. Some of what transpired remained a mystery to me, such as the revelation that the sister of one of the ladies, who resided in Aberdeen, had recently given birth to a stillborn child. When I mentioned to Marie that this fact wasn't in the file, she just shrugged and said Mr. C liked to keep a few surprises up his sleeve. Then there was Lillian's trance. In the past, her medium act typically entailed summoning the spirit of a recently deceased person whom most participants would be familiar with yet not know especially well—a local person of prominence or some such. Neither Marie nor I foresaw her broadcasting the unsuspecting sisters' secret—another fact not contained in the file—much less in such a bizarre voice. When I asked Lillian about this, she said she'd decided to improvise. "I was feeling particularly dramatic," she said and laughed. And when I questioned her about *Ulom*, she said she was simply playing off the discussion about ancient Egypt from earlier in the evening. Ulom was her own invention, she explained. "I pictured her as a goddess of the Nile. All powerful and all knowing."

"And she likes to chant her own name," said Marie, ever the smart aleck, eliciting another laugh from Lillian.

All I could think of was how the letters in the name, when transposed, spelled out Lou M—for Lou Morton.

I tried to forget about it and move on with our usual activities at Rialto Beach. Yet, two days after the séance—fifteen days since the incident on the beach—when Charlie had still not heard a word from Lou and neither had his brother in Los Angeles, Charlie asked Mr. C whether they should contact the county sheriff. I was in the closer of the two treehouses at the time and could faintly hear their conversation as it unfolded on the porch of the main house.

"I should have never hired that fellow," Mr. C said, responding to Charlie's concern that Lou might have just gone for a walk and become lost and that maybe a search party should be gotten up to find him. "A person couldn't get so much as a 'good morning' out of him, and I didn't like how he looked at the twins."

"I apologize for that," Charlie said, "and you're probably right, he wasn't the right man for the job. Still, Mr. Conlin...I brought him here and I feel responsible. The man could be out there with a broken leg or starving or who knows what else."

"No law," said Mr. C, putting his foot down. "If you want to talk to Mr. James about putting some men together, maybe getting John Huelsdonk to help track him, I won't stand in your way. Yet if I hear of the sheriff getting involved..."

He didn't need to finish his sentence. Charlie knew good and well his backside would be dirt if he went against Mr. C's directive and called in the authorities. As everyone associated with Mr. C understood, he had a special wariness of law enforcement. A decade or more ago, as the story went, when Mr. C still went under the stage name of Astro the Magician, the District Attorney in San Francisco came after him for swindling a theater owner out of thousands of dollars. With a warrant issued for his arrest, Mr. C went on the lam for two years until the police finally nabbed him and threw him in jail. He posted bail at the excessive sum of ten grand and hired a hotshot lawyer with an office on O'Farrell Street. By the time the trial date arrived, though, the theater owner had died and the DA's case fell apart. Following the charges against him being dropped, in an act of magnanimity meant to spite the DA as much as help the city's needy, Mr. C donated the ten grand in bail money to the Society for the Legal Defense of the Indigent in San Francisco. Then, on another occasion, not long after Marie and I joined the entourage, there was his run-in with the tax collector. He and Lillian had just started the mail-order business for Conlin Enchantments when someone—Mr. C never would say who—tipped off the Internal Revenue Service that they weren't paying taxes on various revenue sources of the new business. Without any notice, the federal taxman came to their house in the West Hollywood hills, accompanied by three sheriff's deputies, and seized all the records and account books for Conlin Enchantments. Mr. C immediately hired the best accountant he could find—someone recommended by the famous movie producer Hal Roach, one of Mr. C's Hollywood pals—and a few days later the records and account books were returned and shortly after that the government investigation suspended.

However, it was just a year prior to this current trip to the Olympic Peninsula that Mr. C again came under suspicion with government authorities, this time US Customs, for running booze out of British Columbia to the compound at Rialto Beach. We weren't there when the raid happened, but according to Mr. James, who was also suspected, the Customs men came in and searched the Rialto Beach house and cabins, the Mora Hotel, and even the cannery on the Dickey River, which was where A. J. Sproul worked, the man Mr. James and Mr. C hired once a month to make the pre-dawn run to Vancouver Island in his Garwood cruiser for several cases of whiskey, gin, and other assorted spirits. Mr. James was no rube, though. He wasn't going to be caught red-handed like that. As Tucker told me, he kept his and Mr. C's hooch stored deep in the woods in a well-camouflaged cement bunker. There were also plenty of watchful neighbors in the area who were more than happy to tip him off whenever Customs decided to make an unannounced visit to Mora or Rialto Beach, giving him plenty of time to dispose of any evidence.

While I felt bad that Charlie was worrying about his hired man, I was relieved when Mr. C told him to keep the sheriff out of it. I figured the more time that was allowed to pass, the less likely any trace of Lou's body would be found. The bruises on my back and arms had faded beyond notice, and the abrasions on my knees and elbows were healing. The only mark that remained was the still-searing memory of what had happened that morning. It kept me up at night and when I did finally fall asleep, it wouldn't be long before I would start awake, smelling his urine in my hair or seeing him with that stick. I would remind myself that he was dead, that when I left the rocks he was beneath the water and not moving. But my imagination would play out various frightful scenarios. The one that recurred the most involved my rucksack, which I could not convince myself had been returned to me. As I lay in bed in the dark, I could see my rucksack still on the beach and knew I would have to return to the Hole-in-the-Wall rock to retrieve it, and when I did, Lou, having freed himself from the rocks, would be waiting in the woods, poised to grab me and finish his brutalization. In another scenario, someone found the body and reported it to the sheriff's office, commencing an investigation that would lead straight to me through some bit of evidence discovered on the beach, and as soon as my sleepless night was over and morning arrived, the police would come to the door to arrest me. In yet another, everyone at Rialto Beach, including Mr. C and Lillian, Marie and Charlie, Cook and Epi and Mel, and even Mr. James and Tucker, knew what had happened and for reasons I could not fathom were conspiring to keep their knowledge secret from me.

These fearful nights left me exhausted and in a state of constant apprehension during the daylight hours. I tried to distract myself any way I could. I finished reading *Miranda*. I filled my sketchbook and decorated the treehouse with my drawings. I played whist with Cook and looked over logging maps with Tucker. I tarried at the post office in Mora to talk with Tealie, whom I began to count as a true friend, finding her composed and imperturbable manner reassuring. Being with Tealie was like having an older sibling, someone more mature and wiser, whose good-humored attention I came to count on to lift my spirits.

When I invited her to visit us in Los Angeles in the winter when the rains on the Olympic Peninsula would be at their worst, Tealie said she would be delighted to and would just have to find someone to fill in for her at the P.O. Then, the next time I saw her, she had an invitation for me. She asked if Marie and I would like to accompany her across the river to La Push. She usually went over once or twice a month to run various errands, she said, and planned to go over the next day.

"I would enjoy the company," she said.

Having never been to La Push, I didn't know what to expect, but welcomed the half-day excursion. From Rialto Beach, we could see the village across the mouth of the river—the houses, school, church, mercantile store, and various storage sheds where the fishermen kept their nets and buoys—yet Marie and I had never ventured there. We had no reason to. We tended to regard the Indians in the area as part of the scenery, another feature of the landscape or part of the local flora and fauna. Just as we would spot a deer or eagle from time to time, we would occasionally see an Indian man or woman walking along the riverbank or beach. Sometimes there would be a nod between us and even occasionally a verbal greeting, but more often than not we quietly passed one another without any greeting or acknowledgment whatsoever.

I accepted her invitation on behalf of both myself and Marie and was pleasantly surprised when Marie did not object to going. The next day as we waited for Tealie to finish up some business at the post office, she grew somewhat voluble in telling us about the local Indians, as if she felt the need to catch us up. She said they were different from the other tribes on the coast of the peninsula—the Makah to the north and the Hoh and Quinault to the south. The Quileute, she explained, were related to the Chimacum on the east side of the peninsula, not far from Port Townsend.

"But Chief Seattle wiped out most of the Chimacum men a long time ago and took most of the women and children into his own tribe," she went on as she sorted the last of the day's mail. "Which just left this branch of the tribe."

Tealie had taken over the postmistress job from her mother, who'd come to Mora shortly after the settlement was established two decades earlier. Except for a year at the Normal School in Ellensburg on the other side of the Cascade Mountains—"Where it almost never rains," she remarked—she'd spent her entire life in Mora.

"And the Makah," she went on, "are related to the Indians on Vancouver Island, see, the Nootka tribes, and they and their kin from Canada used to come down the coast on raiding runs for slaves and the Quileute would climb James Island to fend them off. On top of that, the government tried to force the Quileute onto the Quinaults' big reservation not so long ago, but they weren't having any of it and hunkered down in La Push where they'd always been, and eventually the Bureau of Indian Affairs granted them their own reservation. So they're a tough lot, the Quileute."

Tealie was a very attractive young woman. She was a half foot taller than Marie and me, with a well-proportioned figure, including an elegant collar bone and slender neck that were revealed by the loose midday shirt she wore the afternoon we went to La Push. Her skin was fair, and her hair had blonde streaks in it that caught the rays of sun before she put her crumpled straw hat on. She carried a large carpet bag and a leather case that held her box camera. None of us had packed any provisions other than a few apples, deciding if we got hungry we could surely find something to eat in La Push.

The three of us walked down to the dock by Mora and Tealie set her carpet bag and camera case in a dory. The early afternoon sun on the milky blue river made the ripples sparkle like a thousand silver doubloons. As Marie and I climbed into the dory, neither of us questioned Tealie's ability to row us across the river and back again. Smart girl that she was, she had timed our departure with the ebb tide. Likewise, when we returned to Mora, which was upstream from La Push, it would be on the flow tide.

As Tealie unloosed the ropes and pushed us away from the dock with one of the oars, I thought how I would readily trade my life for hers. She seemed so much more self-sufficient than either Marie or me. Indeed, she embodied the ideal of the new independent woman. I had heard her at various times voice her support of Bertha Knight Landes, the Seattle politician, and Margaret Sanger, the birth control advocate. As for myself, I had yet to cast a vote in a single election, even though it had been five years since passage of the Nineteenth Amendment. Tealie, on the other hand, never missed a chance to cast her ballot, even when it meant traveling all the way to Port Angeles to do so.

"Even if it's just for the county dog catcher," she said, "I'm going to vote."

I also admired how Tealie stood toe-to-toe with any man without the least diminishment of her feminine charms. She would wait out Mr. James as he huffed and puffed upon not receiving the package he'd been expecting and threatened to open a post office box in Forks, and then she would tell him, "Perhaps it will arrive tomorrow. If it does, I will deliver it myself." It was especially a pleasure to watch her with

Mr. C, tolerating his tales of life on the road, smiling indulgently at his anecdotes about Hollywood actors, and deflecting his shameless flirtations with her.

Just that very morning, after driving Marie and me up the road to Mora, Mr. C had entered the post office and had the temerity to take Tealie's hand through the grill of the front desk and kiss it.

"My dear," he said, "when can we schedule a private séance for you? Surely there's someone you would like to commune with."

"Really, Mr. Conlin," she replied. "I will not be responsible for any more of your ectoplasm being released into this world. You ought to conserve your psychokinetic urges for the ladies of Port Townsend."

Duly rebuffed, Mr. C smiled wanly at her. "You're a skeptic of the highest order," he said with just the suggestion of a bow. "And I must say, it becomes you."

Tealie handed Mr. C his mail and wished him good day.

"Well then," he said, not so easily deterred, "perhaps you'll come to dinner next Saturday evening after Harold Lloyd arrives to pay us a visit."

Through the metal grill, Tealie looked him in the eye.

"He's a delightful man," he added, seeing that he'd gotten her attention. "He's promised to preview his new picture for us."

From where I stood watching this exchange, it seemed that Mr. C had finally gotten the upper hand on Tealie, that he had finally snared her with the bait of meeting a true Hollywood star.

"I've heard of him," she said, unimpressed, as it became clear I was wrong and that she was having none of it. "Is he as funny as Charlie Chaplin? I love Charlie Chaplin. I thought I heard that Charlie Chaplin would be coming to Rialto Beach." She tilted her head and looked at Mr. C with a kind of simpleton's wide-eyed gaze.

Mr. C kept his composure. "No, my dear," he answered, "you heard wrong. It is Harold Lloyd who's coming to Rialto Beach. Not Charlie Chaplin. And I must inform you that Mr. Lloyd's comedic acting is unparalleled. He's a master of the pratfall, a genius of the madcap. Far funnier than your Charles Chaplin. I'm sure you'll enjoy his company very much if you come to dinner when he travels here from Hollywood."

Mr. C was laying it on thick, and I waited for him to tell Tealie, as he did everyone, how he, Claude Alexander Conlin (a.k.a. the Crystal

Seer), had been the inspiration for Harold Lloyd's picture *Luke, the Crystal Gazer*, one of the comedic shorts in the actor's *Lonesome Luke* series. He didn't, however.

"Next Saturday, did you say?" Tealie asked, leading Mr. C on. "I'd love to but I've promised Ona Fletcher I would help her gather fiddleheads. She puts up several dozen jars each spring season and feeds them year-round to her husband, Arn. He loves them with a little butter and salt and pepper. As do I. I'm told they taste like artichokes, though I've never eaten an artichoke. Have you, Mr. Conlin? That is, ever eaten an artichoke. I wouldn't even know what one looked like."

In a nutshell, that was how Tealie dealt with Mr. C. I almost felt sorry for him as he turned away from Tealie, saw the bemused expressions that Marie and I fought to conceal, and frowned at us. "You ladies enjoy your visit to La Push," was all he said and walked out.

Tealie deftly rowed the dory into the middle of the river, allowing us to drift downstream until, approaching the mouth of the river where I could see the Rialto Beach compound to the right and La Push to the left, she swung the dory toward La Push and rowed us straight into a slough where the Indians kept their fishing boats and canoes tied to a half-dozen narrow docks.

"That was fun," Marie said, seated in the bow of the boat. Her injured ankle no longer hindered her, and as soon as the dory bumped up against one of the docks she jumped out.

After tying the dory to the dock, Tealie explained that her first order of business was to stop at the schoolhouse to deliver the box of first-level primers she had raised the money to buy. The school building had recently received a new coat of white paint. Two slim trees out front, de-limbed and stripped of their bark, served as flagpoles, flying the Stars and Stripes and the green Washington State flag. Class was in session, so Marie and I waited outside while Tealie went in to speak to the teacher, a young white woman who, working for the Indian School Service, had recently come to La Push from South Dakota to take over from the previous teacher, who had quit to marry a logger from Forks.

The village of La Push was twice the size of Mora with five times the number of inhabitants. From the schoolhouse we walked past a row of shacks covered in tarpaper and came to a long smokehouse with grayish plumes billowing from three stove pipes in its roof. A woman in a headscarf sat outside by the door at a makeshift table stringing smelt, which the Indians caught by the thousands with large purse seine nets just off shore. Each string held thirty or so of the small silvery fish on it, and there were a dozen strings hanging between two support poles outside the shack. The woman smiled at Tealie through cracked lips and stained teeth. Tealie leaned in toward her to introduce us.

"Mrs. Hay-nee-si-oos, these are two of my friends, *tillacums*, from across the river. Marie and Marguerite."

We nodded to Mrs. Hay-nee-si-oos and she nodded back, looking from one of us to the other as people often did when Marie and I were introduced to them. She laughed and said, "You don't need a mirror, you girls. Both so pretty."

"Thank you," Marie and I said in unison, and when we both became tongue-tied trying to pronounce her name, she told us we could call her Ella.

She then offered us the smoked smelt, and Tealie told her we would come back for some, but right now we had errands to run.

"Will you go to the meeting tonight?" Ella asked.

"We'll see," Tealie answered, and as we walked away she explained that the Indian Shakers met every Wednesday at six o'clock in the village meeting house. When we asked who the Indian Shakers were, she said that maybe we should just go to the meeting and find out for ourselves. I found this answer rather brusque and figured Tealie was growing weary of explaining every detail of Indian life to us.

We walked to the edge of the village and saw a group of men down along the beach carving up seals, the carcasses splayed open on the rocks, exposing the whitish blubber beneath the dark mottled seal hide. The men sliced chunks of blubber from the seals and handed them to a woman who carried them to a large kettle hung above an open fire. The blubber was rendered down for lantern oil, Tealie said, since only the schoolhouse and mercantile store had electricity. She took her camera from its leather case and snapped several pictures of the men and women on the beach.

Our next stop was the mercantile store, not far from the beach, where we met Mr. Riebe, the store owner, who had arranged to sell Tealie a number of craft items made by members of the tribe. Tealie had started collecting such items years ago. Today she was picking up two large baskets (one woven from strips of cedar bark, the other from twined spruce root), a mussel shell rattle, and a robe made of dog wool, which Mr. Riebe swung over my shoulders so I could feel how soft it was. Marie, meanwhile, picked up the rattle and shook it, creating a sound like water cascading over pebbles.

"These baskets are woven so tight, they can hold water," Mr. Riebe said, handing them to Tealie. "Only a few of the women elders make them any longer."

Tealie inspected the baskets and handed them to Marie and me. She got her camera out again and snapped a photograph of Mr. Riebe and the many craft items arrayed along the back wall of the store. We left and carried the items back to the dory. By now it was late afternoon and we were hungry, so we returned to the village hoping to find Ella and eat some of her smoked fish. As we approached the smoke-house, a throng of children came stampeding toward us. School had let out and they'd heard their friend Tealie was in the village with special guests.

"Twins, twins, twins," they shouted as they stumbled over one another in front of us. The girls all wore simple frocks and the boys knickers. Several children were barefoot. They all had round, dimpled faces and bashful smiles and dark skin and straight black hair.

The children gazed in wonderment from Marie to me and back again. Having been warned in advance by Tealie that the children might take special notice of us, we'd come prepared. When we had first joined Mr. C's act, he would teach us simple magic tricks during the long train rides from city to city. Sometimes he would let one of us go out into the lobby as people entered the theater and perform as "The Lassie of Legerdemain" to help warm up the audience. Though it had been a couple of years since either us had done any of these sleight-of-hand tricks, they were so basic that we never lost the knack for them.

First Marie did the handkerchief-and-egg trick, turning one into the other and back again. I followed with the elevating pencil trick, laying a pencil flat in the palm of one hand and with a wave of the other hand making it stand up straight. Next Marie folded and tore up a piece of paper and, after crumbling the pieces into a ball, restored them to a single sheet. And finally, the one that delighted the children most—I pulled a nickel from each child's ear and laid it in his or her palm—seventeen nickels in all, which I'd been carrying with me the whole while in a small interior pocket of my jacket.

After that some of the children ran off to the mercantile store for penny candy while others trailed behind us as we strolled to the smokehouse. Ella, who lived in a small hut right next to the smokehouse, set out chairs for us between the smokehouse and her hut. She brought us each a plate of smoked smelt and a bowl of boiled nettles. While Tealie went right at hers, pulling the smelt apart with her teeth and slurping up the broth from the nettles, Marie and I gingerly picked at ours. The smelt had a brininess made even sharper by the wood smoke, and the nettles were slimy and left a taste like mildewed hay in my mouth. Ella watched Marie and me with bemusement and after a while took our plates and bowls away and returned with plates loaded with strawberry-rhubarb pie topped with whipped cream, which we gobbled right up.

"Would you like more?" she asked, seeing how we'd cleaned our plates of the pie and whipped cream.

"No thank you," I said.

"The pie was delicious, Ella," Marie chimed in. "Strawberries are my favorite."

Ella had a few chores to attend to before the Shaker meeting, so Tealie and I and Marie, having decided to accompany her to the meeting, stayed by the smokehouse and watched the sun slowly slide toward the ocean horizon. I was both curious and nervous about the Shaker meeting. Tealie admitted that she'd only ever been to one and didn't know a whole lot about the Indian Shakers. She did know that they had nothing to do with the New England Shakers.

"Are they Christians?" Marie asked with some tentativeness.

"Yes, of course," Tealie said. The church, she believed, was started by a Squaxin Indian near Olympia. "I forget his name, but the story goes he was a terrible gambler and drunkard and when he died God met him at the pearly gates and told him the only way he could enter heaven was to return to earth and prepare a church for his people, one guided by very simple precepts like temperance and cleanliness. Then he gave the Squaxin man some bells and candles and sent him on his way."

"And what happened?" Marie asked.

"Well, three days later, just before they were to bury him, he came back alive."

"And why are they called Shakers?" I asked.

"They do a lot of shaking," said Tealie and chuckled. "They say it's part of the healing."

Ella had returned by then and gone into her hut. A little while later she came out dressed in a white linen dress that covered her arms and fell to the tops of her black patent-leather shoes. Tealie, Marie, and I stared at her as if she were some kind of angelic vision.

"Did you tell them about Joe Slocum?" she asked Tealie.

"Yes," she said, "though I'd forgotten his name."

"Oh, he was a bad one. But God gave him a second chance and he used it. He was a smart Indian." With that Ella set off for the church and we followed.

With the afternoon light waning, Ella's white dress took on a radiant orange-red hue. As we walked down the dirt road, a church bell rang, and as we approached the church, a score of people, also dressed in white robes and dresses, converged at the entrance. I looked to Marie and that one look told me that she felt as out of place as I did, given that she and I and Tealie were the only ones not dressed in white—as well as the only non-Indians.

The church building was a simple clapboard structure with a pitched roof, a small steeple, and two windows on each side wall. The one-room interior was unfinished, the joists and lathes exposed. To my surprise, there were no pews, only benches placed along the walls, leaving the entire wood-plank floor open, as if for a square dance. Ella directed us to take a seat on one of the benches, while the Indians who came in gathered in the center of the floor and just stood there. As the light outside the windows diminished and we waited for the service to begin, I noticed the many candles lit throughout the room. They rested on small wooden platforms along the walls, especially toward the front of the room, where at least twenty large candles burned radiantly upon a table that appeared to serve as the altar. The table was also arrayed with handbells of all sizes, as if there was going to be a bell choir like the one that had visited St. Anne's each Christmas. On the wall above the table was the largest cross I'd seen since leaving St. Anne's. It must have been six feet in length. It was a simple cross made of some native wood, not a crucifix, so there was no bloody and emaciated body of Christ to have to stare at. Other than that, the church was bare of adornment, and search as I might, there was not a single Bible in sight. There were no hymnals either. In truth, compared to the ornate Catholic church I'd come to know at St. Anne's, the simplicity of this interior was quite appealing. Sitting quietly on the bench, I began to feel the kind of serenity I'd felt while sitting on the beach log looking out at the ocean in the moments before I was attacked—a feeling that, once I recognized it, took on a heavy sense of foreboding.

Eventually, after more people had assembled in the church, two women stepped forward to lead the service. They faced the cross, each lifting a candle to it, and sang the Lord's Prayer in lovely harmony. Then they turned to the congregation and began to sing some more, and soon everyone in the church was singing with them. They didn't sing in English or Spanish or any other language I recognized. They were singing in the Quileute language, as I would learn later, and sometimes in the Chinook jargon, which Tealie occasionally used in speaking to her Indian acquaintances.

As one song followed another, the congregation's singing went from ordinary to rapturous. After half a dozen songs, the two women each gave a litany in English followed by a prayer of invocation asking for God's forgiveness of their sins and God's blessing on all Indian people. The congregants crossed themselves in unison, just as Catholics do. One of the women at the table then began passing out the handbells and candles to the congregants while another led a procession around the floor. Everyone held the candles aloft, rang the bells, and chanted in Quileute. The sound became almost deafening, and with each turn about the church, two or three people stepped out of the procession, moved to the middle of the vacant floor, and dropped to their knees with their hands held forth in supplication or clasped in prayer. Eventually the woman leading the procession stepped up to a man on his knees and began vigorously ringing her handbell about his shoulders and head, reminding me of how Father Albert, the presiding priest at St. Anne's, would swing the thurible to bless the congregation with incense smoke. As she did so, the procession broke up and members approached the other people on their knees and rang their bells about them as well.

In short order, several congregants began shaking. It started as a mild shivering but soon turned into the twisting and jerking of arms, legs, and torsos. Others began praying aloud. When a thin, frail-looking man who was visibly sweating was led to the middle of the floor and allowed to sit cross-legged, half a dozen members gathered about him and commenced ringing their bells, shaking, and chanting over him. The man was Ella's cousin, who had tuberculosis, and that evening's meeting was dedicated to his healing. Indeed, Ella was one of the more exuberant shakers, keeping up her trance-like dance beside her cousin longer than anyone else.

What happened next, however, nearly undid me. An older man in a white frock-like shirt and white painter's pants who had been steadily circling the room ringing his handbell languorously and chanting in a low murmur stopped right in front of where we sat. In the next instant, he reached down and touched my hands where I held them in my lap. He then let out a wail and began clanging his handbell in front of me, starting above my head and moving down the length of my body until he reached my feet. I wanted to shout at him to stop, to push him away, but I was too scared. I looked at Marie sitting next to me and saw the astonishment on her face. The man chanted something in Quileute, and then a woman, also in white, approached and began convulsing in front of me. Just as I was about to push myself up from the bench and move away, the man stopped ringing his bell and the woman stopped shaking and they drifted back in among the congregants circling the floor.

"I need some air," I said and, seizing Marie's hand to take her with me, hurried out the door.

Not until the cool air outside hit my face did I realize how oppressively hot it had been inside the church. Stars saturated the blue-black sky, and most mercifully of all, the night was utterly quiet.

"What was that man *doing*?" Marie asked. "And that woman?"

I was almost crying at this point, so distressed was I by what had happened inside.

"I don't know," I said. "I don't know." I looked about at the dark empty streets, wondering what we should do—*Should I tell Marie? Was now the time?*—and in the next instant Tealie came out and informed us the service was coming to an end.

"Are you all right?" she asked, touching my elbow.

"I think so," I answered, recovering myself. "It was just so strange." I was far more upset, and more afraid, than I let on. I felt so weak I had to lean against the corner of the church building to support myself.

"And deafening," Marie added. "Those bells are still ringing in my ears."

Ella was among the first congregants to come out of the church. She was quiet at first as we walked back toward her hut and the smokehouse, but eventually Tealie asked her why that man had picked me out the way he had.

"God leads us," she answered. "And we do His works." She didn't say anything more for several moments, but as we approached her hut she stopped and turned to me. "That man is Quinault. He lives in Taholah and goes to services here and all over the peninsula. His name is Horton Mowich. He's a *tamahnus* man, from the old ways. He's very wise, but he should know better than to behave that way with guests. I'm sorry." She appeared bothered and turned her face toward the sky, closed her eyes, and took a deep breath. When she opened her eyes, she smiled and said, "My son, George, he'll take you back upriver in his new boat. He's very proud of it."

With that, Ella went into her hut and we made our way back to the dock. George, a young man in overalls and a plaid shirt, was already there, tying Tealie's dory to the back of his boat. Fishing nets and baskets full of sluckus were stacked on the deck, so we sat in the wheelhouse near the bow. When Tealie complimented him on his new boat, George just grinned and started the engine.

Once on the river, I began to feel better. I took off my hat and let the wind blow through my hair. No one spoke as we crossed the river, but as we idled toward the Mora dock, Tealie tapped George on the shoulder and asked him what a tamahnus man was.

"It's a Chinook word for spirit or medicine man," he said as he sidled the boat up to the dock. "He chases away bad spirits. Some of the old people have a tamahnus man bless their boats before fishing. Whatever helps, right?"

THE TAMAHNUS MAN HAUNTED my sleep that night. I kept hearing clanging bells and would sit up in bed waiting for Marie to wake up from hearing them too. But the room was still, the only sound the surf hitting the beach, the wind tossing in the trees, and my own anxious breathing. I pictured the tamahnus man standing over me, speaking in the voice of Lou Morton, asking me to save him. Then I pictured George pulling up his nets at sea and discovering the bloated and bleached-out body of a large Caucasian man. The sheriff identifies the body and comes to Rialto Beach. A pencil point is found embedded in the back of the dead man's hand, and Lillian remembers how the rucksack had my sketchbook in it but not my pencil. I wait for her to say something to the sheriff, and while I wait I look around for Mr. C so he can tell me how to escape the handcuffs the sheriff is about to slap on my wrists. But Mr. C is off hunting. I then picture us all returning to Los Angeles and on the afternoon of our first rehearsal at the Pantages Theater, Lou appears at the stage door. He talks to Mr. C and Charlie, giving some far-fetched excuse for his disappearance, which they accept, patting him on the back and welcoming him back to the crew. From then on, he's always watching me, or rather me and Marie since he still can't tell us apart. Plus, his confusion has made him even crazier and more obsessed, so to extract his revenge for what happened at the beach, he's going to kill us both. Yet, when I go to Mr. C to tell him that Lou scares me, hoping he'll fire him, Mr. C only gets mad at me for being such a scared little child. "I'm not a child," I shout at him. "I'm twenty-one years old." And then I see Lou, who's been standing behind the stage curtain eavesdropping on us the whole while, and he's standing beside someone who resembles the tamahnus man. They're both looking at me, waiting to see what I'll do next.

Throughout the long night my mind kept reeling, tormenting me with such scenarios. At one point I imagined going down to the kitchen for a glass of milk, bringing my book and an extra blanket and climbing up to the treehouse, but instead I rolled over and kept worrying. Eventually, when the darkness behind the window began to fade and I could make out the fir trees on the parameter of the compound, I dropped off to sleep.

When I woke up, Marie was already out of bed, which surprised me until I looked at my bedside clock and saw that it was nearly noon. I remembered that yesterday she'd told me she and Charlie were going to do something together today, though I couldn't remember what. As I washed and dressed, I felt more haggard from lack of sleep than I had since my ordeal began. I made up my mind to ask Mr. C when we would be returning to Los Angeles, even though I knew he didn't like us asking him that. He liked to say he operated on his own clock and that clock had no hands.

When I finally dragged myself out of bed and downstairs, Cook was the only person still in the house. He told me that Mr. Conlin was on his way to Port Angeles to meet the boat bringing Harold Lloyd from Seattle. He also said that Hal Roach, the producer, would be accompanying Mr. Lloyd. Epi had gone with Mr. C, he explained, and they would be back late tomorrow. Meanwhile, he added, Mel had taken Mrs. Conlin to Forks, and Marie and Charlie changed their plans about having a picnic at the pond near Mora and had wandered up the beach.

I listened to Cook in a daze until he mentioned that Marie and Charlie had gone up the beach. Then I felt as if all my anxiety from the previous night was coming true, that they would discover the body and all would be found out.

"Thank you, Cook," I said and went straight to the study to find the local almanac. In all the scenarios that had played out in my head the night before, not one involved Marie. I located the tide table in the almanac and ran my finger down the column for the month of June and was relieved to see that the next low tide wasn't until later that evening. Surely, Marie and Charlie would return from their walk by then. And surely they wouldn't go as far as the Hole-in-the-Wall. All the same, the momentary shock of what might have been left me drained, and when Cook came into the room to ask if I would like lunch, I told him no and asked if he would bring me a glass of water and some headache powder. I even considered trying to find Mr. C's vial of tincture of opium so I could have some small relief from my anxiety, yet, as I already knew, he took extra care to hide it someplace where only he could find it.

For the next hour or more, I stayed in the study, sitting in Mr. C's leather armchair. When my headache finally subsided, I went into the kitchen—Cook had left—and found some cheese and crackers to eat. I was seated at the tin-topped side table staring at the onions and garlic hanging from a wire basket beside the pantry when I heard an automobile coming down the road. I figured it was Mel driving Lillian back from Forks, but when I looked out the window I saw that it was Tucker driving one of Mr. James's vehicles. The canvas top was down, and in the backseat, springing forward on its hind legs, its snarling mouth revealing its formidable incisors, was the cougar that Mr. Huelsdonk had shot and killed.

I reached the porch just as Tucker was climbing out of the driver's seat. He tipped his hat to me and asked if I would hold the front door for him. He hoisted the large stuffed cat out of the backseat of the car, struggled to get a grip on it, and then tottered up the stone steps with it in his arms. Mounted on a platform constructed to resemble a fallen tree, the cougar was nearly as big as he was.

"I was told to put it in the study," he said as he bumped it against the doorframe and entered the house.

"To the left," I said and followed him.

Tucker set the stuffed cougar in a corner of the room, took off his hat, and paused to catch his breath.

"Geez," was all I could say.

"There's more," he said and went back to the car and a moment later returned carrying a bearskin rug. Its head was still attached, its maw wide open to reveal its incisors (twice as large as the cougar's) and thick red tongue. When Tucker laid it in the middle of the floor with its legs splayed out, it looked like an enormous flying squirrel.

There was already a deer head mounted on the wall, but these two new additions of the taxidermist arts made the room seem like a branch of the Boone and Crockett Club. The study now belonged to the great white hunter, which was no doubt how Mr. C fancied himself whenever he came to the Olympic Peninsula.

"Mr. Conlin told Mr. James he wanted them here in time for his guests," Tucker explained.

"Is that so," I said, wondering how Mr. Lloyd and Mr. Roach would respond to the display. They would certainly know they were no longer in Los Angeles. I could already hear Mr. C bragging about shooting the bear, embellishing the story so that he fires his rifle just in time to avoid being mauled by the charging bruin.

His task accomplished, Tucker seemed at a loss over what to do next. His eyes wandered about the study walls, and it was plain to see he was stalling, that he didn't want to return to Mora just yet.

"Sure are a lot of books," he said. "Mr. Conlin likes to do a lot reading?"

"He likes to have a lot of books," I replied, not sure he took my meaning.

"How much longer you folks going to be up this way?" he asked.

"Mr. Conlin hasn't said," I answered truthfully. "Another few weeks. Maybe longer."

Tucker looked over his shoulder through the doorway of the study and into the sitting room as if to make sure there was no one around, and then, taking hold of my elbow and leaning in close to me, he said, "The reason I ask is this. Some of the boys have been talking about how Mr. Conlin's been stepping out with the Eisely girl in P.A."

For an instant I didn't know what he was saying. I thought he said L.A., and how would the loggers and mill workers know anything about Mr. C's life in Los Angeles? Then it dawned on me—he meant Port Angeles.

"What girl?" I asked, shaking my arm free to let him know I didn't appreciate his gossip-mongering. Maybe he was behaving ugly just to get back at me for not taking that walk on the beach with him. Of course, if I had waited to go with him, I would never have been attacked.

"The one that was here for the ghost talks," he said, referring to the séance. "Pauline Eisely."

Yes, I thought, recalling the two sisters who'd come with their mother, Mrs. Eisely. There was Pauline (the flapper) and Bernice (the dowdy sister)—the ones Lillian, in the voice of *Ulom*, had exposed when she revealed that the dowdy sister was dallying with the flapper's beau.

"I'm no snoop," Tucker said defensively, "but I feel obliged to tell someone here 'bouts. That is, if he wishes to keep outta trouble."

I didn't appreciate the folksy manner Tucker seemed to adopt in order to deliver this bit of information. It was like a screen he threw up to hide behind. I'd had enough.

"Is that so?" I snapped back, my hands on my hips. "Well, let me tell you. Mr. Conlin's business is no one's but his own. He can take care of himself without some two-bit timber cruiser sticking his nose into it."

Tucker shook his head solemnly when I had finished, as if to say he regretted my ignorance of the gravity of the situation. "It's like this," he said more straightforwardly. "Mr. Eisely—that is, Roger Eisely—owns four mills between here and Port Angeles, more than anyone on this part of the peninsula, and he wasn't pleased when he heard from his wife what happened here the night they all came for the ghost talk. Or whatever you call it. *Sea-ants*."

"*Séance*," I corrected him.

"But what made the situation even worse," he went on, "is when Mr. Conlin showed up in town a couple days later when the missus was out of the house and took Miss Pauline for a ride in that fancy automobile of his. A fella who knows Mr. Eisely and works at the lodge at Lake Crescent says that's where they ended up."

"At the lake?"

"No," Tucker said impatiently. "The lodge."

"Maybe he took her to lunch," I suggested. "I hear there's a lovely restaurant there."

I knew better than this, though. Two days after the séance, Mr. C had told us he was going fishing on the Elwah River, about twenty miles from Port Angeles, and would be gone for a day or two. I remember thinking it odd that Mr. James, his dependable fishing guide, hadn't gone with him.

"They took a cabin," Tucker said, "and she didn't return to the house until later that night."

He didn't need to say anything more. He could see now that I understood exactly what he was saying.

"I like Mr. Conlin," he said. "But he picked the wrong man's daughter to have a toss in the hay with. All the trouble stirred up over that business between the two sisters and Henry Sprague had old Eisely steaming already. After he found out about the lodge he told his foremen at the Shuwah mill to put the word out to his men that if a logging truck ran Mr. Conlin's car off the road or some other accident befell him in the woods, well…"

I didn't know what to say to this and sat down in the armchair, eye-level with the bounding cougar. Of course, this wouldn't be the first time Mr. C had gotten himself in an entanglement of this sort. Only a year ago, Lillian had put a stop to the "Ladies Only Matinee" that we typically performed on Sunday afternoons in whatever town we were in, knowing her husband used the special performances to obtain the names, addresses, and well-guarded (or not-so-well guarded) secrets of the town's most susceptible females. I knew that if I told Lillian that I'd been warned of a complication following last week's séance—being as elliptical in my delivery as Tucker had been folksy—she would take my meaning and effect the prompt departure of Mr. C and his entourage from Rialto Beach. But I didn't know whether that was something I could, or should, do. Maybe it was none of my business either.

"Thank you, Tucker," I said, a bit abashed by my earlier outburst. He put his hat back on. "I wouldn't want to see any harm come to anyone," he said. "Especially to you or your sister. Especially on his account."

I told him he needn't worry and thanked him again, then mentioned that we might be leaving sooner than I'd previously thought. Yet, all I could do was wish it were so.

MR. C HAD LEFT a message with Lillian that he wanted Marie and me to look our best when he returned with Harold Lloyd and Hal Roach. He wanted to show us off—his Nartell Twins—like a pair of prized trophies, not unlike his stuffed cougar and bearskin rug. I also suspected he wanted to lure a proposal of marriage for one or the other of us from the star actor. Maybe he hadn't noticed that Marie and Charlie were practically engaged already. Since their return from Victoria—which Mr. C had eventually consented to—they'd been inseparable, and Lillian and I both anticipated an announcement before our stay at Rialto Beach was through. It was no secret either that Mr. C was eager to cozy up to studio bigwigs from Hollywood so he could move into the picture show business once he retired from the stage. As for myself, I was exhausted. There seemed to be no end to, or reprieve from, my ordeal and the constant pressure of keeping my secret. As long as we remained at Rialto Beach, it seemed, I was condemned to be forever speculating about how it would all end. Once or twice I even wondered if I should not just walk out into the ocean myself and disappear.

But all this was beside the point because Mr. C had given us our marching orders and we knew we had better step to. Marie and I dolled ourselves up as best we could in the wilderness outpost that was Rialto Beach. And as we rouged our lips and powdered our noses, primped our hair and batted our false eyelashes, and each tried on several different dresses, my mood lightened. I became excited about the imminent arrival of our Hollywood guests.

When the sedan pulled up to the house, the three of us—Lillian, Marie, and I—stepped outside to welcome them. Like welcoming royalty, Lillian walked down the stairs to be the first to greet the guests while Marie and I remained on the porch. When Mr. C waved us forward, we approached in tandem. In the course of our time with Conlin Enchantments, Marie and I had met many of Mr. C's Hollywood pals—Clara Bow, ZaSu Pitts, Boris Karloff, and others who would attend his shows in Los Angeles—but we had yet to meet Harold Lloyd or Hal Roach. To be honest, after seeing Mr. Lloyd in *Safety Last!* at the Granada Theater a year earlier, I'd developed a bit of crush on the adorable bumbler and wondered how much his real-life person resembled his on-screen persona.

All three men were in a jocular mood despite the long trip from Port Angeles. It was plain to see they'd been nipping at the bottle. After introducing both men to Lillian, Mr. C turned their attention to Marie and me. As they approached, we both curtsied before them like the polite Catholic schoolgirls we'd once been.

"Charmed," said Mr. Roach to Marie as he took her hand and kissed it. "*Enchanté,*" he said to me, kissing my hand as well.

"Pleased to meet you," said Mr. Lloyd with a little more modesty as he shook first my hand and then Marie's. He even appeared to blush a little.

Like the movie characters he played, Mr. Lloyd was rather shy. Mr. Roach, on the other hand, was quite garrulous. Though they were approximately the same age, Mr. Lloyd was slim and fit while Mr. Roach was jowly and a bit hunched in the shoulders. There was something mildly comical about the two as they stood side by side, the tall Mr. Lloyd in his straw boater and round spectacles and the stocky Mr. Roach in his gray fedora and white spats.

Marie and I escorted each man to his designated cabin—Marie led Mr. Roach as I led Mr. Lloyd—and after they had been allowed an hour or so to settle in and change into fresh clothes, Mr. C had everyone convene in the study of the main house so he could show off the cougar and bear. When Mr. Lloyd said the bear reminded him of Mr. Roach when they worked on their last picture together—"I swear, he had a permanent growl," said Mr. Lloyd—we were relieved that Mr. Roach could just laugh it off, remarking how *Safety Last!* was the best picture either one of them would ever make.

As Marie and I served drinks in the sitting room, Mr. Lloyd and Mr. Roach laughed at Mr. C's tale of how the Customs detectives searched the house last summer and how A. J. Sproul outran their government boats between here and Canada every time. "He enjoys the chase," said Mr. C.

"Truth be told, I prefer Canadian whiskey," Mr. Roach remarked. "If we ever get this prohibition repealed, which won't be soon enough, I'm going to stick with it as my way of thanking the Canucks for seeing us through this ordeal."

"I'll toast to that," said Mr. C and raised his glass.

At Mr. C's behest, Cook served elk steaks and wild turkey breasts. Fortunately, he slathered both dishes in heavy gravy to conceal the gamey taste, so even Marie managed to down a few bites.

At dinner I noticed for the first time that Mr. Lloyd wore a beige glove on his right hand. When he saw me looking at it, he took the index finger and thumb of the glove and tied them into a knot with his other hand.

"How's that for dexterity?" he said. I must have looked amazed. He laughed and explained he'd lost his thumb and index finger five years ago in an accident on set. "I don't like to draw attention to it, so I wear the glove."

"And still he does all his own stunts. The man's a true wonder," Mr. Roach piped in. "If you look real close, you'll see the glove when he's holding onto the clock arm three stories above the street."

After dinner, back in the sitting room with a fire blazing in the hearth, Mr. Lloyd revealed to Mr. C and Lillian that he was engaged to the actress Mildred Davis. The news came as a mild disappointment to me, so maybe I truly did feel a little lovelorn in regards to my crush on Mr. Lloyd. More likely, though, I was just lonely, longing for the kind of romantic companionship that Marie had clearly found in Charlie.

"That's delightful news, Harold. Don't you think so, Claude?" said Lillian.

"Positively," said Mr. C.

"It's wonderful news all right," said Mr. Roach and raised his glass to his friend. "Millie is a beautiful and charming girl."

"Congratulations, Mr. Lloyd," I said.

"Thank you," he replied.

"Please, dear," Mr. Roach interjected, "you and your sister—and forgive me if I can't tell you apart—must stop with such formalities. He's Hank and I'm Hal."

"Yes, sir," I replied, and turning to Mr. Lloyd said, "Congratulations, Hank."

"Thank you again, Marguerite," he returned, and I knew right then Mildred Davis was indeed a fortunate lady.

WE DIDN'T SEE OUR guests the next day because they drove off at dawn with Mr. C to go fishing along the Sol Duc River. While Marie took her turn helping Lillian with the mail-order psychic readings, I spent most of the day in the treehouse reading a new book, another from Mr. C's bookshelf, titled *Khaled: A Tale of Arabia*, by F. Marion Crawford. It was about a genie, condemned by Allah to be human, who could only be saved by the lovely Arabian princess he falls in love with. Such nonsense, I thought, and when I put the book down I reminded myself to tell Charlie next time he was in Port Angeles to go to the five-and-dime and pick up a new sketchbook for me. I was going doubly crazy without my drawing to preoccupy me.

At lunch, Lillian informed us that we would all be going into Forks the following day for a late afternoon showing of Harold Lloyd's new picture at the Lumbermen's Hall. Mr. C had rented the hall in advance for this purpose and had invited everyone he knew. Mr. Lloyd, she explained, had been kind enough to bring a prerelease print of the film in eight reels with him from Los Angeles. Charlie and Mel had already retrieved the projector and phonograph from Port Angeles that would be needed for the showing in the Lumbermen's Hall.

That evening after the sun had gone down, the men returned laden with fish. Mr. Lloyd and Mr. Roach each carried a string of three or four hefty salmon. Looking every bit like an over-excited boy, Mr. Lloyd held up his string and said, "How 'bout that?" as we greeted him from the porch.

"Where's Cook?" shouted Mr. C. "We want to get these springers on the grill."

At dinner that evening Mr. C turned to Mr. Roach and brought up his recently hatched idea of Marie and me starring in our own series of comedic shorts under the auspices of Hal Roach Studios. The scenario for the first in the series went like this: The adorably naïve and unsuspecting Nartell Twins arrive in the big city from the Kansas cornfields (or maybe an orphanage). They go to work in a bicycle factory and get caught up with a couple of con men who use them to scam a big uptown financier (who also happens to own the bicycle factory). The financier falls in love with one of the twins. But which one? He can't tell them apart! Meanwhile, the other twin's heart belongs to the simple and honest factory floor worker who shared his lunch pail with her on her first day of work. As Mr. C spun it, the plot was filled with all manner of capers and escapades that befall the darling twins in the big city.

"The girls are very athletic," Mr. C added. "They could do all their own stunts, just like Hank here."

"I like the idea," Mr. Roach said. "You might really have something there, Claude. The twins certainly have appeal." He then winked at us. It was clear—to me, at least—that he was being the gracious guest and humoring Mr. C. How many times each week did some kook rattle off another movie idea to him, expecting the owner of Hal Roach Studios to be his ticket to Hollywood fame? "Let's keep thinking on it," he said to Mr. C, "and talk some more when we return to Los Angeles."

Mr. C appeared satisfied with this response, but one glance at Marie told me she herself wasn't so pleased. She understood there was no real future for us in Mr. C's mind-reading shows, that they were fast becoming a relic of the past. She knew that the real magic, the true world of illusion, was taking place on the big screen. So she wanted Mr. C and Mr. Roach to keep talking about the movies that The Nartell Twins would star in. She wanted our signatures to be on a studio contract, one that guaranteed a separate dressing room for each of us, before Mr. Roach left Rialto Beach.

"What would the movie be called?" she asked, turning eagerly to Mr. C.

"I don't know," he replied. "I'm sure Hal has a team of writers who would think of something very clever."

"We have the best writers in the business," Mr. Roach said. "More than we know what to do with. Ain't that right, Hank?" He leaned back and eyed Harold Lloyd, and for just an instant there was something gangster-like in the way he curled his lip and squinted at Mr. Lloyd.

Everyone—that is, everyone who read *Variety*—knew that Harold Lloyd had left Hal Roach Studios following their last picture together to start his own production company. While the two remained friends, it appeared the split was still a sore point between them.

Mr. Lloyd nodded and said there were plenty of good writers in Hollywood to go around. "If Hal here passes on the project with the twins, Claude, you come see me at Harold Lloyd Productions. We're right there in Culver City." He smiled at Hal Roach, who smirked right back at him.

The next morning was devoted to preparations for the matinee premiere of *Girl Shy*, Mr. Lloyd's first movie with his new production company. As with Mr. C and his stage act, Mr. Lloyd insisted on overseeing every detail involving his picture. This meant he had Charlie, who was serving as the projectionist, and Tucker, who was in charge of changing the records on the phonograph, running around frantically.

Showtime was 3:00 p.m., so Mr. C drove Lillian, Mr. Roach, Marie, and me into Forks shortly after lunch. He'd given Cook, Epi, and Mel permission to go into town to see the picture as well. Mr. Lloyd, of course, was already at the Lumbermen's Hall, as were Charlie and Tucker. I was also happy to see Mr. Huelsdonk, along with his wife and daughter, who came the considerable distance into town from their homestead. Tealie also came and brought Ella, her son George, and Mr. Riebe from La Push, which I thought most kind of her. A handful of other folks from Mora also showed up, including Mr. Ebels (the cannery owner), Mr. Keene (the cannery manager), Mr. Samuels (the store owner), and Mr. Berg (the stable and garage owner), together with their wives and children. Then, too, there was the mayor of Forks, the town council members, and the various mill managers, all with their families. There were also a good many of the regular millworkers and townsfolk in attendance.

Though Mr. C had told Mr. James he could invite whomever he liked, I'm certain he did not expect Mr. James to invite any of the ladies from Port Angeles and Port Townsend who'd come to the séance. So I was stunned when Mrs. Eisely, accompanied by her two daughters, Pauline and Bernice, entered the Lumbermen's Hall. I watched to see whether Mr. Eisely had come with them and was relieved when it appeared he had not. Bernice looked her same dowdy self, yet Pauline appeared entirely different. She'd shed her flapper girl shimmer and was now as plainly dressed as her sister, without a trace of makeup on her. Tucker had told me that their parents were planning to send the two of them across the mountains to Walla Walla to attend Whitman College at the end of the summer. "There's nothing but wheat fields out there," he said. "So they shouldn't get into too much trouble."

I looked about for Mr. C and caught his unsettled look—the furtive cut of his eyes toward the door and the furrow that creased his brow—the instant he spotted the trio of Eisely women entering the Lumbermen's Hall. He then diverted his attention and resumed his casual socializing with those about him. Meanwhile, as the mother and sister seated themselves midway down the aisle, Pauline Eisely remained standing, her hands clutched at her chest as she stared plaintively forward at her secret suitor. Mr. C, though, steadfastly ignored her, and after a few moments more she sat down.

By three o'clock every chair and bench in the Lumbermen's Hall was filled and people were standing along the walls. On Mr. Lloyd's cue that everything was ready to go, Mr. C stepped to the front of the hall and raised his arms to quiet everyone. He then thanked the audience for coming and said what an honor and a privilege it was to have this special preview showing of Harold Lloyd's new picture right here in Forks, Washington.

"This could be big for Forks," Mr. C said and then introduced Hal Roach.

Mr. Roach wore a pinstriped suit with a vest and crisp white shirt. His stiff French cuffs were held with gold cuff links and his red silk tie fastened to his shirt with a gold tie pin. I doubt any man in Forks had ever dressed so formally. As he came to the front of the hall, he pushed his jacket open and stuffed the fingers of each hand into the small pockets of his vest.

"Mr. Lloyd and I have had a most splendid time these past several days up here on your Olympic Peninsula," he began. "Its beauty, and the bounty of its natural resources, is unmatched in these United States of America. Even the weather has cooperated." A few chuckles went up in the hall among the locals, accustomed as they were to jokes about the immoderate precipitation their area enjoyed. "I must tell you," Mr. Roach continued, "that I am as eager as you are to see this new film by my friend Harold Lloyd. Hank and I have worked together for the past ten years making pictures, and I'm confident in saying he is one of the hardest working men in Hollywood—and positively the funniest! Thank you."

Mr. Roach then sat down beside Mr. C in the front row and Harold Lloyd stood up. Instead of stepping to the front of the room and standing before the large screen as Mr. C and Mr. Roach had, he simply turned about and with a meek smile thanked everyone for coming and said he hoped they enjoyed the show.

The lights in the hall were turned off, and Charlie and Tucker, atop a platform set up in the back, started the projector and phonograph. The first big laugh came just seconds into the picture when a woman entered a tailor shop to pick up her husband's pants and was startled by Mr. Lloyd's character, also named Harold, popping out of a bin after the woman inadvertently pinched the back of his leg. Next, when two pretty girls walked into the shop and began flirting with Harold, we could see what a terrible stutterer he was. From there the whole story revolved around what a painfully shy man Harold was around the opposite sex. What made his shyness even funnier was the fact that he'd written a book called *The Secret of Making Love*. In the foreword to the book, he explained how a man can win the heart of any woman provided he knows the correct method. It was then signed, "The Author, One who knows, and knows, and knows." There were then two scenarios from different chapters in the book, each recounting one of the author's presumed seductions. The first was Harold seducing "The Vampire." The next concerned the conquest of "My Flapper." At this, I couldn't help but glance back at Miss Pauline Eisely as the Harold character used his caveman methods to subdue the flitty girl in the flapper outfit. When, in the next scene, he took the train to the big city to offer his book to a publisher, he met and fell in love with a lovely rich girl, played by Jobyna Ralston, and rescued her little dog. The instant Miss Ralston appeared on the screen, I nudged Marie sitting next to me and told her I wanted to do my hair just like hers. Marie rolled her eyes at me.

Hardly a minute passed when Lumbermen's Hall wasn't filled with laughter. Whenever there was a scene on the streets of Los Angeles and we recognized a corner or building or signboard, Marie and I jostled one another and squealed with delight. The most thrilling part of the movie was the long scene in which Harold raced from the countryside into the city to halt the marriage of Jobyna Ralston to the wrong man. He ran, missed the train, stole several cars, got chased by detectives for running booze, rode the back of a fire truck, hijacked a trolley car, took off on a copper's motorcycle, stole a buckboard wagon, and then—when the wheels fell off the wagon—rode the team of horses straight to the rich man's mansion where the wedding was taking place and, crashing in upon the ceremony, decked the groom with a roundhouse punch and carried off the girl. The Lumbermen's Hall cheered him on throughout this whole sequence, and when Harold finally managed to overcome his stutter and propose to Miss Ralston and she said yes, everyone in the hall stood and applauded.

The movie was then over and the lights came on in the hall, and as soon as they did and everyone began to gather themselves up to exit, Pauline Eisely—from five rows back and clearly inspired by the movie—rushed to the front of the hall, flung her arms around Mr. C's neck, and declared her undying love for him. As she begged him to take her back to Los Angeles with him, Mr. C looked more shocked than I'd ever seen him. His face turned red as he tried to wrest the young woman's arms from around his neck.

"Please, Miss Eisely," he said sternly when he at last pulled her off and held her at arm's length. "Restrain yourself."

By this time, Mrs. Eisely had come forward and was trying to extract her daughter from the scene she'd created. Pulling at Pauline's elbow, the mother said calmly, "Come, dear. That's a good girl. Time to go home now," and Pauline, giving Mr. C one more plea-filled look, then dropped her face into her hands and, relenting to her mother's coaxing, allowed herself to be led toward the exit.

Standing beside Mr. C this whole while, Harold Lloyd and Hal Roach could instantly see what was taking place and discreetly backed away to join the rest of the audience making its way out of the hall. Marie and I hesitated, too stunned to move, yet when I saw Lillian standing a little ways off, a scowl on her face and rage seizing her body, I quickly tugged on Marie's sleeve. She just looked at me flabbergasted.

"Let's go," I said and led her outside as well.

Once on the sidewalk, I spotted Mr. Lloyd and Mr. Roach to one side of the theater entrance both smoking cigarettes and speaking to a group of locals. I pulled Marie to the opposite side, away from the crowd gathering around our Hollywood guests.

"Let's see if Tealie can give us a ride back," I said.

"What was *that* all about?" she asked, and I realized I'd never told her about my conversation with Tucker from several days earlier.

"Figure it out," I said, and smart girl that she was, it took her less than half a second to do so.

"He really shouldn't have," she said. "Poor Mr. C. How embarrassing."

"Poor Lillian, don't you mean?" I said and went looking for Tealie.

HAD THERE NOT BEEN guests staying at the Rialto Beach compound, Lillian might have remained and dealt with her husband as she always did—scolding him mercilessly, then forgiving him with a warning that this time would be the last. But it must have been too humiliating for her to have to face Harold Lloyd and Hal Roach after they had witnessed such a scene in front of the entire community. She stayed the night at the Forks Hotel. The next day, after Mr. C had taken his guests to the Hoh River to visit Mr. Huelsdonk's homestead, she returned to Rialto Beach, packed her bags, and had Charlie drive her to Port Angeles. Before leaving she told Marie and me she didn't know what would happen but hoped she would see us back in Los Angeles before too long.

"I know this isn't easy for you girls either," she said and began to cry, something we'd never seen her do in the five years we'd known her. "I just wish he would learn his lesson."

There was nothing we could say, so Lillian just kissed us each on the cheek and said goodbye. As for Mr. C, he'd made no effort to contact Lillian before her departure, but just went about his business as usual. Apparently it was his way after each *affaire de coeur* to just walk away following Lillian's scolding and come back when the dust had settled, pretending nothing had ever happened. When I thought about it, I envied him this approach and wished I could just walk away from my own plight and matter-of-factly ignore the anguish it continued to inflict upon me. I knew I couldn't, though. Physically I could not because I was stuck at Rialto Beach, and emotionally I could not because my severe conscience—a taut, ungiving tether that bound me to my presumed crime—would not let me.

In hindsight, I wish I had told Lillian right then and there, before she left, to stop putting up with Mr. C's hijinks. She was a good, smart, attractive woman and didn't need to subject herself to his philandering ways. He obviously thought he could get away with it just as he did everything else—his mind reading and summoning of dead people and hoodwinking of widows and all the like. But I wanted to tell her no, not if she didn't let him, not this time.

Harold Lloyd and Hal Roach decided to cut their visit short by several days and return to Los Angeles as well. This decision left Mr. C disappointed. He tried to talk them into taking a boat ride with him to Canada, but they insisted they'd had enough adventure in the Great Northwest and ought to get back to work. When I saw Mr. C hand Mr. Roach a manila envelope as he was getting into the car to leave, I thought maybe it contained the photos of The Nartell Twins he'd taken our first day at Rialto Beach, a keepsake for the movie producer of his visit to the Olympic Peninsula as well as a reminder of the series of comedic shorts starring Marie and me that Mr. C had proposed to him.

I now became hopeful that the rest of us would also leave Rialto Beach in short order. While I had certainly been distracted by all the goings-on of the past several days, my fear and anxiety and guilt continued to gnaw at me. An hour rarely passed—waking or sleeping—when I wasn't visited by the vision of that man standing over me and pinning my arms to the ground, or of the ocean waves crashing over his trapped and desperate figure wedged between the rocks. While I was eager to leave Rialto Beach, I knew my departure alone would not allow me to escape these haunting visions. My only hope was that distance—and time—might mitigate them.

Unfortunately, Mr. C was determined to remain at Rialto Beach. He was angry at Mr. James for having invited the Eiselys to the showing of *Girl Shy* in Forks, but Mr. C wasn't the type to hold a grudge, and after a few days of fishing by himself, he invited Mr. James back to the house for cocktails and dinner. As for Marie and me, he put us to work replying to the requests for psychic readings that remained in the mailbag Lillian left behind. We found the task tedious, though, and after half a day of it we recruited Tealie to help us. As we might have figured, she proved remarkably adept at understanding people's troubled pasts, sizing up their present situation, and advising them on the most suitable course to take to ease their worried minds.

As another week passed, everyone at the compound settled into a somewhat somber routine. I had a new sketchbook that Charlie bought me after delivering Harold Lloyd and Hal Roach to the boat in Port Angeles, and so to keep my mind distracted I threw myself into drawing mostly small, detailed specimens from nature—leaves, rocks, logs, insects, birds, and a spotted fawn that appeared at the edge of the compound one morning. Everyone seemed to be waiting for Mr. C to decide what to do next. I had again taken refuge in the treehouse one afternoon to draw when he came out onto the porch of the main house, sat down in one of the wicker chairs, and lit a cigar. A few minutes later, Charlie walked up and greeted him. He told Mr. C that he'd spoken that morning on the telephone to Lou's brother in Los Angeles.

"There's still no word of his whereabouts," Charlie said. He explained that the brother was planning to take the train to Seattle and come out to the peninsula to look for him. "And talk to the sheriff."

"He can do as he likes," said Mr. C and left it at that, unfazed by Charlie's mention of the sheriff.

This news alarmed me, however. It threw me into such a spiral of worry, of uncontrolled apprehension, that I could no longer see what it was I was drawing. I dropped my pencil and, without knowing what I did, began pulling at my hair. The pain inside me seized my whole being, I stopped breathing, and finally I just gasped. When my breath returned, I realized that this was it. The time had come to bring my ordeal to an end. I would kill myself, I thought. Doing so would release me from my conscience and answer for my culpability. I would do it with one of Cook's heavy kitchen knives, here in the treehouse, and leave a note to Marie saying how sorry I was. Yet the thought of her reading such a note horrified me. I couldn't burden her with my suicide. Instead I would go to church, as the nuns had taught me to do, and confess my mortal sin to the priest and surrender myself to God's righteous judgment in the forever-after. Only, the nearest Roman Catholic Church was in Port Angeles. This left me with just one option, which was to take myself to the sheriff's office in Forks, admit under sworn testimony to Lou Morton's murder, and let the county judge sentence me as he saw fit. Whether by execution or life in prison, I would pay for my capital crime. This resolve gave me enough peace of mind that when I laid down on the cot in the treehouse and closed my eyes to rest, and as exhausted as I was, I fell right to sleep.

When I woke up and returned to the house, I decided I needed to do Mr. C the courtesy of telling him first so there would be no unforeseen trouble for him. So after dinner that evening—a rather staid affair with just me, Marie, and Mr. C—I allowed an hour to pass and then made my way to his study where he was reading and asked if I could speak with him. He directed me to sit down in the leather armchair opposite his, offered me a glass of whiskey, and seemed mildly surprised when I accepted. When he handed me the drink, I took two good swallows. Mr. C then sat down with his own glass and I looked at him.

"I know what became of Lou," I said.

He set his drink down. "You do?"

"Yes," I said and finished off the whiskey in one gulp.

I then told him everything. I explained about walking up the beach past the Hole-in-the-Wall rock, how Lou had snatched me up and carried me into the woods, how he tore my shirtwaist open and urinated on me and then went and found the stick. I told him everything, humiliating as it all was, sparing no detail. I recounted my running away and stumbling and being hauled out onto the rocks, certain I was going to die. I told how Lou slipped and fell into the crevice between the rocks, with me on top of him, and how I crawled out and then sat there, refusing to assist him or go for help, waiting as the tide came in, and as it did so, watched him drown.

Mr. C listened without saying a word. His legs were crossed at the knees, and his large hands cupped the ends of the armrests. When I finished talking and began to cry, he reached forward and gave me his handkerchief. I wiped my tears away and said I was ready to go to the sheriff's office the next day.

"So Lou's brother won't have to make the trip," I added.

I waited for Mr. C to respond, to acknowledge my guilt and offer to drive me to Forks to turn myself in. Instead he got up, walked over to the stuffed cougar, and stroked the top of its head.

"It's been taken care of," he said and pressed his finger to the tip of one of the cougar's fangs. "Once or twice I thought to tell you, but Lillian convinced me it was your concern, not ours, and you would settle in your own mind what to do."

"I killed him," I said plainly. The revelation that Mr. C and Lillian had known about Lou's death, if not the exact circumstances of it, for much of the time during which I harbored my secret did not surprise me. I should have expected as much from Alexander, the Man Who Knows, and Lillian, his ever-perceptive spouse. I was simply relieved that my secret was out, that I no longer needed to guard it so vigilantly. At the same time, I felt disappointed. In bringing my crime to Mr. C, I had been prepared to face justice and put my guilty conscience to rest, and yet now he was telling me it was all taken care of—finished and done.

"You didn't kill him," he said and turned to face me. "I killed that bear that's lying on the floor, and Mr. Huelsdonk killed this mountain lion. But you did not kill that man."

"How do you know?" I asked him.

"He was not a good man, and if events occurred as you say they did—and I know you would never speak anything but the truth—then you did nothing that was not right and called for. I'm only sorry I could not protect you, and that you had to suffer as you did."

I had never heard him speak so genuinely. I was silent for a few moments as his words settled over me. Finally I asked, "How did you find out?"

He seemed to balk, as he did whenever asked to reveal one of his stage secrets, and I was ready for him to tell me it was none of my concern and I should not worry myself over it. But as I looked at him he must have seen the suffering in my eyes, how so much secretiveness, so much unknowing, had worn me down, like the surf wearing down the beach stones, and so he sat down again and explained how Lillian had first come to him, expressing her own disquiet about the uneasy mood I'd been in since my walk on the beach. She felt something had happened to me out there, especially when the Indian man returned the rucksack, and together she and Mr. C began to suspect that what-ever it was, it was connected to Lou's disappearance—and that it wasn't good. All the same, they kept their suspicions to themselves.

"We decided to wait and see, to give the matter a little more time, especially as you seemed to be more yourself as the days went by."

But I wasn't, I wanted to tell him. I tried to be more myself, honestly I did, but other than a few moments here and there when I succeeded in distracting myself, I never was. I was never fully at ease. *Never.*

When Lou did not show up, Mr. C continued, he and Lillian con-sulted Mr. James, who recommended Mr. Huelsdonk for his tracking skills. It was he who found the body. According to Mr. Huelsdonk, it had washed up on the beach and been dragged into the woods, likely by a bear.

"*Ursus americanus*," Mr. C said and looked at the bear rug on the floor. "There was not much left of him." He took a sip of his whiskey and added, "Mr. Huelsdonk is a very knowledgeable man, let me tell you, and after the discovery and putting all the pieces together, we could pretty well deduce what had happened—that you'd been assaulted and had fought back, and that the man had paid with his life for his actions. But, as I said, Lillian and I felt it was your secret, not ours, and that if you needed our help you would come to us. And here you are." He smiled at me, and even though I had begun crying again, I smiled back.

"But the brother," I said.

Mr. C then came over to where I sat, took hold of my shoulders, and stood me up. Still holding my shoulders, he said, "The brother can look all he wants, and so can the sheriff, yet I assure you they will never find him."

I pressed myself into his chest, letting his shirt absorb my tears, as he wrapped his arms around me, stroked my hair, and kissed the top of my head. He then pulled away, held me at arm's length, and said that Marie and I should start packing because we would be leaving for Los Angeles the following week.

AFTER THAT I BEGAN to feel better. My secret was no longer my own to bear. It was shared now by people older, wiser, more experienced in the ways of the world than I—Mr. C, Lillian, Mr. James, and Mr. Huelsdonk—all people I trusted. I thought of contacting Mr. James and Mr. Huelsdonk personally to thank them, but knew they would likely prefer to forget the whole matter. What counted nearly as much as unburdening myself of my dark, heavy secret was the fact that our departure from Rialto Beach was imminent. I became more relaxed—lazing about the house reading and drawing and occasionally meandering down the road to visit with Tealie. Not once did I go up to the treehouse. After two days of such indolence, Marie warned me that I was turning into a real slouch.

"Have you been into Mr. C's camphorated tincture?" she inquired.
"I'm just taking my cue from you," I said right back to her from the
settee in the sitting room. "Pass the bonbons, please."

We saw very little of Mr. C for the remainder of our stay. He went
fishing every day with Mr. James and no longer kept company with
local folks in the evenings, as had been his custom. Maybe everything
that had happened, including Lillian's angry departure following his
dalliance with Miss Pauline Eisely, had left him a little shaken after all.
True to character, though, he never broached the topic with either
me or Marie. Nor did he ever again refer to my tribulation with Lou
Morton. Mr. C, after all, was a man of significant reserve, as I suppose
every great showman must be.

Nonetheless, his marital troubles and my ordeal were just below
the surface on the singular occasion—five days after our sit-down
in his study—of his asking to speak to me privately. Not Marie and
me, mind—but just me. I instantly feared a snag had arisen in his
foolproof cover-up of my murder of Lou Morton, but detecting the
worried look on my face, he assured me that was not the case. Then
it occurred to me that his request to speak to me alone and by myself
was a signal that he had finally separated me and Marie in his mind.
Perhaps we would no longer simply be his Nartell Twins. Perhaps,
henceforward, he would interact with us as true individuals, each
her own person.

"I just wish to have a word with you," he said in a direct and open tone.

So that evening after dinner, while Marie went off with Charlie as
usual, Mr. C and I retired to the porch for our appointed talk. From
my chair on the porch, I could see the treehouse and imagined myself,
the self of a week ago, up there eavesdropping on the conversation
about to transpire between my new self and the tall, curious man
who had been the center of my life (and my twin sister's life) for the
past five years.

He seemed shy, tentative even, as he asked, "How are you faring,
my dear?"

"Better," I said, appreciating his solicitude. "Thank you."

"I'm most glad to hear it," he said, and instead of proceeding to
speak his mind, as I expected he would, he fell silent.

After several more moments, I became uncomfortable. I wanted
him to light a cigar or recommend a new novel to me or call out to

Cook to bring coffee, anything to break the awkward quiet that had descended upon us.

As I waited, a cobalt-blue Steller's jay landed on a branch of a nearby rhododendron, pecked at it, cocked its head once, and flew off again. I recalled how, on the evening of the summer solstice three days earlier, Tealie had made the comment that "Long light becomes long night."

Mr. C cleared his throat. Then he reached across the narrow span between our two chairs and took one of my hands in both of his.

"You are a dear," he said and smiled weakly as he stroked the back of my hand. "Myself, though," he went on after a pause, "I'm a very lonely man."

This was strange behavior, I thought, and the look of bewilderment on my face must have surprised him because he didn't seem to know what to do or say next. Nor did I.

"I don't know what will become of Lillian and me once we return," he went on, studying my hand. "Or what will become of any of us for that matter." He raised his head and looked at me, for my reaction, but I'm sure my expression was blank.

I didn't know what was happening. This was not the Mr. C with whom I was acquainted. I well knew he could be overly familiar with his risqué comments, but that was how he behaved with every woman who resided within his sphere for any length of time. It's what I was used to and what, perhaps mistakenly, I had come to accept as part of his general mischievousness and charm. The way he spoke to me now, though, alone together as we were, was quite different. He seemed more vulnerable, yet at the same time more intimating. I wasn't quite scared by the difference; I only wished I knew how to respond to it.

"It pleases me that Charlie and Marie have found one another," he continued. "But what about you? Who will you find?"

If I had known how to, I would have ended the conversation right then and there. The suggestiveness of his questions, at least as I took them, was far too forward and insinuating even for him. A certain degree of fright came over me. What exactly was he implying? The sense of relief I had gained following our last conversation was suddenly evaporating. In its place, I seemed to be breathing in a faint, paralyzing poison that spread throughout my chest, causing me to become increasingly anxious. If I could just pull my hand away...

"Maybe the answer is right here," he said and looked me straight in the eye, still petting my hand. "With you and me."

I nearly panicked. A strange and disturbing polygon appeared in my mind—two lines, Mr. C and Lou Morton, meeting through me, ensnaring me. I could not let the points meet. So I reached out with my free hand and seized Mr. C's wrist.

"No," I said.

I said nothing else. But then our eyes met, and I knew he could see what I saw. I had beaten the Iron Man of the Hoh in the arm-wrestling match—not he, The Man Who Knows—and I had beaten back Lou Morton with his own stick. And I was not now going to let this philanderer, Claude Alexander Conlin, or anyone else for that matter, take from me what was mine and mine alone. My will, my agency, my determination.

He let go of my hand, and I released his wrist. Sitting forward in our chairs, we were both still for a moment, and then I sat back and he did too. The moment had shifted, and he appeared drawn and abashed. I looked out over the porch rail, through the trees to the beach, the surf, the ocean.

Mr. C let out a sigh.

"There's that same jay," I said as it flew straight across my line of vision.

"Are you and Marie packed?" he asked.

"We will be," I answered.

THAT WAS OUR FINAL visit to Rialto Beach. Three weeks after we left, the house and cabins burned to the ground in a fire that, according to a letter to Mr. C from Mr. James, was most certainly arson. Mr. James speculated that someone from one of Mr. Eisely's mills had set the fire, and I figured that, based on what Tucker had told me, he was probably right.

Lou Morton's brother never came to the Olympic Peninsula, and as for Lou's disappearance, that was it, no more questions were ever asked. I knew in my heart that Mr. C was right, that I was not to blame for what had happened. I continued to have disturbing dreams, nonetheless, and I also continued in my mind to relive—sometimes willingly, sometimes not—the attack upon me on the beach that day.

A couple of times my mind even tricked me into believing, for just an instant, that I saw Lou Morton on the streets of Los Angeles. In all, my guilt and shame and anger persisted for several years, even as the sharpest pain of those memories receded.

I found great relief in finally telling Marie almost two years later, when we were no longer in the employ of Conlin Enchantments. The relief was so great that I could not understand why I had been so unable or unwilling to tell her during or immediately after our time at Rialto Beach. In turn, she berated herself for not realizing at the time that something terrible like this had happened to me.

"I do remember your acting strangely," she said when I told her. "But selfish me, I figured you were just bothered by how much time I was spending with Charlie."

I reassured her that there was no way she could have known or even guessed at what I was going through, and then she revealed a little secret of her own, which was that she and Charlie had been seeing one another—"*Intimately*," she emphasized—for several months prior to our visit to Rialto Beach that final time. "So I really was in my own world," she said, and with that I laughed and told her how much I loved her and we hugged.

Immediately after everyone returned from Rialto Beach to Los Angeles that summer, Mr. C and Lillian reunited and traveled to Europe for a month. When they returned, the company of Alexander the Crystal Seer headed out on a long autumn tour starting in the upper Midwest and making its way east to New York City, where we spent the Christmas holiday in a suite of rooms at the Essex House overlooking Central Park. After the New Year, we swung through the Southern states before taking the train from Houston back to Los Angeles. That spring, Mr. C began talking about returning to the Olympic Peninsula to rebuild the compound at Rialto Beach, but Lillian assured us it would never happen. Also that spring, Marie and Charlie got married and moved into a house near Venice Beach. In July, after another one of his affairs, Lillian finally divorced Mr. C. She retired from show business and opened a fabric store in Culver City, filling orders from costume designers from the nearby studio lots.

Two months later, incorrigible as ever, Mr. C proposed to me. He took a very proper approach—getting on his knee, presenting me with a diamond engagement ring, and asking for my hand in marriage.

And while I must admit I was flattered, I didn't hesitate to decline his proposal. It was the first and last offer of marriage I ever received. Ever since leaving Conlin Enchantments, I had been determined to pursue the path of independence, of being a self-supporting woman. I did, nonetheless, accept a small loan from Mr. C—which I've since paid back—to help me start my own small art school for children in Pasadena. Initially we offered classes in drawing, painting, and sculpture, and added lessons in dance our second year. I taught drawing, which I'd thrown myself into more rigorously than ever after Rialto Beach. My drawing had much to do with recovering my sense of who I was following that harrowing summer. It gave me purpose. Just as marriage and eventually motherhood did for Marie, drawing helped me mature into full-fledged adulthood. My work at the art school ultimately led me to being hired by the Walt Disney Studios, where I worked inking and painting celluloid sheets for *Three Little Pigs* and *Snow White and the Seven Dwarfs*. Mr. C eventually bought a house in Seattle and spent the rest of his days there.

Strange as it may sound, I mostly recall the five summers I spent at Rialto Beach with fondness. Tealie and I have remained friends, and we have kept up a correspondence over these many years. In one of her letters, she let me know that Ella Hay-nee-si-oos had passed away and that there was a big memorial for her at the Shaker church. Her son George, she added, now owned three boats and was the most successful fisherman in La Push. In her most recent letter, she announced that she had finally quit her job at the post office in Mora and married the pharmacist in Forks. I sent her and her husband a gift box of assorted citrus fruits with my best wishes.

Finally, almost eight years after that final visit to Rialto Beach, I received a letter from Tucker out of the blue. He said he was doing well. With Mr. James's backing, he now ran his own guide service for fishermen and hunters. He said that Mr. James, who eventually purchased the Rialto Beach property from Mr. C after the compound burned, had recently sold it to the federal government to turn into a national park. He added that the blackberries and salmonberries had grown so profusely around the foundation of the house and cabins along the bluff that these could no longer be seen.

"It's like they were never there," he wrote. "Like it was one of Mr. C's disappearing acts."

AT FORT WORDEN

After three days of interviews, diagnostic tests, and around-the-clock observation, the Assessment Committee told me I suffered from an "inadequate personality." When I asked what that meant, the committee members all looked to the state-appointed psychologist on the committee, Dr. Vernon O. Reinholdt, who cleared his throat and leaned across the conference room table toward me.

"Avery," he said, "the assessment of inadequate personality signals a lack of psychological maturity appropriate to age." He explained that, in my case, it included indications of prolonged unsociability, occurrences of acute irritability, chronic impulsiveness, episodes of aggressive and/or reckless behavior, difficulty adhering to accepted social norms, unrealistic life goals, and general overexcitability, a.k.a. nervous disquiet. He added that since my arrival at the Fort Worden Diagnostic and Treatment Center for Juvenile Delinquency on the day of—and here he glanced at his file—Monday, June 15, 1970, most of the aforementioned symptoms had been observed in me. He noted that these same symptoms had, in all likelihood, been the lead contributory factors to the trouble I'd gotten into over the past several months.

I had to admit it sounded pretty bad, though the only part of his explanation I truly understood was the getting-into-trouble part. The rest was just mumbo jumbo. I'm sure my offenses were all well-documented in the manila folder beneath Dr. Reinholdt's clasped pale hands—the running away from home, the shoplifting from the grocery store, the breaking and entering into a neighbor's cabin, the vandalism of the high school, the instances of drunkenness and drug use (mostly weed, some hashish, speed a few times). All these incidents were made worse, of course, by my blatant disrespect for authority, or more precisely, for the Spanaway Police Department, or, more precisely still, for Officer Leroy Yarnell, who overstepped the line when he confiscated my hash pipe—which, according to the guy who sold it to me, was made of Phrygian marble from Turkey—and then threw it into Spanaway Lake. I was so pissed off at Officer Leroy that I shoved him against his Crown Vic cruiser and bolted across the park. He then ran after me, stepped on a rock, and broke his ankle. All this resulted in me being slapped with a Category II offense that landed me in juvie in historic Port Townsend on the beautiful Olympic Peninsula.

"Avery," Dr. Reinholdt said in a voice more sympathetic than the one he'd used to recite the symptoms of my inadequate personality. I sat in my chair, a hand cupped over each knee, my fingers squeezing my kneecaps. I wanted to cry but told myself not to, no matter what, and stared at the floor. "I know all this may not make sense to you now, but you need to know that in terms of what your residency entails, we're here to help you."

I let go of my knees, crossed my arms, and slumped low in my chair. The one lady on the committee, a staff member named Mrs. Adel, said something about the cottage I would be assigned to while at the Treatment Center. I wasn't really listening. I was instead reviewing my options for escaping and making my way to the coast to live among the Makah. Or perhaps I might find a small uninhabited island in the San Juans where I could live out my life as a hermit. Mrs. Adel chuckled to herself and said something about the cottage's adopted mascot, a foam rubber cat the guys in the cottage had found on the beach and named Flotsam, and I glanced up to see the other committee members smiling bemusedly at this anecdote. Then my eyes went to the window and settled on the gray sky above the green-shingled rooftops of the assorted whitewashed buildings situated across the Fort Worden grounds.

"Our practice entails the use of positive reinforcement—" Dr. Reinholdt explained. I noticed he loved the word *entail*. "—as well as a time-out contingency, when reinforcement fails to effect the necessary behavioral changes."

"What's that?" I asked. There was something remotely threatening in the way he'd said this last bit.

"What's what?" he asked right back.

"'Time-out *contiguacy*.'" As I was growing up in Spanaway, I didn't read much, and I skipped school a lot, so my vocabulary was rather shaky—even for a sixteen-year-old.

"*Contingency*," he corrected me. "The time-out contingency entails separating a resident who has misbehaved from the general population and placing him in an isolation unit where he'll be held without the ability to communicate with his fellow residents until the staff deems him capable of reintegrating in a functional capacity with the general population." He inhaled in apparent exasperation at having to explain himself so extensively and finished by adding, "It's our hope for every new resident that the contingency is never exercised."

Dr. Reinholdt then turned to the other committee members and asked if there was anything further to discuss with "young Mr. Clausen."

I glanced about the room and saw their heads quietly shaking, giving him his answer.

"All right then," he concluded and told Mrs. Adel she could escort me to my cottage for formal admission.

I KNEW THERE WERE worse places than Fort Worden if you were a juvenile delinquent in the State of Washington, and the counselors and cottage parents there never let us forget it. They would threaten to send us to Echo Glen reformatory near North Bend or Green Hill reformatory down in Chehalis. Green Hill was the one we all knew you had to look out for. Kids at Fort Worden described it as a combination Nazi concentration camp and asylum for the criminally insane. It was the kind of place where a young maverick reporter—a Geraldo Rivera type—could show up and do a documentary piece on the cruel and inhumane conditions of the facility, shocking television viewers into outrage and sending state officials scrambling to investigate. At Fort Worden, we liked to scare one another with tales of kids we heard of who'd been sent down to Green Hill.

"This one kid had his toes chewed off by rats when they put him in the hole," Eddy Lockwood said.

"They chain you to the wall at night," Nick Scalpone put in, corroborating the facility's Edgar Allen Poe–like reputation.

It was where the kids who stabbed their parents in their sleep, raped their little sisters, bound and tortured neighbor kids, and set their schools and churches on fire were sent. The *irreformables*, as the counselors called them, letting us know by implication that we were a better class of delinquent. We played rough, but we weren't savages. Our IQs were higher, and we were a lot savvier. Our lot ran away from home, got into fights, broke into homes and businesses, slashed teachers' tires, tortured the occasional house pet (mostly cats), did a variety of street drugs, *threatened* to kill our parents, vandalized municipal property, jacked a car now and then, or just drifted about until someone decided it was best to put us away before we did any real harm.

Once in a while a kid from Echo Glen or Green Hill would get a reverse-transfer to Fort Worden, and for the next few weeks that kid would carry a menacing aura about him. The kid knew this and would use it to his advantage, hunching over and glaring at you in a way that let you know he'd been through far worse than Fort Worden, so keep your distance. Scarier still was the kid who transferred in from one of these places who never looked at you, didn't talk, didn't give any sign that you or anyone else existed, but holed up inside himself instead like some kind of beaten-down animal. This kind of kid was unnerving because he was so unreachable. The typical tough guy at Fort Worden always wanted to prove how badass he was by getting up in your face at the smallest provocation. But the "trauma kid," as I came to think of him, seemed dangerous in ways none of us could quite grasp. So we left him alone. But inevitably one or another of us would be egged on to test him, like being the one appointed by your gang of friends to touch the electrified fence to see if juice is coursing through it or not.

As it happened, it was my turn to test the electric fence, and the kid was a strange one. His name was Prosper. Just four months into my own residency at Fort Worden, he was transferred from Green Hill and placed in our so-called *cottage*, the old army barracks where they housed us. I bided my time for my chance, waiting until no one was around and the cottage was quiet. It was one of those mid-September days that are both warm and cool. Most everyone was out on the parade grounds playing flag football or drifting about in small clusters. I wasn't out there because I'd gotten hold of a Hershey's chocolate bar, one of those really big ones, from a kid in another cottage in a trade for a half pack of Winstons I'd stolen from a kid in my own cottage. I was retrieving it from underneath one of the bathroom sinks where I'd stashed it when this Prosper kid from Green Hill walked into the john. He strolled straight past me as I was crouching on the white tile floor, and he entered one of the stalls without a word. I just grabbed the chocolate bar and got out of there, thinking that if he asked me later what I was doing I'd give him one of two answers: A) I was praying to God not to let me beat the crap out of him for asking such a stupid question, or B) I was retrieving a large Hershey's bar that I would happily share with him if he didn't beat the crap out of me.

I stashed the chocolate bar in my pillow case and returned to the cottage lounge to act like nothing had happened. I was flipping through a copy of *Boys' Life* when he came into the lounge, dropped himself into one of the aluminum-framed Naugahyde chairs, and sat there with his hands in his lap. Physically he didn't look like a kid anyone would have to worry about. He was tall, just shy of six feet I'd say, with a slight build, like someone who might have run cross-country or done high jump for the track team. His face was bony but pliant-looking, with his heavy lips and long-lashed eyes. Bunches of dark hair sprang from his head like thick dog fur, and an Adam's apple the size of a ping-pong ball protruded from the middle of his long neck. His complexion was the color of cigar ash.

It drove me crazy to have him just sitting there. He didn't look at me or say a word. He just stared off into the corner of the room as if hypnotized by the structural angles where the floor and ceiling met the two walls.

"I think that sink in there is leaking," I said finally, looking at him over the top of the magazine I held in my hands.

He blinked a couple times, as if his trance had been broken. "Huh?" he uttered and glanced over at me.

"The sink," I said. "It's got a leak."

He nodded, his eyebrows lifting a bit and wrinkling the skin of his forehead, where a fair number of pimples made their mark, and then he looked away again. He'd been in the cottage nearly a week, yet my remark about the sink in the john was probably as much as any resident had said to him. So, having put myself out to make this effort, I wasn't going to let him just blow me off. I'd been at Fort Worden four months already and deserved acknowledgment, certainly more than just a nod.

"So that's your real name?" I asked him.

He looked straight at me this time.

"It's my real name," he said without the least bit of challenge in his voice, and after a moment added, "My grandfather was named Prosper."

"It's different all right," I said.

"Avery's kinda strange too," he said after another pause.

It surprised me that he even knew my name.

"Yeah," I said, "I suppose. But not as strange as yours."

These would have been fighting words for nine out of ten kids at Fort Worden, and I was ready to jump to my feet to defend myself the instant he made a move. But he didn't budge. He stayed where he was, and his thick eyebrows went up as if he was conceding the simple truth of my statement. And this was how my friendship with Prosper began.

Of course, I say *friendship* even though a person didn't really have friends at Fort Worden. You had someone you hung out with, maybe sat in the mess hall with, traded comic books with, walked around the parade grounds with, that kind of thing. But this kind of camaraderie had its limits, which was just as well since kids came and went at the Treatment Center, some after only a few weeks. You didn't want a situation where you stood up for your friend—maybe even got into a fight for him—and a week later your friend gets sent to another reformatory or a foster home and there you are with no one to cover your back like you'd covered his. So friendship wasn't a very wise stratagem.

All the same, because I was the first person in our cottage Prosper had said two words to, he and I started hanging out. Several days later when he asked me what I'd been doing kneeling by the sink when he came into the john, I told him straight up, though the Hershey's bar was long gone, consumed over the course of three nights under my bed covers, the wrapper eventually flushed down the toilet. He then let me know he'd been sent to Green Hill in Chehalis because he'd stolen a bunch of clothes from a department store in Olympia where he was from and where both his parents were government employees.

"That doesn't seem like a big deal," I said. "Most kids do a lot worse than steal some clothes." It did strike me as a bit odd that anyone would want to steal clothes. Like most kids at Fort Worden, I'd done my share of shoplifting. I usually went for small-fry stuff—a flashlight from the hardware store, a transistor radio from the variety store, a package of Oreos from the grocery store, comic books from the drugstore, cigarettes from the gas station, that kind of stuff. The closest I ever came to stealing clothes was a belt I lifted from the men's clothing store in downtown Spanaway when I was in fifth grade. It was made of extra-wide hand-tooled leather and had a big square metal buckle stamped with the scene of a bear fighting a cougar. I knew no one else at school had anything like it, and for a month afterward I hid the belt beneath a rock near my house and on my way to school removed my usual skinny belt and put on the belt with the big flashy buckle. A month or so later, after only a few kids noticed it anyway, I grew tired of the routine and threw the belt in the trash behind the middle school.

"They were really expensive clothes," said Prosper. "I was going to give them to my mother for Christmas. But instead of returning them to the store like my parents told me to, I burned them."

That seemed rather strange to me as well. Maybe I'm just selfish, but it never occurred to me to steal something as a gift to give to someone. When it came to shoplifting, it was all about personal gain. On the other hand, his getting rid of the evidence by burning the clothes made sense, even if he had already been caught.

"And what happened?"

"My father wouldn't pay for them, especially since I was wearing one of the dresses when I burned them in our backyard, and so the store pressed charges and I was sent to juvenile court."

"Why were you wearing one of the dresses? Were you high?"

"No," he said. "I just did."

I realized what Prosper was telling me was a confidence that, if any of the other Fort Worden residents found out about it, would ruin him. He'd be dead meat. I suspected he knew this as well, but he told me anyway. I was flattered by his trust in me, yet I wasn't sure I was worthy of it. So I didn't press him for any more details and chalked the whole story up to his being the world's biggest momma's boy. And for the next few days I avoided him.

This was easy to do since he basically remained the same brooding loner he was before we struck up our acquaintance. He didn't play football or kickball or do any of the things most of us did out on the parade grounds when we weren't sitting in class or enduring a counseling session. He didn't speak when we ate in the mess hall, and in the evening, he didn't play ping-pong or pool or watch TV with the rest of us. Instead he usually went out to the front porch and read a book. Also, to my relief, he didn't glom onto me with some newfound sense of us being pals, as I worried he might. He respected my keeping my distance, and I respected him for that.

All the same, it's not as if I was a *duke*, one of the half dozen kids who ruled the roost at the Diabolic and Treacherous Center for Juvenile Dip-Shittery. A duke sat wherever he wanted in the TV room, had first dibs on the ping-pong or pool tables, could mooch cigarettes and candy from anyone he wanted, was always captain in picking sides for football, and generally was fiercer and more reckless than anyone else in his cottage of twenty or so kids. I, on the other hand, was somewhere in the middle of the pack, wishing I could rise in the ranks, setting my eyes on dukedom but not really tough enough or ambitious enough to make it happen. Mainly I was content to not sink lower than my current level, somewhere between Bobby Felton, the duke of dukes at Fort Worden, and Marcus Donaldson, the weakest of the weak. This status allowed me to associate with kids on a sliding scale—which meant I could participate in the schemes plotted by the top-rank kids, those who got into the greatest trouble, and also take it easy at times, slumming with the lowliest kids, who preferred as much as possible to disappear.

Working both sides of this divide caught up with me, though, when I learned about the plan to hold a blanket party for Prosper one Friday night. Blanket parties were a risky business because you could get three or more days in "the hole" if caught, or even sent to Echo Glen or—God forbid—Green Hill. They were infrequent occurrences, reserved for kids like Prosper who didn't fit in anywhere with anyone. I knew that objecting out loud to his hazing was out of the question, and as Friday rolled around, I hoped that I could just avoid it altogether. But that wish fizzled when Bobby Felton assigned me to the lookout position at the top of the stairs leading down to the bedroom of Mr. Higman, our cottage parent, on the ground floor.

The party started at 3:00 a.m., half an hour after the night guard made his last round of the grounds and cottages before returning to the guard house and dozing off at the front desk. Bobby Felton shook me awake and pointed toward the door where I was to take my position. I slipped my feet into my sneakers and did as instructed. From where I stood holding the door partially open to keep an eye on Higman's door at the bottom of the stairs, I could see the entire dormitory floor. I watched as six guys wearing gym shorts and T-shirts (instead of pajamas) sprang from under their covers and gathered at the foot of Prosper's bed. The six included the biggest and meanest kids in our cottage—Bobby Felton, Del Emmons, Pete Munson, Jack Moore, Nick Scalpone, and Stewart Parks.

Like killer ants attacking a slender worm, they went to work. When Del lifted the covers off Prosper's sleeping body, Bobby yanked him to the floor. Pete and Nick then pounced on him with the blanket, and while Stew and Jack pinned his legs to the floor, Bobby and Del wrapped a rope around the blanket from his shoulders all the way to his waist, ten times at least, pinning his arms to his sides. The tussle woke some kids up, and as they sat up in bed to see what was happening, I gave them the hush sign. Then, as Prosper's muffled screams grew louder, I saw the first sock come out. I don't know what was in it—maybe sand, maybe a bar of soap—but when Bobby swung it across the spot in the blanket where Prosper's head was, it landed with a thud, and I could hear Prosper groan as he slumped beneath the blow.

That's when Bobby waved me to leave my post and open the emergency exit door that led out to a metal staircase attached to the outside of the building's west side. No one spoke the whole while, everything done with hand signals.

The guys lifted Prosper to his feet and, dazed and no doubt half suffocated, he complied. He was hustled out the emergency exit door and down the staircase. Once on the ground, the group took off in the direction of the old theater, giving the guard house a wide berth, and after ducking behind the maintenance shed, they began moving up Artillery Hill. Meanwhile, I trailed a few yards behind, keeping a watch over my shoulder to make sure no lights came on either in our cottage or the guard house.

"I can't breathe," Prosper kept saying as he was pushed and dragged up the hill. By now everyone but me had a fully loaded sock and was taking swipes at Prosper's back and rear end to keep him moving.

"Shut up, weirdo," Pete ordered.

"Keep moving," Jack piped in.

It was dark as we trudged up the poorly paved road that encircled the hill and led to the half dozen battery installments from when Fort Worden was actually a military base. I continued to lag behind, telling myself I was just going along to watch and make sure nothing really terrible happened. Yet, instead of going to one of the concrete batteries as I expected they would, the group suddenly veered to the left off the road. We were now bushwhacking through the dense woods, everyone tripping over roots and logs in the dark, tree branches slapping back into our faces. Artillery Hill was strictly off-limits to residents, yet many of us knew our way around it pretty well. But on this particular night I don't think anyone knew where we were going. The best I could figure, the idea was to go deep enough into the woods and then leave Prosper to try and find his way back.

When Bobby put his hand up like one of those cavalry captains in the old westerns signaling his troop to halt, we all gathered around him. Del gave a kick to the back of Prosper's knees and he collapsed to the ground.

"Now what?" Nick asked, looking around at the other guys.

"Get his pants," Bobby ordered.

Prosper started kicking as soon as he felt two guys grab his legs and start pulling at his pajama bottoms. When they got them off, he rolled to his side and did his best to curl up into a ball. He was whimpering now, his white skinny ass visible to everyone standing around.

"Shut the fuck up," Stew yelled and kicked him in the lower back.

Another guy not from our cottage, who must have joined us once we got outside, started whacking Prosper on the rear end with a stick, and Prosper screamed.

"Shut *the fuck* up," Stew shouted again, getting really ticked off.

It didn't matter how much Stew shouted at him; by this point Prosper couldn't stop blubbering, letting out giant, gasping heaves.

"Shut it, you pussy," Stew shouted one more time and then seemed to lose it. He took a white athletic sock from his back pocket, dropped what looked like a cue ball from the rec room pool table into it, and began wailing on him. Prosper couldn't cover his head with his hands tied down, so he rolled over and, like a sow bug, curled up into a ball as best he could.

Stew got in a half a dozen swings before Bobby stepped in.

"Are you fucking crazy?" Bobby shouted and pushed him away.

I noticed that with the last couple of shots Stew landed, Prosper had ceased curling up. He was just a clump of blanket and rope and bare legs.

"Hey douchebag," Bobby said to Prosper and nudged him with his foot.

We were all standing around waiting for him to respond, waiting for his whimpering to resume, but there was nothing—no sound, no movement.

"*Fuck*," I heard Bobby mutter, and then more loudly, "Take the blanket off him."

Several guys untied the rope and pulled the blanket away from him, no longer concerned if he saw their faces. His eyes were shut, and we all thought he might be dead. Then, perhaps because of the cool night air reaching him once the blanket came off, he gave a snort and started coughing like a person pulled from the water moments before drowning. As Prosper came to, Bobby gave the word to scram, and everyone raced back through the trees toward the road.

When I reached the road, though, I stopped and looked back into the woods. Just because he was breathing didn't mean he was okay. On the other hand, if I went back and checked on him, I might make myself suspect to the other guys. They might think I could give them up during the grilling everyone in the cottage was sure to get once word got around what had happened. Yet, because the other guys had already run down the hill and were out of sight, I decided to risk it and trudged back into the woods to see if Prosper was moving at all.

When I reached the spot where we'd left him, however, he was gone. The blanket was on the ground, his pajama bottoms flung up into a tree. I stood on the tamped-down area where he'd been curled up ten minutes ago and scanned the dark woods. I was about to call out his name when I saw his spectral figure about thirty yards off stumbling through the trees. He was moving up the hill, away from the road.

"Shit," I let out, knowing I had to go after him. There were plenty of stories of kids falling off the bluff at the top of the hill, a hundred-foot drop to the stone-strewn beach below that left heads crushed and limbs mangled. I picked up the blanket and thrashed through the woods, making my way toward him, and when I got within a few feet I called out his name.

He didn't turn around at first, but when he did I could see that he was not all there. I don't think he even recognized me as I grabbed his wrist and led him back down the hill to the road. Only after we'd stepped onto the pavement did he finally say anything. First he yanked his arm away. Then—barefoot, no pajama bottoms on, his pajama top torn, leaves and twigs tangled up in his thick hair, a blank look still on his face—he asked me what I was doing.

I was ready with my answer. "They told me you were up here and I should come get you," I said, and this seemed to satisfy him. He took the blanket I handed him to wrap around his waist and then followed me down the hill. When we reached the maintenance shed and passed beneath a streetlamp, I could see that his feet and legs were nicked up pretty bad and that the glazed look on his face had returned.

"You okay?" I asked, but instead of responding, he just bent over and hurled.

It took him a couple minutes to finish, but when he was done I led him to the guard house and sat him down in one of the metal chairs on the porch.

"Remember," I told him. "You didn't see me." I rapped three times as hard as I could on the door of the guard house, and then leapt off the porch and sprinted back to my cottage.

THE NEXT MORNING BEFORE any of us were even dressed, word went around the dormitory that Prosper was in the infirmary with a severe concussion, heavy bruising, and multiple lacerations. Immediately following breakfast our entire cottage was put on restrictions, which meant there would be no ping-pong, no pool, no TV, and no flag football on the parade grounds. In the afternoon after classes, we were taken one by one into the cottage parent's office downstairs and "interviewed" by Superintendent Lindquist, Director of Counseling Mrs. Adel, and Mr. Higman, our cottage parent. It was understood—as it's been understood among the criminal kind from time immemorial—that you didn't squeal, and if you did, the consequences would be far worse than anything the overlords at Fort Worden could dish out. So it was hard to account for why I was the only guy of the more than half dozen involved in the incident who got fingered. Was I being set up as the fall guy? How was Mr. Higman able to say two people—he didn't say whether they were residents or staff—reported seeing me on the grounds last night before dawn? At any rate, I was the only one held accountable for the episode. The whole cottage received a lecture on the wrongs of hazing and were made to do litter patrol for the entire grounds the next ten days, while I received two days of isolation and two weeks of disciplinary probation, which meant if I had another violation within that period my case file would be reviewed for reassignment, which meant being booted from Fort Worden and possibly sent to Echo Glen or Green Hill.

"If you wish to discuss who else was involved, we would take into account your cooperation and suspend your time in isolation," offered Superintendent Lindquist.

"I was just getting some fresh air," I said, "'cause I couldn't sleep." Lindquist was generally a nice guy, liked by almost everyone at Fort Worden, so I felt bad for lying so blatantly to him—and so lamely—and making him have to play the heavy.

"Okay then," he said as he rose from his chair, causing me to wince with shame at the note of resignation in his voice.

Wait, I wanted to call out as he left the office. *I'm the one who went back and got Prosper and probably saved his life.* But this would have amounted to a full-fledged confession of my involvement, and if I didn't want to get sent to Green Hill or Echo Glen, I would then have to squeal on the other guys, which would mean looking over my shoulder for the rest of my life waiting for Bobby Felton to get me in one of his notorious choke holds while the other guys bludgeoned me with their blackjack socks. I couldn't do it. Honor aside, my sense of self-preservation was too strong.

It would be my first time in the hole—so yeah, I was kind of scared. Whenever we talked about the hole, guys would take on the stern, husky voice of Carr, the floorwalker in *Cool Hand Luke*, and even if you'd never seen the movie, which I hadn't, the joking around about it was hilarious—and terrifying. Pete Munson had the part of Carr down pat with his cigar-chomping, floor-pacing, no-nonsense manner. But instead of saying "in the box," Pete said "in the hole": "There's no playing grab-ass or fighting in the building. Any man playing grab-ass or fighting in the building spends a night in the hole. Last bell's at eight. Any man not in his bunk at eight spends the night in the hole. There's no smoking in the prone position. Any man caught in the prone position spends a night in the hole. Any man with dirty pants on sitting on his bunk spends a night in the hole. Any man don't bring back his empty pop bottle spends a night in the hole. Any man loud talking spends a night in the hole."

Pete could also do a good rendition of the sadistic warden from the movie, with his slithery gestures and Southern hauteur. "Now, it's all up to you," Pete would say in a flannel-mouthed drawl, tipping back his ball cap. "I can be a good guy, or I can be one real mean sonofabitch."

By noon everyone in the cottage had learned I'd gotten two nights in the hole, starting that afternoon, and Pete gave his best rendition of the warden ever and had everyone in the cottage holding their gut from laughing so hard.

But when it came to Bobby, he wasn't laughing at all. Instead of patting me on the back and thanking me for taking one for the team, as I thought he might, he wanted to know why I hadn't come straight back to the cottage with the rest of them last night.

"Where'd you go?"

His suspicion of me was loud and clear, and everyone on the dormitory floor settled down to hear how I'd answer. It seemed that every day at Fort Worden I became a better liar than I was the day before, quicker and more convincing, and so I didn't flinch.

"I thought I dropped my sock back there," I told him, "so I went back for it." Just like in *Cool Hand Luke*, at Fort Worden every resident had to write his initials with a permanent black marker on every article of clothing he owned—every sock, pair of underpants, pair of pants, T-shirt, sweatshirt, jacket, you name it. I amused even myself with this smooth-as-Farina lie since I hadn't even brought a sock with me, having never wanted to pound Prosper senseless in the first place.

"You idiot," Bobby said, changing his tone. "Did you find it?"

"Naw," I said. The fool didn't even think to ask if I'd seen Prosper when I went back into the woods.

"You better hope they don't find it," he said.

"Yeah," I said, and with that I walked to my bunk, opened my foot locker, and put a pair of clean underpants, a clean T-shirt, and my toiletry kit into my gym bag and headed downstairs where one of the guards was waiting to escort me over to the guard house to start my sentence.

"See ya," Pete Munson said, and a few other guys chimed in with "See ya's" as well, while one wise guy piped in with "Have fun in the hole, asshole."

FORT WORDEN WAS ONE of three forts at the north end of Puget Sound that included Fort Casey on Whidbey Island and Fort Flagler on Marrowstone Island. The three forts were collectively known as "the triangle of fire," all built during the Spanish-American War. They were meant to guard Admiralty Inlet from enemy ships entering Puget Sound and attacking the naval shipyards in Everett, Bremerton, and points south. It was a good idea, but ultimately unnecessary. Not a single shot was ever fired in battle from the enormous guns in the heavily fortified battery placements that lined the bluffs of each fort. The Treatment Center moved into Fort Worden sometime in the late '50s when, following the Korean War, the military decommissioned it. The hole was in the basement of the guard house, which, like every other building at the fort, was almost a hundred years old.

I was escorted to the guard house by Officer Buehle, a young guard who was popular with the guys because he badmouthed administrators, talked dirty about girls, and gave cigarettes to his favorites. I didn't like him, though, or any adult for that matter who used the little bit of authority allotted them to swagger about like they ruled the roost. And Buehle knew I didn't like him because he didn't say a word as he pushed me through the front door of the guard house. He asked me if I was hiding anything and then patted me down and turned my gym bag inside out.

"Because if you are, Clausen, you'll be in a shitload more trouble," he said, making a point of calling me by my last name, which he didn't do with other kids, and then handing me back my gym bag. "Let's go." He shoved me on the shoulder again, and if I had been a different kind of person, the kind described by Dr. Reinholdt during my official assessment, let's say, I might have turned around and wailed on Officer Buehle, which would have been just what he wanted, and I would have doubled my time in the hole.

But I wasn't that kind of guy. Never was—my incident with Officer Leroy of the Spanaway PD being the one exception. So I took the shove from Buehle and headed down the stairs into the basement, which was made up of three rooms separated by cinderblock walls. Buehle gave me my mattress, folded up into a heavy roll, and a set of sheets and a wool blanket. He unlocked the metal door of one of the rooms and jerked his head to signal me to get in. Then he locked the door behind me and looked in through the square grate.

"You'll be checked on every hour. Meal time is the same as usual. If you have to use the can or need anything else, you don't yell, you wait for the guard to come down. Understood?"

I nodded. *But what if there's an emergency?* I wanted to ask. What if I get diarrhea from the swill they feed us and no matter how hard I try to hold it wet poo starts squirting out my bunghole? Do I still have to wait for the guard to come check on me, Officer Buehle? What if

I'm allergic to the mildew on the damp walls and start bleeding out of my eyeballs, or a rabid rat gnaws on my ankles and I start foaming at the mouth? Can I yell for help then, Officer Buehle?

"Good," he said and returned upstairs.

And that was it. I was in the hole.

The particular room I was put in—as I would learn from subsequent stints in the hole—was identical to the other two. The outer walls were the building's stone-block foundation, plastered with thick gobs of concrete mortar and discolored from generations of mold. The floor was concrete slab and the eight-foot ceiling had sweaty sewer and water pipes running across it. In my room, a square plexiglass window the size of a Monopoly board and six feet off the floor gave a view of a shrub right in front of the window and a few patches of gray sky between its leaves and branches. There was a metal bed frame against one wall and a table and chair against another. The sole lighting was a 60-watt bulb in a metal-wire cage in the center of the ceiling. There were stories of kids hanging themselves from the pipes and cutting their wrists from the glass of a broken light bulb, and I'm sure those options passed through the head of every kid who was ever placed down there, so I was surprised the light bulb wasn't better shielded and I was allowed to keep the laces on my high-top Cons.

I was now officially "in isolation." Decades later when I did a little research, I would learn that this was the most forward-thinking method of dealing with unruly and recidivist behavior among juvenile delinquents, especially those who were wards of the state. It was the disciplinary seed of what would come to be known as "time out." Instead of physically punishing a kid, you deny him the reinforcement he's come to expect from his misconduct, whether that be positive reinforcement from the approval of his peers or negative reinforcement from the punishment administered by authorities. Dr. Vernon O. Reinholdt, the head psychologist at the Treatment Center, who came over to Port Townsend twice a month from his day job as head of the psychology department at Western Washington State College in Bellingham, wrote a couple of articles on the subject. Apparently, as a follower of expert shrinks like Eric Ericson and B. F. Skinner, Dr. Reinholdt was all about behavioral modification. He believed that prescribed isolation served to disrupt harmful reinforcement without producing what he called the "frustration effect," whereby an organism fearing extinction reacts even more forcefully—be it bacteria, beast, or boy.

The first thing I did once Officer Buehle returned upstairs was to unfold the mattress on the metal springs of the bed and put the sheets and blanket on it. The pillow I'd been given was a thin piece of foam, and the pillowcase I put on it did nothing to soften it. I sat on the bed and realized I was the only one down there, that the other two rooms were empty, and when I thought how this must be what solitary confinement was like in prison—which is where I was probably headed once I turned eighteen—such an overwhelming wave of misery and self-pity came over me that I began weeping and did actually consider cutting my wrists or hanging myself. Here I was, after all, locked in this dank basement by myself. It couldn't get much worse.

I thought of my parents. Would they be told of this disciplinary action? Would they approve, or would they see the punishment as an injustice and indignity done to their beloved son and rush to Port Townsend to demand my release? Not likely. They would probably figure I'd been up to my old tricks again and gotten what I deserved. They would feel bad for me, maybe, or perhaps just sorry for themselves and all they'd been put through because of me. Mom might send a tin of cookies with a note urging me to try to be on my best behavior from now on so I would be allowed to come home for Christmas, and that would be it. Dad would maybe tell himself to send me some cash for the commissary but then forget to.

My crying jag didn't last long, and when it ended I got up and walked to the table. I was told I needed to bring my school books with me, but I'd deliberately left them back at the cottage, figuring I wasn't going to let them lock me up *and* make me do homework. There were several books stacked on the table, so I sat down in the chair and looked them over. The first was a paperback copy of *A Separate Peace* by John Knowles. The cover was a drawing of a young guy standing beneath a tree, an ivy-covered tower in the background. I'd seen kids reading it in ninth grade, but it looked kind of slow and moody for my tastes. Next was *Dune*, the big thick science fiction novel that everyone at Fort Worden raved about. People said it was the greatest book ever written and that the author, Frank Herbert, was from Tacoma, as if that made any difference. So I opened it and read the first sentence—"In the week before their departure to Arrakis, when all the final scurrying about had reached a nearly unbearable frenzy, an old crone came to visit the mother of the boy, Paul."—and put it down. The next book was a hardback copy of *In the Pocket: My Life as a Quarterback*, the autobiography of Earl Morrall, the backup quarterback for Johnny Unitas with the Baltimore Colts. *Who cares?* I thought, never much interested in jock stories. The last book was *The Grapes of Wrath*. I'd picked up Steinbeck's *Of Mice and Men* a few months before and liked it well enough to finish it, and so even though *The Grapes of Wrath* was a much bigger book than any I'd ever read before, I took it back to the bed, lay down, and cracked it open.

After Officer Buehle came down the stairs the first time to check on me, I stopped paying him any mind and didn't even look up from my book the next couple of times. I didn't have a watch and there was no clock in the hole, so I had no notion of time. After some while of reading *The Grapes of Wrath*—and, to my amazement, breaking the one-hundred-page mark—I dozed off. When I woke up, I had to pee really bad but didn't have a clue when the guard would be down next. Holding it in became painful, and I paced the room with my ears tuned to the sound of the basement door opening. The gurgling of water through the sewer and water pipes above my head didn't help. Then, through the metal grate in the door to my room I could see a drainage hole in the center of the basement floor, with the concrete slab sloping toward it to facilitate the draining of water when the basement flooded. I thought I might relieve myself beneath my door and let it flow straight toward the drainage hole. Fortunately, though, just as I was preparing to execute this plan, the basement door opened and I zipped back up.

"I gotta go," I called out when he looked through the grate of my door.

It was Officer Dorn this time. He was a short, mild-faced man who was nonetheless a black belt in kung fu *and* karate and taught popular classes in both at Fort Worden on Saturday afternoons. At one of the classes I attended, he recounted modestly how he once went up against Bruce Lee at Lee's Jun Fan martial arts studio in Seattle. At that time, Bruce Lee had yet to make his really famous movies, and we only knew him as the guy who played Kato on *The Green Hornet* TV show, but that was more than enough to impress us. So, even though he wouldn't say who won in the bout, we admired Officer Dorn for even taking on Bruce Lee / Kato.

"The match was not about victory," he said, "but about understanding your opponent and coming to know yourself better."

We groaned at this lame explanation and later among ourselves agreed that Kato had probably given Officer Dorn a wicked beating.

"Come on," Officer Dorn said and unlocked the door to let me out.

I followed him upstairs to the only bathroom in the guard house, which was just a two-room building—one room with a couple of desks, some wooden file cabinets, and a large metal cabinet I figured was for rifles, tear gas, and other anti-riot gear. On one of the desks, there was a two-way radio that quietly crackled. As I used the bathroom, which was just a toilet and sink, Officer Dorn waited outside the door, and when I came out he asked if I wanted some fresh air.

"Sure," I said, nervous that I might run into Officer Buehle, who would surely give me and Officer Dorn a hard time for violating the rules of my isolation, which limited a person to only an hour a day outside, a half hour after breakfast and a half hour after lunch.

But Buehle must have been tooling about somewhere in the security jeep or else off-duty because I didn't see him the entire time I sat on the top step of the front porch while Officer Dorn sat in one of the two metal chairs—the same one I'd set Prosper down in less than twenty-four hours earlier. We must have sat there for almost an hour.

"That kid got beat up pretty bad," Officer Dorn said at one point.

"I know," I said, and wondered if he was going to try to wheedle some kind of a confession out of me.

"He could've died up there on the hill," he went on, "but someone brought him back to the guard house."

I didn't say anything. I rested my forearms on my knees and looked out toward the parade grounds filled with kids walking around, playing football, tossing a Frisbee, some kids off to the side clustered in small groups, the usual. It was early evening, and even though the guard house was in shade, the parade grounds were still in full sun. Beyond them I could see the shimmering blue-and-white waters of Admiralty Inlet, and beyond that the hay-colored bluffs of Whidbey Island, and beyond *that* the hazy dark-blue outline of the Cascade Mountains.

"Is he going to be all right?" I asked, turning around just enough to make eye contact with Officer Dorn.

"Sure," he said and went quiet for several minutes. Then he leaned forward in the chair and asked, "Do you know what Buddhism is?"

"Yeah," I said, "sorta," though I really had no idea. I knew it was a religion and that was it.

"The first precept of Buddhism is to refrain from violence and protect all life. It's kind of like the policeman's creed: *To serve and protect.* It all comes down to compassion."

I let his words rest between us and then asked, "Are you a Buddhist?"

And right then, oddly enough, the dinner bell rang, echoing across the grounds of Fort Worden, and suddenly everyone on the parade grounds was making a beeline for the cafeteria.

"Not really," he answered. "I've just been reading up on it." He got up from his chair and I knew it was time to go back inside.

Shortly after delivering me back to the basement, Office Dorn carried down a covered tray with my dinner on it—a plate of Hungarian goulash, a bowl of creamed corn, two slices of buttered Wonder Bread, a squishy plum, a thick brownie with walnuts in it, and a tall glass of milk.

I slept soundly my first night in the hole, and the next day I ate all three meals there, made three trips to the toilet, and kept reading *The Grapes of Wrath.* The time away from the noisy cottage with the constant jockeying and clamor was actually a reprieve of sorts. My second evening in the hole, I heard Buehle and Dorn talking for a while upstairs as one shift ended and another started, and later Officer Dorn let me sit out front again. Then, as I ate my dinner back in the basement, I heard him talking on the phone, his transistor radio playing in the background.

If the purpose of the isolation was to have me "think about what you've done," as Mr. Higman indicated, that goal wasn't being achieved—at least not in the way he or Dr. Reinholdt imagined. It was just me and my book, and I was too preoccupied with what the Joads were doing—or rather having done to them by the heartless bankers, greedy orchard owners, and cruel sheriff's deputies—to ponder the error of my ways. From here on out, I figured, it would be me and Tom Joad fighting injustice: "Long as I'm a outlaw anyways," as Tom says to Ma. The line became my mantra.

FROM THEN ON, YOU could rarely find me anywhere on the grounds of the Fort Worden Diagnostic and Treatment Center for Juvenile Delinquency without a paperback in my hand or sticking out of the back pocket of my state-issued khakis. In other words, the hole had made a reader out of me.

I finished *The Grapes of Wrath* about two hours before Officer Lockwood, who was chief of security, came down to the basement mid-afternoon of my third and final day and let me out. Upstairs, Mr. Higman was waiting to escort me back to the cottage where I would be allowed to shower and change my clothes before having a counseling session with Mrs. Adel in her office.

When I told Mrs. Adel that I'd left my textbooks in the cottage and wasn't able to keep up with my schoolwork while in isolation, she became angry with me for neglecting my studies and not requesting my textbooks be brought to me, and then she blamed the guards for not seeing that I used my time wisely. Even when I told her I'd read all of *The Grapes of Wrath*, all she said was, "Yes, well, that's fine. But you're behind in your schoolwork."

I soon found out that Prosper had been released from the infirmary that morning and after lunch had gone to class. I wasn't eager to see him, but as it turned out, our meeting wasn't as awkward as I thought it might be. I was in the common room downstairs in the cottage, looking at the dozen or so paperbacks on the mantle above the bricked-up hearth—all books I'd mostly ignored for the past four months—when he walked in, sat down on the couch, and asked me how my time in the hole had been. He wasn't even being sarcastic.

"Nothing to it," I said as if I was James Cagney and had just gotten out of the slammer. "How was the infirmary?"

"Boring," he said. "I slept most of the time. And played Chinese checkers a few times with Nurse Wong and another girl who was there. Tammy. She's over in one of the girls' cottages. Nurse Wong told us Chinese checkers aren't from China at all, but that a German guy invented it."

"Weird," I said, taken aback by how chatty he'd become, afraid he might be setting me up so he could slam me later for my part in the blanket party.

But he never brought it up—not then in the common room, not ever. And later the thought passed my mind that Prosper's hazing had in some ways worked. He was no longer in the shell he'd been in his first week at Fort Worden, and all the badass guys in our cottage like Bobby Felton and Stew Parks now let him be. He still didn't play ping-pong or pool or any sports with most of the rest of the guys, but everyone was pretty much all right with him. He got a job at the infirmary assisting Nurse Wong and that way became friends with some of the female residents at the Treatment Center who otherwise, with the exception of class time, were kept strictly segregated from the guys. As for me and Prosper, we did become kind of friends, and he even helped me catch up with my schoolwork.

But even after catching up on school work, I kept reading on my own. Over a couple of weeks I read John Steinbeck's *The Red Pony*, which was too sappy for my tastes, and *Cannery Row*, which made me want to take off for Monterey Bay. I also read *Big Jim Turner* by James Stevens, which wasn't great, though I liked it all right, mainly because parts of it reminded me of *The Grapes of Wrath* and it was set in the Northwest woods.

When my disciplinary probation ended, autumn was coming on for real. One storm after another rolled in from the Pacific during October. The inlet was torn up with white caps, and ferry service to Port Townsend was stopped several times. One storm had such crazy winds that it brought down trees across Point Wilson, where Fort Worden was located, and caused a power outage. This meant that instead of school the next day, we were all marched outside in army-surplus ponchos to clear the grounds of wind-downed branches. Then when the maintenance guys finished bucking all the fallen trees with their chainsaws, we loaded the rounds onto the back of a truck to be hauled off and sold for firewood in town.

I DIDN'T GET INTO any trouble or even do anything wrong for weeks on end—which was new for me. But then, without even giving it much thought, I learned about escaping from Fort Worden. One Saturday afternoon, when hanging out with a couple of guy from another cottage, the three of us decided to just slip off the grounds and go for a walk. We strayed all the way to the Motor Movie Drive-In out on Route 20, snuck under the perimeter fence, and lay on the grass up front watching *Shalako*, a western with Sean Connery and Brigitte Bardot. And after the movie we went back. The escape was no big deal—since we didn't get caught—though it helped me realize how easy it was to actually flee if I wanted to.

So, not long after that, I really took off after having a serious run-in with Mr. Larrison. He was a World War II veteran, a former gunnery sergeant in the marines. A real tough guy. And he taught math, my least favorite subject. He didn't like me, and I didn't like him—the usual story. Rather than explain what a function was or how a particular notation worked, he would tell me to look it up in the textbook and then throw more problems at me.

"It's simple, Clausen. Just use your head." Like Officer Buehle, Mr. Larrison called residents by their last names unless they were his favorites.

I could do the equations when I had someone like Prosper to help me, but on my own I was lost nine times out of ten. I would get so frustrated I would clinch my jaw and grind my teeth until my whole head hurt. I would bite my fingernails until the cuticles bled and start bouncing my right leg uncontrollably. When we came to the chapter titled "Negative Power and Powers as Numeric Fractions," I tried my best to follow what Larrison was doing up at the chalkboard. I even raised my hand and asked a question. But when it came to doing the problems in the workbook, my frustration only mounted. When he came over to my desk, stood over me, and asked to see my work, I showed it to him.

"Two problems. That's all you've done this entire time is two problems?" He bent over my desk with his red pencil in hand and corrected my work. "Look at these," he said, "and figure out what you're doing wrong."

They say Albert Einstein never memorized his multiplication table, which I always took comfort in, since neither did I. And now they say that multiplying in increments in your head, as Einstein probably had, is okay. Do one pair of numbers, then the next, and so on, which makes perfect sense to me. But solving linear, literal, and radical equations in algebra just took more than I was cognitively capable of doing under Gunnery Sergeant Larrison's command. I would rather have faced a whole squadron of Nazi panzers with flamethrowers on top than try to solve another math problem.

"Fuck," I let out involuntarily as I tried to figure out his corrections.

Everyone in the classroom stopped and looked at me. Larrison was at another kid's desk two rows over. He stopped what he was doing too, pushed his way over to me between the rows of desks, and ordered me to stand up.

"I don't get it," I said and remained seated.

"There's no swearing in my classroom," he replied. "And you don't get it because you're not trying. Now stand up."

I hunched over my workbook, deliberately defying him, and pretended to start on another problem. That's when he gripped the back of my neck, squeezed like a vise, and tried to make me stand up. He was strong, that was for sure, but I was desperate. I snatched up my workbook and hurled it across the room and in doing so broke free from his grip. I then slid out of my chair, ducked between three rows of desks, and ran out of the classroom and out the front doors of the building. I sprang down the steps and started across the parade grounds toward the cottages. When I looked back, Larrison was at the top of the steps.

"You'd better be headed to the guard house, Clausen. That's where I'll expect to find you when I'm done here."

I raised my right hand, gave him the finger, and kept walking. Instead of going to the guard house, I made a wide loop around it and headed into the woods just above the West Gate. And kept walking.

This became the first time I'd truly *rambled*, as we all called it—leaving the grounds with no intention of coming back. Unlike sneaking out to the drive-in and sneaking back afterward, when you rambled you just kept going. Usually the Treatment Center security officers, with help from the Port Townsend Police, nabbed kids who went rambling before they got very far. But I was lucky that day. I walked south-southwest, cutting through backyards and fields, avoiding the roads whenever possible, until I reached Route 20 at the top of the hill. At the pace I was walking, this took me less than half an hour, so I figured my absence had probably not even been reported yet. Then, as soon as I stepped onto the main road and stuck my thumb out, an old farmer stopped in his ancient Dodge truck, and I climbed into the passenger side. As he drove, he told me he'd just been to Theriault Building Supply and the lumber in the bed of his truck was for a hen house he was going to build. When he asked why I wasn't in school,

I told him my uncle in Seattle was sick and my parents were already there at the hospital with him, so I got permission to leave school, and since the bus was so slow, I was going to hitchhike to the city to join them before my uncle died.

"I'm sorry to hear that," the old man said. He wore a tan felt hat that was stained white with dried sweat around where the hatband should have been. He was kind of shrunken up, or at least appeared so as he gripped the big steering wheel of the truck with his gnarled hands and lifted his chin to peer over the dashboard. He wore baggy overalls and hadn't shaved in probably a week. "Seattle's a long ways," he said.

"I think I can get there before night if I'm lucky."

That's when he offered to drive me all the way to the Hood Canal Bridge if I would help him unload the lumber in the bed of his truck first. I turned and looked into the back. It wasn't a big load, and I figured it wouldn't take more than twenty minutes to unload. So, knowing I could spend that same twenty minutes or longer on the side of the road waiting for my next ride, I told him sure thing.

His farm was about five miles past Chimacum, in the narrow valley between the coastline and the mountains. It was a big place, too, though fairly run down. The two-story frame house needed a paint job and the front porch sagged terribly. The barn seemed to be leaning to one side and looked like it could use a new roof. As we started unloading the lumber, he told me he'd gone from raising a herd of dairy cows two decades ago—"Twenty head," he said—to just one cow and a bunch of goats a few years ago. "But now all's I got is a couple a goats and a passel of chickens that need a henhouse so the coyotes don't keep getting them."

We finished unloading the lumber in no time and got back in the truck. He was far from being the taciturn farmer you read about in Robert Frost poems. This old man could talk, and he started telling me how he bought his farm during the war with the money he'd made working in the Crown Zellerbach paper mill in Port Townsend, putting in twelve- and fourteen-hour shifts because of the labor shortage and wartime demand for paper. "I guess the army goes through a lot of paper," he said. He also told me how his wife of forty-two years had died last year and their thirty-eight-year-old son was a longshoreman down in Portland. "Now there's a union for ya," he added. "My boy makes more money than most lawyers."

As we approached the Hood Canal Bridge—which I'd crossed for the first time when I was brought to the Treatment Center—I could see the smooth blue water ahead bisected by the floating bridge that spanned the mile-wide canal. The old farmer was telling me about his son and how he hoped he would come back to the farm once he saved up enough to quit longshoring. When he noticed the bridge coming up, he said, "What the heck, I'll take you to the ferry," and we barreled across the bridge. Then, at the Kingston ferry dock, he pulled a five-dollar bill out of his crusty leather wallet and told me to get something to eat. I thanked him and we shook hands.

Maybe he knew I was lying to him about my uncle and that I was dead broke. In any case, that fiver was a godsend since I had no way of paying for the ferry. I bought my ticket and still had plenty left over for clam chowder and french fries from the food concession on board. When the ferry docked in Edmonds, I ran off to get in front of the car traffic and instantly caught a ride from a UW student going all the way down I-5 to the University District. After he told me he was from Bonney Lake, not far from Spanaway, we got to talking and eventually he said I could crash the night at his fraternity house if I wanted to. I said sure and felt as if I'd made the cleanest, most effortless break from Fort Worden probably in all of history.

THE FIRST TIME I went to Seattle I was nine years old. The trip was to visit the '62 World's Fair. My father didn't want to take me, saying it was too expensive and I was too young to appreciate it. Yet every kid I knew was going, so from the Fair's opening day in April I kept up a steady whine about it. Finally, in August, he relented and the next weekend we got in the car and drove the hour and a half to Seattle. We had a good time. My father really got into the exhibits, like the glass-enclosed Bubbleator ride that took you into "The World of Tomorrow," where we were presented with images of Marilyn Monroe, flying cars, and mushroom clouds. We rode the Monorail, "the future of transportation," and the gyrocopter, which my father and I both marveled at. He said as soon as the gyrocopter hit the dealerships, we'd be the first family in Spanaway to get one. "It'll be worth it," he said, "given how the price of gas keeps going up." Later that afternoon, at my mother's insistence, we went to the Playhouse to hear Nat King Cole sing and play piano with his band. Afterward she said she would rather listen to Nat King Cole any day of the week over Elvis Presley, who'd been at the fair earlier in the summer to make a movie. We ate hamburgers and milkshakes in our car at Dag's Drive-In after the Nat King Cole concert and stayed the night in a nearby Travelodge.

The next day we visited some of the more educational exhibits like the Mercury space capsule, the display of Northwest Indian art, and the nation pavilions of Japan, India, and Mexico. We got lunch at the Food Circus, and afterward I was allowed to go on three rides (and three rides only!) at what was called the Gayway, the fair's version of a carnival midway. To cap off our visit, the three of us rode one of the Union 76 Skyride gondolas that let us ogle all the fairgoers swarming below, and then, with night coming on, we drove back to Spanaway.

Since then, I'd been back to Seattle three times—once to go shopping at Frederick & Nelson department store with my mother, once to visit a divorce lawyer in the Smith Tower with my father, and then when I first ran away from home at age thirteen. That first trip to Seattle, however, could never be topped, and even though I never knew the pre–World's Fair city, it seemed to me that Seattle had changed once the Fair was over. That's what everyone said, pointing out how much busier and congested and fancy the city had become. Whatever the case, like any big city, Seattle could always be counted on to be a rough place for a kid on the streets, which is what I was the morning after my escape from the Fort Worden Treatment Center in 1970.

Even after polishing off nearly a case of Oly the night before with the guy who drove me to Seattle and two of his fraternity brothers, I woke up early, snatched a box of Pop-Tarts from the kitchen, and left. I didn't know where I was headed or what I was going to do, so I just started walking. In the distance I could see the Space Needle—which we never went up in '62 because my mother felt it couldn't possibly support all the people riding the gold-capsule elevators to the top—and I headed in that direction. It was a chill November morning and I was glad to have the standard-issue blue windbreaker from the Treatment Center. I zipped it up, stuffed my hands in my pants pockets, and walked across the University Bridge, along the length of Lake Union, past the Travelodge where my parents and I had stayed, and headed downtown. By now, Superintendent Lindquist would have put out a bulletin to all the appropriate child care and law enforcement agencies, including the Seattle PD, that I'd gone AWOL.

It was almost noon when I reached Pike Place Market. I walked around looking at the fish tables and produce stalls and tables of flowers. I bought two twenty-five-cent hot dogs, loaded them both up with sauerkraut, onions, relish, and mustard, and ate them on the landing next to the entrance to the Place Pigalle Tavern. The tavern was already open and several people came and went as I stood there chomping on my hot dogs.

I was licking my fingers clean and wiping them on my pants leg when a middle-aged guy in a blue blazer, gray slacks, and an open-collar yellow shirt with a red silk ascot around his neck came down the landing. He was about to open the door of the tavern when he paused and said, "Are you John?"

Even though there was no one else on the landing, I looked around to see who he was talking to, then realized he was talking to me.

"No," I said.

"You're not John from Renton? The guy I'm supposed to meet here?"

"Afraid not," I said. "I'm from Spanaway."

"Okay then," he said. "My mistake." I thought he was going to enter the tavern at that point, but instead he let go of the door and came up to me and asked, "So what's your name?"

I told him my name.

"I'm Roger," he said. "Good to meet you, Avery." He put his hand out and so I shook it. "Since John's not here, how 'bout I buy you a beer?"

I thought he just wanted to have a beer with someone—John from Renton, me, whoever—so I told him okay, he could buy me a beer. I had nowhere I needed to be.

We went into the dim tavern and sat at one of the small booths in the back next to a window that looked out over Elliott Bay toward the Olympics. As he went up to the old wooden bar, I watched another guy with long braided hair and a blue bandana around his head get up from the bar and go to the jukebox against the wall. He dropped a quarter in the slot and started punching numbers, and a moment later a Creedence Clearwater Revival song came on. Roger came back to the booth with a schooner of beer for me and a tumbler of wine for himself.

"If the bartender asks," he said, leaning across the table and putting a hand on my forearm, "you're twenty-one."

"I am twenty-one," I said. Why did he think I wasn't? I hadn't told him I wasn't. I knew plenty of kids who passed for twenty-one, so why shouldn't I?

"That's good," he said with an amused smile. "That's very good." He took a sip of wine. "So where's this place you said you're from? Spam-something?"

"Spanaway. It's by Tacoma."

"Well, what brings you to the big city? And don't tell me you're visiting a sick grandmother."

"Uncle actually. He's in the hospital."

"Oh *really?*" He gave me a look of mock sympathy, as if my feeble attempt at lying disappointed him. "I'm so sorry. Which one?"

He had me there. I took a swig of beer and said, "What's it matter," and looked about the tavern as if I'd grown bored with the conversation. I bounced my head to the CCR tune and sang the lyrics to myself: *"Down on the corner, out in the street."*

It occurred to me I needed a plan. Yesterday all I wanted to do was escape from Fort Worden, get off the Olympic Peninsula, and haul down to Seattle. But now that I was in Seattle, what was I going to do? The more he talked, the more I realized I couldn't hang out with this Roger guy. He was probably in his forties and kind of strange. He resembled Charles Nelson Reilly from the show *The Ghost & Mrs. Muir*, minus the enormous glasses. I need to find a job, I told myself, and a place to stay. I figured I'd set myself up here in Seattle since it seemed like a good place to hide out. Or, if it didn't work out here, I'd head down to San Francisco. It was less than twenty-four hours since I'd fled the Treatment Center and I was tired, so I was staring off into space when Roger asked me if I wanted another schooner.

"What?" I said and blinked a few times, and he repeated the question. "Naw," I said. "This is enough."

He went to the bar and brought back a refill of wine for himself and another schooner for me anyways. "In case you change your mind," he said.

"Thanks," I said and mindlessly finished my first glass and started on the second.

"Do you have a place to stay the night?"

I shrugged.

"If not, there's a place I'm associated with where you can get a clean bed, hot shower, and something to eat." He explained how he belonged to a group called the North American Man-Boy Support Alliance, otherwise known as NAMBSA. "It's a group of mature men, like myself, who support and mentor boys and young men in need." He explained that the group had a house in the Capitol Hill neighborhood, not far from where we were.

"I don't know," I said, thinking, *Hadn't I just fled a place where mature men were supposed to be supporting and mentoring boys and young men?* I didn't know what this group's spin was—not then anyhow—but I did know that I had just a short while ago eaten two hot dogs and wasn't that hungry at the moment, and also that I could go as long as I needed to without a clean bed or hot shower. Besides, I'd figured out by this point that there was no John from Renton and that ol' Roger from the Support Alliance was making a move on me.

"Let me take you up to Capitol Hill and show you," he said. He was smiling more nervously now. "Once you see it, you'll like it. I'll introduce you to some of the other alliance members."

"I gotta go," I let out. Then, when he reached across the table and laid his hand on my forearm, it reminded me of Mr. Larrison grabbing the back of my neck in math class the day before, and I pulled away. He looked surprised, and a bit sad, as I slid out of the booth.

"Take the address in case you change your mind," he said.

"Thanks for the beer," I replied and headed toward the door. The bartender stood leaning against the back bar, flipping through a magazine. The Dead's "Uncle John's Band" played on the jukebox.

The market had become much busier in the half hour or so I'd been in the tavern. It felt good to have people jostling around me, to lose myself in the crowd. I passed a stand selling pot stickers and curry buns and, suddenly feeling hungry again, dug into my pocket for the few coins I had left. There was about thirty cents. I held my hand out with the change in my palm and asked the Chinese man behind the steam table what I could get for this. He handed me a small paper bowl with three pot stickers in it, and I dumped the change into his hand.

"Thanks," I said and strolled away filling my mouth with the steaming hot dough and savory filling.

As I made my way down to the waterfront, I took my jacket off and tied the sleeves around my waist. On the abandoned Salt Dock, straight down the hill from the market, half a dozen men dangled fishing rods over the water. One of them had a tin pail with some kind of brownish flat fish in it. I asked what it was, and he said it was a flounder. After that I found a spot away from the fishermen and sat down. As the warm boards of the dock and the pungent smell of low tide started to make me drowsy, I bunched up my jacket for a pillow, stretched myself out, and fell asleep.

WHEN I WOKE UP, the afternoon sun was in my face and a cool breeze was blowing off the water. I sat up, groggy still, and put my jacket on. Then I saw somebody across the dock going from fisherman to fisherman, panhandling and being shooed away. When the person ambled over to where I sat reclined against a horizontal beam, I noticed it was a girl, a really pretty black girl, rail thin and kind of gangly. She stood right at my feet in front of me, the sun behind her back making a perfect silhouette of her figure.

"You got a cigarette?"

I shook my head no. I put my hand over my brow and squinted up at her.

"You got any change?"

"Nothing," I said. "Flat broke."

"Are you sure?"

"Pretty sure," I said and laughed.

She stepped aside, leaned over the edge of the dock, and let a big gob of spit drop from her lips into the water. The angle of her cheeks gave her smooth skin an almost purplish tint. With a clear view of her now, I could see she was about my age or maybe even younger. A multicolored, baggy hand-knit cap was on her head. She also wore an army fatigue jacket with the name Johnson patched on the top right pocket and faded denim jeans that were tight around her hips and butt but splayed out like tent canvas around her legs, the ragged cuffs dragging on the ground. When she turned and sat down on the large beam I had my back against, I could see that she had leather-strap sandals on her sockless feet.

"Do you need a couple bucks?" she asked me.

I didn't understand the question at first. One minute she was asking me for spare change and the next offering me a couple bucks. I had to look to my left and over my shoulder to see her face. Her eyes were light brown and speckled, and I wanted to keep looking at them.

"Well do you?" she asked again, her eyes wide in exasperation.

I pushed myself up so I was sitting on the beam too. "Naw," I said. "Thanks anyhow."

Now she laughed at me. "Well which is it? Either you're broke and need a couple bucks, or you're not and you just lied to me about not having any change."

I didn't have an answer to this. She yanked the knit cap off her head and her hair sprang loose in short, frizzy coils that had a reddish tint to them.

"My name's Brenda," she said, "and all I'm saying is if you're hungry or anything, I have a few dollars."

"Thank you," I replied. "I ate something a little while ago."

"That's steady," she said, and she scratched her head and put the cap back on.

"Who's Johnson?" I asked and pointed to the name patch on her jacket.

"I don't know," she said. "Just some guy, I suppose. Maybe he's dead now."

As we sat there for a few minutes without saying anything more, just looking out across the sparkling surface of Elliott Bay, I realized I'd never exchanged so many words with a black person in all my life. There were a lot of black people in Tacoma, but not in Spanaway, at least not that I knew of. There were a few black kids at the Treatment Center, but they were in cottages other than mine. I knew who they were from school and playing sports on the parade grounds, but I never spoke to any of them. They seemed intimidating, or at least that's how I saw them, especially when they hung out together as a group, which they usually did. So maybe it was because Brenda was a girl, or because she'd approached me, or because I had nowhere else to go, or all these things combined, that made it easy for me to sit there with her, waiting for whatever happened next, which turned out to be a stronger breeze coming up and the air turning suddenly cooler as the sun slid down behind the mountains.

I stood and zipped up my jacket. A ferry was coming in, slowing down as it approached the waterfront, its lights reflecting lime green on the glassy water.

Seeing the ferry reminded me of the last time I'd been to the Seattle waterfront several years earlier. After the visit to his divorce lawyer, my father and I came down to the waterfront and ordered fish and chips at the walk-up window at Ivar's Acres of Clams. When we were done eating, we walked through the nearby ferry terminal and watched several ferries come and go. We didn't say a word to one another the whole while, and eventually he said it was time to go, and we drove back to Spanaway, where my father dropped me off at our house, the house he'd already moved out of two weeks earlier.

"Maybe we should go sit in the ferry terminal," I suggested. "It'll be warmer." Brenda stood up then and started walking, and I followed. "I'm Avery, by the way," I said as I tried to keep up with her fast pace.

"Hi Avery Bytheway," she said and smiled at me.

The ferry terminal was busy with rush-hour commuters, so Brenda set about panhandling again while I sat down on one of the wood-slatted benches, picked up a discarded newspaper, and flipped to the Help Wanted ads. I could hear my father warning me about being a freeloader, so I told myself there was no way I would start begging, and located half a dozen notices for dishwashing jobs, no experience required, including one right next door at Ivar's. When Brenda came back, she showed off by jangling in the pocket of her army jacket all the change she'd gotten and offered to buy me a hot chocolate from the coffee stand. I said sure.

For each ferry that came and went, Brenda dove back into the throng of commuters and each time came away a little richer.

"It's a goldmine," she said, and admitted she'd never thought of coming here before and thanked me for suggesting it. At one point she asked me to hold some of the change for her. Another time she said some guy offered her ten dollars for a BJ and she told him to fuck off. "He had on a suit too," she said. "I hate people in suits."

As the evening wore on and the number of ferry riders thinned out, she spent more time sitting on the bench with me. This is when she started to ask me questions about myself, and I told her straight out about running away from the Treatment Center in Port Townsend and hitching down to Seattle.

"So that's why you're dressed like that," she said, glancing at my khaki pants, white T-shirt, blue windbreaker, and black high-top Converse.

"I guess so," I said and then turned the tables and started asking about her.

She said she was the sister of one of the players on the SuperSonics, which was the NBA team Seattle had gotten a few years earlier.

"Which one?" I asked. I wanted her to say her brother was Lucius Allen, the Sonics guard who'd played with Lew Alcindor at UCLA and won the NCAA championship, but she wouldn't tell me his name. She did say that her brother didn't live with her and her mother, and that even though he made loads of money, they still lived in the Yesler Terrace public housing just up the hill from where we were. She said her grandmother, who was a Jehovah's Witness, also lived with them and that she, Brenda, used to go door to door all over Seattle with her Memaw passing out copies of *The Watchtower*, which might be why she found it so easy to go up to people asking for change. Her real father was hardly ever around, she said, and her mother had a new boyfriend who was turning her mother into a junkie and hitting on Brenda whenever he came over, so that's why she spent most of her time on the streets now.

"What about school?" I asked, wondering why she hadn't been picked up for truancy and sent off to someplace like the Fort Worden Diagnostic and Treatment Center.

"What about it?" she asked right back, and said she hadn't gone in three weeks. "I'm thinking of going to New York."

"What for?"

"I don't know," she said. "Because it's not Seattle." The brightness in her eyes seemed to dim, but then she recovered herself and pronounced, "I probably have enough for a bus ticket with what I got here tonight."

She dropped down to the floor, dumped all the loose change and bills she'd panhandled between her outstretched legs, and started counting. The total, which included a five-dollar bill, came to over twenty-seven dollars. She said we should each carry half in case anything happened and one of us lost theirs, so we divided the coins and bills between us and went down to Ivar's for some fish and chips. On the way, I mentioned maybe applying for the dishwasher job, and she said I should.

After we ate, we walked north along the waterfront and then angled up toward the Space Needle. I told Brenda how I'd gone to the World's Fair with my parents as a kid, and she said that she was still living in St. Louis then, which was where her Memaw was from. Then she said she knew someone with an apartment near the Space Needle and we should see if he was there. So we continued walking up the hill and before long were standing in front of a three-story brick apartment building. Brenda tossed a pebble at a second-floor window, and a moment later the window opened.

"Sweet baby Brenda," a shirtless guy with long red hair called down as he leaned out and looked at us. "Come on up," he said and dropped a set of keys out the window.

Brenda caught them, and a moment later we were walking up the stairs and down the hall to where a door had been left ajar. As soon as we entered, the lanky red-headed guy came up and gave Brenda a big hug. He then turned to me—"Hey, man, I'm Jay. Welcome."—and gave me the soul brother handshake.

"Avery," I replied.

He was like a stick figure, he was so skinny. His chest seemed concave, like a heavy weight had been dropped on his ribcage as a child, and his pale skinny legs stuck out of his cut-off jean shorts. Wavy red locks framed his face and fanned out about his shoulders, and he had a spotty orangish beard on his chin and hollow cheeks. And he was barefoot.

It was a one-bedroom apartment with a frayed couch against one wall, next to it a lamp with an Indian batik cloth draped over it, and in the other corner a torn leather recliner. A scuffed coffee table was in the middle of the room. There were several concert posters tacked to the walls: Monterey International Pop Festival, the Grateful Dead at Fillmore East, the Steve Miller Band in Golden Gate Park. The four black-and-white portraits of John, Paul, George, and Ringo that came with the *White Album* were taped to a narrow portion of wall above the window frame. A small corner table had a stereo tuner and turntable on it and a wood crate filled with albums underneath. Two speakers were set on either side of the table. From the archway leading into the kitchen hung a round object made of wood, leather, feathers, and beads, which Brenda later told me was a Hopi dream catcher she'd given Jay for his eighteenth birthday.

Before we even sat down, Jay handed Brenda a bulbous-shaped bottle, and she took a swig and handed it to me. I glanced at the label—Mateus Rosé—and took a swig. It was warm and tasted dreadful but almost instantly set my head abuzz. Brenda and I dropped onto the couch and Jay sat cross-legged in the recliner. That's when I noticed the three small painted turtles in the shallow glass bowl on the cluttered coffee table. Two of them sat on a rock and the third floated in the water. They seemed content enough.

"Do you get high?" Jay asked me.

There was weed at Fort Worden, and I knew for a fact that at least two guys in my cottage, Bobby Felton and Pete Munson, smoked it regularly. But I'd never been offered any, and didn't dare ask Bobby or Pete for some, so it had been a while.

"Yeah," I said, "All the time."

"Let's do it up then." Jay unfolded his legs, dropped his feet to the floor, and reached forward to pick up a wad of aluminum foil no bigger than a matchbox that lay on the coffee table. He reached into his pants pocket and pulled out a polished marble pipe that looked like the one I used to have before Officer Leroy threw it in Spanaway Lake.

"I used to have a pipe just like that," I said.

"Cool, man." He peeled back the aluminum foil, broke off a corner of the brownish-green square that lay in it, and placed it on the screen in the bowl of the pipe. "The best hash comes from Afghanistan," he said. "That's where this comes from."

"I've never smoked hash before," said Brenda, as Jay took out his lighter.

"Baudelaire loved it," he said.

I didn't know who that was, but when Jay lit the pipe, took a long drag from it, and passed it to me, I straightaway put it to my mouth and sucked in. I started choking almost instantly but then settled down, took another pull, and this time kept the dense white smoke down before passing the pipe to Brenda. She took a small, cautious hit and let it out slowly, but when she tried to take another hit, she erupted in laughter and snorted smoke out her nose. The pipe passed between the three of us a couple more times before the piece of hash in the bowl was reduced to a small bit of ash.

As Brenda flipped through Jay's album collection, Jay pulled his legs up, rested his head on the back of the recliner, and asked me where I was from.

From, I thought. My mouth was dry and my eyes burned. "I don't know," I said, unsure what he was actually asking me.

Jay stroked the hairs on his chin and laughed knowingly.

"You're from Span-*away*," Brenda volunteered as she came back to the couch. An enchanting woman's voice began to flow from the stereo speakers. "My father knows her father," she said, holding up the album cover.

"I am," I said.

"Your father knows Judy Collins's father?" Jay asked.

"I'm from Spanaway," I said. "Who's Judy Collins?"

"Never mind," said Brenda and took a swig from the bottle of Mateus. "Here," she said and handed it to me.

The wetness of the wine felt good in my mouth, and it tasted better now too. I was falling in love with the music filling the room and so closed my eyes, sank down into the couch, and let the melodious voice bathe me. Brenda and Jay were talking, but I couldn't hear what they were saying.

After a few songs, Brenda nudged me.

"Are you falling asleep?"

"No," I said.

"Then tell Jay what you told me about that place you ran away from yesterday."

I sat up and ran my hand through my hair. I looked at Jay, who had his hands clasped behind his head, making the ribs in his chest push out from his translucent white skin.

"Do you have a beer?" I asked him.

"Just wine," he said. "Brenda said it was like some kind of prison you were in, or something fucked up like that."

"It's called the Fort Worden Diagnostic and Treatment Center for Juvenile Delinquency," I said with due deliberation.

"So that makes you a juvenile delinquent," he announced, then laughed and reached down and scratched his foot. "What's it like, man? Do they mess with your head, make you do all kinds of crap you don't want to do, force you to obey and all that shit?"

"It's just a place," I answered, but then regaled them with some of the worst things I'd ever seen or heard about the Treatment Center, like the kid hanging himself in the hole or a girl getting raped by a counselor or the guy setting his mattress on fire and nearly burning down his cottage—pretending like all this had happened in just the last month alone. I even mentioned Prosper's blanket party. I told them about the stint I did in the hole last month, and for full effect finished by saying, "You get used to it."

By this time, though, Brenda was curled up in her corner of the couch and already asleep. But Jay, to show his commiseration with me, broke off another small piece of hash, lit the pipe, and passed it to me.

"That's some heavy shit," he said, and then told me he was going to crash since he had to get up to go to work the next morning—he worked, he said, at the Elephant Car Wash—and then told me that Brenda and I could stay as long as we wanted. "Help yourself to the fridge," he said as he shuffled off into the bedroom.

I went into the kitchen and saw from the oven clock that it was nearly 1:00 a.m. I wasn't tired, but I was hungry. In the freezer I found a half-full carton of black walnut ice cream, sat down at the kitchen table, and ate straight from the waxed container with a fork I found in a drawer. A box of magazines and paperbacks was on the chair beside me, so while I ate I leafed through old *National Geographic*s and read the back cover of a tattered copy of *The Picture of Dorian Gray*. After I finished off the ice cream and dropped the empty container in the trash, I stuffed the copy of *Dorian Gray* in the pocket of my windbreaker and then, back in the living room, fell asleep on the couch at the opposite end from Brenda, our legs touching in the middle.

IN THE MORNING, BRENDA and I found an umbrella in Jay's front closet and walked back downtown. The streets were slick with rain, and the whole of Puget Sound was a wall of fog. When we reached Pike and Third, I told Brenda to wait for me on the sidewalk and then entered the Woolworth's and came out just a few minutes later, hurrying Brenda down the block toward the market.

Once beneath the main arcade and in among the produce stalls, I reached into my jacket and took out a pair of heavy wool socks and two boxes of doughnuts: one powdered, one cinnamon.

"Here," I said and handed Brenda the socks. "To keep your feet warm."

"Thanks," she said, and as she kicked off her sandals and pulled on the socks, I tore into the box of powdered doughnuts.

As we crouched with our backs against the wall of the arcade and watched people pass by, I asked Brenda how she knew Jay and she told me they used to be neighbors on Mercer Island, which is a well-heeled little enclave that sits in the middle of Lake Washington.

"I lied about living in Yesler Terrace and all that," she confessed. "I didn't know if I could trust you or not."

I shrugged and said, "No big deal," though to be honest I felt a little hurt. Why wouldn't she think she could trust me?

Then she gave me the real story of who she was. Her father was a doctor at St. Cabrini Hospital. They moved to Seattle from St. Louis when she was eight, and her Memaw did live with them and was a Jehovah's Witness, but Brenda had never gone door-to-door with her. Her Memaw wanted her to, but her father wouldn't allow it, not on Mercer Island at least, where doctors, lawyers, bankers, and Boeing engineers mostly lived, and which was 99.99 percent white. As for her mother, she was a housewife, and on Tuesdays and Thursdays she volunteered at the local library.

"And what about Jay?"

"Jay lived next door to us in the cul-de-sac. And Jay's not his real name." He was nineteen, she said, and was drafted a year ago after graduating from high school.

I brushed some powdered sugar off my jacket. "So he's a draft dodger?" I asked, thinking of my father, who had fought in the Korean War and scorned anyone who refused to do their duty and serve. When I started getting into trouble, the first thing he told me was, "Wait 'til you turn eighteen. Then we'll let the army straighten you out." I knew the draft was out there, I knew I would have to register for the Selective Service in just over a year, and I knew that I could be sent to Vietnam. But I did my best to put that prospect out of mind. I would deal with it when the time came, I told myself, and tried to remain oblivious—though by the end of 1970, with the war dragging on and my seventeenth birthday just around the corner, obliviousness was less and less an option.

"The Vietnam War is a crime against humanity," Brenda shot back at me for my insensitive question about Jay being a draft dodger. "Nixon and Kissinger should be sent to prison as war criminals for all the innocent people they kill every day. Haven't you been paying any attention?"

Her jaw tightened and she looked irate. I had to confess that, no, I hadn't been paying much attention, not to the war in Vietnam, not to Nixon and Kissinger, not to the mass protests. In all, I was oblivious to a lot more than just the war. I would hear about stuff that was happening—assassinations, race riots, Jimi Hendrix and Janis Joplin OD'ing—but none of it registered with me as anything more than passing headlines, something Walter Cronkite would lead the nightly news with, the kind of stuff adults clamored over but then forgot about when the next big crisis came along, which it seemed to do on a weekly basis. Plus, all this stuff seemed mostly to be happening elsewhere, far from our distant corner of the Northwest. So until I was sent to Fort Worden and began hearing other kids talking about some of these goings-on—especially the war, which loomed even larger for the older guys—I could never quite grasp what any of it had to do with me. Or perhaps, given my broken home and legal troubles, I just didn't want to have to deal with anything else.

"The war's terrible," I said in a feeble effort to regain Brenda's approval.

"Jay's parents pay his rent," she explained. "They don't want him to get killed in the jungle over there, and they don't want him to have to go up to Canada either." She seemed to calm down and leaned into me, resting her shoulder against mine. "He lets me stay with him whenever I want...and never once came on to me."

I had to wonder why she was here with me at this moment and not back on Mercer Island in her pretty house in the cul-de-sac, but not wanting her to stop leaning into me, I didn't ask. I let my left leg lean sidewise until our knees touched. This was the most physical contact I'd ever had with a girl, and I wanted it to last.

The morning was going very well, in fact, until two Seattle cops in tight-fitting powder-blue uniforms walked up to us and asked who we were and what we were doing and before we could even answer told us to stand up.

As soon as we got to our feet, though, Brenda took off running. Just like that, she bolted, surprising me as much as the two cops. As one of them went after her, the other cop grabbed my arm. I saw Brenda's rainbow-colored knit cap dashing between people in the crowded arcade and then she turned and cut between two produce stalls and out to the cobbled street, where I lost sight of her. The cop that chased her was no match for her fleet-footedness, and after several minutes he came back into the arcade breathing heavily. He picked up the half-eaten box of powdered doughnuts and the unopened box of cinnamon doughnuts.

"Where'd you get these?"

"I don't know," I said. "I just found them."

"Let's go," he said and took my other arm, and he and his partner led me out of the market and back up the block to Woolworth's, where the floor manager said I was the one he saw put the doughnuts in my jacket.

"There was something else he took too," the manager added, though he couldn't say what it was, so one of the cops patted me down while the other jotted something in his black notepad. He asked me my name and where I lived and I told him, happy to be thinking of Brenda getting away, her feet warm in the socks I'd shoplifted for her.

It didn't take the police long after they brought me down to the station to figure out I'd run away from the Treatment Center. They sent me to juvenile detention, adjacent to the city jail, where I was charged with shoplifting. They also questioned me about the girl I was with, but I told them I'd just met her that morning and I didn't even know her name. They failed to say whether they'd contacted my mother in Spanaway or my father in Tacoma, and I felt certain I was headed for Echo Glen or Green Hill. Yet, after one night in the Seattle juvie, I was loaded into a station wagon with two other teen delinquents and driven up to Port Townsend and back through the gates of Fort Worden.

IN SOME WAYS IT felt good to be back on the fort grounds and off the streets of Seattle, even though I missed Brenda and wondered what she was doing and if she was thinking about me. As I was processed back into the center, I still feared my double offense—running away and shoplifting—might get me sent to Echo Glen or Green Hill. Superintendent Lindquist informed me, though, that Prosper had come to him and revealed in strict confidence that I'd been the one who helped him out of the woods on Artillery Hill and brought him down to the infirmary.

"Prosper is very grateful to you for that," Lindquist said. "And so some of us here don't think you're as incorrigible as you make out to be." He told me I would have one day in isolation followed by another two-week period of disciplinary probation. So thanks to Prosper's commendation, my Seattle excursion had cost me next to nothing. I was even allowed to keep the fourteen dollars that I had in my pocket when the police nabbed me in the market, loose change from Brenda's panhandling at the ferry terminal and money I could now spend in the commissary on potato chips and soda.

I also kept the copy of *Dorian Gray* I borrowed from Jay's apartment and read it while in the hole. Dorian's desperation and debauchery made me think of the beer I had with Roger in the Place Pigalle Tavern, the hashish I smoked with Jay, and even the Pop-Tarts I took from the fraternity house and the doughnuts I stole from Woolworth's. What kind of depraved narcissist was I becoming? I wondered. What other vices would I indulge in if given half a chance? Was Brenda my Sibyl? Prosper my Basil? The novel was a great read, but by the time I came to its suspenseful end I'd been lying on my bed for four hours straight and suddenly had to pee almost as badly as I did that first time in the hole. So, as soon as I heard Officer Buehle coming down the stairs to check on me, I put the book down and called to him to let me have a bathroom break.

"You're awful quiet down here, Clausen," he said as he led me upstairs. "You been diddling yourself this whole while?" He had an idiotic smirk on his face.

I went into the bathroom without saying a word. After relieving myself, I washed my hands, leaned over the sink, and studied my face in the mirror. In three months I would turn seventeen, and, unlike Dorian, I could see the creep of advancing age on my face. Light-colored hairs sprouted unevenly along my jawline and chin—not quite whiskers, but not quite peach fuzz either. When I opened my eyes as wide as I could, my brow furrowed, and when I squinted, three lines spread out from the side of each eye. I raised my upper lip and examined my front teeth. I'd never noticed before but they seemed kind of yellow-ish—perhaps from the hashish I'd smoked—and I vowed to brush at least three times a day from then on. I studied my eyes, the reflective black of the pupil, the mottled blue of the irises, the not-so-perfectly white whites. I looked haggard and felt tired.

A knock on the bathroom door made me pull away from the mirror. "I'll be right there," I said with plenty of grievance in my voice, then turned on the faucet, splashed my face with cold water, and rubbed my skin raw with a paper towel.

Buehle was not standing there when I opened the door, so I walked up front to find him, while at the same time hoping I might run into Officer Dorn. I hadn't seen him in a couple of weeks, and I thought that if he came on duty he might let me sit outside on the porch with him again.

Buehle was at the front desk smoking a cigarette, and when he saw me he stamped it out and got up. "Back downstairs," he said and put his hand on my upper arm and made me do an about-face. As I walked back down to the basement, I asked when Officer Dorn was coming on duty.

"Dorn?" he said as if he was trying to place the name. "That guy's probably on patrol somewhere near Cambodia by now getting sniped at by Charlie."

"What do you mean?" I asked as I walked into my basement room.

"He was in the reserves and his unit got called up. Sent to 'Nam. A lieutenant, I think, infantry, so he'll be walking point. Which means about a three-month shelf life."

Goddamn Vietnam, I thought as Buehle closed the door, gave the handle a jiggle to make sure it was locked, and returned upstairs. For the first time, far more than when Brenda told me about Jay, I could see why people hated the war so much. *Maybe I won't wait to be drafted before fleeing to Canada*, I told myself, fuming at the injustice of someone like Officer Dorn being sent to fight and perhaps die, or maybe I'll enlist and make it my mission to find him over there, and when I do we'll both sit down someplace quiet and meditate, as he told me he tried to do every morning.

I crouched on the floor beneath the plexiglass window with my knees pulled up and my arms wrapped around my legs. I recalled all the families in Spanaway and thereabouts with sons and brothers who had enlisted or been drafted. Even though my parents knew some of those families, I didn't. Officer Dorn was the first person I knew to be sent to Vietnam. I replayed in my head the short exchange I'd had with Brenda about Jay and wondered why Officer Dorn didn't do like him and just hole up somewhere in Seattle. Why not just sit out the war working at the car wash, getting high, drinking cheap wine, and listening to albums? I thought of the times in my cottage how, when someone turned on the TV in the common room, we flipped right past the news, which was often about the war, to get straight to *The Twilight Zone* or *Star Trek* or *Hawaii Five-O*. Then there was our social studies teacher, a guy who told us on his first day that he was a Quaker and had Conscientious Objector status. He was serving his country, he said, by teaching at the Treatment Center. A couple times he tried to explain what the war was about: French colonialism and American imperialism, the Cold War and how the Soviets and Americans used third-world countries like Vietnam as their proxies, the myth of the domino effect, the megalomania of Nixon and Kissinger, the grassroots protests gaining momentum every day, Walter Cronkite finally turning against the war, and so on. But throughout all these explanations, I had, up to this point, preserved my obliviousness. Until now, none of what I ever heard about the war had the effect of making it real to me. While some of the guys at the Treatment Center bragged that they were going to join the marines and kill Charlie as soon as they turned eighteen, I never saw the point of such bluster. A few guys had older brothers who were in Vietnam, and one guy was at Fort Worden because he'd stabbed a Filipino man he thought was Vietnamese after his brother was killed in the war. I especially remembered the photograph our teacher who was the CO showed us of the Buddhist monk in Saigon immolating himself to protest the persecution of Buddhists as the war escalated. You could see him through the flames and black smoke sitting cross-legged and erect in the middle of street, the white gas canister carefully set down beside him. I tried to recall the Buddhist saying Officer Dorn shared with me the time I sat with him on the porch of the guard house. Yet, because I was so upset thinking about everything else I knew about the war but had ignored until now, I couldn't remember what it was.

I finished *Dorian Gray* and spent the rest of the night wondering what I would do if I was drafted, and finally I figured it out. I wouldn't go to Vietnam. I figured Officer Dorn wouldn't want me to. Instead, I would find Brenda, and the two of us would go deep into the Olympic Mountains to escape the world's mayhem. We'd live off the land like

Jeremiah Johnson in the Vardis Fisher novel I'd read—in harmony with nature and one another. We'd practice Buddhism and never return to civilization. And when Officer Dorn returned from the war—*if* he returned—we would welcome him to stay with us. It was a good plan, and I committed myself to seeing it fulfilled.

THE NEXT DAY I was back in class, further behind than ever. Larrison, the math teacher, didn't say a word to me, though all the other teachers told me they were glad to see me back. At recess, all the guys wanted to know where I'd gone and what I'd done. Some said they'd heard I'd made it all the way to San Francisco and was picked up in Haight-Ashbury tripping on peyote.

"Is that true?" Del Emmons wanted to know.

"No, I was in Seattle," I said. And I don't know why, but I didn't say anything more about my ramble. I didn't tell them about Brenda or Jay, or Roger or the fraternity guy or the farmer from Chimacum, who I thought if I ever got the chance I might visit again. I pretended instead like I'd spent my three days in Seattle poking around by myself, hungry and bored. I did mention how I stole the two boxes of doughnuts from Woolworth's and that's how I got nabbed by the cops in the farmer's market, but that's all.

Another two days passed before I finally spoke to Prosper. It was Saturday, and the cottage parents had organized a beach cleanup for the guys and a grounds clean-up for the girls. Each cottage was assigned different portions of the beach stretching from Point Wilson to Cape George. It was a bright, windy day, the air crisp and clear except for a thin strip of haze hovering over Admiralty Inlet. Other than the occasional car tire or tangle of fish net or chunk of Styrofoam, there wasn't much trash to pick up, so mostly we skipped stones, whipped one another with strands of bull kelp, and looked for hermit crabs and other tidal creatures under big rocks we'd overturn. The cottage parents overseeing us tried to keep us corralled into a group, but this was almost impossible with the older kids hanging back, knowing the more they lagged behind the longer they'd get to stay on the beach. At one point I smelled marijuana and saw Bobby Felton and two other guys crouching near a large piece of driftwood passing a joint around.

That's when I saw Prosper a few yards ahead of me, walking along the edge of the gently lapping water, stooping down now and then to examine something, and decided to catch up with him.

"You find anything good?" I called to him before he even noticed me approaching.

"Just rocks," he said, "but they look so amazing when they're wet. It's like the water brings out all the colors in them."

I scooped up a handful of the wet pebbles, and he was right. They were green, purple, red, and orange. Even the duller ones, brown, gray, and black, seemed luminescent when wet. Some were striped, others speckled. Some were shiny, some translucent, and some a soft matte.

"Mr. Higman told me if you soak them in fresh water the salt will leach out and leave them brighter when they dry."

"That's really cool," I said and took another look at the pebbles in my hand before tossing them into the water.

"I'd love to find an agate," Prosper said. "They're supposed to be all over the place around here." When I asked what an agate was, he said they were a kind of quartz formed by volcanoes. "They're practically gems."

Prosper, I'd come to realize, was full of all kinds of facts like this. He'd won the geography bee in social studies class hands down. He knew that Ouagadougou was the capital of the Republic of Upper Volta in Africa.

I poked along down the beach with Prosper for a while longer, asking him now and then if he thought this rock or that was an agate, and he usually said he didn't think so but that it was pretty all the same and I should keep it. So before long both of my pants pockets were filled with multicolored pebbles.

Behind us, Bobby and the other two guys who'd been toking up had their shoes off and were wading in the water. Up ahead, Mr. Higman saw what was going on and shouted to them to get out of the water and put their shoes back on.

"I think they're high," I said to Prosper.

He stopped walking and looked back at them. "Really?" he said in a combination of disbelief and amazement. "How do you know?"

"They were toking on a joint back there." I don't know if this information disappointed him or what, but he just turned around and went back to looking for agates. I changed the subject.

"Thanks for telling Lindquist about that night," I said kind of dopily. He glanced over at me as if he wasn't sure whether I was being sarcastic or not. So I added, "I mean it. If you hadn't told them I would probably be at Green Hill right now."

Then there was some silence between us for a few minutes. There was more I wanted to say to him, and finally I managed to.

"I'm sorry about what happened that night," I said. "I mean, really sorry." I suppose I could have been more forthcoming, more detailed, about my role in the hazing, but I let myself off the hook by figuring he probably knew already.

"Assholes," he said and looked back at Bobby Felton and the other two guys scornfully. I could tell he didn't include me in this condemnation.

"Anyway," I said again, "thanks."

From then on I gave more credence to my friendship with Prosper. He continued to help me with my homework, especially in math, and convinced me I could pass the GED exam if I wanted to. He still kept to himself most of the time, but in the weeks leading up to Thanksgiving, he and I teamed up in woodshop to build a trebuchet big enough to hurl apples. Another group of guys caught on to the idea and built one as well, and then the battle was met. With Mr. Binford, the woodshop teacher, overseeing the contest, we each gathered a dozen apples from the neglected orchard in a corner of the Fort Worden grounds and carried our trebuchets out to the parade grounds to see who could fling their apples the farthest. Because the other guys called their trebuchet "Warwolf," Prosper and I had to come up with a name for ours as well, and after much debate we settled on "The Agate Blaster." But when the guys on the other team called it a faggot name, I almost got into a fight with one of them before Mr. Binford broke it up.

"This dispute, gentlemen, will be settled on the field of battle," he declared.

As it turned out, the other team knew almost nothing about tension and torque and the physics of counterweights, and so our apples outdistanced theirs nearly every shot, and by a considerable margin. This meant Prosper and I were triumphant in the contest of medieval weaponry.

"Design and trajectory beat brute force every time," I remember Prosper saying proudly.

We reveled in our triumph all the way to Thanksgiving, at which time the mood at the Treatment Center began to turn more subdued. While many kids were given leave to go home, just as many of us were denied it or else had no real home to go to and were stuck at Fort Worden for the long holiday weekend. My mother had written me two weeks earlier to tell me she didn't think it a good idea for me to come all the way down to Spanaway just for Thanksgiving but hoped things might work out for me to come home at Christmastime. I didn't hear from my father.

On Thanksgiving Day, some of us played touch football on the parade grounds in the morning, and at one o'clock that afternoon the staff served everyone turkey and stuffing, mashed potatoes and gravy, green bean casserole, cranberry sauce, and apple pie with vanilla ice cream in the cafeteria. On Friday and Saturday I hung out with Bobby Felton and a few other guys, sneaking up into the woods on Artillery Hill and sampling the difference between Thai Stick and sensimilla.

Prosper went home to Olympia on a four-day pass, but the visit with his parents didn't go so well, and when he came back Sunday afternoon (driven by his father) he was moodier than ever. He was even more withdrawn than when he first arrived at the Treatment Center, and by the middle of the week after Thanksgiving, we'd hardly exchanged three words. So during recess one day I asked him if he wanted to haul The Agate Blaster out after class and do target practice on the cars in the parking lot. He said he wasn't into it anymore, so I just shrugged.

As we had this conversation, Prosper and I stood outside the class-room building, along the side wall. A drizzle was falling from a dark sky and I was getting cold. When I looked at him, he was standing like one of those stiff Greek statues we learned about in Western civ. class—the kouroi—his head and back erect but tilted slightly forward, arms clamped to the sides, both legs straight, looking like he was standing at attention. His teeth were chattering and his lips were blue.

"It's freezing out here," I said. The wind came up and lashed a spray of rain across my face. I turned away from it and made to leave. "You coming?"

"I'm not going home for Christmas," he said, stopping me from going any farther. I figured this decision was based on how bad his visit over Thanksgiving had gone.

"Well, I probably won't be either," I told him. This was the truth too. My mother's tepid encouragement about my coming home for Christmas got me asking myself why I should even bother, and I was already thinking I might take a holiday ramble down to San Fran. For a fleeting moment I thought, *Maybe Prosper and I could be road buddies*, but then let the idea drop just as fast as it came. He wasn't the road buddy type. He seemed too effete—a word I'd just learned—and complained about too many things besides.

"Do you think they would let me change my name?" he asked, totally out of left field.

I pulled my collar up and came and stood beside him again. "You mean will your old man and old lady?" I asked, figuring he was sick of the name "Prosper." And who wouldn't be? It was one of those wishful-thinking kind of names people sometimes give their kids, as if naming your kid after some trait or thing like "Joy" or "Summer" will automatically give the kid those qualities. But then I remembered him telling me once it had been his grandfather's name, so that hippie-dippy sort of thinking wasn't the source of it at all. It was an old family name, probably from way back in Puritan times when people trotted about in their buckle shoes with names like "Prior" and "Cotton" and "Kindred." In either case, I could understand him wanting to change it.

"No," he said. "Here. Lindquist. If I asked Lindquist, do you think he would let me change my name?"

"I don't know," I answered, now thinking that he meant to change his last name, to disassociate himself from his parents. The same notion had crossed my own mind a few times. Instead of Avery Clausen, I would be Avery Averson (for the alluring alliteration) or Avery Whitman (for the great poet of unscrewing doors from their jambs who I'd discovered that fall) or Avery Lord (for the sheer audacity of it). "What would you change it to?" I asked him.

"I'm not sure," he said. "I know a guy in British Columbia whose name is Laurie. It's short for Laurence. And another guy I read about once was named Robin."

"Those are kinda girl names."

"They can go both ways," he said and looked at me hesitantly. "At least some places."

"I always dug the name Reed," I said. It was the name of my mother's brother, my Uncle Reed, who was probably the only adult I'd ever gotten along with. He moved to San Francisco when I was eleven, and I liked to imagine he would take me in if I made my way down there and happened to show up at his door. He was a carpenter, but he also played a Hardanger fiddle that he'd inherited from his grandfather, my great-grandfather, who'd come to America from Norway when he was just a teenager.

"Never mind," Prosper said and headed inside.

I didn't give the name change business any more thought, not realizing that there was more to it than just having a stupid name. *Just be yourself,* I wanted to tell him as I followed him back into the classroom building. *Be Prosper and live long.*

We both passed the Christmas holiday at Fort Worden. I read *East of Eden*, and even though it made me want to run away to California more than ever, I stayed put. For the first week of the holiday break, the Treatment Center was almost like summer camp. We didn't have to go to class and were free to play as much ping-pong and pool as we wanted to. Then we were totally beside ourselves when the staff brought in a brand-new foosball table. The day-long tournaments that followed were fierce. Half the kids were gone on holiday leave, and the staff were relaxed and willing to bend the rules a little for those of us left behind. They even let us bring snacks up to the dormitory floor.

Then, in the week between Christmas and New Year's Day, two big things happened. First, a winter storm moved over the Olympic Peninsula and dropped almost a foot of snow on us. Everyone went wild. The staff lined us up and distributed parkas—the kind with the battleship-gray shell, orange nylon liner, and hood trimmed with rabbit fur—and rubber boots, blue skull caps, and wool gloves. Out on the parade grounds, guys built snow forts and had epic snowball fights, while the girls made snowmen and snow angels. Superintendent Lindquist gave the maintenance crew permission to use their trucks to pull a couple of long toboggans around the unplowed road that encircled the parade grounds, with up to six kids crammed onto a toboggan at a time. The cafeteria staff set up a table and brought out trays of cookies and urns filled with hot chocolate, and all day we kept saying how the kids who went home for Christmas were missing the best day ever at Fort Worden.

The other big thing that happened was that Brenda arrived.

AT FIRST I WASN'T sure it was her because in Seattle I'd rarely seen her without her colorful knit cap and baggy army fatigue jacket. Plus I was all the way across the parade grounds when I saw her walking with one of the lady cottage parents from the administration building toward one of the girls' dormitories. I wanted to shout out to her and run across the snowy field and say hello, but I didn't want either of us to get in trouble. I knew I could find out in the cafeteria through the grapevine what was going on, and so the whole rest of the afternoon I was anxious for the dinner bell to sound. I wanted to find a way to speak to her. I wanted to know if she was all right, and why she was here. Did she remember that Fort Worden was where I'd escaped from when we met in Seattle? Did she get herself sent here, just possibly, to seek me out?

The cafeteria later that evening at dinner was noisier than usual because of the excitement over the snow. But with many kids having gone home for the holiday, it wasn't nearly as crowded, so I was able to spot Brenda right away.

"Brenda," I called in a hushed voice across several rows of metal tables. I had just gotten my tray of food and was walking toward the table where I always sat with Prosper and a few other guys from our cottage. There was too much noise, though, and she didn't hear me. So I put my tray down and walked back to get a glass of water, this time making a detour right past her table. "Brenda," I said.

When she looked up, she smiled in recognition but then shooed me away since guys were not allowed on the girls' side of the cafeteria.

"I'll meet you outside when you're done," I said.

"They told me I had to go straight back to my cottage," she answered, no doubt still scared after having run the gauntlet of official assessment, admission, and orientation. She wore the mandatory khaki skirt and light blue blouse, both freshly pressed.

I just signaled toward the door and kept walking. Back at my table, I watched to see if she was getting up to leave. One of the girls sitting at her table was talking to her, her head leaning in toward Brenda's, but Brenda just sat straight and didn't reply.

The fact was, the Treatment Center staff didn't do a great job of keeping the guys and girls segregated. Their main strategy was to restrict the movement of the girls far more than the guys, especially since there were far fewer female residents. All the same, guys were always sneaking over to the girls' cottages or meeting them in some hidden corner of the grounds. Occasionally we'd hear of a guy—Bobby Felton, for one—getting it on with one of the girls. Meanwhile, among the guys, there was no end to the rumors about what went on in the girls' cottages. We were always saying how the girls got special favors because they flirted with the staff members and teachers—male and female alike. When the recreational coordinator, a guy in his thirties, left the Treatment Center in the middle of December, everyone said he was fired for having sex with one of the girls in the field house. One thing, however, was certain: if anyone thought the guys were rough and foul-mouthed, you only had to stroll past one of the girls' cottages and hear what they yelled at you from the upper windows to realize these girls were no shy, delicate creatures. They were tough, and they could be as crude and rude and outright vicious as any guy. So I felt bad for Brenda. She was a spunky kid, but now she was in with girls who had actually grown up in places like Yesler Terrace public housing, and so she had good reason to be on edge. On top of that, she was one of only a handful of black kids at the Treatment Center—though if she grew up on Mercer Island, she was used to those kind of numbers.

I wolfed down my food and got up to leave, hoping she would take my lead. As I bussed my tray, I saw that Brenda was just sitting there with her hands in her lap and her head down. When the girl sitting beside her nudged her in the side and nodded in my direction, Brenda obediently got up and carried her tray to the conveyor belt as I went outside to wait for her.

I stood at the front corner of the cafeteria building. Aside from the noise emanating from inside the cafeteria, everything outside seemed remarkably still and quiet. A half-moon above the inlet illuminated the snow into an iridescent blue. There was a street lamp nearby, lighting the front of the building, so I stepped over to the opposite corner of the building where it was dark.

Brenda came out the front door and looked around.

"Hey," I whispered, and she scurried over to me and stood real close. She had a parka on, the hood with the rabbit fur trim pulled up over her head. Suddenly I didn't know what to say.

"What cottage are you in?" I asked.

"Danielson." Then she started walking in that direction, and I walked beside her.

"I can't believe I got sent back for stealing doughnuts," I said, and she laughed at this.

"And socks," she reminded me.

"The way you ran...that was something. That cop was never going to catch you."

She could probably tell I was curious to know why she'd gotten sent to Fort Worden, so she just came out and told me how she'd broken into a gas station. She'd actually broken into three different gas stations before getting caught. "For cigarettes," she said, "and maybe some candy." She explained how she would take the cartons of cigarettes she stole to the ferry terminal and Greyhound station and sell them by the pack for half price. But she finally got caught at a gas station on Mercer Island, one of only two on the island. The guy with Down's syndrome who pumped gas for the owner slept in the back room, which Brenda didn't know, so when she broke the side window and climbed inside, he woke up. Plus he knew who she was since her father and mother had been getting gas there for years. "I'm telling," he said to her as the two of them stood by the counter inside the gas station in the middle of the night. But Brenda convinced him not to tell, saying how much trouble she would get into. "And you don't want that, do you, Cyrus?" Yet the next morning when the gas station owner came in, he asked what happened to the window, and Cyrus told him, and the owner turned Brenda in to the police. They picked her up that morning trying to hitch a ride back into Seattle, and within the week—after her fingerprints were taken—she was tied to the other two gas station break-ins as well.

"Poor Cyrus," she said. "He really is a sweet guy."

We reached Danielson, and standing there with her almost felt like the end of a date. I wanted to kiss her, and maybe I would have, but I could see other kids coming out of the cafeteria and already walking toward us.

"Do you need to borrow my diaphragm?" one of the girls shouted ahead to Brenda.

"Anyway," she said, trying to ignore the remark yet squinting in agitation at it, as if realizing this kind of intrusion into her personal life was going to be routine from now on. As for myself, I had no idea what a diaphragm was. "I'll see you around."

A couple of girls from Brenda's cottage came up to us and put their arms through hers. "Leave our new girl alone," one of them said to me and pushed me away.

"See ya," I called to Brenda as the girls led her up the stairs and into their cottage.

For the next several weeks I took every opportunity to place myself as near to Brenda as possible and spend a few minutes with her whenever I could. Staff members repeatedly blew their whistles at me during recess and meals when I would drift over to the girls' end of the parade grounds or their side of the cafeteria. Guys started making fun of me for getting jungle fever and having a taste for brown sugar. Then one guy, Trey Withers, a real mean-spirited sort I'd always kept my distance from, went too far and called me something so offensive—to me, but most of all to Brenda—that I wasn't sure at first what it actually meant. I just knew it was bad.

"Go fuck yourself," I shouted back at him and walked away, though I seethed over the slur all afternoon. *What if Brenda had heard it*, I kept thinking.

So later that evening when I spotted him walking to his cottage, I ran up and sucker punched him in the back of the head. He crumpled to the ground and when he rolled onto his back I leaned over him like Cassius Clay over the fallen Sonny Liston, taunting him with my clenched fist.

"You say one more word about her and I'll kill you," I said.

The asshole reported me all the same, and I got a day in the hole, leading Officer Buehle to comment on how I was becoming one of his regulars. This time I read Hermann Hesse's *Demian* and wondered, Was I Emil Sinclair, the confused youth trying to free himself from his own sheltered existence? Or was I his alluring friend, the dark and mysterious Max Demian, willing to defy authority to attain a greater, more profound insight into the world? *Which would Brenda be more attracted to?* That was the real question. In a secret code using a combination of initials, abbreviations, hieroglyphics, and obscure allusions to my reading—which is to say, utterly meaningless to anyone but myself—I scratched onto the stone and mortar walls of the guard house basement my declaration of love and devotion to Brenda.

And maybe there was something to my declaration, some silent signal that was transmitted to Brenda, because at some point in the middle of the night after I'd finished reading *Demian* and turned off the light and was staring into the dark, a knock came on the plexiglass window. I got up and tried to peer out to see who it was, but the plexiglass was nearly opaque with age and other kids' scratchings.

"Avery," said Brenda.

"What're you doing?" I said. I could now make out the faint outline of her head through the plexiglass. There was a scraping sound, and then I could see that she was jimmying the window with a crowbar. She pried the flat end of the crowbar between the plexiglass and the rotted wood frame that held it in place, and when she leaned back and kicked the other end of the crowbar, the plexiglass popped right out. Then she stuck her head through the opening.

"Holy shit," I said, which made her laugh. It was like some kind of Bonnie and Clyde jail break. I was shocked by how brazen it was for her, still a relative newbie at Fort Worden, to do what she was doing. Brenda's move could get us both sent to Green Hill, but I didn't care. I was smitten. In the Warren Beatty–Faye Dunaway movie, Buck Barrow, referring to Bonnie, asks his brother Clyde, "Is she as good as she looks?" And Clyde answers, "Better."

Brenda was smiling down at me with her smooth cheeks, bright eyes, and wide grin. "Should I come in or do you want to come out?"

My answer was to snatch up my jacket and slide the chair over to the window.

"Get the blanket," she said. This was more like the mischievous Brenda I knew from Seattle than the shrinking, bashful girl she seemed to have become since arriving at Fort Worden two months earlier.

I pulled the scratchy army-surplus blanket off the bed and handed it up to her. Then I climbed onto the chair and hoisted myself up through the window frame, sprawling onto the wet ground next to her. The big rhododendron in front of the ground-level window concealed us perfectly, and I would have been content to stay right there, huddled behind it, but Brenda wanted us to move on. I wondered if she had a full ramble in mind, the two of us escaping together and going off to the mountains as I'd imagined or maybe—my Plan B—making our way down to San Francisco.

"Let's go up the hill," she said. "I brought a bunch of food." She raised a brown grocery bag rolled up at the top. "You carry the blanket and I'll carry this."

We peered out from the thick leaves and crooked branches of the rhododendron to make sure the coast was clear and then ran as fast as we could toward the base of the hill and kept running straight up the road that led to all the battery installations. There was that soggy late-winter cold in the air, and when we finally stopped running and looked about, white clouds billowed from our mouths and nostrils like horses' breath. I knew we had to get off the road because the security guards, when they had nothing else to do, would sometimes drive their jeep up Artillery Hill. Once when one of the guys found a discarded *Hustler* magazine and a slew of empty Oly cans near one of the batteries, we figured a guard must have been having a private party up there. The frayed copy of *Hustler*, of course, made the rounds of the guys' cottages for about a month until a house parent found it lying on the floor in one of the bathrooms.

"Let's go this way," I said to Brenda and cut into the woods to our right. A lot of guys liked to go into the abandoned batteries to hide out. They were placed across the hillside, and some of the batteries tunneled a long ways into the earthen berms in which they were dug. There were also all kinds of smaller rooms, above ground and below, where ordnances were once kept. But now, and especially if you didn't have a flashlight or candles, the damp, graffiti-marked concrete enclosures could be pretty scary. So I guided us past a couple of the batteries, across the grassy swards that lay in front of them, and onto a short, narrow path that led through a thicket of rose hip and snowberry bushes and came out finally onto a high, exposed bluff overlooking the Strait of Juan de Fuca.

"Wow," was all Brenda could say.

The moonless sky had that winter sharpness that made the stars appear especially bright and gave the black water below a distinctive shimmer. A yellowish emanation was visible on a portion of the horizon, and I said it was probably Victoria, BC.

"Prosper wants to go live there so he can change his name to Laurie," I said, and regretted the crack as soon as I said it. Brenda, though, was too awed by the view to bother responding.

"Let's sit down," she said and moved forward and then stumbled, and when she reached back and grabbed my arm, I told her to be careful. We were only a few feet from the edge of the bluff.

"Here," I said and stomped down a patch of dune grass to make a soft place for us to sit.

We sat side by side with the blanket over our shoulders, leaning against one another like we had at the market in Seattle. Brenda unfolded the paper bag she brought with her and we ate Hostess CupCakes and Lay's Potato Chips. We talked some. I asked how she was making out in the girls cottage and whatnot, and she said okay. And then I asked if she knew how long she was assigned to Fort Worden for, whether her assessment committee had told her anything, and she said they hadn't. Her parents, she said, were working to get her released as soon as possible. I didn't know how to respond to this. I felt bad that she had to be at Fort Worden at all. I felt her loss of freedom more than I did my own. But I also didn't want her to leave. Or, rather, I wanted us to leave together—and stay together.

Brenda again must have been picking up on my thinking because when a cargo ship passed through the strait heading out to the Pacific, she said how we should run away from Fort Worden, go to Harbor Island in Seattle where all the cargo ships docked, and become stowaways.

"Do you want to?" she asked.

"Sure," I said and meant it. I would do anything she wanted me to.

We sat there for a long time, and when a trace of blue appeared in the eastern sky over the Cascades, we decided we should probably go back. After midnight, the guards never checked the basement rooms hourly as they did during the rest of the day, but I knew one would be down not long after dawn. As Brenda and I stood up, stretched, and brushed the grass off of one another, we vowed to keep our rendezvous a secret. I wanted to kiss her, wanted to so badly, but I didn't know how to and finally settled on holding hands with her as we walked back down the hill.

Sunlight was just hitting the top of the tallest fir trees when I crawled back into the hole. Brenda then said "See ya," restored the plexiglass to its frame, and returned to her cottage.

THE NORMAL PERIOD OF residency at the Fort Worden Diagnostic and Treatment Center was between two and twelve months. I'd arrived June 15, 1970, so that meant that March 15, 1971—the Ides of March, which I first heard of reading Shakespeare's *Julius Caesar* in English class at Fort Worden—marked nine months that I'd been there. When

I had my monthly meeting with the Assessment Committee on that very day in March and Dr. Reinholdt asked me if I felt ready to go home—that is, get along with my parents, return to my regular high school, and generally be a cooperative member of my community—I answered flat-out, "No." I told him that if I got sent back to Spanaway I would just run away again and get into even worse trouble.

I knew there was no reason for me to return to living with my mother in our old house in Spanaway. From what I could gather from the intermittent communications I'd had with her and my father, my mother had basically become a shut-in ever since my father remarried and moved with his new wife, who was expecting, to Longview, Washington. I didn't think my mother or father would be very happy if I showed up at the doorstep of either one.

The directness of my answer obviously flustered Dr. Reinholdt, who slap-closed the folder in front him (my case file), dropped his pencil, and said, "Well then, Avery, what do you propose we do with you?"

I didn't have a ready answer. I just knew I didn't want to leave the Treatment Center and face never seeing Brenda again. All I wanted to do anymore was be with her, and even though this wasn't so easy given the Treatment Center's rules and restrictions, we found our ways around them. Just the week before, on perhaps our most daring rendezvous, we snuck into Alexander's Castle—the oldest building at Fort Worden, a small sandstone house complete with a crenulated tower that stood apart from the main grounds—and were there for an hour making out before a security guard caught us.

"I don't know," I replied. I knew well enough what the official options available to the committee were. We all did: Green Hill, Echo Glen, Forestry Camp, foster care, or the Treatment Center. And even though I knew I wanted to stay at the Treatment Center, I didn't just come out and say so. I didn't want to tip my hand as to why I wanted to stay.

Dr. Reinholdt reopened the manila folder in front of him, scanned a few pages, and said, "Tell me about Brenda Johnson."

I didn't have a response to this either. What did he know about us? Obviously there was something in my file. Which only made sense given that every resident at the Treatment Center knew about me and Brenda. All I could figure as I sat there was that he had better not say anything bad about her. If he did—Green Hill be damned—I would fly across that table so fast and smash his fat face with my fists so hard he wouldn't know what happened until he came to in the infirmary.

"Are you and she friends?"

"Yeah, kind of," I said. I wanted to say we were more than just friends, we were in love, were soulmates, were bound together in the celestial heavens to live our lives in bliss as one upon this cruel and forsaken planet...but I knew better than to open my mouth.

"As you know," he went on, "the Center has policies about male and female residents commingling. Furthermore, it's not because you and she are different races that I say this—let me be clear on that point. Rather, it's that the Assessment Committee does not believe you and Miss Johnson are a positive influence on one another. You have half a dozen curfew and grounds violations between the two of you...and so we're perplexed as to what to do about this situation."

What situation was he talking about? Not a positive influence? How did he or anyone else know what the kind of influence Brenda and I had on one another? We were the best possible influence. Everything about her and about our being together made me better—happier, calmer, and even smarter. In her company, I was less aggressive, less unsociable, and less impulsive. She helped me achieve a far more adequate personality than I'd ever had in my entire life. So I didn't want to sit there and listen to what the Assessment Committee thought our influence on one another was. They didn't have a clue. It was just like Brenda said, paraphrasing Angela Davis: political and spiritual enlightenment were the establishment's worst enemy, and whenever the thinking of any person or group became too free, the Man imposed himself on that individual or group to stomp out that freedom. I sat in my chair glowering across the table at the committee members and not saying a word, knowing that anything I said to protest their opinion of Brenda and me would be misconstrued and ultimately used against us.

"I can see the subject's upsetting to you, Avery," said Mr. Higman. "You have to believe that we wouldn't bring it up unless we thought it was absolutely necessary."

"What's necessary?" I said back at him. "Is this necessary? Any of this?" I waved my arm to indicate the five of us seated at the table—me, Reinholdt, Higman, Lindquist, and Mrs. Adel. During my exchange with Reinholdt, the others had remained quiet.

"We believe so," replied Superintendent Lindquist in his ever-so-calm manner. "We're not running a summer camp here," he reminded me, a line he used routinely on residents.

"Or Woodstock," said Mr. Higman. The *Woodstock* movie had been playing at the Motor Movie Drive-In for the past two weeks, and so a lot of people—including our social studies teacher, the Quaker CO—were talking about it. Brenda and I were already hatching a plan to sneak off the grounds some night to see it.

My composure was disintegrating, and I was on the brink of lashing out the way I had at Larrison over algebra that time. Just thinking about Brenda, however, had a stabilizing effect on me, and keeping her in mind I maintained my cool and waited them out.

Dr. Reinholdt leaned forward across the table toward me. "What it entails is this," he said. "I have made the recommendation to the committee that you and Miss Johnson should be kept strictly apart from one another for the duration of your time at the Treatment Center, and the committee has agreed. We are speaking to Miss Johnson tomorrow and will make this determination clear to her as well."

"The incident in the castle counts as one strike against both of you," Superintendent Lindquist added. "One more strike and we'll have to exercise whatever options are available to us to ensure you're kept apart. In other words, there will be no strike three. Two strikes and you're out. Do I make myself clear, Avery?"

"But we haven't done anything," I said, feeling as if the committee was engaging in an arbitrary exercise of power and intimidation. Brenda was probably right when she'd said it bothered many people more than they would ever admit to see a black girl and a white guy together. She mentioned the Loving case about miscegenation as proof—and when I said I didn't know what that was, she explained it to me.

"And that's how it will remain," said Superintendent Lindquist, asserting his supervisory authority in a way I'd never seen him do before.

He looked at me sternly as Dr. Reinholdt closed the folder for a final time and Mr. Higman stood from his chair to escort me from the room.

"We know you and Brenda are both good kids," Mrs. Adel put in.

And with that I went back to my cottage and imagined all the ways Brenda and I could escape—this time for good. Between the two of us, we were clever enough and daring enough to pull it off. And once we did escape, maybe we would get married, just to show them, and have a bunch of dark-skinned, blue-eyed babies. Richard and Mildred Loving would be their godparents.

My mind was racing when Bobby Felton strolled into the dorm. When he came up to my bunk and asked if I wanted to walk down to the beach and get high, I sprang to my feet and said, "You know it."

AFTER THE ASSESSMENT COMMITTEE prohibited Brenda and me from even being in proximity to one another, we began passing notes through the help of other kids in our cottages. Prosper proved especially useful in this regard since everyone viewed him as such a goody-two-shoes. Brenda let me know through one of these notes that when she met with the committee she threw a fit and yelled at them, calling them ignorant bigots and fascist camp commandants. I loved her for that and wrote back that I'd do something soon to get sent to the hole so she could break me out again. Every resident at the Treatment Center now knew about the window that could be jimmied from its frame, and yet security still hadn't caught on.

As spring arrived, the rhododendrons and dogwoods on Artillery Hill began to bloom and the grass on the parade grounds turned a vibrant green. For every three or four days of rain there would be a day of unstinting loveliness, and it became impossible to sit still while inside on such days. It was on just such a beautiful spring day that the Black Panthers showed up at Fort Worden. It was after the last school period, around 3:30 p.m. A handful of us were tossing a Frisbee in the small field next to the chapel when we saw the dark Lincoln Continental enter the main gate. My first thought was that it was some kind of state official, maybe Governor Evans himself, coming to meet with Superintendent Lindquist. But as the vehicle turned onto the road that circled the parade grounds, I could see there were three black men in the car, two in front and one in back, all wearing black clothes and looking straight ahead with a severe military bearing.

Someone said, "They're Black Panthers," and with that we dropped the Frisbee and ran across the road to watch where the car was headed. As it approached the administration building, I kept waiting for the white security jeep to come racing up to meet it. Other kids caught on that something was up and began to gravitate toward the administration building. When the car came to a stop, we all stopped too and waited for the guys inside to get out. But they stayed in the car, hardly moving. The driver lit a cigarette, and the guy in the passenger seat turned around and spoke to the guy in the back. Otherwise they just sat there, as if they were either waiting to pick someone up or about to rob a bank.

"Maybe they're going to shoot the place up," someone said. "Remember what Cedric said?"

Cedric Rudolph was one of the twenty or so black kids at the Treatment Center. A couple weeks ago he got into a scuffle on the basketball court with a white kid, Brian Klimmick, over who was the better guard, Walt "Clyde" Frazier of the Knicks or Jerry "Mr. Clutch" West of the Lakers. Cedric said Frazier and Brian said West, and the argument turned into a fight after Brian fouled Cedric so hard he knocked him to the pavement. When they were finally separated, Cedric was shouting threats at Brian, saying he was going to call his Black Panther friends in Tacoma to come show Brian's lily-white ass what Black Power was all about. So now, to our astonishment, it seemed that Cedric had made good on his threat, and we all glanced around to see if Brian was anywhere in sight.

Then, simultaneously, both front doors and a back door of the Lincoln Continental opened, and I half-expected the three men to step out fully armed, just like in the photographs of Black Panther rallies in Oakland, California, that I'd seen in *Time* magazine in the Treatment Center library. But if the men were armed, their weapons weren't visible. The man who'd been in the front passenger seat appeared to be older than the other two. He was also the one who looked most like an authentic Black Panther, wearing a shiny black leather jacket, the requisite black beret, and dark shades. The backseat passenger, who seemed not much older than any of us, was a skinny guy in a black turtleneck and black jeans, also wearing dark shades. The driver, meanwhile, wore a black T-shirt and black jeans and had neither a beret nor shades, but did sport a big Afro with a pick stuck into the back of it.

As the three men approached the steps to the administration building, Officer Buehle came out the front door to meet them. I figured the security jeep was parked in the back and he'd been inside watching the men in their vehicle the whole time. Buehle rested both hands on his tactical belt. In fact, as the other kids and I sidled closer, I could see that the flap over the sidearm in his holster was undone, and I'm sure we all thought there was about to be a shoot-out. It was just unfortunate that it had to be Buehle on duty when the Black Panthers showed up, instead of Chief Lockwood, for instance, or Officer Barris, the first woman to be hired by security shortly after Dorn left. The whole vibe of the encounter would have been different.

Fortunately, before Buehle could open his mouth, Superintendent Lindquist stepped out onto the landing and told him he'd take it from there, and then turned to the three men, each standing on a different level of the steps leading up to the entrance, and said, "I'm Alfred Lindquist, the superintendent of the Fort Worden Treatment Center. How may I help you gentlemen?"

The man near the top of the steps was the older-looking man. Right behind him and to his right stood the driver, and behind him, three steps down, the skinny, younger-looking backseat passenger. The man near the top of the steps indicated the skinny guy and said, "We've come to see his sister."

"And what's this man's sister's name?" asked Superintendent Lindquist.

"Brenda Johnson," the driver answered and stepped up level with the other man.

I heard the name spoken, but it was just a name, not a person, and I didn't immediately think of Brenda—my Brenda, the Brenda who resided only with me, in my world, the two of us together, alone, without parents or siblings or any relations or associations whatsoever beyond the few friends/allies/cohorts we had at Fort Worden. Neither of us liked to talk about our other lives, the lives we had before being sent to the Treatment Center. In my mind, we were two beings in a synchronous orbit, without moons or rings or man-made satellites (other than, recently, the members of the Assessment Committee) to clutter our closed binary system.

"Did you hear that?" Pete Munson said, nudging me. "That guy's Brenda's brother."

"Shut up," I said back. It was the only way I knew to get control of the situation presenting itself to me. Plus I wanted to hear what was being said.

"I see," said Superintendent Lindquist.

"We want to take her out for a hamburger in town," Brenda's brother, the guy in the black turtleneck and black jeans, said. "We'll bring her back before dark. I haven't seen her in almost a year. I was still in the VA hospital when she was sent here." He looked around, as if expecting Brenda to appear, ready to go. I looked around, too, thinking the same.

"Well, Mr. Johnson," Superintendent Lindquist began, his calm demeanor prevailing once again, "I'm sorry you had to come all this way. I know what a long drive it is. Yet I'm afraid we're unable to release a resident into the temporary custody of anyone other than a parent or legal guardian."

Neither Brenda's brother nor the other two men on the steps said anything in response to this clear denial of their wish to take Brenda out for a hamburger. Instead, a rather tense quiet came over everyone. Superintendent Lindquist waited, with Officer Buehle standing behind him, not taking his eyes off the three men. If guns were going to be drawn and start blazing, this would be the moment.

But that's not what happened.

"What do you want to do?" the older man asked Brenda's brother.

Brenda's brother looked up at Superintendent Lindquist. "Can I see her? Maybe we can just sit here on the porch and talk for a while."

Superintendent Lindquist looked genuinely sympathetic to this request, and I half-expected him to tell Buehle to go find Brenda and bring her around. But he shook his head, frowned, and said, "You have to remember that this facility is part of the Department of Juvenile Delinquency, which is part of the state corrections system. We have very strict rules about visitations. Not just anyone is allowed to visit with a resident. An application must be submitted and approved and specific visitation guidelines followed. I appreciate very much your wanting to see your sister, Mr. Johnson, but the best I can do is invite you to submit an application. Again, I regret that you had to drive all this way to hear this. I'm sure it's disappointing to you."

Another silence followed.

"All right then," Brenda's brother said with a note of resignation in his voice. "Can you tell her I was here?"

"I will do that," said Superintendent Lindquist, "most certainly. And thank you for understanding."

"Maybe I'll come back later for one of those applications," he said, and then the three men turned around and walked down the steps. A couple dozen residents, both guys and girls, were standing around by this point, yet the men ignored us and walked straight back to their car. I kept looking at Brenda's brother, studying him, trying to detect any resemblance between him and her. It was there in their frame certainly, their mutual lankiness, but even more than that, there was a kind of self-possession that expressed itself in both his face and hers, in the way the mouth was set and the eyes unwavering.

As the men got back into the car, I suddenly regretted that Brenda wouldn't be able to see her brother. The only brother she'd ever mentioned having was the unnamed player for the Seattle SuperSonics, and as I knew, that was a lie. This guy was her real brother. He said he'd been in the VA hospital, which meant he was a vet, and then I remembered the army jacket Brenda had been wearing when I met her on the Salt Dock in Seattle last fall. I remembered the name on it: Johnson. She'd been wearing her brother's army jacket.

As the Lincoln Continental headed back toward the main gate, Superintendent Lindquist ordered us all to return to our cottages. Within minutes, as we walked across the parade grounds, the buzz about the Black Panthers coming to Fort Worden gained mythic proportions. Someone said he saw the outline of a gun in the jacket of the man near the top of the stairs, the older guy. Someone else said they probably had hand grenades and Uzis in the trunk of the Lincoln Continental and would come back after dark and start blasting up the place until they found Brenda.

"What if there are more of them just outside of town?" one guy pondered.

"Lindquist had better call in the state troopers," another said.

The scenarios kept getting crazier and more violent until finally the four black kids among the group that had watched the whole thing, not saying a word the whole while, just peeled off by themselves.

"Where are they going?" someone walking beside me asked.

"What do you care?" I said, a bit huffy, and went upstairs to my bunk to write Brenda a note.

BRENDA AND I HAD been using Prosper as our go-between ever since the Assessment Committee had banned us from seeing one another. Yet in the days and weeks following her brother's appearance at Fort Worden, and after almost daily notes from me, he kept returning to our cottage empty-handed, saying he'd given Brenda or one of her friends my latest note but she didn't have anything to send back. I couldn't figure out why. When I first wrote explaining how I'd seen her brother, describing the two guys he was with, recounting the exchange with Lindquist, and even asking whether her brother was the one whose army jacket she used to wear in Seattle, I expected her to write back excited, eager to meet me somewhere so I could give her all the details. So her not responding left me wondering if I'd done something wrong, if I'd offended her somehow. Then I got to thinking…maybe the guy wasn't her brother at all, maybe he was her boyfriend, and his showing up at Fort Worden had thrown her into a total puzzlement about *us*. While there had always been a number of small mysteries surrounding Brenda, starting with the story she had first told me about where she lived, I'd always looked past them. They were part of her allure, along with her being black, I suppose, and maybe if she'd been white I would have pushed her further on them. On the other hand, if she'd been white, three guys looking like Black Panthers probably wouldn't have shown up in a Lincoln Continental asking to take her out for a hamburger. I ultimately decided the guy was actually her brother.

By the third week, when Prosper began complaining about being my messenger boy, I resolved that if Brenda wasn't going to acknowledge my notes I would go see her myself—to hell with the Assessment Committee's ban. I considered various options for waylaying her in order to maximize privacy as well as the amount of time we would have. But I never got the chance to carry out any of these plans. Brenda was now almost always in the company of several other black girls at the Treatment Center and collectively they seemed to ward off anyone who approached them. She and her group of friends also began milling around some of the black guys who were residents, which didn't appear to concern the staff nearly as much as my hanging out with her did. Suddenly it seemed as if she was insulating herself from me, as well as all the other white kids at the center, knowing that none of them would be bold enough to walk up to a group of six or eight black kids and just start talking to them. But I was desperate and needed to know whether she'd written me off for good or not.

So one day when I saw her and her friends sitting in a circle near the grove of rhododendrons behind the chapel, I made my approach. I knew a few of the other kids with her and nodded to them and then asked Brenda if we could talk. They all looked at me like I was crazy. Then Yvette, a girl in Brenda's cottage who wore an immense Afro with a headband pushing the hair up off her forehead, told me to go away.

"I want to tell you something," I said to Brenda, though actually I wanted to do more asking than telling. She looked about at her friends as if embarrassed by me. *What have I done?* I wanted to blurt out at her. It now felt to me as if my being white was the issue.

"She don't want to talk," Yvette said.

I felt awkward standing while they all remained sitting. "Why not?"

"Because that's why, whitey," said one of the guys, Eddie, whose nickname was "Trap" because he was at Fort Worden for stealing a drum trap from a music store. Eddie jumped to his feet and got right up in my face. I held my ground.

"Trap, leave him alone," I heard Brenda say. She was looking at me now, and I knew by that single look—somewhere between annoyance and disinterest, with maybe a touch of pity—that for whatever reason she wanted nothing to do with me anymore.

"Just leave, Avery," she said.

I took a deep breath, felt it catch in my chest like I might choke on it, and blinked several times. "I like you, Brenda," I heard myself saying. I wanted to say *love*, I truly did, and I might have if we were alone. But we weren't alone, and I didn't say it, and I was forever after sorry.

Yvette wailed in derision. "He *likes* you, Brenda," she said, mocking me. Trap laughed too and high-fived another guy sitting in their group. "What'd you do to this white boy, Bren?"

Brenda just shook her head, staring at the ground. "Just leave, will you?" she pleaded, and I cringed to think how uncomfortable I must have made her among her friends.

I managed to start breathing again and stammered, "What'd I do?"

That's when Trap gave me a hard shove and I stumbled back and fell onto my rear. "The sista said *leave*, motherfucker."

I got up. "Okay," I said, and with one more look at Brenda caught her eye and added, "never mind."

That evening I skipped dinner in the cafeteria and afterward wandered about the grounds. I walked past the infirmary, past the administrative building, and over to the lower battery installments situated just above the parade grounds where a raucous baseball game was taking place. The curfew, I knew, was 7:30.

Unlike the larger batteries on Artillery Hill, these smaller ones weren't off-limits to Treatment Center residents, mainly because they were well within sight of the other buildings and their openings were barred with large metal doors. I climbed up onto the farthest one and sat on its concrete edge, looking out across Admiralty Inlet to the bare bluffs of Whidbey Island. A few days ago when I'd come to the same spot with a few other guys, we'd eyed a half-submerged submarine making its way south and one of the guys said there was a nuclear submarine base at Bangor on Hood Canal. He knew, he said, because his brother was in the navy.

"And if the Russians ever attack us," he warned, "the base will be one of the first places they hit with their nukes. They'll hit Bremerton and Everett too, my brother told me. And just like that we'll all be toast. Totally obliterated."

"Not me," another guy said.

"Yeah, you too," said the first guy. "All of us, you can count on it."

When I heard the curfew bell being rung and saw the baseball game breaking up, I stood up. I then scurried over to the bluff and slid down the sandy slope. I walked along the beach out to the Point Wilson lighthouse, still stunned by Brenda's rejection.

When I finally returned to my cottage several hours later, I ignored Mr. Higman's reprimand for missing curfew and went to bed and dreamed of nuclear annihilation. I survived the attack by ducking under a wooden rowboat that was left overturned on the beach. When the attack was over, there was no more beach and no more Puget Sound. As I peered out from beneath the rowboat at the vast arid wasteland littered with industrial debris, the only living thing I saw was a single malformed figure stumbling about in a daze in the far distance.

I GOT A DAY in the hole for going AWOL that evening. This time around I didn't read at all. Bradbury's *The Martian Chronicles* and Kerouac's

The Dharma Bums had been left in the room, but I wasn't interested. Instead, I stared at the plexiglass window waiting for Brenda to come and pry it off so we could have another nighttime tryst. At one point I climbed onto the chair and pushed at the window to test it, but it was set tight into the frame, maintenance having finally fixed it.

Following this last stint in the hole, I was pretty depressed and grew irritable easily. I snapped several times at Mr. Higman and was warned by Superintendent Lindquist that I was walking on thin ice. I even became mad at Prosper. After I told him what had happened with Brenda and her friends, he said he wasn't surprised.

"That's the direction it's going with Black Nationalists these days," he said. "They're cutting off all association with white people. Even CORE, in Seattle, voted to not have white members any longer."

"What's that?" I asked.

"CORE? It stands for Congress of Racial Equality. It's a civil rights group."

"You know too fucking much, you know that," I said and stormed out of the common room where we'd been hanging out. I knew he probably was right, that the Black Nationalist stuff was probably what was going on with Brenda. As with the Vietnam War, I'd paid very little attention to civil rights issues. I knew who Martin Luther King Jr. was, that he'd been assassinated, that there had been riots afterward. And of course I knew about the Black Panthers, or at least what I read in *Time* magazine about them. I also understood generally that black people were pretty upset with how things had been going for them for the past couple hundred years or so in America. So maybe they were right to wash their hands of white people. Brenda had probably never had so many black friends as she had now at Fort Worden, and so I figured some peer pressure was also involved in her freezing me out.

I spent more time over the next few days thinking about race relations than I ever had before. Then, in another little talk with Prosper, he pissed me off again when he shared with me the rumor that the Treatment Center was going to close.

"Everyone's going to be reassigned," he said, looking worried. "Or else sent home." This second option seemed to frighten him more than the first. The idea of being around his parents was unthinkable to him. Unlike the self-assured Prosper who could deliver salient facts about civil rights or any other topic at the drop of a hat, the Prosper who had to reckon with the prospect of being sent home was a simpering twit.

"That's bullshit," I snapped back, almost as bothered by the idea as he was. I told myself if the Treatment Center was going to close, surely I would have heard about it already—certainly before Prosper. I also told myself that if the rumor was true, I for damn sure was going to bolt for San Francisco.

The next day when I asked Bobby Felton about it, he said he didn't know and didn't care, and added that he had more important things to think about. He confided in me that he was meeting a guy from town later that night near the West Gate to score a sheet of windowpane. He'd give me a few tabs if I wanted, he said as if testing me, and so, just to make sure he knew I was cool with dropping acid, I told him sure, I'd take a few hits off his hands. To be honest, though, I wasn't keen on taking LSD. I knew what it was, but I'd never done it or known anyone who had. In Spanaway the main means of getting wasted were Green Death (a.k.a. Rainier Ale), cheap Cali weed, and speed in the form of little white or pink pills that made you so edgy you kept downing tallboys of Green Death to level out.

Yet, for better or worse, I never got to experiment with Bobby's windowpane since he took most of it himself that same night. He and Del Emmons. And together they broke into the maintenance shed, made off with a couple full gas cans, and went on a spree setting fires through the upper grounds of the fort. As all the residents were waking up to the sound of sirens from fire engines barreling through the main gate, Mr. Higman came rushing into the dormitory shouting at us to get up and get outside. No one knew yet who was starting all the fires or where they might strike next, so we were ordered to gather in the middle of the parade grounds and not move.

This worked out well for us because we had a perfect view of the half dozen fires burning in the brush along that stretch of the upper grounds. More than one kid said he hoped it would spread to the administration building. The cottage parents brought blankets out to us, and we sat on the grass and watched as if we were at a campfire. I looked over toward where the girls were huddled, hoping to see Brenda, but I couldn't spot her.

"Who do you think did it?" Prosper asked me. He wore a pair of pajamas that were pink from his having put them—mistakenly, he said—in the washing machine with a brand new red bandana. He took a lot of razzing for them from all the guys in the cottage, and I told him he should throw them out and sleep in his underpants like everyone else, but he just kept wearing them.

"I don't know," I replied, thinking about Prosper's pink pajamas mainly because the laundry building was now ablaze. Two other outbuildings were also burning.

Before long, word went around that it was Bobby Felton and Del Emmons who were responsible for the incendiary havoc being wrought on Fort Worden. When several Port Townsend police cars went tearing up the Artillery Hill road, we speculated that's where Bobby and Del were now, and sure enough, when new flames accompanied by thick gray smoke appeared in a couple spots along the hillside, our speculations were confirmed. We all rooted for them to keep lighting fires *and* get away.

Once the fires on the lower grounds were extinguished and all there was to see from the upper grounds was smoke, the staff marshaled us back to our cottages. By then it was well past four o'clock in the morning and no one was going to go back to sleep, and when this became clear to the staff, they let us turn on the lights and just hang out in the dormitory until the morning wake-up bell rang at six. As several of us clustered around Del Emmons's bunk, I related how Bobby had gone to buy acid from some townie the night before.

"They must've taken a shitload," Pete Munson said.

"Maybe it wasn't any good, and they had a bad trip," someone said.

"No shit, Sherlock," said someone else.

"Obviously they flipped out," said Pete.

"That's why I'm sticking to weed," another kid remarked, and we all nodded at the sagacity of this pledge.

Eventually the dawn light began to show through the window, and when the breakfast bell rang letting us know we could make our way to the cafeteria, Mr. Higman announced from the doorway that classes and all other scheduled activities were cancelled and that we would be confined to the cottage for the entire day.

"So just settle in," he told us as a collective groan went up.

"Did they catch 'em yet?" came a shout from the far end of the dormitory floor.

"Never mind," said Mr. Higman and let us know the kitchen staff would be bringing egg sandwiches and orange juice over soon.

THERE WAS A SHAKEDOWN of all the cottages that day, including footlockers, with the staff and security looking for drugs and mostly finding (in the boys' cottages anyhow) contraband cigarettes and copies of *Playboy* and *Penthouse*. The next day an assembly was held on the evils of drugs and the severe correctional measures anyone caught with them would be subject to. And then we were back to our routine. The laundry building was a mound of rubble and ash, and so we had to wear dirty clothes longer than even we wanted to. But other than that, the damage from the various fires was not as devastating as we'd thought it would be. After a few days, a consensus story about what had happened to Bobby and Del took hold. They'd been apprehended by the Port Townsend police while holed up in one of the batteries on Artillery Hill, still tripping their brains out, half naked and screaming uncontrollably, their hair singed and third-degree burns on their hands. Then, once restrained by the police, they were transported to Northern State Hospital, the big mental hospital near Sedro-Woolly, where they were put under twenty-four-hour observation. Eventually reports circulated that Del was now a babbling idiot who shit and pissed himself, and Bobby, once the toughest kid at Fort Worden, was a blissed-out fool with glazed-over eyes and a simpleton's smile frozen on his face.

Frankly, the whole episode had me scared straight for the next month or so. I laid low, spending most of my time reading *David Copperfield* and then *The Old Man and the Sea*, followed by *A Farewell to Arms*. I also resolved, as part of my effort at self-reform, to try to move on from Brenda, especially since she'd obviously moved on from me. The notion of doing so, of giving her up, was agonizing to me. Why did the world have to be so fucked up? I tried to believe that maybe somewhere down the line, just as we did after Seattle, Brenda and I might find each other again. In the meanwhile, I told myself, I would respect her wishes and make a point to avoid her. Some people said she and Yvette were lesbians, but I didn't believe it. *Besides*, I told myself with my new resolve, *what did I care?*

The one time we did come upon one another and say a few words, it was amiable enough. We passed each other in the cafeteria. She asked me what I'd been doing lately, and I told her I'd been reading a lot, and she said, "That's cool. Me too," and showed me the thin little volume she was carrying in her purse: *Malcolm X on Afro-American History*. I'd learned who Malcolm X was a few weeks earlier in social studies. To me, the most significant fact about him was that he'd been friends with Muhammad Ali.

"Is it good?" I asked her.

"He talks about the Omacs, the first Africans to come to North America, long before Christopher Columbus. Long before any white people."

"That's amazing," I said. I noticed she was growing out her hair, which she was working into dreadlocks. She also wore a thick bracelet of woven leather strips dyed green, yellow, and black, which I figured probably violated the Treatment Center dress code.

"Take it easy, Avery," she said and moved on.

I appreciated that she said my name, as if there were no hard feelings between us, and later that afternoon I went to the school library to find any books by Malcolm X, so I could talk to her about him next time our paths crossed, but none were listed in the card catalog.

That same week a woman from the Jefferson County School District met with all the Treatment Center residents who were sixteen and older in the school auditorium to explain that the district was launching an initiative to help "at-risk students" like ourselves prepare for and pass the GED exam. She said the initiative was part of a joint program with the Junior League of Washington State, which assisted young people in entering the workplace, and the Getting Started program at Central Washington State College, which helped kids like us go on to higher education.

Someone among us later said that if you went to college you could get a deferment from the draft. "That's how all the rich people do it," he said. "Only poor people and delinquents get called up."

Still, I wasn't interested in the GED program—even though, having turned seventeen by this point, I was less than a year away from facing the draft. All I really wanted to do was lie beneath the big linden tree near the maintenance shed and read and maybe get high now and then. I didn't want to have to think about anything else. Prosper, though, was gung ho about the program and wanted me to sign up as his official "study buddy" so we could take the exam together in June. So I did. Workbooks were provided as well as separate study areas, and eventually those of us who registered for the program were moved into a smaller barracks where we each had our own desk and chair for doing homework. Now, in the evenings, instead of playing ping-pong or foosball in the common room, I either sat at my desk studying or at one of three round tables where we could receive tutoring from Port Townsend retirees who volunteered their time.

Despite my initial resistance, I began to like the GED prep program and the handful of perks that came with it. The idea of going across the mountains to Ellensburg to attend college—along with getting the draft deferment—was starting to appeal to me. I had no idea how this would be accomplished but decided to speak to someone from the Getting Started program the first chance I got. Prosper, meanwhile, was really good at math, and said he wanted to go into business and makes gobs of money. "If you're rich enough you can do whatever you want—be whoever you want—and everyone else can go fuck themselves," he proclaimed. We were sitting on the front porch of the GED prep cottage.

"What do you want to be?" I asked, thinking he would say banker or accountant or stockbroker or something else that involved making tons of money.

"I want to be me," he answered.

I looked to see if he was being serious or what.

"How's that pay?" I said, laughing at him. "Can I be you too? You know, if it pays really good?"

"No, you can't," he said, unamused. "You just have to keep being the same old douchebag you've always been," and with that he got up and went inside.

Prosper's hissy fit ticked me off, so instead of risking the chance that I might punch him in his prissy little face if I saw him again inside, I walked back to my old cottage where I found Pete Munson watching a ping-pong game and asked what he had. He took me outside around the side of the cottage, checked to see if anyone was watching, then pried back a loose siding board and pulled out a plastic baggy with about twenty tightly rolled joints in it. And that evening, instead of studying, I got really stoned.

We were only three weeks into the new GED prep program when it became official: The Fort Worden Diagnostic and Treatment Center for Juvenile Delinquency would close in August. According to our social studies teacher, the State of Washington, like most of the country, was in dire fiscal straits, forcing the state government in Olympia to make drastic budget cuts, especially to social programs. Boeing, the state's biggest employer, was laying off people in droves, and the governor, Dan Evans, had to call an emergency session of the state legislature to deal with the crisis. Furthermore, our teacher told us, talking to us like adults, the US Congress was about to pass the Juvenile Justice and Delinquency Prevention Act, which would allocate grants to state and local agencies to assess programs like the one at Fort Worden and encourage the creation of newer, more community- and family-based approaches to dealing with juvenile delinquency. The Fort Worden Treatment Center, it seemed, wasn't forward-looking enough for the new law.

We could tell that staff members were upset by the news. Some, like Mr. Higman, were downright bitter and made little effort to mask their feelings to the kids they oversaw. When I went over to my old cottage one afternoon to visit with Pete again, I spotted Higman in his first-floor office, loudly and sarcastically singing the lyrics from "Gee, Officer Krupke," the song from *West Side Story*, without a care in the world who heard him:

> Gee, Officer Krupke, we're very upset;
> We never had the love that ev'ry child oughta get.
> We ain't no delinquents,
> We're misunderstood.
> Deep down inside us there is good!

When he saw me standing in the foyer, he grinned and called out, "Heya, Clausen. You better pass that goddamn GED exam or it's off to Green Hill for you." Then he just laughed and slammed his office door closed.

That week Superintendent Lindquist held an assembly where he explained to all two hundred residents that each of our cases would be reviewed in detail and we would individually meet with our Assessment Committee to discuss the options for reassignment prior to the final closure of the Treatment Center. He assured us that every effort would be made to return us home or place us in a suitable foster home or facility comparable to the Treatment Center. For most of us, all of the options sounded like shit. We wanted to stay at Fort Worden. But none of us knew what we could do to alter the course of things.

With so much uncertainty casting a pall over the Treatment Center, I was even more glad to be in the GED prep cottage. It was an oasis from the unruliness breaking out elsewhere. There were a lot more fights among residents, and at least once a week someone busted out a window in one of the buildings or set fire to a mattress or took a swing at a cottage parent, and security was constantly chasing down another kid who'd gone rambling. Two guys stole a car off the lot of the Kruse Car Center out on Route 20 and drove it all the way to Port Angeles before being caught. A whole gang of guys broke into The Hilltop Tavern one night and stole several cases of beer. They were drinking down by the bay when one of the guys dove off a pier and slammed headfirst into the submerged remnant of a pylon and broke his neck, paralyzing him from the waist down. When the annual Rhododendron Festival took place in downtown Port Townsend, a group of Fort Worden kids, both guys and girls, snuck off the grounds and ended up getting into a brawl with a group of kids from town.

The transgressions weren't limited to the residents either. Mr. Higman's little display was just the start of staff members coming unhinged. One of the counselors was sacked for groping several female residents. One of the maintenance crew was busted for buying weed from Pete Munson, who got busted in turn and was sent straight to Green Hill. Mr. Larrison, the math teacher, finally lost what little control he had and punched a kid, breaking his cheekbone, and was immediately fired, while our social studies teacher, the Quaker Conscientious Objector, just upped and quit, telling everyone the Selective Service System could rot in hell, he was moving to a commune in Oregon. Meanwhile, a general moroseness descended upon everyone employed at the Treatment Center, from cottage parents to kitchen staff, as they counted down the months and weeks to the inevitable.

AT THE END OF July, with three weeks to go before the GED exam, a handful of residents got a respite from all this gloom. A group of two young men and one woman from the Seattle branch of the Outward Bound program came to Fort Worden to recruit eighteen kids, male and female, for a four-day version of their wilderness curriculum in confidence building and interpersonal skills. By this time, the administration had started to regard me as one of the more exemplary residents, in that I hadn't been in any trouble in two months. So I was picked for the program, as was Prosper. And I was hoping Brenda would be picked as well, but she wasn't, and Yvette, who was picked, told me Brenda was probably going to return to her parents' house on Mercer Island in a week or so. When I asked her if that's what Brenda wanted, all she said was, "I guess so."

The three Outward Bound instructors were serious, athletic-looking people. Even though we were going backpacking for just two days, with only one overnight, they had our group spend two full days doing team-building exercises, learning about the gear we'd be using, and studying the terrain we would be traversing, including its flora and fauna. By the second day, this approach was working, and the eighteen of us who were selected for the adventure began to bond, interacting with one another in a way we never had before—with confidence and a level of maturity that at times was embarrassing to our more adolescent selves. When the two-day orientation was completed, the instructors roused us out of bed at dawn, loaded us into a small bus (to be followed by a van carrying our gear), and drove us to a trailhead on the west side of the Olympic Peninsula. Before most of us were even fully awake, we had our orange nylon packs on and were trudging through the woods. We'd learned the day before that the trail we were on led to a place deep in the Olympic Mountains called the Enchanted Valley.

Within the first hours of hiking up the trail with the thirty-five-pound packs strapped to our backs, kids were complaining about the strain on their shoulders, the chafing of their thighs, and the burning of blisters on their feet. The instructors would help individual group members make adjustments to their pack or give them a Band-Aid for their feet, but mostly they ignored the whining and pushed on.

I'd been in Mount Rainier National Park twice with my father, but the forests around the perimeter of the park, not far from Spanaway, could not compare to the lush forests in the lower stretches of the Olympic Mountains. The trees here were wider, taller, and mossier, as was all the vegetation. The trail followed the East Fork of the Quinault River for a couple of miles, rising gradually through thick stands of cedar, hemlock, and yew. When the terrain turned steeper, the group became quiet as everyone's breathing became more labored. Everyone was also sweating pretty heavily, trying to keep up with the pace set by the instructors.

When we all had to cross a narrow suspension bridge, below which the turbulent, milky-blue river coursed down a deep ravine, a kid from our group named Nick became panic-stricken halfway across. He just froze, gripping with both hands one of the guidewires, staring down at the water, and refusing to move either forward or back. The instructor who took up the rear came forward, walked onto the bridge, and tried to coax him off, but failed to budge him one inch. His breath coming in gasps, Nick kept shouting, "I can't. I can't," over the roar of the river. It was a pitiful sight. Some of the kids who'd already made it across tried to cheer him on, telling him it was all right, he could do it, and so on, but the added attention seemed to increase the pressure he felt to move, and he became even more locked in panic.

The lead instructor worked his way around the kid and was on the other side consulting with the other two instructors about what to do when out of nowhere Prosper slid his pack off and walked out onto the bridge. Apparently he was friends with Nick, and we all watched as he went up to him, leaned on the cable beside him, and started talking to him. I could see Prosper's lips moving, but because of the noise from the cataract of water, no one could hear what he was saying. I could see Nick shaking his head no and then Prosper putting his hand on Nick's shoulder and just letting it rest there. Everyone backed away from the bridge, even the instructors, and waited, until finally Nick straightened up and looked around. "Don't look down," I imagined Prosper saying as he leaned in close to Nick. Nick released his white-knuckled grip on the guidewire and turned to face the other side. Prosper kept speaking to him and then finally Nick took a step forward, and then another, and another, one very deliberate step at a time, always the right foot first, followed by the left. It took a few minutes, but eventually he reached the other side, at which point everyone broke out in cheers. Then one of the instructors waved his arm in the air, shouted "Hikers Ho!" and signaled for those of us still on the other side of the bridge to move across it single file.

After that episode the complaining subsided and we found our rhythm. We had become a single cohesive unit, which was like nothing I'd ever experienced before—a genuine collective experience, brought about by mutual purpose and exertion. About every hour the instructors shouted down the line that it was time for a break. We weren't allowed to take our packs off, so we'd get someone to fish the canteen and bag of gorp from one of the side pockets and then recline on our packs for the duration of the short break. At noon when we stopped to eat lunch—peanut butter and jelly sandwiches we'd made the night before, carrot and celery sticks, and a carob bar each—we were finally allowed to drop our packs on the ground. There was some moaning that followed, but most of us were too tired to even speak and ate our lunches in silence, listening to the distant drone of the river and the wind moving through the tree tops—the two sounds nearly indistinguishable.

As the day wore on and the trail gained in elevation, the morning fog burned away and sunlight streamed through the boughs of the trees and made the moist woods glisten. At one point someone began singing the work song from Snow White and the Seven Dwarfs, and before you knew it we were shouting out all those heigh-ho's at the top of our lungs, no doubt scaring every creature large and small for miles around. After that someone started singing "This Land Is Your Land," but most of us knew only a few of the lyrics, so after the song fizzled out one of the instructors began in on the John Henry song, with all the kids from the Treatment Center heartily coming in on the chorus after each verse—"Hammer's gonna be the death of me, Lord, Lord / Hammer's gonna be the death of me"—and on and on as we marched up the trail.

At one point we all had to sit down and take off our boots and socks to traverse a frigid cold creek. After that the trail leveled out and eventually met up again with the East Fork of the Quinault, and not much later we reached our destination—a long narrow valley with a large open pasture. The river, flattening out at this point and strewn with freestones, carved a meandering path through the pasture, while on either side of the valley, steep mountain slopes with clumps of trees and granite outcroppings, as well as the occasional waterfall, slanted upwards toward the clouds. Not one of us had ever seen anything like it. At the head of the valley there rose a jagged wall of snowy peaks with an enormous glacier dead center, like a keystone of ice supporting the peaks on either side of it. We all stopped and stared.

"Goddamn," one kid muttered, and everyone laughed at how perfectly the utterance summoned up the awe we all felt.

"That's Mount Anderson," one of the instructors said, pointing to the largest peak. "We'll hike up that way tomorrow morning. But first we need to make camp."

The walk through the valley was easy. We spotted a small herd of elk along the sandy banks of the river, but as soon as the bull elk lifted its head with its rack of antlers and saw us, it cantered off, its harem of smaller cow elk following close behind.

Before long, we came to a clearing along the back edge of which, just in front of a cluster of alders, sat a weathered three-story building with a moss-covered pitched roof. The instructors called this "The Chalet" and said it was an old ranger station built by the Forest Service back in the '30s.

"Is that where we're going to sleep?" Alex, a kid from the GED cottage, asked.

"Yeah, shitface, that's why we hauled tents on our backs all this way," another kid answered sharply. Yet, whereas a few days ago we all would have guffawed at this sarcastic comeback, no one did so now. Instead, we listened as one of the instructors explained that we would set up camp a dozen or so yards from the structure.

We made our way forward to this spot, dropped our packs, and immediately set about making camp near a circle of river rocks previously set up for a camp fire. We were in teams of three, which meant Prosper, me, and Alex would share a tent. We barely had time to pitch our tent before the sun went down behind the mountains and the valley was cast in shadow. Also, with each passing minute, it became a lot colder. The instructors allowed us to retrieve some of the wood stacked beside the chalet—"*The wood was gray and bark warping off it / And the pile somewhat sunken,*" as Robert Frost wrote in his poem "The Wood-Pile"—and before the last light in the sky had disappeared we had a good-sized blaze going in the fire pit.

For some kids, mostly those like Yvette who grew up in the city, this was their first time camping and the darkness that quickly closed in around us kept them huddled close to the campfire. For others, like me, who'd spent a fair portion of my life outdoors in semi-wild places not far from Spanaway, I felt right at home. A few of us took our flashlights and poked around the pasture, even as the instructors warned us that black bears liked to graze the pasture at night, a tidbit of info that ensured we kept the campsite within view.

Initially, when arrangements for this backpacking trip were being made, it had an aura of finality to it. Once we hit the trail, though, most of us were able to put all that business out of mind and just appreciate being in the wilderness. For me certainly, my past thirteen months at the Treatment Center no longer mattered. Each misdeed and subsequent punishment, each precarious friendship, each razor cut to the heart, each frustration and uncertainty, big or small, seemed to disappear as I took in deep lungfuls of mountain air and looked up at the swirl of stars in the black night sky.

In the morning, Prosper, Alex, and I were the first ones up. I yanked myself out of my sleeping bag, pulled on my shorts, jacket, and hiking boots, and tumbled out of our tent and into the quiet, misty morning, and they soon followed. The campfire was still smoldering, though just barely. There were birds beginning to chatter in the trees, and at one point I thought I heard the big bull elk bugling in the far-off distance. At the head of the valley, the tips of the peaks were pink with alpenglow, while below that point, a thick white cloud had settled in between the ridges, obscuring the view of the glacier and the tops of the trees. Below the cloud line, meandering just past the alder with their leaves already tinged yellow, the river produced a mist that lifted into the air. In the pasture below us, a large roundish creature bent its head toward the sedge grass. Alex saw it first and signaled Prosper and me to look.

"Should we wake up the others?"

"No," I said, not daring to take my eyes off the bear—and wanting to preserve the moment for ourselves. "Not yet."

Eventually one of the instructors unzipped the flap of his tent and saw us standing there and then saw what we were looking at. He got out quickly and rustled everyone else out of their tents to have a look, and within a few minutes everyone was gathered around watching the bear. For most of this time, it simply ignored us. It raised its head once or twice to look in our direction, but otherwise it went about its business of intently foraging, and only when two of the instructors decided they needed to get the campfire going and started making noise did the bear finally amble off into the woods.

After gobbling flapjacks, dried banana chips, and Tang for breakfast and just poking about the campsite for a while, we were corralled by the instructors and ordered to break camp. We set about rolling up sleeping bags, breaking down tents, and cramming everything back into backpacks. We then stored all the packs in the chalet to keep them away from curious black bears, filled our canteens at the river (dropping chlorine tablets in first), and set off on an exploration of the glacier moraine at the base of Mount Anderson. After crossing a creek that raced through a boulder field, we reached the first snow bank and everyone went crazy, breaking into a snowball fight, kids versus instructors.

A recent rockslide had blocked much of the trail leading through the narrow pass that led toward Mount Anderson, but once we negotiated our way over and around the slide, the way opened up and we stood below the edge of the glacier. Because of the risk of falling into crevasses, the instructors prohibited us from climbing onto it. We were told that traversing a glacier required crampons and ropes, and while I listened, staring at the looming wall of ice and gravel, I secretly vowed to myself that someday I would come back with the right equipment and climb to the top of Mount Anderson. For now, I was content to sit with the group at the base of the glacier and look out at the valley below. We hardly spoke the whole while we sat there, and nobody once mentioned the Treatment Center. When one of the instructors eventually stood up and said it was time to get back, a collective sigh went up, and we all begged to stay a little longer. But he reminded us that after we returned to the valley floor, we still had a twelve-mile hike down to the trailhead.

On the tramp back into the valley, Prosper and I lagged behind the others. I was as reluctant as anyone to be going back to Fort Worden and kept thinking how I would wait a week or so and then take off, making my way back to the valley, where I would bivouac in the chalet until the winter. I didn't think about how I would survive all those weeks before the first snowfall, probably imagining I would graze off the land like the black bear we'd seen that morning. Those were just minor details, and what mattered was getting back to this unreal place.

It was just after we'd forded the creek again and were almost back to the valley floor when Prosper told me he'd decided what his new name would be.

The topic caught me off guard, having entirely forgotten our conversation from so long ago, and my first thought was that he was setting me up for a joke. "Something douchey, no doubt," I said.

"*No*," he said, sounding offended. He didn't say anything more and I realized he was being serious.

"You mean you're really going to change your name?"

He looked at me without any trace of joking around and said, "Yes, I am."

So I said that was amazing. "I mean it," I added, "Really," and then asked him what he was going to change it to.

He waited a moment—whether for effect or out of nervousness, I don't know—and then answered, "I'm going to change it to Tracy."

"That's a girl's name," I said almost immediately, just like the first time, not knowing what else to say.

His response was the same as that first time as well. "It's a guy's name too. It's both."

"It is?"

"*Yes*," he said, then turned quiet and seemed to withdraw. In other circumstances, I might have worried he was going to cry. But that wasn't the case now. He was going to keep it together.

At the time, all I could figure was that he must really hate the name "Prosper" and really like the name "Tracy." He'd obviously given it a lot of thought. But why he would pick a name that for most people was just as strange—at least for a guy—made no sense. He would probably get as much ridiculing for "Tracy" as he ever had for "Prosper," if not more. The significance of the two names he'd proposed being both girl names didn't register with me. I just took him to be—as I basically always had—the sensitive, creative sort who preferred doing things differently than everyone else.

"It's unusual, that's for sure," I replied. I didn't want to get into any kind of harangue with him about it. "But you know, it's kind of cool too. Like Dick Tracy or Spencer Tracy." The Treatment Center staff had shown us *The Old Man and the Sea* with Spencer Tracy for movie night a couple of months ago. It wasn't as good as the book, but I liked the way Spencer Tracy played the old man.

"Those are last names," Prosper said, and then maybe realizing I had just given the name my approval, weak as it was, he added, "It just sounds right."

"I guess that's all that matters," I said. "It's your name, right? You have to live with it."

He smiled then and proceeded to try it out, getting giddier with each new iteration. "'Hi, I'm Tracy Sutton.' 'My name is Tracy Sutton.' 'You can call me Tracy.' 'And the award for the highest score on the GED exam goes to...Tracy Sutton.'"

"Okay, okay," I said. "I get it."

But he wasn't done. "'It was announced today that Tracy Sutton is the richest person in the world. Richer than Howard Hughes. According to his spokesman, Tracy Sutton has purchased Fort Worden, in Port Townsend, Washington, and plans to rename it the Avery Clausen Center for Juvenile Propinquity.'"

Propinquity had been one of our GED vocabulary words. He was laughing so hard now that several kids and one of the instructors farther down the trail looked back at us.

"You're nutso," I said and shook my head, wanting to laugh along with him but also kind of embarrassed by his goofiness.

"I guess this valley just has me *enchanted*," he said, starting to calm down as the chalet came into view. Then, as we approached the building, he turned to me and asked me to say his new name.

"Why?" I said, a little put off by the request.

"So I can hear how it sounds." He could see I was balking. "Just once," he said.

Ahead of us the others were already dragging their packs outside and helping each other put them on.

"Whatever you say, *Tracy*," I said in return, and he smiled when he heard me say it. "Do you want me to call you that from now on?" I asked sarcastically.

"No, not yet," he said, and leaving it at that we retrieved our packs.

Maybe it's the fatigue factor, but the return part of any hike always seems longer to me than the hike in, even though it's usually faster. This was the case with our hike out of the Enchanted Valley. All the same, keeping a steady pace and taking fewer breaks, our group reached the trailhead well before nightfall, and by eight o'clock we were rolling back through the main gate at Fort Worden. It took us an hour or so to unpack and return our gear to the Outward Bound equipment van and then, after profuse thanks and goodbyes to our three instructors, we all returned to our respective cottages, dead-tired and ready to sleep through the end of the world.

I SPOKE TO BRENDA once more before she left the Treatment Center to return home to Mercer Island. We bumped into one another in the makeshift laundry facilities in the basement of the old army band barracks, where I was washing my clothes from the backpacking trip. It was hard seeing her, the pang of being in her presence almost more than I could bear. She asked me how the trip was and I gave her a few of the highlights. She said that Yvette thought it was the best thing she'd ever done in her life and that she wanted to become a park ranger now.

"That would be great," I said. Then, changing the subject, I asked Brenda how she felt about going home.

She said she thought it would be all right. "My parents aren't so bad," and she explained how her plan was to finish high school, even if she was a year behind, and afterward join VISTA to help inner-city kids.

"That's great too," I said. I had been thinking she might join the Black Panthers like her brother. I wanted to ask about him but didn't. Too much distance had grown between us.

"And you, Avery?" she asked.

What about me? I wanted to say.

I had decided that going back to my mom's house in Spanaway or my dad's place in Longview was not an option. Neither was Green Hill or Echo Glen. Nor Forestry Camp or foster care. I still had the GED exam ahead of me, and the Getting Started program, so perhaps Central Washington State College in Ellensburg lay in my future. Until I turned eighteen, though, I would still officially be a ward of the state. Which meant that running away to live in the chalet in the Enchanted Valley was still probably my best option.

A blank look must have come over me because when I didn't answer, Brenda finally said, "Never mind," and added in a somewhat sullen tone that if I was ever in Seattle I might look her up.

"Okay," I said dumbly and was surprised when she came forward and gave me a kiss on the lips and then hugged me before carrying her basket of laundry back to her cottage.

A couple days later when I saw Yvette, she told me Brenda's mother and father had picked her up that morning. Immediately after hearing this, I trudged back to my cottage, sat down in one of the bathroom stalls, and cried with a kind of hurt I'd never known until that moment. Only when I heard someone walk in did I try to pull myself together.

Without Brenda, without Bobby Felton, without even Del Emmons and Pete Munson and a few of the other guys I used to hang out with regularly, nothing at the Treatment Center was the same. It became a whole lot duller. I was one of the oldest residents now and one of the longest there—more than a full year. My cohorts now were Prosper, who'd never once spent a night in the hole, and Alex, our tentmate on the backpacking trip. Alex was obsessed with playing board games like Risk and Stratego, so that's what we mostly did with our free time now.

Although life at Fort Worden became very uneventful, I was able to really prepare for the GED exam. On the appointed Saturday morning, those of us in the GED prep cottage, including Prosper and Alex, were bussed to Port Townsend High School to take the exam. Just entering the halls and classrooms of a regular high school made me itchy, but once the test proctor handed me the booklet with the exam questions, the answer sheets, and two sharpened no. 2 pencils and several sheets of scrap paper, the test-taking skills I'd developed with all those sample tests during the past several weeks clicked in and I settled down to the task at hand. I struggled with the math, but got through it, and with the language arts portion I was particularly pleased to be able to readily answer the two John Steinbeck questions:

1) In what Depression-era novel does the character Tom Joad migrate with his family from Oklahoma to California?

Too easy! And then,

In what part of California is John Steinbeck's novel *East of Eden* set?
a) The Mojave Desert
b) Los Angeles

c) Monterey

d) The Salinas Valley.

I instantly knew Monterey was a trick answer, being where *Cannery Row* is set, and filled in the bubble for d) The Salinas Valley.

At the break, Prosper, Alex, and I sat outside on a low brick wall and exchanged answers with one another as we ate our bologna sandwiches and bags of potato chips. Prosper seemed to have nailed all the questions. He corrected me and Alex on some of our answers but then reminded us that we only needed 40 percent correct to pass. He was confident we'd gotten well above that. Plus, he said, the next two subjects (history and geography) were easy ones.

When the exam was over later that afternoon, we were dizzy with relief at simply having put it behind us. To celebrate, our cottage parent, along with several of our tutors from town, took the whole group out for ice cream on Water Street in downtown Port Townsend. Then, on the short bus ride back to Fort Worden, one guy from our group asked probably the most obvious question of all: Why would anyone sit through four years of high school when you could just take the GED exam? All of us agreed with the irrefutable logic of this rhetorical question, no doubt exasperating our cottage parent, who kept his mouth shut as we basked in the glory of having completed the exam.

It was another week before I received word that I had passed and would have the Certificate of General Educational Development bestowed upon me. In fact, all twenty of us in the GED prep cottage passed the exam comfortably, with the highest pass percentage being 96, which we all knew was Prosper's. Our cottage parent suggested we consider taking the SAT exam next, but most of us, including me, said it was too soon, our brains were still fried from the last exam. Besides, as we said among ourselves, the Treatment Center was going to close in six weeks and we wanted to see where we ended up first. "Why should I study for another exam if I'm going to be locked up in Green Hill?" someone said, and we all concurred.

In the coming days as residents met with their Assessment Committee, everyone began to learn what their fate would be. A good many kids at the Treatment Center were going to be sent to a new facility in Vancouver, Washington, down along the Columbia River, which was rumored to be more like Fort Worden. The worst cases among us, as expected, would be going to Green Hill or Echo Glen. There weren't that many of these kids, though, and a number of them, when presented the option, chose instead to go to the Forestry Camp, located in the Cascade foothills outside Sedro-Woolley, where they would learn to maintain the state's forest preserves and fight summer wildfires. As for the GED cohort, some were being sent home, some to foster homes, and some to the new place in Vancouver. That's where I was assigned. Prosper, on the other hand, was told he would be going home.

This news didn't sit well with him—not at all. He wanted to take the Junior League of Washington up on its offer to help him enter the workforce (so he could begin making his millions, he told me). That way, he said, he might be able to live on his own. Or maybe he could figure out a way to be sent to Vancouver with me and the others. But Dr. Reinholdt and Superintendent Lindquist said that neither option was viable in his case and that the best recourse would be for him to go home to Olympia, find a job there, and live with his parents until he turned eighteen. The prospect of returning home, however, freaked him out. We were sitting in the common room, just the two of us, almost like that first encounter we'd had shortly after he arrived at Fort Worden, but this time he was raging about how unfair it all was, how Reinholdt and Lindquist didn't know shit, how his parents were total assholes, how we were all lied to about the great advantages of getting our GEDs, and how the whole world was a big, fucked-up mess when it came right down to it. I'd never heard him cuss so much. Even during his hazing in the woods last fall, I don't think he swore once.

I wanted to tell him that if it was me and I was as pissed off as he was, I would just take off. But I didn't want him to get into trouble, and so instead I tried to persuade him that going home maybe wouldn't be so bad. Maybe after getting a job in Olympia he could find his own apartment and he wouldn't have to stay very long at his parents' house.

"You're going to be eighteen in seven months, right? Also, don't they have a college there? Maybe you can take classes."

"I already told you," he shouted back at me as if I were threatening him somehow. "I don't want to go to college." Veins bulged from both sides of his neck. His face was flushed, his eyes wet and bloodshot, and he kept wiping tears off his cheeks with the sleeve of his shirt.

Prosper had always been the guy you could count on to keep his cool, so seeing him like this was unnerving. Unlike most of us, who were on a sliding scale of hotheadedness, he never threw violent tantrums or went on a tear breaking things or needed physical restraint by security. It was one of the qualities I admired most in him. But at the same time, it made me wonder about him—how he could remain so calm and collected all the time. Didn't everyone need to freak out once in a while? To lose control? Wasn't it your right as a human being? I recognized early on that whatever anger Prosper did harbor he usually directed at his parents. He complained that his straightlaced, prim-and-proper, churchgoing mother and father couldn't understand that not everyone was like them, that their way wasn't the only way, that the world was changing, people were changing. Rants by residents against parents were not unusual, but most kids at Fort Worden railed against their parents (as well as teachers and local cops) to showcase their untrammeled rage to their fellow residents. Not so with Prosper. His rage seemed more private, more intensely personal, and a lot more embittered.

I wasn't having any luck reassuring him, and eventually he got up, wiped his face one last time, and walked out of the common room without a word, leaving me sitting there. I didn't know what more I could do. Should I petition Reinholdt and Lindquist to let Prosper come to Vancouver with me? It was unlikely I could have any sway with them, especially Reinholdt, the expert on juvenile mentality and motivation. Finally I figured if Prosper really didn't want to be sent home, he could go into town and steal a car or break in to a gas station or vandalize some public property and get sent to Green Hill. Ultimately I was convinced—this being my own fallback plan—that simply taking off would be his best bet, even as I knew Prosper just wasn't the rambling sort.

Nonetheless, he went rambling that afternoon. It was a Sunday when residents were allowed more leisure and freedom of movement than usual. Just the same, our cottage parent noticed as soon as Prosper didn't show up for dinner. Those of us from the GED prep cottage were immediately enlisted to look for him. While everyone else went looking around the lower and upper grounds of the fort, I decided to go farther afield and without permission slipped past the maintenance building and up the road to Artillery Hill. I had a hunch that Prosper hadn't really taken off, hadn't entirely left the Fort Worden property. Plus, as I knew from experience, the hill was the default place to go if a kid needed to get away without actually going AWOL.

The hill made up a large area, though, so if he was up there the odds of me finding him weren't great. So instead of trying to cover the whole area, I decided to take a tour of the various batteries. First I checked out the batteries along the bluff, including the one near where Brenda and I spent our predawn morning together wrapped in a blanket watching cargo ships pass through the strait. I walked along the ramparts of each battery, poking my head into the different rooms and chambers and calling out Prosper's name, thinking he might be squirreled up in the dark recesses of one of these. Then I made my way to the interior of the hill, where the larger batteries with their ordnance storerooms were located. This is where, more as a lark than anything else, thinking Prosper might get a kick out of it, I started calling out the name "Tracy."

I didn't expect to hear a response, and when I did hear something after my fourth or fifth time calling out, it wasn't like any kind of sound a human would make. It sounded more like a couple of tree branches scraping together, making that eerie high-pitched whine you hear in the woods sometimes. So I called out "Tracy" a few more times, and then I was certain that it was a human sound.

"Where are you?" I yelled.

There was no answer. I was standing in the grassy center of a horseshoe-shaped battery that had several entrances, each marked by a heavy metal door through which a horse-drawn wagon or caisson carrying munitions could fit. Some of the doors were rusted closed and some pried partially open. Maybe I was just imagining I'd heard something, I began to think. But then there came a groan and I kept turning about trying to detect from which direction. I didn't really want to go into one of those doorways without knowing what was in there.

"Prosper?" I called out.

"Go away."

It was faint, but I heard this utterance distinctly. Hidden behind a gnarled old apple tree, there was a square concrete blockhouse about the size of a tool shed. The large iron door on its entrance was pushed all the way open. I walked up to it and peered inside, with just enough light to see all four walls, and found Prosper crouched in one of the back corners.

"What're you doing?" I asked him.

He had his knees pulled up to his chest and his arms wrapped around them. His shoulders were slumped forward and his forehead rested on top of his knees. He raised his head just enough to look at me.

"Go away," he said again.

"Are you tripping?" I asked, thinking maybe he'd gotten hold of some of the same bad acid Bobby Felton and Del Emmons had taken, even though I knew Prosper never did drugs. "Everyone's looking for you. Man, you're in a shitload of trouble."

I walked into the blockhouse and coming nearer noticed that his pants looked stained around the crotch, almost as if he'd peed himself. I didn't know whether to offer him my sympathy or make fun of him. I saw how pale he was, more than usual, and then I saw that the wetness on his pants and on the concrete floor where he sat was something else.

"Is that blood?" I could see plainly now that it was. He was groaning again, and clearly in a world of hurt. "What happened? Are you all right?"

"I cut myself," he managed to get out.

At first I thought he meant he'd maybe fallen and cut himself, which was easy enough to do horsing around the old batteries—there was jagged metal and chunks of broken concrete everywhere—but when I took another step forward and told him to let me see so I could get an idea of how bad it was, he flinched and said no.

"You can't just sit there bleeding," I said.

"Here," he said with a note of stubbornness in his voice and opened his right hand, showing me the small pocketknife that lay in his palm. Both knife and palm had blood on them. "I did it with this."

I figured he'd probably tried to slit his wrists or commit hari-kari or something stupid like that. In my time at the Treatment Center there had been three suicide attempts. One, by a sixteen-year-old girl named Lisa, had succeeded. She had sliced open both her forearms in a zigzag pattern from her wrists to her inner elbows.

"Did what?" I asked as his head wobbled back down to his knees. He was passing out, and I stepped up to him as he tipped over. That's when I saw how bloody his pants were. I still couldn't imagine what he had possibly done to himself, but I knew it was bad.

"That was nice of you to call me Tracy," he mumbled, coming to. "'Cause that's who I am."

I didn't know what to do. I was scared now and really confused. It came to me that I had to do one of two things: run down the hill for help or carry him down myself. It didn't seem right to just leave him there, not knowing what else he might do to himself, so I told him I was going to piggyback him down to the infirmary. As I got him to stand up against the back wall, I noticed that in addition to being totally bloody, his pants were undone. I ignored this as I turned around and crouched low so he could clasp his arms around my neck. As I straightened up, I reached behind, hooked my hands beneath his butt, and hefted him onto my back. He let out a scream at this sudden motion and kept on groaning as I adjusted his weight to get a better grip. I staggered with him out of the blockhouse and then took off in a kind of shuffling walk down the hill, moving as fast as I could while making sure he didn't slide off my back.

As soon as I reached the bottom of the hill, a couple of kids spotted us, saw how much blood there was, and ran ahead to the infirmary and guard house. Two security guards immediately came sprinting up to me and lifted Prosper off my back and carried him the rest of the way. I tried to follow them into the infirmary, but they ordered me to stay out front. "We need to talk to you," one of them said. From just outside the front door, I heard the nurse order one of the guards to bring her iodine, sutures, and gauze from the supply room and then tell the other guard to call an ambulance. "He needs to go to the hospital," she said, and I began to think Prosper might die.

Superintendent Lindquist came running to the infirmary and arrived just before the ambulance did. Together we watched as Prosper, unconscious and with an IV in his arm, was wheeled out on a gurney and placed in the back of the ambulance.

A few moments later, Officer Barris came outside carrying a couple of chairs, set them on the grass, and asked me to sit down with her. She could not have been more straightforward and no-nonsense. "It appears your friend Prosper castrated himself," she said. I didn't fully comprehend what she was saying, more out of incredulity than anything else, and she could see this. "He cut off his penis and testicles," she said more bluntly. "So I want you to tell me how this happened and where. Starting at the beginning."

IN MY OTHER COTTAGE, the one before the GED prep cottage, there would have been vicious and unrelenting ridicule of Prosper, and me too probably, over what had happened. But in the GED prep cottage, the response remained subdued. Everyone there liked Prosper. He was the smartest one among us and had helped each of us, to some degree, prepare for the exam. No one spoke about what he'd done to himself, though privately of course everybody wondered about it, including me. And even though the situation was so bizarre, given the nature of the injury and that it was self-inflicted, I asked Superintendent Lindquist the next day when I saw him out on the grounds if I could go visit Prosper in the hospital. He denied my request, though, and after a couple of days I heard that Prosper had been moved to a hospital in Seattle. I was mad and upset that I hadn't gotten the chance to see him and considered making a run for Seattle. I decided, however, to take a more conventional approach, thinking I might win the day that way, and took my grievance directly to Lindquist in his office.

"He's my best friend here," I said, standing in Lindquist's office with him sitting behind his desk. I had never owned up to this fact, not even to myself, and as soon as I said it I started bawling. I didn't care, though. I told Lindquist I wanted to visit my friend.

"I appreciate that, Avery."

This was one of Lindquist's expressions we'd all grown used to. If he told you he appreciated something—the kind of person you were, your point of view, the situation you were in, anything like that—you could count on him turning you down for whatever you were asking for. "You've proven your friendship to him time and again. But we can't allow it."

I got a grip on myself, wiped my tears, and said I knew how to get to Seattle on my own. "I'll be back in two days," I said. "I promise."

Lindquist said no and then explained that Prosper's parents weren't allowing any visitors. "They're very upset," he said, his hands clasped tightly in front of him on his desk. He didn't show it, but I could tell he was rather upset himself. "I'm truly sorry."

I left his office totally dejected, and that afternoon I slipped into a deep funk—first Brenda, and now Prosper, both gone. I sat behind the cottage by myself for hours, virtually catatonic, my back against the stone foundation. As I sat there, it finally and unambiguously came to me what Prosper—from stealing dresses and dyeing his pajamas pink to changing his name and ultimately castrating himself—had wanted all along. He wanted to be a girl. He put up with being called a homo and all manner of vicious slurs by the more macho and bullying kids at Fort Worden, but they had it all wrong, which is maybe why he always seemed impervious to the name-calling. I then began to wonder if someday I might be walking down the street, maybe in Seattle, maybe somewhere else, and recognize Prosper/Tracy. I would do my best, I told myself, to address him as Tracy, as awkward as the name change still felt to me. "Whatcha been up to, Tracy?" I would casually say. Maybe, too, Prosper/Tracy would be dressed as a woman—*presenting*, in today's discourse—and from then on I would simply begin to think of *him* as *her*. We would then reminisce about Fort Worden. I would tell her about what I was doing—whatever that happened to be—and she would tell me about her many successful business ventures. Then together we would look up Brenda, who would be doing some kind of community organizing in the city, and the three of us would go to Ivar's on the waterfront for lunch.

The next day I ducked out of the GED prep cottage and went over to my old cottage and peeled back the siding where Pete Munson had once hid his stash, hoping he'd left something behind after being busted. But there was nothing. Different scenarios once more began playing out in my head. I could go live with the old farmer in Chimacum and help him raise chickens, or hitch down to Seattle again and live in the NAMBSA house, or move in with Jay the hippie draft dodger in his apartment near the Seattle Center, or, reverting to my original plan, make my way back to the Enchanted Valley and live as a hermit in the chalet. I rejected the notion of letting myself be transferred to the new state facility for juvenile delinquency in Vancouver, since I'd had enough with being a ward of the state. I ruled out San Francisco after my mother wrote me a letter to tell me she was planning to sell the house in Spanaway and move to the Bay Area to be closer to her brother, my uncle. She said maybe I could visit.

So, about two weeks after the incident with Prosper—and about a month before the Treatment Center was scheduled to close its doors—I was again sitting behind the cottage when I just stood up and started walking. I'd escaped once before, but, to be honest, I'd been lucky. Geographically speaking, Port Townsend is not an easy place to sneak away from. It's on the Quimper Peninsula, which is located on the Olympic Peninsula—so a peninsula on a peninsula—which means there's a lot of water pinning the place in, and for this reason most Treatment Center residents, when they went rambling, were picked up before they got past the city limits.

The solution, however, was an easy one, and why it had never occurred to me or any of my fellow residents before was beyond comprehension. But now the idea hit me—and stuck—and I didn't need to go far to act on it, just down the bluff and up the beach toward the lighthouse to the boat dock where a number of Fort Worden employees, as well as townspeople, tied their skiffs and small boats. I just had to make sure no one was around and that I wouldn't be seen, which wasn't difficult since the morning fishermen had all returned by noon and the evening period for going back out didn't start for several hours.

Once on the beach, I lay down behind a large driftwood log about fifty yards from the dock and waited for the last person to leave. In the next half hour or so of lying in the sand, I realized this was my moment—one of those now or never situations. I also recognized that in some undefined way I was acting on behalf of the others as well—Prosper and Brenda, absolutely, but also all the other residents I'd come to know during my stay at Fort Worden—all of us hamstrung and confused and just longing to break free. To where or what, none of us could say. I knew that my own future was about to become more uncertain than ever, and that in all likelihood my friends' futures would remain forever obscure to me. But at this particular moment, seized by this singular intention, I had perfect clarity.

I watched as an old guy in rubber boots who'd been lingering about the dock finally picked up his white bucket and lumbered away. As soon as he drove off in his truck, I sprang to my feet, dusted the sand off my pants and jacket, and as casual as could be walked out onto the dock. Looking over the score of boats tied to the dock, I knew I didn't want anything with a motor on it since it would just run out of gas. So I picked a medium-sized aluminum rowboat that not only had oars and oarlocks in it, but also, beneath a tarp near the bow, a fishing rod and reel, tackle box, metal ice chest, and faded orange life vest. I stepped into the boat, untied the front and back ropes from the dock cleats, tossed the two bumpers into the stern, and pushed away from the dock. Once I got seated, set the oars, and dropped them in the water, I had to decide which way to go. Straight ahead would bring me across Admiralty Inlet to Whidbey Island. To the right would lead south toward Marrowstone Island. And to the left would take me north around Point Wilson and then westward into the Strait of Juan de Fuca.

Anyone growing up near Puget Sound hears about the fierce tides and treacherous currents that can mess with even the most experienced yachtsman. As I guided the rowboat toward the Point Wilson lighthouse, I didn't care squat about any of these dangers. I put my back into pulling on the oars and in no time had rowed around the point and into the strait, where immediately the wind picked up. The water turned choppy and spray came off the white caps. As I kept rowing, making my way farther into the strait, I could feel blisters rising on my palms and fingers. Eventually my shoulders started to ache, and there was a slight cramp in my right calf. But none of this mattered. I felt good, and I was going to keep rowing. I was going to row all the way to the Pacific Ocean.

And from there, who knew where to?

OUT OF SHELTON

The first time I had the dream I was in junior high. The next day, with it still fresh in my mind, adding an aery sense of wonder to my morning, I had an appointment with the guidance counselor, Mrs. Quiblat, who was from the Philippines and had two posters depicting the country on her office walls.

"Chris, what do you want to be?" Mrs. Quiblat asked after some small talk about my classes.

"I want to be a crooner," I said. "Just like Bing."

"Like who?"

"Bing Crosby."

"You mean the singer?"

I nodded.

She then asked me about my interest in singing and music, sidestepping the whole Bing Crosby question. So I told her about my dream. In it, I could fly if I sang. The more I sang, the higher I soared. Humming wouldn't do. Humming was like gliding and I would gradually lose altitude. In a pinch—"If I forgot the lyrics," I explained—I could always sing scat. Singing scat maintained lift.

Mrs. Quiblat said it was an interesting dream and suggested I join the school choir. I told her I would—and so I did, spending two years in the choir and learning many music fundamentals in that time. I then started to ask Mrs. Quiblat if she'd ever listened to Bing Crosby, but she interrupted me, saying she had another student to see. So I never got to tell her how my grandmother was practically grooming me to be the next Bing Crosby.

According to Grandma's plans, I would attend Gonzaga University in Spokane and be in the Glee Club—"just like Bing," a phrase I often heard from her. Grandma even took me to Spokane on a Bing Crosby pilgrimage when I was twelve. We stayed near the Gonzaga campus at a hotel on the Spokane River and visited the Crosbyana Room in the Crosby Student Center, a room next to the entrance filled with Bing Crosby paraphernalia—from his gold records to the many products he endorsed, the packaging of each emblazoned with his smiling, pipe-smoking image. Then we walked over to the Crosby Alumni House, the large Arts and Crafts–style bungalow on the edge of campus that Bing grew up in after his parents moved to Spokane from Tacoma, where he was born. There were photos of him on the walls at the Alumni House, and Grandma and I were allowed to wander through the upstairs, where we speculated on which bedrooms had belonged to which family members. We decided the small room with the sloped ceiling and two dormers facing south toward the Spokane River had been Bing's. It seemed like the kind of room where a precocious young boy, not unlike me, could dream away his time. Now it served as the office for the alumni magazine. The magazine's editor sat at her computer at a desk near one of the windows as my grandma and I contemplated where Bing's bed might have been. She smiled and confirmed that it had been Bing's room.

Before we left, the work-study student working as the receptionist downstairs gave us each a medallion embossed with Bing's profile, which Grandma said made the whole trip worthwhile. That night we went to a production of *Seven Brides for Seven Brothers* at what is now called the Bing Crosby Theater downtown, and the next day we drove home, a seven-hour drive, listening to Bing Crosby cassette tapes the whole way. Grandma loved whenever I sang along. "You sing just like him," she said encouragingly, and I believed her and dropped my twelve-year-old voice to sound even more like his. I sang duets with Bing across the wheat fields of eastern Washington, the scablands of central Washington, up and over the Cascade Mountains, past the gray dome of the state capitol building in Olympia, and up the eastern side of the Olympic Peninsula, past Eld Inlet and Totten Inlet, all the way to our house in the old mill town of Shelton.

I AM WHO I am in large part because of my grandmother. She raised me after my mother died in childbirth. *Complications* was all I was ever told, though there was a lawsuit against the hospital and my father received a sizeable settlement, which the judge placed in a trust for my care and maintenance. After just six months, Child Protective Services came to the house, my derelict father disappeared, and the same judge granted my grandmother custody of me and appointed her my trustee. I always knew if I wanted to I could track down the public records for all this—find out exactly why my mother died, why my father was deemed legally negligent, and so on—but I've never really wanted to. You could say I prefer to dream my troubles away. And that, right there, has been my problem.

So Grandma raised me, but she had a big assist from Bing Crosby.

When I think of all those teenage girls down through the ages shriek-ing, pulling their hair, and fainting over the likes of Elvis, the Beatles, David Cassidy, Justin Bieber, One Direction, whoever, I can't help but think how they have nothing on my grandmother and her devotion to Bing. Just ask my Uncle Lillis.

"*Please,*" he implored the first time I brought the subject up with him when I was in my twenties, not long after Grandma died. "It was rough, all that Bing Crosby crapola."

Uncle Lillis was a marine. He'd fought in the rice paddies and jun-gles of Vietnam. The back window of the Super Duty Crew Cab on his F-350 has two small round stickers on it: one the insignia of the United States Marine Corps, the other the emblem of the National Rifle Association. "Lillis," by the way, was Bing's middle name. His full name was Harry Lillis Crosby.

"I don't know how I survived." He wasn't talking about Vietnam; he was talking about my grandmother's obsession with Bing Crosby. "And poor Dad had it worse than me. And now you, Chris. Look what she's done to you."

It's true that, like my dearly departed grandmother, I have an uncommon love of Bing Crosby. My earliest memory is of Grandma patting me dry with a towel after my nightly bath, dusting my toddler body with baby powder, putting me in flannel pajamas still warm from the clothes rack near the wood-burning stove, and softly trilling "*Too-Ra-Loo-Ra-Loo-Ral.*" So Uncle Lillis was right: I owed my attach-ment to Bing to my grandmother. But unlike Uncle Lillis, who shut the whole Bing business down early in his life, my relationship to the crooner has been more involved—and more complicated.

"Just try not to do so much singing on the job," he told me after I started working at the mill when I was still in high school.

Uncle Lillis took over the mill from Granddad when he died twen-ty-two years ago, and despite the near-collapse of the timber industry on the Olympic Peninsula in recent decades, he's managed to build up the business. For me, the benefit of being part of a family busi-ness—and having such an understanding uncle—has always been having a job to fall back on. What's more, he never got on my case about my Bing Crosby obsession. And even more important, he and my Aunt Sherrie always adored Lencie and her son, Rory, accepting them as family right from the start.

I'VE KNOWN LENCIE SINCE Shelton High School, but that's not when we hooked up. While we were friendly in school, we never hung out. Mainly we were friendly because we were both mildly freakish. I liked to slick my hair back with Brylcreem and wear a cardigan sweater or sometimes a plaid sport jacket over my button-down white shirts. I'd get called a fag and after each instance reassure myself that I was no more gay than Bing, who had six children with two wives. Lencie, who was mildly cross-eyed in one eye, was spared ridicule because she was such a nice, smart girl who everyone liked—and because, quite honestly, her cross-eye made her look adorable! I might not have fallen so gaga in love with her had both eyes been looking straight ahead. But the asymmetry from the slight inward turn of her right eye made her dimpled, girl-next-door face that much cuter. It made her seem more trustworthy, like a person could really confide in her and she'd listen. And like Uncle Lillis, she accepted me for who I was—Bing and all. That is, until the obsession became too much even for her.

The problem was never really with Bing, though. The problem was me. Or perhaps more accurately, the problem was my grandmother. According to Uncle Lillis, Grandma played her old vinyl recordings of Bing to me every day while I was in my mother's womb, ignoring my mother who begged her to please stop. Because my mother lived with my grandparents during her pregnancy, my grandmother had unlimited access to me in utero. My father was who knows where most of this time, and so Grandma just wrote off her deadbeat son-in-law, who eventually was never seen or heard from again. My birth came five years after Bing dropped dead of a heart attack in 1977 on a golf course in Spain. And my grandmother, though a church-going woman, apparently believed I was the reincarnation of the great crooner. The umbilical cord had hardly been snipped and my bottom slapped and my first cries cried before my grandmother was exclaiming that my big elfish ears and thin hair looked just like Bing's. In later years, she always said the trill of my infant's wail would slide right down into that deep vocal valley where Bing's melodic intonations were their richest.

"I wish I could have met her," Lencie said.

It had been ten years since Grandma's passing. Lencie and I were in a room at the City Center Motel in Shelton. We'd just had sex for the second time, the first being the night before after we checked in. Now we were lying between the sheets in a post-coital cuddle watching

Dr. Phil on morning TV. He was speaking to a group of older women who were all admitted "hover-grannies," which brought up the topic of my grandmother.

"She would have liked you," I said.

"Was she really like these ladies? They seem insufferable."

Even in high school I admired Lencie's vocabulary, which was always more grown-up than anyone else's. No one else I knew used the word *insufferable*.

"She was sufferable," I replied. "In some ways, she was the perfect grandmother."

"Do you miss her?"

"Sometimes," I said, trying to be honest. I unconsciously started humming the melody to "Galway Bay," one of Grandma's favorites. Her father had come from Ireland, so she had a special love of Bing's Irish songs.

Lencie slapped my arm. "Stop that humming," she said. She then straddled my waist and looked down at me with that sweet cross-eyed look of hers, her hair falling softly over the sides of her face and brushing the top of her small breasts. She ran both her hands through my hair.

"I like your hair," she said. "The color and all."

It was brown and straight—quite ordinary.

"You know I'm going bald," I said.

"You look like Prince William. He's your age and he's going bald too. It doesn't seem to bother Kate Middleton any."

"Who?" I said. I then grabbed her butt, and as Lencie began undulating her hips over me, I closed my eyes.

An hour later, after showering together—and just before the noon checkout time—we left the motel and went to the Dairy Queen a few blocks down for lunch. After my night with Lencie, Shelton looked like a brand new town. I was reminded of the romantic mountain village where Bing falls in love with the exotic Franciska Gaal in *Paris Honeymoon*. We ate in a booth at Dairy Queen, and then Lencie said she had to pick up Rory at her mother's house. As for me, it was my day off from the mill, so I was free as a jaybird. As we walked back out to the parking lot, I said I'd call her later and crooned, *"Da da dee, da da dee dee,"* and she smiled and gave me a kiss.

L&H PRECISION LUMBER HAS been operating since the end of World War II. That's when Granddad, home from the war, acquired a twenty-five-acre lot just outside of Shelton, built a large shed on it, placed a 1936 Newman bandsaw and planer in said shed, and began supplying structural lumber to the postwar housing boom. Uncle Lillis keeps the Newman bandsaw and planer in the original shed and sometimes starts them up for old times' sake. They can still do the job, though not half as efficiently as the modern machinery, much of which is laser-guided and computerized and has virtually made the sawyers of old obsolete.

"Are you going to work today or you just going to sing some more of your pretty songs?" said Roger, the log yard supervisor. "We need you on the wheel loader."

I'd already figured out as much when I drove into the yard. A load of Doug fir—solid second-growth sawtimber—had been dropped in the log yard from three trailers the day before and needed to be moved to the scaling bay.

"I want you to scale and grade 'em and haul 'em to the log deck," Roger went on. "We need 250,000 board feet cut by Saturday."

Roger had been with L&H Precision Lumber for twenty-five years. He was also a Vietnam veteran and, according to my uncle, the best journeyman millwright on the peninsula. His white beard made him look like the kindly sort, a Burl Ives–type, yet he was a mean and bitter sonofabitch. His red face and beer gut the size of a half round from a tree trunk gave away the fact that he drank a half rack of Hamm's every night after work. He and I didn't always get along, but I did what he told me to do and he put up with me because I was the boss's nephew. He also put up with me because he knew I could get the job done. I had practically grown up at the mill and knew the operation inside and out. Plus, I had my heavy equipment license from the local community college, where I'd also picked up a general associate's degree right out of high school. I could operate every piece of equipment in the yard, from wheel loader to knuckle boom, canter saw to drum dryer. There was also the fact that I loved the work. It was semiskilled labor, and it was satisfying. I like to think my granddad would be proud to see me doing it.

"I'm on it," I called back to him, donning my orange vest and yellow hard hat and walking through the mud toward the idling wheel loader.

Roger squinted at me, spat on the ground, and walked off toward the pile of culls at the back of the yard.

In the cab of the wheel loader, I got the heater going to take off the morning chill, checked the hydraulics, maneuvered the front fork and clamp, and drove over to the log yard.

A log yard, it shouldn't need to be said, is a dangerous place, and taking shortcuts or horsing around can get you killed. So even with a rush job hanging over our heads, Uncle Lillis insisted his workers go slow and do the job right, which was why the safety record at L&H was so good and the inspectors from Labor and Industries loved Lillis. So working slowly but steadily I moved the logs to the scaling bay. Balance and maneuvering are everything in hauling logs from one end of a yard to another, and once I had the fork and clamp around half a dozen logs, they weren't going anywhere I didn't want them to. The whole job took over two hours, and when I was done, I parked the wheel loader and headed into the breakroom where there was always a large box of maple bars and apple fritters from the local Safeway next to the coffeemaker. There was also usually someone hanging around who would ask me to sing—just like in all of Bing's movies, where he's always the modest, unobtrusive fellow, happy to stay out of the limelight until someone insists he give the gang a song.

My cousin Jennifer, who was working on her MBA with an emphasis in environmental economics at UW Tacoma, was on spring break, which meant she was helping out in the front office, processing invoices and purchase orders while Carli, our bookkeeper and all-around office manager, took the week off. Jennifer always wanted a song. During the summer when she'd been working in the office full time, she and I worked up a few duets modeled after the songs Bing sang with the Andrews Sisters. We sang them only if no one else was in the office or break room. Uncle Lillis, I knew, would rather see me sell meth to his daughter than lure her into singing Bing Crosby duets.

Jennifer looked up from the computer monitor on the desk where she sat. Charley and Ed were in the breakroom yukking it up over something or another. Charley liked to remind me how he once dated my mother in high school. Ed was a Quinault Indian, and he'd been working at the mill almost as long as Roger had.

"What's with those guys?" I asked her, taking off my hard hat.

"You should know better," she said. "A small town like this." She took a drink from the 24-ounce plastic cup of Diet Pepsi that she always had with her. She was a little overweight—like our grandmother had been—but pretty, with the silkiest, shimmery-est long brown hair you've ever seen. She would swing around on the office swivel chair and, in a single fluid motion, send her hair over one shoulder like in a shampoo commercial. When I didn't reply, not knowing what she meant, she put her cup down and looked me dead on. "Lencie Howell? The City Center Motel? I would think you could do better."

"Better how?" I asked. "The hotel or Lencie?"

"The hotel, you idiot. Lencie's great. I love Lencie. You do know she has a kid?"

"Yes."

"And her ex is an asshole?"

"Yes."

"Okay then," she said. "I just wanted to make sure. But don't expect to keep your private life private if you're going to conduct it so openly in a burg like this. I swear, did you just get off the boat?"

I went into the breakroom, took a maple bar from the box, and told Charley and Ed to shut the fuck up.

"Heya," Ed said, "I see how they've got free internet now at the City Center Motel."

"Yeah, it's a classy place all right," said Charley.

I dropped my head in exasperation and walked back to the front office. I wasn't really that bothered. So what if the whole town knew I'd hooked up with Lencie? She was a fine person, and it wasn't like we were kids fresh out of high school anymore.

Jennifer was back at her computer. She took a sip of pop and without looking up said, "I need to get the estimates for those three loads to the distributor by this afternoon."

"I'm going to scale and grade them right now," I said. I took one bite of the maple bar and tossed the rest in the trash. "Where's Uncle Lillis?" I asked as soon as I heard Charley and Ed leave the break room. I watched out the front window as they walked across the yard to the circle mill, where the logs would go after I scaled them to determine the precise board feet each would give. I took pride in being an exact and honest scaler, keeping the mill owner (Uncle Lillis), the contractor

234 | PETER DONAHUE

(the logging company), and the distributor (the lumber wholesalers) happy with my estimates.

"He went up to Port Townsend to meet someone at Zellerbach."

I waited.

Jennifer made a few more rapid keystrokes on the keyboard and then swung about, throwing her hair over her shoulder. "Sing me a song," she said, giving me a silly smile.

"Aw, I don't know if I should. You see, I have a lot of work to do," I said. It could have been a line from a dozen different Bing movies.

"Oh, come on."

"Well, all right."

I cleared my throat and started slow, with scat—"De dee da boo"— to warm up the pipes and make like I was thinking of just the right number to sing. When you don't have a band to back you up, a few notes of scat can serve as well as a trumpet for your lead-in. Then I gave Jennifer the irresistible droopy-eyed Bing look and started singing...

It was a lucky April shower,
It was the most convenient door.
I found a million dollar baby
In a five and ten cent store.
The rain continued for an hour,
I hung around for three or four.
Around a million dollar baby
In a five and ten cent store.

I threw in a little whistling between the lyrics and then sat on the corner of the desk and resumed singing...

Incidentally,
If you should run into a shower,
Oh, step inside my cottage door,
And meet my million dollar baby
From the five and ten cent store.

...and closing with some more scat, I picked up Jennifer's hand and gave it a kiss.

She applauded, then glanced about the office to see that no one was around, and giving me a conspiratorial look said, "Let's do one together."

"How about 'Stardust'?" I suggested without hesitation, and launched right into the torch song, letting Jennifer chime in on the refrain.

It was a wonderful duet, and we both laughed when we were done.

"You've got a nice singing voice, kid," I told her. I put my hard hat back on and opened the door.

"I hope it works out for you and Lencie," she said. She then reached for a nail file on her desk. "Remember, Chris, I need those numbers by this afternoon."

I left the office with a small notepad and pencil, retrieved my fifty-foot tape measure, scaling stick, and hatchet from the large tool shed next to the office building, and headed back to the scaling bay to look for knot clusters and checks and calculate volumetric units. Even today, in 2015, with lasers and computers and magnetized scales, it still takes someone like me with a well-trained eye and a keen appreciation for quality lumber to properly size up a load of logs.

WHEN I THINK WHAT it must have been like in Shelton in the '30s and '40s when my grandmother was young, I can imagine how she must have felt when she first heard Bing Crosby sing. At the start of the twentieth century, the town had a dozen mills, dominated (then as now) by Simpson Timber. The town was the heart of the Sawdust Empire. The stands of fir, hemlock, cedar, and spruce were still abundant. The national economy was healthy in the decade following the first World War, and the mills operated around the clock, coating every surface within a ten-mile radius with coal soot and sawdust. Company shacks lined the tideflats, while farther up the hill, company managers and owners built their large houses and sent their children off to college in California. When the Great Depression hit, nearly all the mills closed—which in some ways was just as well, since by then all the surrounding hills had been stripped of their timber and were nothing more than what Granddad called "stump ranches"—and Shelton got hit hard.

So when my grandmother tuned in to the radio station out of Seattle and heard Bing singing, what dreamy wonder his deep melodious voice must have cast over her glum soul in that damp, claustrophobic corner of the Olympic Peninsula. Add to this having to see her husband—my grandfather—go off to war a year after they'd been married. She became pregnant with my Uncle Lillis during his only leave before shipping off for the Pacific, so it's easy to see how Bing became such a great source of solace for her. She probably felt he was singing just for her, just as millions of young women across America felt, and whenever a Bing Crosby movie happened to come to the only movie house in town, she probably felt as if he'd come all the way to Shelton just to serenade her. So when people my age and younger complain about what a drab place Shelton is to live in and make plans to move to Seattle or Portland or San Francisco—they have no idea how good they have it. When I was born in the Mason County General Hospital, the town was still in the dumps from the downturn in the economy in the '70s, but it was nothing compared to my grandmother's day. By the time I was growing up in Shelton, the air was clean, the clear-cut tracts had long ago been reforested, and even the oyster beds in Oak Bay were making a comeback after being decimated by decades of discharge from the old pulp mill.

Lencie always said she liked Shelton, and unlike many people we knew, she never felt the need to escape and live elsewhere. I liked Shelton too—and still do. It was where we both grew up, where we both had family, the town we knew better than any other, the place that *unequivocally*—one of Lencie's words—felt like home.

We went slow our first few months together. Her divorce wasn't settled yet, and we wanted time for her son, Rory, to get to know me. He liked to hear me sing, so we were off to a good start. Plus he was an adorable kid. Her ex, on the other hand, as my cousin Jennifer had pointed out, was a real asshole. When I found out from Lencie that he was blackmailing her, threatening to post photos of her naked on the internet unless she agreed to take less than half of what she was asking for in spousal maintenance as part of the divorce, I decided to go see my friend Stiles for some legal advice.

Stiles had been a defense attorney in Seattle before being disbarred after it was discovered he'd been sleeping with the district judge presiding over several of his cases. "Talk about ex parte communication," he said one time when I asked him about it. "The poor girl got kicked off the bench."

He was a few years older than Lencie and me, but we both remembered him from high school where he'd been famous for producing zines by the dozens, a new one every week. He must have socked away a chunk of change from practicing law in Seattle because he didn't work or have any apparent income. Of course, one didn't need much to live in Shelton, and Stiles certainly lived modestly.

"Funny finding you here," I said when I entered Annabelle's Tea Room and Consignment Shoppe on Railroad Avenue. He spent a lot of his time at Annabelle's, preferring it to the local Starbucks. Annabelle's had Wi-Fi and comfortable old couches, so with his laptop at the ready, it became his de facto office. "Can I take a seat?" I asked.

"Take a seat," he answered, barely glancing up. He epitomized hipster chic in his vintage bowling shirt, straw fedora, and soul patch.

"What's up?" I said. I looked about the shoppe at the clutter of vintage clothing, costume jewelry, antique furnishings, candle sticks, tea sets, crocheted items, and dusty clothbound books.

"Just a second." His fingers flew across the keyboard of his laptop. "I'm posting."

"What about?"

He didn't respond, but just kept typing, then stopped, looked at what he'd written, hit the enter key, and pulled the screen down.

"What was it you asked?" he said.

"What you were posting."

"You don't want to know."

He was probably right. Stiles maintained several blogs and websites on top of his multiple Facebook and Twitter accounts, none of which I bothered to friend or follow. There was his *Stylin' with Stiles*, a kind of TMZ fashion / celebrity gossip blog; *Bloozer*, his blog on the alternative music scene in the Northwest; *Legally Yours*, his legal advice blog; and *AngelCloud*, his softcore porn blog, maintained under the nom de internet "Fuller Diaz," where he reviewed softcore sites for the discriminating web surfer.

I explained Lencie's situation to him, and his response was, "Call the sheriff. It's extortion, case closed. Who's her attorney?"

"She doesn't have one. Him either."

"They're pro se? That's absurd. Everyone loses." Then he asked, "Have you seen the photos?"

Coming from anyone but Stiles, I would have been offended by the question. But Stiles, on point of principle, refused to exercise tact—ever.

"No," I answered. "Does it matter?"

He looked at me like I was an idiot.

"Let's put it this way," I said, "she told me they go beyond the usual yearbook portrait."

He tore off a corner of the scone on the plate in front of him, popped it into his mouth, and washed it down with a swig of tea.

"I've never seen a cross-eyed girl pose before," he said. He looked out the plate glass window as his brain's algorithms searched his internal database for a matching thumbnail image. "No Results Found," he said. "And I bet she has a fantastic body." He looked to me for confirmation.

"She does," I said. I couldn't hide my pride. "She *absolutely* does."

Changing his tone, he asked, "The ex. Who's he?"

I told him how the ex worked at the prison—excuse me, "Washington Corrections Center," one of the town's largest employers—and that he lived out on the Olympic Highway. Then he said he thought he knew who he was, had seen him a few times in the taverns around town.

"A real shit, as I recall," he said. "How'd a nice girl like her get tangled up with trash like that?"

"She was young."

"Yeah, weren't we all once?"

At thirty-one, or even now at thirty-three, I liked to think of myself as still fairly young—pre-early middle age. Of course, by the time he was my age, Bing already had his first record deal, so I had some catching up to do.

"Like I said," Stiles went on. "Call the sheriff. I didn't vote for him, but he's all right. If your girl doesn't want the sheriff involved, she should get a lawyer and sue her ex's ass. I recommend Kirchner. She's fresh out of law school and still hardworking. Her office is on Alder. And if that doesn't work, we could always go over and rough him up."

I thanked him, not taking this last suggestion seriously, and pushed myself up from the sofa. I went to the front counter, bought a chocolate-dipped biscotti and a large drip coffee to go, and put a dollar in the tip jar.

"Hey, Bing," Stiles called out as I opened the door. He was the only one who called me that—half-mockingly, of course. "You know where you should go with your shtick? Seriously? You want to know?"

It was impossible to anticipate what Stiles was going to come up with next, and telling him no was useless, so I just said, "Sure. Where?" "Japan. You should go to Japan. I was reading they love Bing Crosby over there. You could do an act. They're into all kinds of crazy shit over there. We have no clue."

I KNEW ALL ABOUT the Japanese fascination with Bing. I knew because several dozen Japanese Bing Crosby fans followed me on my own Facebook page called *Bustin' out with Bing*. They commented on the page regularly. I had an open invitation to visit my Japanese friends—and even perform for them. One follower offered to arrange a tour for me of karaoke clubs from Seagaia to Sapporo. He'd shared my YouTube video (of me singing Bing, of course) with his friends, who all loved it. He assured me people would come to see me. Then I had to take the page down because of licensing and proprietary issues with the Crosby estate. It took some doing to convince the estate I was sincere in my fandom, that my page wasn't some kind of strange satire, and that I was actually paying homage to a man I truly admired. Eventually they gave me their permission and I put the page back up.

When I wasn't preoccupying myself with Bing, though, I was thinking of Lencie and the dilemma she was in with her ex. She wasn't the confrontational sort, so she didn't want to take the matter of her ex and the photos to the sheriff. Who could blame her? Word would have gotten all over town. She did see the attorney Stiles recommended, however, and the attorney told the ex to back off his attempts to blackmail her. But then he told Lencie he might just post the photos anyway, regardless of the divorce settlement, saying it was freedom of speech and there was nothing she could do about it. When I checked this out with Stiles, he affirmed the guy's position.

"Freedom of speech and net neutrality are the hallmarks of the internet," he said. "You've seen all the sex tapes—Kim Kardashian, Paris Hilton, et cetera, et cetera—from years back, right? Same deal. There's talk in the legislature about passing a 'revenge porn' law, but the First Amendment folks keep blocking it."

The whole situation brought Lencie to tears every time I saw her. She worried that if the photos got out, CPS might take Rory from her. I assured her that would never happen. Then she started talking about moving. But when I asked her where, she couldn't say. "Maybe Port Angeles," she said, "Or Tacoma. I don't know."

"Bing's birthplace," I said with a laugh.

"Port Angeles?"

"No, Tacoma," I replied. She looked at me in exasperation.

We sat in our usual booth at the Dairy Queen and shared a large order of fries. Lencie loved Dairy Queen. She'd worked there throughout high school, mastering the art of the dip cone.

"It's all in the wrist," she said once. So we went to DQ two or three times a week.

I felt like an idiot for my remark, and said, "Maybe we could move to Seattle."

Lencie had just plunged a fry into the little paper container of ketchup in front of her. She left it dangling in the ketchup and wiped her fingers on a napkin. Then she put both elbows on the table and rested her head in her hands. I looked at the top of her head, her hair pulled back into a ponytail and held with a scrunchie.

"I'm sorry," I said.

She inhaled through her nose and breathed out slowly through her mouth—a sigh for the ages—then raised her head and looked at me across the table. In the last two months she'd been doing special therapy for her cross-eye, trying to realign it, straighten it out, and the difference was apparent. Instead of her left eye looking at you while the right eye looked across the bridge of her nose, now both eyes looked at you, just from different angles.

"It's not that easy," she said. "I have a child. And his father's such an asshole, I don't know if he would let me move."

"I care more about Rory than he does," I told her. She nodded, knowing this was probably true. "You'll get custody and then you can take him wherever you want."

"Maybe," she said, and then looked at me. "Are you ready to take care of a child?"

I'd already considered the prospect at some length, ever since that first night with Lencie in the City Center Motel.

"Yes, I am," I said—and meant it.

"He really loves you, you know," she told me and lowered her chin, still looking at me.

She was tearing up.

"I love him too," I said. I started to tear up too.

We finished the fries in silence. Then we each ordered a Blizzard and started making plans to move to Seattle. She would apply to a dental hygiene program, something she'd wanted to do for a long time, and I would try to make a go of it with my singing, something I'd wanted to do for a long time as well.

OVER THE NEXT TWO months Lencie and I took a couple of exploratory trips to Seattle to check out neighborhoods and rental houses. The situation with her ex, though, was bothering me more by this point than it seemed to be her. Maybe it had to do with my manhood and the new role I would be taking on with respect to Lencie and her son. In any case, I began to feel like a weenie for just packing up and leaving town without trying to settle the matter first. I had to confront the ex about the photographs. So a week before we were set to rent a U-Haul truck and move, I talked Stiles into driving out to the ex's house with me to see if we could reason with him.

"What do you need me along for?" Stiles wanted to know. He sometimes reminded me of Bob Hope, Bing's impossibly feckless sidekick in all those road movies they did together. After all, the idea of confronting the ex—even roughing him up some—had been Stiles's originally. "Especially if you're just going to *reason* with him."

"Because," I said, trying to think of why I needed him along, "you can get all lawyerly on his ass. Put the fear of the judicial system in him." This tactic hadn't worked with the attorney Lencie hired—at $250 an hour, which her parents paid—but, of course, Stiles had a different approach to the law than most attorneys.

The prospect of acting as my legal eagle appealed to him, and so the next afternoon I picked him up at Annabelle's at 3:00, the time each weekday when a group of Shelton ladies calling themselves Annabelle's Belles came into the shoppe for the proprietress's High Tea Special.

We drove out on the Olympic Highway looking for the place where Lencie and her son used to live. It was a trailer home set back from the road. Lencie's ex had built a large shed roof over it, and to one side of it there was a pole shed with maybe four cords of fire wood stacked underneath. Toward the back of the lot was parked a white F-150 pickup.

"The rig *de rigueur* of the lower peninsula," Stiles said, looking at the vehicle.

We agreed we would simply go to the door and I would politely ask Lencie's ex, as the decent thing to do for the mother of his son, to delete the photos of her. I didn't know if he would or not, and it really didn't matter. Mostly I wanted him to get the message he couldn't keep threatening to post them on the internet.

Yet when Stiles and I walked up to the trailer and I knocked on the aluminum door, there was no answer. After two more tries, it became obvious he wasn't inside.

"Maybe the truck's not his only vehicle," said Stiles.

I shrugged. "Maybe."

Then Stiles reached around me and said, "Hey, looky." He was holding the doorknob with the door slightly ajar. "It's open."

"Forget it, Stiles," I said, ready to leave.

"Just go in and delete the files."

"I'm not going in there," I said. "Maybe he's asleep. Next to his shotgun. And his pit bull."

"Don't be a pussy," he said. "Do you want to help your lady or don't you?"

I looked about the property. The ex could be anywhere. But then again, Stiles was absolutely right. I was there to help Lencie out. So I asked myself, *What would Bing do?* It was something I'd started doing a while back whenever I was faced with difficult decisions. *WWBD?* It was a joke, of course, but there was something to it, since Bing almost always did the right thing.

"Stop wasting time," Stiles said. "I'll keep a lookout."

Again, he sounded a lot like Bob Hope.

"Okay," I said and pushed the door open enough to see in.

I was already sweating, and hardly breathing, and started humming "Pennies from Heaven" to calm my nerves. Though not a lawyer like Stiles, I was pretty sure this was breaking and entering—a goddamn felony. I stepped inside.

"Hello?" I called out. "Anyone home? Lencie asked me to come by and pick up a few things."

The inside of the trailer looked about how you might expect: a worn couch, a scratched coffee table, and a Seahawks pennant on the wall. There was also a massive flat screen TV flanked by three-foot-tall speakers, probably from the Aaron's rental center in town.

"Look," Stiles said. He was standing right behind me. "The guy's got the new Xbox One."

I didn't care that Stiles was no longer keeping a lookout because, as I peered across the room, I saw a laptop on the counter of the kitchen island. I wasn't about to sit down on one of the counter stools and try to log on to the guy's computer, so I pulled the cord from the socket with one hand and scooped up the laptop with the other and said, "Let's go."

Stiles gave me a look of astonishment, a look I'd never seen on the uber-cool hipster's face, and then he smirked. "Right on," he said, and in the next instant he had the Xbox in one hand and the controller in the other. We then dashed for the door.

We got in the car and tore out of the drive, the back wheels spitting gravel, and as we sped down the Olympic Highway, Stiles kept twisting about to look through the back window. He didn't settle down until we bounced over the railroad tracks that separated downtown Shelton from its outskirts. I dropped him off at Annabelle's, but not before first slipping the Xbox and controller into a couple of plastic bags that were on the floor of the backseat.

"Call me if you need help getting into his computer," he said, leaning over the driver side. He then slapped the hood of the car as if we were in some kind of '80s cop show and strolled into the Tea Room.

As I turned the corner, I became excited—in my own devious way—to get home and boot up the ex's laptop.

At the time, I lived in the small apartment above the two-car garage adjacent to my grandmother's house where my Uncle Lillis and Aunt Sherrie resided. I had a rent-free arrangement and paid only utilities, which came to about $120 a month excluding internet since I could pick up the wireless signal from their house. In the two-and-a-half years I'd been living there and working for my uncle at the mill, I'd been able to put aside a good portion of my paycheck each month, resulting in a sizeable nest egg to get me and Lencie and Rory started in Seattle.

I'd fixed the place up nicely too, especially the kitchen, since I liked to cook. About once a month I would log on to the Williams-Sonoma website and order a new pot, utensil, or small appliance, such as the automatic bread maker or saltless ice cream churn. The rest of the apartment was comfortable as well, with the matching armchair and couch Aunt Sherrie had given me when she and Uncle Lillis bought a whole new living room suite for the main house. I also kept the apartment tidy, knowing Grandma would never have tolerated a slob living there.

Once I got back, I didn't waste any time. I grabbed a bottle of beer from the fridge, plugged the power cord in, and sat down in the armchair with the laptop. It was a PC and wasn't password protected, so in a few moments the background image of Lencie's ex in camo holding a rifle and lifting the head of an eight-point buck appeared on the screen. I went straight to the pictures folders to search for the photos of Lencie. There were more than I'd expected, a couple dozen at least, some racier than others but nothing too weird or raunchy. They were just nudie shots, hardly worse than what you would find in the pages of *Maxim* or the *Sports Illustrated Swimsuit Issue*—though Lencie was not nearly as buxom as those models. I thought for an instant of saving them on my flash drive but then thought better of it and dragged them all over to the recycle bin and emptied it. Task complete.

I felt good. I'd done right by my "lady," as Stiles called her. I took a couple swigs of beer and then started snooping through the rest of the files on the ex's computer. There were only a few Word documents. They appeared to come from classes he'd taken at one point at Olympic College a year ago when, as Lencie had told me, he'd tried to get into the state trooper training academy. One of the papers, from a psychology class, described different kinds of phobias and mental disorders. Another, with the file name "shittiest essay ever written," was about how he learned to change the gaskets on a truck engine. I clicked on the music folder, but there were only the sample songs that come with the computer. Then I clicked on the videos folder and saw where the ex's real interests lay. He had five separate folders labeled "Anal," "Facial," "DP," "Lesbo," and "Others." Each had a dozen or more video files in it, and as I clicked on one, I could hear Grandma chastising me when I was sixteen—long before the boom in online porn—after she'd discovered a *Penthouse* magazine stashed beneath my bed. The words she used—*smut, filth, trash*—wouldn't do justice to the eighteen-minute video I proceeded to watch on the ex's computer. I'd clicked on a few porn sites on my own computer in the past—who hasn't?—but I always felt creepy about it, and I certainly never typed in my credit card number to view more. When Grandma found the *Penthouse*, she said, "A real man doesn't need that kind of filth, Christopher. It makes him ugly."

It certainly wouldn't be in character for a suave and easygoing fellow like Bing Crosby. So I pressed my finger on the power button and forced the computer to shut down. Then I put it in a brown paper grocery bag and drove halfway to Olympia with the windows rolled down, letting the cold air clear my head of the images of magnified genitalia, and threw the laptop into a dumpster behind a roadside bar and grill.

OVER THE NEXT FEW days I kept wondering whether Lencie had watched all those videos or whether they were just the ex's dirty little secret. There was obviously a link between his porn collection and the nude photos of Lencie. Maybe he'd wanted her to make a sex tape and that's where she drew the line. I could never bring myself to ask her, and just as well. We had our own thing now. The sex was great—we both said so—and we would soon be moving to Seattle.

When I let Uncle Lillis and Aunt Sherrie know Lencie and I would be leaving at the end of July, they were understanding.

"Lencie and her family are nice people," said Aunt Sherrie.

"You always have a job at the mill," added Uncle Lillis. "When you're done with Seattle, that is."

He hated the city. He'd gone to Seattle twice in his entire life—once when my grandparents took him and my mother to the '62 World's Fair, and again a couple decades later when he took Sherrie, his fiancée at the time, to a Mariners game at the Kingdome. He didn't like to leave the Olympic Peninsula, much less venture into the metropolitan corridor that stretched from Olympia to Everett. So I knew better than to suggest that he and Aunt Sherrie could come visit us once we got settled in Seattle. I knew it would never happen.

"You'll come home for Thanksgiving and Christmas, right?" asked Aunt Sherrie.

"Of course," I said. And I meant it—because, truly, a person couldn't ask for a better aunt and uncle than I had in Aunt Sherrie and Uncle Lillis.

Lencie's parents were another story. They didn't like me, and they especially didn't like the fact that Lencie was moving with me to Seattle before her divorce was final. I suppose I can understand how they felt. Their daughter was just extricating herself from one really bad relationship, and they didn't want her jumping into another. *Take your time*, they probably told her, even though it had been a year and two months since she'd moved out of the trailer on the Olympic Highway and back into their house. *You can stay here as long as you like*, I could hear her mother, a substitute teacher at the middle school for the past twenty-five years, saying to her. *We love having Rory and you with us.*

I can also imagine Lencie cringing at these words and wondering if she would ever have a life of her own again.

Lencie's parents, furthermore, could not comprehend my passion for Bing Crosby. "I don't get it," was all her father said when I tried to explain Bing's appeal.

"I like other singers too," I tried to say, but then I couldn't think of any off the top of my head. The fact was, I didn't listen to much music, especially contemporary music. I had Grandma's old LPs and cassette tapes of Bing, and I'd downloaded most of his discography from iTunes, and that was almost all I listened to. Stiles once burned a CD of Jim Reeves, the classic country-western singer, for me to listen to. "Gentleman Jim," he said. "You'll like him." So I listened to the CD, kind of got into two songs—"Four Walls" and "He'll Have to Go"—and then went back to listening to Bing.

"I like Jim Reeves," I told Lencie's father, but he didn't know who he was. Then when Lencie talked me into singing a Bing number for her father, I chose Bing's one Seattle song, "Black Ball Ferry Line," and before I was halfway through, he was looking at me like I was the sorriest, most pathetic excuse for a person he'd ever laid eyes on. Lencie's mother, meanwhile, remained neutral on the whole matter of my preoccupation with Bing Crosby.

Rory, on the other hand, at the precocious age of four, loved whenever I sang to him from the Bing songbook. He couldn't get enough. I would sing "You Are My Sunshine" every time I saw him, though his favorite tune, bar none, was "Pistol Packin' Momma." He started to learn the lyrics and sing along with me, and I liked to imagine him returning to his grandparents' house, climbing onto his granddad's lap, and crooning a few Bing numbers to the old grouch.

After two more weekend trips to Seattle, Lencie and I found a rental in the Greenwood neighborhood, a two-bedroom, one-bath house shoehorned between two other squat houses. The rent was doable, and the location was relatively convenient. Greenwood Elementary School and Greenwood Park were nearby, and one transfer on the bus would get Lencie to and from Seattle Central Community College on Capitol Hill, where she'd applied and been accepted into the dental hygiene program. As for myself, I still wasn't sure what I would be doing in Seattle. I'd decided that somehow, someway, I wanted to start performing to see if I could launch a singing career for myself. But that's all I knew.

In the weeks before our departure from Shelton, I saw Stiles only once. He'd rigged up the Xbox One he'd stolen from Lencie's ex, started playing a *Call of Duty* game, and couldn't stop. He no longer went to Annabelle's Tea Room and was not only neglecting his Facebook, Twitter, and other online obligations, failing to post and update and whatnot, but was letting himself go physically as well. When I saw him coming out of the corner Chevron with a twelve-pack of Hefeweizen under his arm, I honked and pulled up to him. He was rumpled and red-eyed and told me he couldn't "tarry." He had to return to the mission. "War's a bitch," he said. "Domed two dudes this morning. Got thirty-two kills." Before I could ask what "domed" meant, or how he was doing, he just shuffled off down the sidewalk.

That weekend Lencie and I loaded all of her and Rory's stuff into the seventeen-foot U-Haul, then all of mine, and attached the car tow dolly with my vehicle on it—Lencie having sold hers for cash in hand. Then the three of us piled into the cab of the truck and headed to our new life in the big city. And even though Lencie and I glanced at one another with a pang of nostalgia as we drove out of Shelton, we gave each other a big high-five—and Rory too—once we hit Highway 101.

WE HAD ONE WEEK and four days before Rory's preschool class started, and another two weeks after that before Lencie's dental hygiene program began. So until that time, we spent our days unpacking and exploring the neighborhood. Rory liked everything about the new living arrangements and new neighborhood. Before the first week was out, he even had a playdate with another little boy down the street, whose parents we'd met in the neighborhood park.

On Saturday morning Lencie and I walked Rory down to their house. As the boys played in the backyard, the four adults sat on the deck drinking coffee. The Keoghs were about our age, maybe a couple years younger. Christine worked in elder care as an activities coordinator for a chain of retirement homes in the Puget Sound area. Rob developed investment apps for a software company in Fremont. When they asked what we did, Lencie told them about starting the dental hygiene program at SCCC and I said I was a musician. Immediately they both asked what I played.

"I sing," I answered, and then they wanted to know what kind of music.

"Jazz mostly," I said and left it at that. I was shy about explaining the whole Bing Crosby business to just anyone, especially people I'd only just met. For starters, if they were under thirty, as Rob and Christine probably were, they might not even know who he was.

"We'd love to hear you sometime," Christine said, and I replied that I'd let them know when I landed my first gig. Then she offered to arrange for me to sing at one or more of the retirement homes where she worked—that is, if I ever wanted to. They paid $200 for an hour's entertainment, she added, and I told her I would keep the offer in mind.

The Keoghs were nice people, and despite our obvious differences in education (and income), it seemed like we could get along. And, most important, our kids could play together a couple of times a week at one house or the other, allowing the parents to spot one another for a morning or afternoon for whatever—wild sex on the kitchen floor or just watching some uninterrupted daytime TV.

Eventually Lencie and I began to get our bearings in Seattle. One afternoon while she met with her program advisor at SCCC, I explored Capitol Hill. I remembered visiting the neighborhood years ago with some buddies from Shelton, all of us rubes from the tulies bent on getting drunk. It was the mid-90s, and I loved the carnival atmosphere of Broadway that night. Now the neighborhood seemed smoothed out and sanitized. Whole blocks of old one- and two-story buildings had been replaced by sleek structures several stories high. While the skateboarders and longboarders, buskers and panhandlers, dopers and deadbeats were still about on the periphery, they'd mostly been crowded out by young professional types, many pushing baby joggers that drove you off the sidewalk worse than any cluster of street kids. I did appreciate that the Dick's Drive-In was still there, and when Lencie was done at the college, we got a bag of cheeseburgers and fries and ate them in the park across the street.

For the next two weeks as Rory started pre-K and Lencie geared up for her dental hygiene program, I kept wondering what the heck I was going to do with myself. It wasn't as if I could get on craigslist and find a band looking for someone to sing 1940s standards. There was always busking, but performing on the street was problematic. It required a license, and you risked getting pigeonholed as just another street performer. There were a lot of talented musicians on Seattle streets, no question, but once people knew you as the guy on the street corner, it was impossible to get them to come see you in a club. In other words, once a busker, always a busker. And I had higher aspirations, even though these were as yet undefined.

So I decided to go for the next step up: talent shows. If you counted the competitive karaoke circuit, you could say talent shows were two steps up from busking. There were two or three shows any given week in the Seattle area. They were held in community auditoriums, neighborhood theaters, and nightclubs throughout the city. There were a lot of really bad performers, as you might expect, but there was genuine talent as well. According to the Facebook page that tracked the city's talent show scene, talent scouts from *American Idol, The Voice, America's Got Talent, So You Think You Can Dance,* and all those other shows attended them regularly to recruit performers—mostly singers. Record producers and small label owners came as well. Some talent shows were wide open—comedians, fire-eaters, magicians, contortionists, jugglers—while others were just for musicians. I limited myself to these.

At first, I didn't even sign up, I just attended, getting a feel for the whole scene. The show I went to at the Neptune Theater in the U District was a raucous event. It had a battle-of-the-bands format and was emceed by the guitarist from Ink Bone, a local band that hit it big in the '90s. But not all the bands were rock or punk. A bluegrass group did a wonderful rendition of the Beatles' "Lovely Rita," and a string quartet played a piece by Debussy.

I went to two other talent shows, both dominated by singers— would-be divas, with a few Sam Smith–types thrown in. They could all belt out a number, but that wasn't my style, so I worried about putting myself out there. Besides, what did I expect to gain? The biggest first place purse was $3,000, which was sizeable, but not a reliable source of income—which I didn't need right now, fortunately, but would eventually. There was always the chance a television producer might invite me to audition for some reality show, but when was the last time you saw a genuine crooner on one of those?

I knew I had to do something, though, so I signed up for a music-only competition at the Columbia City Theater, located in a quiet neighborhood in the south end of Seattle. I debated whether to enlist an accompanist and finally decided to go solo, singing the way I always had to my grandmother at home in Shelton.

When I told Lencie about the show, the first thing she wanted to know was whether she and Rory could come. I'd already pondered that and decided this was something I needed to do on my own. So I said no, I'd rather they didn't.

"Why not?" She was wiping the kitchen counter with a sponge and stopped to look at me.

"I'm too nervous as it is," I said. "Maybe next time."

"Rory loves hearing you sing," she said.

It was true that Rory was my biggest fan. In fact, in some ways I had begun grooming him, just as Grandma had groomed me, to sing just like Bing. He did a splendid version of "You Must Have Been a Beautiful Baby"—absolutely darling! I kept telling myself I needed to record and post it.

"I'll sing for Rory anytime he likes," I replied.

Rory was in the living room watching TV, and hearing this conversation he came into the kitchen to ask me to sing something for him. I sang him "Swinging on a Star," one of his favorites—one of mine too—only too glad to avert having a squabble with Lencie.

THAT FRIDAY NIGHT WAS my first public performance—my first time in front an audience other than family or friends.

The way it worked was each performer pulled a number before the show to determine the order they would go in. I was number eight out of fourteen acts, meaning I had to go first after intermission, which made me nervous. I was plenty nervous already, having to sing solo before a full house, especially since it was a raucous crowd, with lots of whistling and heckling. But then on top of this they would all be making their way back to their seats just as I took the stage. Having to go after intermission, however, turned out to be not such a bad thing. It meant I didn't have to follow the impressive jazz flutist, the beautiful Shakira look-alike, the stunningly talented classical guitarist from the Iberian Peninsula, or the jug band complete with washtub bass, spoons, a two-gallon jug, and someone in overalls clogging.

As I took the stage, people were still returning to their seats, just as I'd feared, but I told myself to be brave and went forward. My only concession to the Bing look was to wear a lightweight tweed jacket over dark slacks—no bowtie, no Biltmore hat, no plaid shirt, no briar pipe. I didn't want people thinking I was simply a Bing impersonator in the mode of Elvis impersonators, most of whom hang their act on parodying the King with the overly large pompadour and glittering jumpsuit. I wanted to honor Bing, not parody him. I wanted to woo the audience with his reassuring baritone, heartfelt lyrics, and genuine charisma—not make them laugh at him. Instead of the audience thinking, *Hey, he does a good imitation*, I wanted them to experience Bing.

The applause was polite as I took the stage and stepped up to the microphone stand. After standing there for a moment looking out over the house to bring everyone's attention center stage, I took a deep breath and went into "I Surrender, Dear." And then it no longer mattered that this was my first time singing on stage. I trusted the song's inherent charm, relishing its hypnotic melody and singing it beautifully. For my next number, thinking of Rory, I went upbeat with the toe-tapping "You Must Have Been a Beautiful Baby," whistling my way through the instrumental portion while I held my hands behind my back. I was feeling good as I finished it. I could see faces smiling in the first few rows. So to close, I came up extra close to the mic and began humming the opening bars of "Please," one of Bing's earliest hits, before taking up the song's pleasing alliterative lyrics:

Oh, please.
Lend your little ear to my pleas
Lend a ray of cheer to my pleas
Tell me that you love me too.

I held the final note a little longer than usual, then said a simple thank you and gave a short bow before walking off the stage.

The applause let me know my performance had been appreciated, and backstage my fellow performers gave me their earnest congratulations.

"Your voice made me cry," said the young woman who looked and sounded just like Shakira. She then gave me a hug.

I took a bottle of water from the cooler near the backstage steps and returned to my seat to watch the remaining acts. I felt good, knowing I'd sung well. At the same time I told myself not to get my hopes up.

The judging followed the *American Idol* model: a panel of three judges combined with audience voting. It took half an hour following the final performance—an accordionist who sang *corridos*—for the SMS votes to be tallied and the judges to confer. Eventually, all the performers were invited back on stage so the emcee, a tall skinny fellow with a bushy mustache and strong radio voice, could announce the winners. I was pleased when the Shakira singer, whose name was Nicole, was named second honorable mention. She took home a check for $50. The jazz flutist took first honorable mention ($100), and a doo-wop trio took third place ($200). When the emcee called my name for second place, I could hardly believe it, and as I stepped forward to receive my $500 check, I kept thinking how happy my grandmother would have been. First place went to the classical guitarist, Oscar Galdós, who took home $1,000.

After the show, some of the performers headed to the brewpub around the corner. I sat with Oscar and Nicole. Oscar was rather shy, but not Nicole, who was positively giddy with her honorable mention and kept looking at her $50 check.

"Wait till I call my folks back in Idaho," she said. "They won't believe it."

I was glad to have someone there who was at least as big a hick as me. Yet it was nearly midnight, so after just one pint, I excused myself from the gathering. I shook hands with Oscar, gave Nicole a hug, waved to everyone else, and left.

Lencie and I celebrated just ourselves when I got home that night. She was asleep on the couch, but when I woke her up and explained that I'd gotten second place, she squealed with delight. As I told her about the whole evening, she opened a bottle of wine, and after a couple of glasses each, we hurried to the bedroom for celebration sex.

"Hullabaloo and Timbuktu!" I exclaimed to Lencie and Rory the next day when I took them to the Space Needle restaurant for lunch so the three of us could celebrate. "What a view!"

"Look," Rory shouted, pointing down at something. He was on his knees in his chair, his forehead pressed to the glass.

Lencie leaned over to look where he was pointing. "That's the monorail," she told him.

"Can we go on it?" He turned around and looked at us.

"Of course," I said. "But let's eat first."

He was thrilled by how the whole restaurant rotated almost imperceptibly, and when our appetizers arrived—potato wedges for him and his mom, oysters for me—he could hardly stop looking out the window.

"Here's to the second-place winner!" Lencie said. She raised her glass of water and clinked it with mine.

"Thank you," I said, feeling pretty good.

"Next time Rory and I want to go," she said as our sandwiches arrived.

"Absolutely," I said.

THE LIFT I FELT from my second-place win at the talent show was weighed down a few days later when I received a text message from Stiles telling me that Lencie's ex knew it was us who'd stolen his laptop and Xbox.

"How could that be?" I texted back, flabbergasted.

"Don't know," Stiles almost instantly replied. "He's a fucking prison guard. Maybe he had a security camera." He then recounted how, in violation of prison policy, the ex had entered the Harbor Tavern still wearing his gray Corrections Center uniform and confronted Stiles, who was sitting at the bar.

"He threatened me," Stiles wrote, "and there were witnesses."

Witnesses. As if Hank, the Harbor Tavern owner, or any of his half-soused clientele would testify to anything other than outrageous gas prices, Obama coming for their guns and ammo, or the shitty fourth quarter the Seahawks had in last Sunday's game.

"He threatened you too," Stiles went on in a separate text message.

"So I told him the superintendent of the Department of Corrections was a personal friend of mine and if he wanted to keep his job, he'd get out of my face."

Stiles talked tough, but reading between the lines I could tell he was rattled. He knew a lot of people—maybe even the superintendent of Corrections—but he didn't have a whole lot of friends. There was Annabelle from the Tea Room, and me, and that was probably it—and I was never sure exactly why I was friends with him except perhaps for the reason that I didn't have many friends myself. I could never figure out why Stiles stayed in Shelton, why he didn't move back to Seattle or to Olympia or Bellingham or any place else that was a little less closed-minded. It was a mystery to me, though at the same time I kind of admired him for sticking it out in our old hometown.

I decided not to say anything to Lencie about Stiles's message. The ex had conceded custody of Rory in lieu of paying any spousal maintenance, though the judge wouldn't let him off the hook for child support. By the end of September, the divorce was finalized. All the same, I didn't want to worry about running into the ex when we went back to Shelton for Thanksgiving. So I told myself he'd just have to get over it and, like Lencie, move on with life. He wasn't getting his laptop or his Xbox back, that was for sure.

The next two talent shows I signed up for were smaller than the one in Columbia City, and even though I sang well at both, I didn't get so much as an honorable mention in either. Following the second show, the emcee told me someone in the lobby was looking for me. My first thought was that it was Lencie's ex, that he'd come to Seattle to have it out with me. Yet I knew that was highly unlikely.

Quite a few people were still milling about the lobby, so I stood in the corner, near the side exit, scanning the room. After a few minutes, a middle-aged man approached me. Mist beaded the shoulders of his tan raincoat. He had on a black felt hat with the brim curled up all the way around. He also wore narrow rectangular glasses and had a goatee, like a German scientist from a 1930s movie. I guessed him to be in his mid-forties, a little old for the hipster set. He took his right hand out of the pocket of his raincoat, shook my hand, then asked me to excuse him for leaving me waiting—"I ducked out for a cigarette," he said—and introduced himself as Atzel Gott. "I'm owner of the Amethyst Club. Have you ever been?"

I'd never heard of it.

"Sorry," I replied. "I'm still new to town."

"It's in Belltown on First. Jazz," he added.

I knew of Belltown. Like Capitol Hill, it was nothing like it was a decade or so ago. It was all high-rise condos and nightclubs now. Stiles had lived in Belltown. "It's like Miami's South Beach," he once told me. "Only soggier."

"I like the way you sing," Atzel said. "I'd like you to come down to the club sometime. We have half a dozen house musicians who play on Tuesday and Thursday nights. Maybe you could sit in with them. Let me know the numbers you'd like to do, you know, a few days ahead, and I'll see that they have 'em ready for you." He brushed the beads of mist off his raincoat and removed his hat and brushed the mist off it as well. "You'll like these guys. And I think they'll like you."

I thanked him for the invitation. "I can do that," I said, and getting excited asked what day he would like me to come down.

"Today's Saturday, right?" He took his smartphone from the pocket of his raincoat and poked at it, and as he did so, I looked across the lobby, saw Ian, the jazz violinist who'd performed right after me, and nodded to him.

"Let's do this," said Atzel. "Send me your list of songs, half a dozen, by Monday. The guys can then have a little time to rehearse them, and you can come down on Wednesday and try them out on stage. Sound doable?"

"Absolutely doable," I said.

He then handed me his business card and said he looked forward to getting the songs.

"I really like how you sing," he said again. "What a wonderful singer Bing Crosby was. I bet few people even know who he is anymore. And if they do, they don't know what kind of singer he really was. How talented he was."

"Sadly," I said.

"Maybe we'll change that," he said, and we shook hands.

All the way home I thought of how to tell Lencie about this development. I figured I should downplay it, especially since there'd been no mention of money. This Atzel Gott fellow was probably just looking for talent to fill the off-nights at his club. He knew someone like me would be so flattered at the chance to perform at the Amethyst

Club, they'd do it for free. But it meant exposure, and that's what I needed. Plus it meant singing with a real live band! The prospect thrilled me. It also scared the bejesus out of me. I would have to play it cool. I knew Bing's music as well as anyone, but I didn't play an instrument and couldn't read music very well, which I knew was a deficit. I would have to take my cues from the real musicians—and not get too full of myself.

Such thoughts zigzagged through my head as I drove back to Greenwood. The car must have been zigzagging too, because when I got off I-5 and was heading west of Eighty-Fifth, a cop hit his lights and pulled me over. I turned in to a gas station, rolled down my window, and readied my license, registration, and insurance.

"Do you know why I pulled you over, sir?" the officer asked.

Poor pitch? I wanted to say, still in a pretty good mood about meeting Atzel Gott, owner of the Amethyst Club. "No, I'm afraid I don't," I said instead. "Was I speeding?"

"You drove straight through the stop sign back there," he told me and took my documents. "Have you been drinking at all tonight, sir?" He aimed his flashlight onto the passenger side floor and then into my eyes. I looked at his badge: Officer Gwozdek.

"No," I answered. I wanted to explain that I was simply jacked about getting the chance to play with a real band. Which six songs, of the more than two-thousand songs Bing recorded in his lifetime, would I send Atzel?

"Okay," he said. "I'll be right back."

As I waited for the officer to run my name through his databases, the paranoid notion suddenly came to me that Lencie's ex might be involved in this routine traffic stop. Didn't these guys have each other's backs? Weren't they all brethren? Couldn't he have just put something out on the wire, or whatever it was law enforcement used to communicate with one another, to tip this cop off that I was someone to harass? As I glanced in the side-view mirror and saw the cop walking toward me, I readied myself for whatever sort of mistreatment he had in store for me.

"Here you are," he said and handed me my documents. "It's a four-way stop back there."

"I must not've seen it," I said lamely.

"Shelton, huh?"

I still hadn't gone down to the Department of Licensing to obtain a new driver's license.

"You've been?" I asked. Every cop in the state knew of the Corrections Center. Maybe he'd make some crack about it—*I've given a few guys bus tickets there*, that kind of thing.

"Can't say I have," was all he said and let me go with a warning.

As I drove the rest of the way home, I thought how if the gig at the Amethyst Club worked out and I became a regular, I might invite Officer Gwozdek and his significant other down to the club as my special guests.

LENCIE WAS ALREADY THREE weeks into her dental hygiene program when I got the invitation to perform at the Amethyst Club. By then we had a routine, especially with Rory—because kids need routine. Dropping him off and picking him up at pre-K were my jobs since Lencie just couldn't do it. She had to leave the house by 7:30 a.m. to catch the bus so she could make her 9:00 class. At 3:30 when she got home, we would take Rory to the park if it wasn't raining too hard, or maybe we'd have the Keogh kid over (or Rory would go over there), and around 6:00 p.m. or so we would eat dinner. I did most of the cooking, trying out recipes from the Epicurious website, though sometimes, admittedly, it would come down to Stouffer's mac and cheese and steamed broccoli, or maybe cube steaks and baked potatoes from the microwave.

I liked walking the five blocks with Rory to his school each morning. Other kids, with mom or dad trailing, would converge on the school from the surrounding neighborhood. Like a bunch of coyote pups, the kids would scamper around on the grass berms on either side of the school entrance. Eventually several of the less raucous kids would go stand near the door. A few minutes before the bell rang, a teacher would step outside and from the top of the stairs tell all the kids to line up. Then the bell would ring and the kids would turn to wave goodbye to their parents, and the teacher would lead them all into the school building.

With the whole day before me, I would go to the café a few blocks away and read for an hour or so. Eventually I would return to the house and drink some coffee (while checking email and Facebook), eat some lunch (leftovers usually), take a nap (no more than an hour), and then I would sing. I would start with vocal exercises that I remembered from high school choir and picked up from YouTube videos. (I once totally disassembled and reassembled a chainsaw from watching YouTube videos.) The exercises helped me warm up, control my breathing, stretch my voice out, and move between different registers. Then I would rehearse a dozen or more Bing songs. By then it was time to return to the school and pick up Rory.

He would bolt from the doors with the rest of the kids, dragging his jacket by the sleeve, and I would scoop him up and give him a big hug. Then he would see one of his friends—maybe his new best buddy Stephen—and squirm loose from my arms and race off to join him. I waved to Stephen's mom, and after a few minutes we'd each call out to the boys and they'd have to say so long to one another.

One time as we walked home, Rory told me that Stephen and him and another boy named Jared all had Hot Wheels, and the next day they were each going to bring their favorite one to school.

"Which one are you going to bring?" I asked him. When we moved into the Seattle house, we arranged Rory's bedroom just how he wanted it, which meant setting up the Hot Wheels track with its timer-triggered catapult starter and loop-de-loop at the foot of his bed. He had a dozen or more Hot Wheels cars that went with it.

"The red one," he said.

He had three or four red ones. "The Camaro?" I asked. "With the racing stripe?"

"Yeah."

We walked along for a few minutes without saying anything. It was a warmish afternoon, late September. I could see the Olympics down one street. Having grown up directly beneath them on the Olympic Peninsula, I felt like I was peering into my own backyard, which gave me a tinge of longing for Shelton.

A block from our house, Rory took my hand in his, which he sometimes did even if we weren't about to cross a street. He gave my hand a tug, and when I looked down at him he asked, "Are you my daddy now?"

I didn't know what to say. His biological father—Lencie's ex—was pretty much out of the picture at this point. The divorce settlement gave him visitation rights (Wednesday afternoons and every other weekend), but these were basically voided by our living in Seattle. He certainly didn't seem interested in making the trip to come see his son. However, Rory wasn't asking for my legal opinion. I made his PB&J sandwiches, cut his carrot sticks, sliced his apples, wrapped his Fig Newtons in cellophane, and put it all in his Hot Wheels lunchbox every weekday. I walked him to school every morning and walked him home every afternoon. I took turns with his mother giving him baths on Sunday, Wednesday, and Friday evenings after dinner and on the other days scrubbing him down with a washrag. I regularly read to him at night before Lencie and I put him to bed. I also felt responsible for him and loved him like my own flesh and blood. What more was there to being a daddy? Yet, at the same time, I didn't feel right saying yes, not wanting to risk crossing out the kid's biological father in his eyes.

"Well, Rory," I said, fumbling for words and trying to sound wise at the same time. "I'm kind of your daddy. I do a lot of daddy things and I love you like a daddy…" As I looked at him, he absentmindedly shredded a big yellow maple leaf he'd picked up from the ground. It was clear my answer was unsatisfactory, and that's when I let my daddy instinct take over and said to myself, *Screw the ex.*

I put my hands on Rory's shoulders, bent down on one knee so I was eye level with him, and said, "Yes, Rory, I'm your daddy now." No hedging, no qualifying—no nothing. I knew I was making one hell of a serious pledge to a susceptible little boy and just wished to God I could keep it.

LENCIE WAS EXCITED WHEN I told her about Atzel Gott's invitation to play at the Amethyst Club.

"You *really* are an amazing singer," she said, looking meaningfully into my eyes before giving me a kiss. After putting Rory to bed that night, we made love on the couch in front of the TV, and the next morning, a Sunday, the three of us ate blueberry pancakes and sausage links before going to the Woodland Park Zoo. As we *ooh*'ed and *aah*'ed at the lions and giraffes, I thought how lucky I was to have such a stable, ready-made family life.

All the while that splendid Sunday, though, I was nervous about the upcoming Amethyst gig. What songs would I give Atzel? What if my lack of musicianship—true musicianship, beyond my so-called natural abilities—really showed itself? What if I was exposed as the buffoon singer I sometimes feared I was?

I would just have to find out, I told myself, and on Monday I emailed my finalized selection of songs to Atzel—all Bing covers, of course—including two of my grandmother's favorites, "I'm a Fool to Care" and "Keepin' Out of Mischief Now." Then I started rehearsing my selection. After dropping Rory off, I came straight back to the house instead of going to the café. I first listened to the songs, plugging my old iPod into a pair of speakers. I hummed along to Bing's vocals to get in time with his rhythm, then I harmonized with him, and finally I sang each song on my own and then listened to Bing's version again, back and forth like that until I was confident I had his timbre and every intonation down pat. I knew the songs sounded good and, in a moment of chutzpah, genuinely wondered if, in a blind listening test, a person could distinguish my voice from his.

That afternoon Atzel emailed me back saying the selection looked good, though he wasn't familiar with half the numbers and was worried the band might not be either. So I forwarded him MP3 files for all eight songs, and he replied thanking me and adding that he'd already ordered the sheet music from an online distributor. I wrote back saying I looked forward to coming down to the club, and he replied saying I was welcome to bring a friend.

Lencie loved the idea when I told her and phoned the babysitter, a Seattle University student that Christine and Rob had recommended.

"I'll have to study every minute between now and then," Lencie let me know after arranging the babysitter, and went into the kitchen with her armload of books while I took Rory to his room to play with his Hot Wheels.

Two nights later we spruced ourselves up and headed downtown. She wore a hip-hugging, thigh-length blue dress—one I'd never seen before that looked great on her—and I wore a new white dress shirt (purchased the day before at JCPenney), a green and gold silk tie, and a light tan jacket—"Bing chic," I called the look.

It being a Wednesday night, Belltown wasn't terribly busy. Lencie and I ate dinner at the Queen City Grill—appletinis and coho salmon.

It made me happy to see her having a good time. Her program at SCCC was harder and more stressful than she'd ever imagined, and just one month in, it was getting her down. When she was done with her first drink, she ordered another and asked if I wanted another too. I took a pass, though, since I had to sing.

When we were done, I helped Lencie with her coat, and we walked the three blocks north on First Avenue to the Amethyst Club. It was a smallish place, basically a storefront in a three-story brick building. The bar was on one side of the narrow room and the stage on the other, with tables the length of the room. It was dark, fitting for a jazz club, with fluttering candles in glass bowls on each table. Framed photos of jazz legends hung on the wall—Dizzy Gillespie, Chet Baker, Billie Holiday, and even, to my surprise, Mildred Bailey, the little-known singer from Spokane who had been such a big influence on Bing's singing style.

It wasn't even eight yet, so the musicians were still setting up. A young woman carrying a tray of drinks saw us looking around after entering and told us to sit wherever we liked. I took Lencie's elbow and guided her toward the back of the room and away from the stage lights. Then I looked around for Atzel. When the waitress came over, Lencie ordered a Long Island and I got plain cranberry juice. The club was maybe a third full when a slump-shouldered, middle-aged guy in a sweater sat down at the piano and started doing a slow play on "Take Five." It was a sweet rendition of the classic and seemed to put everyone in the mood for more music. Meanwhile, the other musicians quietly took the stage. The drummer was a woman with a purple Mohawk. As she sat patiently behind her trap, she rolled the sleeves of her denim jacket up over her thick forearms. The tall bass player, with a newsboy cap pulled low over his brow, leaned over his upright bass, which nestled into his shoulder like a dance partner. The three horns—saxophone, trumpet, trombone—stood side-by-side-by-side to his left. When the piano player finished the Brubeck number, he acknowledged the applause from the twenty or so people in the club with a nod and pulled the microphone arm forward.

"Thank you and good evening, everyone. We're so glad you could join us tonight at the Amethyst Club," he said, looking over the audience. "We're going to keep with our tribute to the late great Dave Brubeck with one of my favorites, 'I May Be Wrong.'"

The whole band took up the number and was brilliant—smooth

and syncopated, swinging and sophisticated. It scared me how good they were because I knew they would expect me to be just as good. The big city jazz club scene was new to me, a mill punk from Shelton with sawdust still behind his ears. Yet, I'd imagined it would sound and look something very much like this—though a lot smokier—based on the black and white photos of New York City jazz clubs I'd seen in old copies of *Life* magazine my grandma had stored in the attic when I was a kid. Back then I even dared occasionally to picture myself as part of such a scene, though I hardly believed it would ever happen. And yet here I was, not only in the audience listening, but waiting to sit in with the band and sing.

Lencie smiled pleasantly and swayed to the rhythm. The band was into its third Brubeck number when I saw Atzel come through the front door. In his sleek black overcoat and black ascot cap, he looked every bit the jazz impresario. I pointed him out to Lencie and she raised an eyebrow.

The band picked up the tempo with its next few numbers. It wasn't until they were wrapping up the set that Atzel, having removed his coat and cap, made his way to our table. Without speaking over the music, he shook hands with me, then Lencie, and sat down at the table next to ours. Each musician in the band took a short solo, and when they finished, the piano player brought the piece to a close with an artful flourish back to "Take Five."

"We're going to take a short break," the piano player said over the applause. "Remember, show your waitress some love. Tip generously."

With that Atzel pulled his chair up to our table and formally introduced himself to Lencie. I could see he was taken by her darling face, including her adorable cross-eye. He laid his hand on my forearm and said, "I'll introduce you to Jerry and the band."

For the remainder of the break, he kept waving musicians over to our table to meet me, and finally Jerry, the piano player, came over. Atzel introduced me as the guy who'd sent the songs, who'd be singing with them after the break.

"Hey, right on," said Jerry, reminding me of Tony Bennett, the mellifluous way he had of enunciating his words. "The band played around with a few of those numbers on Monday," he said, "and they're good. I like your taste. I especially got a kick out of 'Keepin' Out of Mischief Now.' I haven't heard that one in years."

Jerry was a natural-born band leader. He had such ease and confidence. I knew I'd be in good hands when I took the stage.

"So whenever you're ready, kid," he said. "You just step up when I introduce you." He then told Lencie it was a pleasure to meet her, slapped Atzel on the back, and made his way back to the stage.

Atzel said he had some business to take care of, excused himself, and walked off to his office at the back of the club. When he was gone, Lencie leaned over and kissed me on the cheek. She was nearly finished with her second Long Island and was feeling it. I was glad I'd stuck with cranberry juice, because the preperformance jitters were coming over me. It was like the first talent show I'd done a month ago, when I just didn't know what I'd gotten myself into. So I took several deep breaths and tried to relax. I thought of Bing. He would be puffing on his pipe right about now, looking calm and composed—Bing as Buddha—so I tried to take on that aura myself. Lencie could see that I was nervous, though, and jostled my shoulder. "Just do what you do," she said and kissed me again.

As the band started the second set, I felt okay. As the set continued, though, one number after another, I began to wonder if maybe Jerry had forgotten about me. That's when I heard my name announced and saw Jerry stand up behind the piano with a welcoming gesture. Lencie gave me a nudge. "Go," she said.

I trotted up to the stage, shook Jerry's hand, and gave a nod to the other musicians. "You got this," I heard the trumpeter say, smiling through his heavy beard as I stepped up to the mic.

As soon as I turned to the audience, Jerry began tickling the piano keys. The drummer came in with her steel brush on the snare, the bass player added a subtle bass line, and just like that I began singing, and when the horns broke in midway through the first verse, I knew that, yes, I had this. It was freedom. I could feel my voice rising, gaining strength and control. And what a feeling to have a full band backing me! Such depth, force, and control. The instrumentation complemented and enhanced my vocals. After the second chorus, I stepped back and the trumpeter stepped forward and took a solo. When he rejoined the other horns to the appreciative applause of the audience, I stepped up to the mic again. I don't know how I knew to do all this, to interact with the band so well, but I did. I guess it was all those years—decades really—of listening to Bing and performing to an imaginary audience in my bedroom back home in Shelton. My phrasing was perfect, and with *"Really am in love and how,"* I raised a hand to my brow and found Lencie though the glare of the stage lights, then looked over my shoulder at the band with *"All the world can plainly see"*…and with the crescendo—*"Keepin', keepin' out of mischief now"*…and one, two, three, we're out.

The audience loved it. And so did the band. They were applauding right along with the audience. I bowed and mouthed thank you to the band. The drummer pointed one of her sticks at me. The bass player kept saying, "Right on, right on." And the audience kept applauding.

That's when Jerry broke in to say that maybe the young man with the satiny voice could be persuaded to do a few more songs, to which the audience gave its approval with renewed applause. Then Jerry put his hand over the piano mic and looking at the band said, "My Blue Heaven."

He looked at me. "Got it?"

"Got it," I said, no doubt left in my mind, and without a moment's hesitation, Jerry signaled the horns, which kicked the number off with a big brassy opening. And just like that I was at the mic again crooning my heart out.

The song was a hit, and we did two more. When I returned to my table at the end of the set, people were still applauding, and Jerry took the liberty of telling everyone I would be back on the Amethyst stage next Thursday evening. Lencie had tears in her eyes as she stood up and gave me an exuberant hug.

"I never heard you sing so wonderfully," she said, and I realized she'd never heard me sing to anyone other than herself and Rory. She had wanted to make it to one of the last two talent shows, but her studies had made it impossible.

The room was nearly spinning as I sat down, and when the waitress came around, Lencie ordered another Long Island and I ordered a double scotch. I was so charged I didn't see Atzel approach.

"He's really something, isn't he?" he said to Lencie. He patted me on the back with one hand and extended the other to shake.

"Those guys are amazing," I said. "How'd they learn those songs so fast?

"They're good all right, that's all I can say. A lot of credit goes to Jerry. He knows how to bring 'em along." He then sat down and turned toward me. "Listen, you heard Jerry just now. We want you to come back next Thursday. That's a better night for us anyway. So why don't you send another six songs, and we'll have you do a whole set."

"Six more songs?" I was a bit incredulous.

"That's right. You got that many?"

"Yeah," I said. "Of course." I could do the whole Bing catalog if he wanted me to. "No problem."

"The audience likes you." He turned to Lencie. "You could see that, right?"

"They loved you," said Lencie and leaned in and pressed her cheek to my shoulder.

"That tells me something," said Atzel.

"Thank you," was all I could think to say in response.

Atzel then walked back toward the bar and on his way stopped to have a word with the waitress. Jerry and the other musicians all came around to our table and congratulated me, and I thanked them profusely for making me sound so good. By that time, it was already well past when we'd told the babysitter we'd be home. As Lencie phoned her, I signaled the waitress over for the tab, and she told me Atzel had taken care of it.

I LISTENED TO A lot more Bing than usual that week. I sent Atzel six new songs, and I rehearsed them over and over. But I also made sure not to overdo it since every singer, even the most gravelly, needs to take care of their voice. This is especially true for a crooner, who can't settle for anything less than perfect pitch. So, in addition to rehearsing each day, I did warm-up exercises, drank lots of water, and rested if I felt any scratchiness in my throat.

On Saturday, Atzel emailed asking if I could substitute two of the numbers I'd chosen. According to Jerry, who'd been working out the arrangements, one had too extensive a string section for him to bridge with the piano and the other relied too much on a chorus of backup singers. I immediately sent him two new songs. It was also agreed during our email exchange that I would come in on Monday to rehearse the whole set with the band.

Some Seattle musicians refuse to play on Mondays. It's their one day off. But that seems to hold more for classical musicians than it does the jazz world, so all the musicians who'd been on stage the previous Wednesday night were back at the Amethyst Club for rehearsal on Monday, the one night each week the club was closed. There was a guitar player and a clarinetist this time around as well. Atzel appeared briefly but then disappeared, which made no difference to the rehearsal since it was Jerry who was in charge of the music.

"You've seen the arrangements," Jerry said to everyone, giving them the playlist and nodding in my direction. "These are *his* songs. So from here on, he's calling the shots with them."

I stared at Jerry. Was he referring to me? Because if he was, I sure as hell was in no position to be calling any shots!

"You ready?" he asked me.

I looked at him and then thought, *What Would Bing Do (WWBD)?*— and knew instantly. Bing would go with it, easy as you please. He'd be cool and relaxed and ready to make some sweet music. So I replied, "Ready as ever, maestro," and turned to the band and said, "Let's start with 'Get Happy,' shall we, gang?" and everyone laughed, perhaps picking up on how I was channeling Bing. I told them which key, and then I counted us in and started off with some scat.

We worked our way through all twelve songs on the playlist, yet it hardly felt like work at all. We had to tweak our timing now and then, but it was no big deal for these talented musicians. Jerry was still the guy with the most experience and know-how, so when he asked if I would like to stretch a note another half beat or have the horns come in sooner or let the clarinet take a solo, I said, "Absolutely, great idea." Plus, the more I went along with Jerry's suggestions, the more I learned what making good music was all about.

"There was a lot more clarinet back when these songs were recorded," he remarked at one point, "before the sax bullied it aside." The saxophonist squawked his horn in response to Jerry's remark.

That's how the whole rehearsal went—serious and on point when it came to the music, but otherwise relaxed and playful. It only made sense. These musicians were professionals. Some of them had played together for years. Jerry had started out in New York, played in Paris (where he met Nina Simone), then came back to the States and settled in New Orleans for a stretch before moving to San Francisco and then up to Seattle, where his first gig was playing the old Jazz Alley in the U District. "Played with Ornette Coleman there," he told me during our break. He knew I was basically a musical novice, so I appreciated his patience and subtle mentoring of me.

Then he asked about me, how a kid from—"Where was it? Shelstein?"—ever got into Bing Crosby.

"Shelton," I corrected him, and replied, "My grandma. She loved Bing like no one's business. She even hinted once she'd had a fling with him. A fling with Bing. But I don't think so since she rarely left Shelton in her eighty-seven years."

"I like that," said Jerry.

"Wishful thinking on her part, I suppose," I said, and explained how Grandma raised me and passed her love of Bing's music on to me.

It wasn't until after the rehearsal when I was driving home that the story of my passion for Bing struck me for the first time in my life as really rather unusual. What kind of parent or grandparent raises a kid to be totally preoccupied with a once-great, nearly forgotten crooner? And what kind of parent or grandparent brings the kid up to essentially become a clone of the crooner? Was Grandma just another self-centered stage mother? Was I living out some kind of Gypsy Rose situation? Instead of pictures of rock stars or athletes on my bedroom walls, I had pictures of Bing. Toward the end of her life, Grandma would special order video cassettes of all his movies, and we would watch them together in the basement where, as a teenager, I should have been getting wasted with friends while blasting out Nirvana and Soundgarden.

"You know, I never could figure why everyone's so nuts over Frank Sinatra and that Rat Pack group while no one listens to Bing anymore," Jerry said after hearing my story. "Like they say, Bing was the first white guy to be cool. Sinatra could be brash. But Bing, baby, he could sing."

"You and Grandma would have gotten along great," I said, and with that we went back to rehearsing.

We kept at it for another hour or so, closing with "Nice Work If You Can Get It," one of my favorites, making me go more tenor than baritone, with the horns punctuating the high notes in Jerry's arrangement. By the end of the rehearsal we all felt pretty good and ready for Thursday night.

As I came off the stage, Atzel waved me over to the bar where he was sitting. He wore clear plastic-rimmed glasses that gave his eyes a kind of halo effect.

"You want a drink?"

I said no, and he placed his hand on a manila envelope on the bar and pushed it toward me.

"Here's a contract," he said. "It's for every Thursday between now and New Year's. So that's four Thursdays before Thanksgiving and four after. Eight in all. Five hundred a night. Then we'll see where we go from there." He nodded at the manila envelope. "Look it over, and if it checks out, sign it and bring it back on Thursday."

"Sounds great," I said. I hadn't expected anything more than maybe a few bucks under the table and free drinks like Lencie and I had gotten the first night.

"Also, did Jerry talk to you about the union?"

I shook my head.

"The contract says you have to be a member. Musicians' Association of Seattle, Local 76-493."

I was already familiar with unions. I was still a member of the International Woodworkers of America, Local 3-38, Shelton. In fact, my card was in my wallet as I spoke to Atzel. It had been there since I graduated high school and went to work for my uncle, because out on the peninsula, whether you worked in the woods or at a mill, you joined the union or else you didn't work at all. That was a fact of life. There was a lot of history there and a lot of struggle—heads cracked, blood spilled, lives lost, all for the sake of organized labor—so it made no difference if your uncle owned the company. If you wanted to work, you joined the union.

"I'll sign up tomorrow," I told Atzel.

LENCIE COULD HARDLY BELIEVE it when she saw the contract. She didn't even know musicians had contracts—and for that matter neither did I. Her excitement amused me. But on the drive home, I'd already figured out I would make $4,000 in two months, which wasn't much in Seattle, where the cost of living was outrageous compared to Shelton. On the other hand, it would nearly cover two months' rent, sparing me from taking it from my savings, which life in the big city was steadily whittling away. But, I also thought, did I really think I could ever possibly support myself—myself and Lencie and Rory, that is—on singing

Bing Crosby songs? I knew I would have to get a day job eventually, as most musicians did. I figured I could probably get hired in the lumber department at just about any Home Depot or Lowe's. But did I want to go down that road just yet? I thought about this most of the next day and finally answered no, I didn't. I would give myself these next two months at the Amethyst Club to develop my music, and then if nothing more came of it, I would start filling out applications.

Meanwhile, Lencie's dental hygiene program was taking its toll on her. She studied every night at the kitchen table until midnight. She studied on the bus going to school, between classes with her various study groups, and on the bus back home. She was really dedicated and really smart, so she was doing extremely well in all her classes—even Dental Anatomy and Morphology, the one she cursed daily—but she felt forever harried by the next test or the next big due date.

It was Wednesday evening, one day before my first official show at the Amethyst Club, and we were putting the dinner dishes in the sink to soak. Rory was watching TV in the living room. I told Lencie she could go join him if she wanted to, but she stayed in the kitchen.

"You've heard me talk about Cheryl, right? She's in my A&M study group."

I vaguely remembered. "What about her?" I asked.

"She failed the first major exam!"

"That's not good," I said and started filling the sink with hot water.

"It's terrible. It was 20 percent of the course grade. She's already talking about dropping out of the program."

To see the worried look on Lencie's face right then, the way she bit her lower lip and winced, would have made anyone think it was her and not her classmate who had failed the exam.

"How'd you do on it?"

"I got an A," she said with exasperation, as if she'd barely passed.

"That's great," I said. I turned off the water and dried my hands on a dish towel. "I guess you got a lot more out of the study group than Cheryl did."

Lencie ignored this comment, as though she didn't have time for such flippancy, and turned to unpacking her book bag. She set a textbook as big as a butcher's block on the kitchen table.

"I'm just worried, is all," she said, then sat down, opened the tome, and hunched over it with a highlighter poised above the page.

I went into the living room and watched the rest of *Fanboy &* *Chum Chum* on Nicktoons with Rory. In this episode, Fanboy and Chum Chum were burying their dead electronic pet in the Digital Pet Cemetery. It then came back as a digitized zombie to terrorize the neighborhood. At the commercial break, Rory asked me what a zombie was.

"Well," I said, stumped as I often was by the near-impossible questions a four-year-old can come up with, "they're people who come back from being dead." Then I thought twice about this answer and added, "But they're not real."

"What happens when you die?" he asked. He was curled into the corner of the couch holding a pillow in his arms.

"This is a good question for your mommy," I said. I craned my head over the back of the couch to peer into the kitchen. "Lencie, Rory wants to know what happens when you die?"

Lencie didn't hesitate. "The cells no longer get oxygen, so accelerated autolysis occurs, which leads to chronic tissue necrosis. That's why zombies have such hideous faces. Their flesh is disintegrating. We covered all that in the histology unit."

"Thank you," I said, and then *Fanboy & Chum Chum* came back on and Rory returned to watching.

THE LIVE MUSIC AT the Amethyst Club started at 8:00, so I arrived an hour early the next night. I was the first musician there, so I sat at the bar, sipping a club soda, and waited, watching each time as the door opened and someone new came in. I wanted a standing-room-only (SRO) crowd but, at the same time, dreaded the thought that anyone at all would come. In addition to the poster in the window announcing that week's performers, Atzel had put my name on the club's website and Facebook page. He'd also sent out a reminder to his email distribution list. As I flipped through the *Seattle Weekly* at the bar, I also found my name listed under the music calendar. This sent me out to the corner to find a copy of *The Stranger*, the city's edgy alternative weekly, to see if I was listed there as well, and sure enough I was, with a star recommendation no less, though on what basis I had no idea, given tonight was my first official gig.

"You're not nervous, are you?" asked Tess, the waitress.

"Who, me?" I answered and made a twitchy face gesture.

She laughed and said, "You'll do great. You look good too. The bowtie's a nice touch."

"I didn't think you'd notice," I said. I had Bing-ed myself up for my debut show. This included wearing a black bowtie with white polka dots, my gray-and-black plaid tweed jacket, and a white cotton handkerchief folded with three points in the breast pocket of the jacket. Plus, I paid Rory a dollar to put an extra bright shine on my black Florsheims. The real kicker—which had Lencie in stitches when I came out of the bathroom—was my pomaded hair. I'd gotten a short, very tidy haircut the day before and now used hair gel to comb it straight back.

"Where's the pipe?" she wanted to know, and then laughed and said, "On the other hand, maybe you should stay clear of fire with all that grease in your hair."

Instantly I began worrying I'd overdone it. Lencie made a crack about putting putty behind my ears to push them forward but then must have seen the distress on my face and stopped teasing me.

"You look great," she said. "Really." She reminded me that it was my singing that counted, not how I looked, which left me wondering about this point. Could I dress as me and still sing Bing as well or as convincingly? Probably, I thought, but why would I want to? "I wish I could be there," she added. We'd decided not to spend the money on a babysitter, and anyway she had to study.

In the end, it was a shame she couldn't attend because the show was a smash. By the first chorus of the first number, my preshow jitters dissolved and the band and I sounded like we'd been playing together all our lives. Though maybe not SRO, it was certainly a full house, and I held them. There was none of the typical chatter at the tables, and no one got up to go to the restroom or duck outside to smoke. Tess stopped serving drinks for most of the set, while at the bar Atzel sat watching and listening from first note to last.

At the break, several band members congratulated me on a wonderful performance. Tess brought me a scotch, and Atzel invited me to have a seat with him at the bar.

"You're better every time I hear you," he told me.

"It's a great band backing me," I replied, with typical Bing deflection, ever so polite and self-effacing.

"Don't be so modest."

"I don't know about that," I said, still with the Bing shtick.

Atzel signaled the bartender for a refill on his coffee. "I have a feeling we're onto something here," he said. "A revival of classic crooning."

I took a sip of my drink. In the past week or so, I'd started to see other aspects of Atzel, not just the music appreciator and club owner, but the manager and businessman as well.

"I'm not just talking about the voice here," he went on. "It's the songs too. All those fabulous songs. Berlin, Waller, Porter, Kern, Cahn, Mercer. Those guys knew how to write lyrics."

I took another sip. Atzel was letting me in on his thought process, so I wasn't going to interrupt him.

"Crosby had the phrasing like no one else. The lyrics and the phrasing. He married the music to the lyrics. The whole mood of those songs. Tender, romantic, sweet. Funny, too, some of them. I think people enjoy listening to that kind of music, I really do, even though most folks have never even heard it. But that's only because it hasn't been around. Not since the man himself sang those songs. But maybe it's also because no else could do it the way he did."

"I wish you could have met my grandma," I said in that mildly wry manner that Bing had.

"I would have liked that," he said, sounding like he meant it.

I could just picture it. Atzel would come to Shelton, and Grandma, bless her, would cook him a big ham supper, with no notion that a guy with a name like Atzel Gott might not eat pork. Or maybe Grandma would have come to Seattle and Atzel would wine and dine her in Belltown and make her the guest of honor at the Amethyst Club for the night. Grandma would have enjoyed that.

"I was watching tonight," he went on. "You could see it in the way people listened. Those songs spoke to them. People have been through some rough times lately, even the people who come to a place like this. And it's not just their personal lives either, not just the economy. It's the wars, the politics, the shootings. All of it. They just want a little sweetness back in their lives, some sentiment, a nice turn of phrase, a melody they can hum. And a voice that can carry it off."

Atzel had been looking straight past me as he spoke, gazing through the front window to the wet street outside. He was clearly into it.

"Michael Bublé," I said. "Like that?"

He turned to me. "*No,*" he said in disgust. "Not Michael Bublé. Not at all. Too much flash. No authenticity. I'm talking about *you.* You've got that voice."

Was he for real? He seemed to be. And even so, should I buy what he was selling? I knew the songs I sang that night were good, but he seemed to be getting a little nutty. Was he saying I was better than Bublé? More authentic? The real deal? Was he saying I was the next Bing Crosby? I believed he was.

"This is just your first night," he said, calming down a bit. "So we'll have to see." Then he clinked his coffee cup to my glass of scotch and said, "Cheers."

MY NEXT TWO SHOWS at the Amethyst Club were just as successful as the first. On Monday of both weeks, the band and I rehearsed. I felt as though I was inhabiting Bing's songs as never before. Each show seemed to confirm Grandma's instinct that I was, positively, *just like Bing.* I felt more confident working with the band and even occasionally took the liberty to make suggestions, such as opening a particular song a certain way or closing out another some other way. I also rotated in a couple of new numbers.

Jerry kept making suggestions as well. Sometimes these were directed at me, as when he told me to hold a note longer on "I Can't Begin to Tell You," and sometimes his suggestions were directed to other band members, as when he asked Kiran, the drummer, if she might try half time on "It's All Right With Me."

"We need to slow it down," he told her.

"But Jerry," Kiran complained, slumped on the stool behind her trap. "I can only count to four. I can count to four fast, or I can count to four slow. Do you want me to count to four slow?"

"Yes, darling," replied Jerry, who routinely let it be known he thought Kiran was the best jazz drummer on the West Coast. "Be a sweetheart and count slow."

I loved Monday rehearsals as much as the shows on Thursday. Atzel was rarely there for rehearsals, but he never missed a show. The Thursday crowd was growing as well, which he liked. He was working hard to get the word out, but the shows apparently were generating buzz all on their own, which was astonishing to me. By the third Thursday, I was outdrawing the better-known musicians Atzel booked for Friday and Saturday nights. Tess confirmed that I was getting a following when she mentioned that some people had come to all four shows.

"Folks tip better at your shows too," she said, which I took as a compliment.

The Amethyst Club would be closed for Thanksgiving, so I had a break coming up. Lencie and I had promised our families we'd come home for Thanksgiving. It would be our first trip back to the peninsula since leaving. Back to Shelton. Back to the trees and peaks and rivers and fog and windy roads and still more trees—all of which I sorely missed after just a few months in concrete-swollen, car-congested, pedestrian-packed Seattle. Shelton might seem like a shabby town to some, but it was my town, where I grew up, and that fact alone—once I was away long enough—lent the town its greatest charm. Call it homesickness, call it nostalgia, but I was missing Shelton.

We left Seattle early Wednesday morning and passed Olympia well before noon. From the highway, I took the Route 3 exit and then turned into the viewing area at the top of the hill so we could take in the town, mill, and bay from above.

"It's so small after living in Seattle," said Lencie after we got out of the car and stood at the edge of the bluff looking down.

Shelton was small all right. A few new businesses had opened downtown over the years, and up on Northcliff Road, we had the community college and the hospital and a Walmart Supercenter, but Shelton was basically the same as it had been in the early '90s when I would ride my bike from one end of the town limits to the other. It was also, and always would be, a working town. And a fairly poor town as well. Most residents made below thirty grand a year, and a good many were on public assistance. The Simpson panel mill, right there at the heel end of the bay, remained the main employer, and people always said that as long as smoke was coming from its stacks, they knew the town would be okay.

"Where's grandma and grandpa's house?" Rory asked.

"You can't see it from here," said Lencie. "But we'll go there right now."

Because we weren't married, Lencie's parents didn't want us sleeping together under their roof, so the plan was for Lencie and Rory to stay with her parents and for me to stay with my aunt and uncle. Lencie agreed her parents were being irrational, but she didn't want to quarrel with them about it—or with me.

We drove into town, both a bit surprised to realize how much our lives had changed in the past four months.

"Can you believe it!" Lencie said as we drove past the City Center Motel. "Did we actually stay there?"

"Best night of my life," I said, and asked her if she wanted to stop at the DQ.

"Can we?" Rory shouted from his safety seat in the back.

"We're going to grandma and grandpa's first," Lencie told him.

Her parents lived in a two-story farmhouse on the outskirts of town. Its white siding seemed more chipped and mildewed than it had just a few months ago when we left, and the front porch seemed to sag more as well. Her father's Dodge pickup was parked in the gravel drive. At the back of the five-acre property, the rusted front end of a maroon Grand Marquis stuck out from a thicket of blackberries, its back half entirely overtaken by the thorny tendrils. It had been the family car when Lencie was a kid.

Since she had called ahead from the viewing area, her parents were in the yard ready to greet us as we turned in to the drive. They were both in their late fifties but looked a lot older—a far cry from the well-heeled, athletic fifty-somethings jogging and cycling hither and thither in Seattle. Lencie hugged her dad while Rory raced into his grandma's arms. Then they switched, and when they were done hugging each other, I shook hands with Lencie's father and gave her mother a peck on the cheek.

"It's so far away and we never see you," her mother complained as she led us into the house.

"It's not *that* far, Mom, and it hasn't been *that* long," said Lencie.

"Well, we're just glad you're here, and glad to see Rory again. He's grown so."

I had been inside their house only twice before, each time to pick up Lencie for a date. The living room had a sofa and matching armchair, worn beige carpeting, an antique secretary stand, and four shopping center paintings representing the four seasons on the wall behind the TV. In the kitchen, the main gathering place, Lencie, her father, and I sat at the light blue wood table, another holdover from Lencie's childhood, while Rory stood and watched the song bird clock on the wall, waiting for the American robin to chirp the hour.

Lencie's mom served lunch—split-pea soup and cheese sandwiches—and most of the conversation as we ate revolved around Lencie's dental hygiene program and Rory's pre-K school. I knew her parents had no interest in my singing—"the whole Bing Crosby thing," I could remember Lencie saying—so I didn't expect them to ask me about it. At one point, her father asked me how my uncle was doing, and I said he was doing fine.

"I don't see him around much," he said.

"Working hard," I replied.

"Has a lot more to do since you left, I imagine."

"Any shed rat could do my job," I shot right back. Of course, this wasn't entirely true. When I started at the mill, I was assigned mostly grunt work, but as I learned the operation and became more adept at handling the machinery, my tasks became more difficult, requiring more skill. My remark was mainly intended to justify to Lencie's father—and perhaps to myself as well—my decision to quit the mill and move to Seattle to pursue my singing.

After lunch, I thanked Lencie's mom for the wonderful meal, shook her father's hand again, and said I'd be heading over to my family's place now. The plan was for me to have dinner there, spend the night, and then return the next afternoon for Thanksgiving dinner.

"Goodnight," I said to Lencie and gave her a big, mouth-mashing kiss right there in the kitchen for both parents to see. "See you tomorrow, tiger," I said to Rory and gave him a hug.

On the drive to my aunt and uncle's, I took the road north of town that led out across a high prairie area that early settlers once farmed. It was a large flat that now served various purposes. The airport, fairgrounds, motorsports park, water treatment plant, state trooper academy, and state prison were all up there. As one approached the prison, signs warned of no parking along the road. The whole compound was encircled by a double row of cyclone fencing with razor wire atop each and more razor wire laid on the ground between the rows. The one- and two-story buildings inside the perimeter of fencing were white with a sickly aqua-blue trim. Many of the buildings had a strangely decorative lattice design made of concrete on their exterior.

"Brutalist with a touch of lanai," as Stiles once described the prison's architecture.

At each corner of the prison compound stood a guard tower. These were square columns topped with glassed-in lookouts. As I drove by, I could see a guard in the lookout of the west tower. He looked out across the prison yard where forty or so inmates in white jumpsuits were milling about, playing basketball, or walking the fence line. I wondered if the guard was Lencie's ex, but I couldn't get a good look at him, and as I drove past the prison, I realized how much his threats to Stiles had been on my mind leading up to my return to Shelton.

I felt better, though, when L&H Precision Lumber came into view. The mill's muddy yard, mounds of sawdust, stacked logs, metal office building, and various sheds were such a familiar sight. And a welcome sight, I had to admit to myself, realizing as I drove past that I actually missed the place. I knew that Uncle Lillis had likely sent everyone home at noon for the holiday, so even though I thought about stopping to look around a bit—I still had the key to the front gate—I decided to wait and headed straight to the house instead.

Walking through the rush of their three dogs as I got out of the car, I greeted Uncle Lillis and Aunt Sherrie standing on the front porch. It was wonderful to see them. Aunt Sherrie had baked a batch of oatmeal cookies and brewed a fresh pot of coffee, so the house smelled warm and inviting. We sat in the living room surrounded by Aunt Sherrie's abundant crafts: needlepoint pillows, wool rag rugs, afghan throws. Like many peninsula women, she had the homesteading instinct in her. She also kept a garden, canned her own fruits and vegetables, raised and butchered chickens, and kept a freezer full of deer and elk meat that Uncle Lillis hauled home every hunting season. It had been a good many years since my grandma's passing, so the house was all Aunt Sherrie's now with the exception of a few pieces of furniture and a signed and inscribed photo of Bing Crosby that hung in the hallway. It was actually a still from the movie *Waikiki Wedding*, one of Bing's seventy-five movies. Grandma won it as part of a promotion. In the photo, Bing is wearing a white tuxedo with a black bowtie and a captain's hat with an anchor insignia. He's in mid-croon as he stands before the microphone. The inscription reads, "For Frances, In the Aloha Spirit. Best Wishes, Bing Crosby." She was a teenager when she received the photo, and for the rest of her life it remained one of her most treasured possessions.

When Aunt Sherrie saw me looking at it before dinner, she asked if I wanted to have it.

I had to laugh. "You mean it's not your most prized possession? You don't cherish it?"

"Weeeellllll," she said, trying to be delicate.

"That's heresy," I protested. "So maybe we should leave it where it is so we don't offend Grandma's spirit."

By the end of dinner, we had all caught up with one another. Uncle Lillis and Aunt Sherrie thought it was great that I was performing at the Amethyst Club and wanted to know when they could come see me.

"Any time," I said. "I'll have three more shows before Christmas."

"Are you going to do the Christmas songs?" Uncle Lillis wanted to know.

"I'm not sure," I said. "I haven't been asked."

Ah, the Christmas songs. They're probably Bing's only lasting legacy with respect to the general public. The only Bing movies you'll ever see on TV are *White Christmas* and *Holiday Inn*. The only songs you'll ever hear on the radio are "Silent Night," "It's Beginning to Look a Lot Like Christmas," and "I'll Be Home for Christmas." And right there is the whole problem. His music has been cheapened by dreary Christmastime cheer. And so even though Grandma loved having me sing the Christmas songs to her during the holiday season, privately I had maintained a moratorium on singing them ever since her passing. I wanted to expand people's appreciation of Bing, not narrow it. I wanted them to recognize him for his full artistic breadth and versatility.

"Why don't you give us a song," said Uncle Lillis. Of course, he was being a real card with this request because he knew that I knew he could not care less about Bing Crosby.

"No Christmas songs before Thanksgiving," I insisted.

"Give us one you do in Seattle then," said Aunt Sherrie. "Or maybe one your grandma liked."

I took a moment to consider, then stood up, walked over to the fireplace, and put my arm on the mantle. "Here's one that I do in Seattle *and* that Grandma absolutely loved," I said, and started humming a few bars to find the right key. "It's a little number called 'The Nearness of You.'"

A lot of singers have recorded this slow, lovely song. Norah Jones did an especially sweet version of it. But Bing's version was the best. I liked to sing it at the Amethyst because Jerry's piano accompaniment was always so great. As I sang the song for my aunt and uncle, I could see they were moved by it. Aunt Sherrie wiped her eyes with the sleeve of her sweater, and Uncle Lillis looked at me with admiration.

"Your grandma would be really pleased," he said without a trace of sarcasm when I was done.

I gave a polite bow and said thank you. And truly, coming from Uncle Lillis, the compliment meant a lot to me.

The next day, as planned, I spent the morning with my aunt and uncle and then returned to Lencie's parents' house for Thanksgiving dinner. After stuffing ourselves on turkey and all the fixings, we sat Rory down with his grandparents to watch Laurel and Hardy in *March of the Wooden Soldiers*, and Lencie and I went out for a walk. We walked down along Goldsborough Creek, the long, slithering stream that follows the railroad tracks for miles through the southwest portion of town before it empties into the bay. It was drizzling and the path beside the creek was muddy. Several wood ducks—the males with their forest-green caul, the females with their white-spotted eyes—swam in the creek. I told Lencie how I sometimes saw river otters in the creek when I was a kid. She then reminded me of the time years ago when a middle-school girl was raped alongside the creek. She also mentioned that she'd spoken to her ex the night before, after I left.

"Does he want to see Rory?" I asked. This seemed the likely reason for his calling her, even though, as far as I knew, he hadn't expressed any interest in seeing his son for the past four months.

"No," she said. "I called him."

"*Why?*"

Her initiating contact with this creep made no sense. It was one thing for him to ignore his son and threaten to run me out of town, but why did Lencie have to go calling him?

"Do you want to see him?" I asked her straight out.

"Don't be an idiot" she said. "Of course not. But I did think he might want to see his son. Or at least know how he was doing."

"It seems to me, based on every indication he's given so far, that he's more or less renounced all paternal obligations," I asserted. "As well as fatherly affections."

"That's harsh," she said.

"Why harsh?" I came right back. "So now you're going to defend the guy to me? *That's* harsh."

"Because he's Rory's father," she said.

The little conversation I'd had with Rory a couple of months ago while walking him home from school came back to me. *Wasn't I Rory's daddy now?* Why should her ex get paternal preference over me? Just because he'd impregnated her? Maybe it had even happened during one of their photo sessions. When was the last time Mr. Bio Dad had made a PB&J for Rory's school lunch or washed the poop stains from his Spider-Man pajamas? I felt slighted, as if my role in Rory's life had been reduced to little more than parental water boy.

"Maybe that's how *you* see it," I replied, trying to imply that Rory saw it otherwise. I tore a switch off an alder and started whacking the tall sedge grass along the creek bank.

"It doesn't matter anyway," she said. "There was a lockdown at the prison yesterday and he has to work double shifts through Thanksgiving."

"That's convenient."

Lencie ignored my sarcasm. "He said he wants to see him at Christmas, though."

"Touching," I said.

After that we walked back to her parents' house in silence. When we entered, Lencie went straight upstairs to her bedroom and I went into the living room where Rory and his grandparents were still watching the movie. Bo-Peep and Tom-Tom were fleeing Barnaby and had just entered the caverns of Bogeyland, where they ran into Ollie and Stannie. I sat down on the couch next to Rory to watch, yet Lencie's disappearance, as if it were me who had somehow done or said something wrong, left me stewing.

"I'm going," I said abruptly, getting up just as Barnaby was about to release his army of bogeymen.

"Bye," Rory said. He waved to me and then turned his attention back to the TV.

"Don't you want some leftovers?" asked Lencie's mother.

"No thanks," I said. "I'll have some at my uncle's." I grabbed my jacket and walked out of the house, intentionally not saying goodbye to Lencie.

I drove straight downtown to Bob's Tavern, a one-room

hole-in-the-wall where some of the folks from L&H sometimes gathered. I figured shooting the breeze over a beer or two would take my mind off Lencie and her asshole ex. It was Thanksgiving evening, so the bar was crowded, yet to my astonishment—had I been away *that* long?—I didn't recognize anyone. Nonetheless, I sat down at the end of the bar, threw back a shot of Pendleton and downed a beer, and then headed out again.

An hour later, as I dozed in Uncle Lillis's recliner with one of Aunt Sherrie's throws over me, I heard my phone blip. It was a text from Lencie. She wanted me to know she was sorry. I texted back that I was sorry too and added "I ♥ u."

This was the worst squabble Lencie and I had had since getting together. It wasn't much, yet it felt significant—to me at any rate—not only in my staking my place in Rory's life but in laying claim to our little family unit, such as it was.

THE NEXT DAY I picked up Lencie and Rory, and the three of us took a hike along the Duckabush River. The trail was wet and mossy, and the cedar and hemlock boughs soaked us every time we brushed against one. Even this late in the season, with the snowpack already building up at higher elevations, the river roared down from the mountains so forcefully we could barely hear ourselves speak when we reached its banks. I carried Rory on my shoulders for most of the hike, and Lencie and I held hands now and then.

We met with my uncle and aunt for lunch at the Pine Tree Restaurant downtown, their only chance to see Lencie and Rory during our short visit. When we were done, Uncle Lillis picked up the check, and out in the parking lot he and Aunt Sherrie took turns hugging Lencie and Rory and saying how good it was to see them and that they looked forward to seeing us all again at Christmas. They seemed to have forgotten about coming to see me at the Amethyst Club, which I figured they would.

Then, after we got into the car and were pulling out of the parking lot, I looked across the road and spotted Lencie's ex, wearing his gray guard uniform, stopped at the intersection in his white pickup. He saw me too—no doubt about it—and gunned his truck, turning the wheel hard and screeching up North First. Lencie, who was leaning over the backseat to adjust Rory's safety seat, didn't see a thing. I took a deep breath and turned left in the opposite direction, and all the way back to Lencie's parents' house I couldn't help wondering whether this encounter was pure coincidence or if he'd actually been following us.

After I dropped them off, I decided to track down Stiles. He hadn't replied to the email I'd sent him a week ago or the text message I'd sent on Thanksgiving Day, so I decided to look for him at the only two places I could think of. I went to Anabelle's Tea Room first, but it was closed. Then I went to the only place I'd ever known Stiles to live, the somewhat scary Decochet Hall apartments, just off of Railroad Avenue heading out of town. Once upon a time, the Decochet was probably an attractive building. But no more. The three-story stucco-sided structure was shaped like a Chinese block puzzle, an assortment of squares intersecting with one another. It had once been painted white, but age and weather left it looking as dull and gray as the November sky. A few weeks earlier, while in Seattle, I'd been playing around on Google Maps, dragging the cursor around the streets of my hometown, and tried to find Decochet Hall. The Google car guy had picked the perfect day for driving around Shelton, wet and dreary, but he never drove past Decochet Hall.

I parked on the street and walked up the chipped concrete steps to the double entrance doors. I checked the residence board for Stiles's name, but only half of the apartment numbers had names next to them. I tried the door, but it was locked. Yet when someone came out—a Latino guy with a mustache, followed by his wife carrying a baby—I grabbed ahold of the door and went in. The hallway floors were linoleum tile, the walls scuffed, the staircase carpet stained and worn. There was an open window on the landing to the second floor with an empty beer bottle on the window ledge. I found 211, the apartment that for some reason I thought was Stiles's, and knocked.

"Hey, Stiles, it's me. I saw the ex about an hour ago. I think he was following me." I knocked again. "You in there? Should I call the EMTs? Or the coroner?" I put my ear to the door but couldn't hear a thing. "Come on, man. I'm leaving town tomorrow." I knocked again and waited a couple minutes, but nothing. It might not have even been his apartment. So I tried the doors on either side and got the same non-response at one and at the other an old guy shouting at me to go away. I then gave up on Decochet Hall and finding Stiles.

The next morning, as arranged, I arrived at Lencie's parents' at 10:00. I loaded Lencie's and Rory's bags into the trunk, and as I waited in the car for them to say goodbye to the grandparents, I chewed on the stem of the pipe I kept in the glove compartment. By 10:30, we were on our way. *So long, Shelton*, I thought as we left the town behind, understanding now why such holiday visits always leave people feeling so uncertain about their hometowns.

BACK IN SEATTLE, THE period between the holidays was hectic. Lencie had finals, and I had a few new numbers I wanted to work into my remaining performances at the Amethyst. When I showed them to Jerry, he said sure and suggested an additional song, one by Vince Gill, the country songwriter. I was doubtful at first. I wanted to sing Bing and hadn't bargained on expanding the repertoire to include anyone other than Bing. But Jerry assured me that the Vince Gill number was one Bing would have loved, being how Bing was always willing to try out new songwriters. So I agreed to give it a go at Monday's rehearsal—and it was great. It fit right in with the Bing songbook, the sentiment, the phrasing, the tonality, everything.

"Do you think people will know it?" I asked Jerry during a break. I'd only ever sung Bing Crosby covers, songs that most people didn't know. Though written by others, they always sounded so original to Bing, and since most people today had never heard them, they also sounded original to me. So I worried that if I started throwing in a lot of contemporary numbers that people were familiar with—what next? A Beatles tune?—they would start thinking we were just another lame cover band.

"Not unless they're huge Vince Gill fans," he replied.

I then asked him if he thought Atzel would sign me to a new contract after Christmas, and he laughed. "Are you kidding? He's already told me you're our New Year's Eve act. And when you re-sign, make sure he gives you more money."

This response was one reason everyone in the band loved Jerry so much. He knew how to make great music and he looked after his people. We did the Vince Gill number that Thursday and got a big applause for it.

The next Monday, Atzel showed up toward the end of rehearsal. Then, when we were done and everyone was packing up, he signaled me to the bar and pushed another manila envelope in front of me.

"If you want to sign it now before you leave, that'll be fine. I'll be back in the office if you have any questions." He then walked away and left me there to read the new contract.

As I read through it, I had to look up periodically to process it all. This one was for a full year, beginning December 31. I would perform a minimum of once a week, Thursdays definitely, but also a Friday or Saturday now and then. For Thursday performances, I would receive $700 a night, and for Friday and Saturday performances, $1,000. Furthermore, I would have to be willing to travel to bookings in other cities, these dates to be scheduled by Atzel in consultation with me, with all travel arrangements to be made by Atzel.

About halfway through reading the contract, I looked around the club. The horn players were cleaning and packing their instruments, joking among themselves. The bass player, Ronel, was still on stage, in his own world, improvising on his double bass as if in a slow dance with it, tickling the strings with his left hand along the unfretted stringboard and slapping at them along the instrument's belly with his right. Meanwhile, Jerry and Kiran were in a tête-à-tête over drinks at a back table.

The next part of the contract really bowled me over. The terms stated that within the first six months of signing, I would record a full-length album in the studios of the recently formed Amethyst Records, song selection and arrangement to be determined in consultation with Atzel Gott and Jerry Parrington. I would receive a $1,000 advance on the album and 10 percent of all sales. In other words, I was going to be a recording artist.

The contract far exceeded my expectations, so I put away any notion of bargaining with Atzel for more money. The union, however, recommended members have any contract reviewed before signing it, so when I entered Atzel's office, I thanked him first and expressed how excited I was about touring and recording and performing more regularly at the club, and then told him I'd have the signed contract back on his desk by Thursday.

"That's fine," he said. "I think we're going to make a lot of beautiful music together."

Driving home on I-5, I can't say what it was, but rather than being excited about the new contract, suddenly something came over me and I was overtaken by a storm of doubts like I'd never experienced before. They came in the form of a monumental sense of inadequacy, a certainty that I was neither prepared for nor deserving of such a dramatic uptick in my so-called singing career. Mired in this mood, I drove past my exit and headed toward Northgate, then Alderwood, then Edmonds. Was this really happening, I wondered, or was someone (Atzel, Jerry, or someone else entirely, like my Uncle Lillis) playing a massive prank on me, taking me for the fool that I was? Success was throwing itself at me and instead of embracing it, I wanted to duck for cover. I even began to fear telling Lencie about the new contract. The trip to Shelton and the ongoing ordeal with her ex still left me questioning, especially after our squabble, our relationship and what kind of future we had. Was it time for us to get married and for me to officially adopt Rory? Oddly, we'd never discussed either possibility. At this point in her life, it seemed like all that mattered to Lencie was her dental hygiene program. It seemed I was increasingly relegated to the role of daycare provider, housekeeper, and academic cheerleader. But if I was going to accept this new contract with Atzel, things would have to change. By the time I reached Everett, I even started thinking I might be better off on my own.

I exited at Marysville, talked myself down while pumping gas into the car, and got back on I-5 South. *Easy there, fella*, I told myself, channeling Bing. I thought how every performer probably gets scared while also fantasizing about fame and fortune. You couldn't tell me Bing, anxious as he might have been upon leaving Spokane, didn't anticipate a glorious future for himself when he headed down to Los Angeles chasing his star. Maybe my voice—or was it his voice? I sometimes got confused on this point—would be my ticket to such success as well.

I started humming, then sang a little scat, then whistled some, and by the time I reached the Greenwood exit, I'd calmed myself down. It was just a mild panic attack, I told myself. I got overexcited, is all. Nothing I couldn't handle. I should absolutely go for it. It was now or never.

LENCIE, OF COURSE, WAS experiencing her own success. She earned straight As in every class, made the dean's list at the end of the fall quarter, and joined the honor society for community college students. When she applied for the supervised clinicals at public dental clinics throughout Seattle, she was one of only two first-year students selected. What's more, the position paid. The only hitch was it meant we wouldn't be going to Shelton for Christmas, not even for the one day.

"They're assigning me to an emergency clinic," she said, "and it's open every day, even on Christmas. That's the whole point."

I didn't pretend to show much disappointment about not returning to Shelton for Christmas. While I would miss seeing my aunt and uncle, the fact was, if I never had to deal with Lencie's cranky parents or her unstable ex again, it would suit me fine.

"We'll have a wonderful Christmas right here," I said. It would be just the three of us, which would be great. We'd get a tree and decorate it, hang stockings, drink hot cocoa, and open presents on Christmas Eve, and the next day when Lencie came home from the clinic, I'd have a turkey dinner waiting.

"Will Santa know where we live now?" Rory asked when we told him we'd be staying in Seattle for Christmas.

"Of course," I told him. "Santa knows where every little boy and girl lives." I planned to get him the expanded Hot Wheels track that he wanted so badly and also surprise him with a five-gallon fish tank and half a dozen goldfish to put in his bedroom. It was going to be the best Christmas ever, I told him.

THE NEW YEAR'S EVE show at the Amethyst Club was SRO. Atzel couldn't have been happier. The crowd was all sorts and ages—hipsters, professionals, baby boomers, oldsters—and a lot of them were dressed to the nines. I wore a black suit with silk lapels and a black bowtie for the performance. I also put extra gel in my hair. The new numbers we added to the playlist sounded great. The band and I were in perfect sync with one another. Everyone's timing was on, and I never felt in greater command of my own voice. I owned the stage, and the audience members could tell. They applauded more enthusiastically than ever. Faces were beaming, and some people even cheered. Man oh man, was I ever feeling it! I was in full Bing mode, becoming one with my crooning idol. I was on top of the world, reaching for that star!

My only regret was that Lencie couldn't be there. She had the night off, but finding a babysitter on New Year's Eve was impossible. *Did she even know what kind of talent she was living with?* I thought after the first set when I called her and wished her Happy New Year. Did she recognize the effect I had on an audience? She'd been to a couple of my earlier shows, but they were nothing compared to this. The New Year's Eve show marked a turning point.

The next morning—New Year's Day—I had an email from Jerry, sent at 4:37 a.m. All it said was, "You were great! We need strings."

He was right. I was great and we needed strings. Adding a couple violins, maybe a cello, had always been in the back of my mind. They played a big role in Bing's music. Jerry's arrangements were stupendous, but a string section, even a small one, would turn our little ensemble into an orchestra. And Jerry then could be a bona fide bandleader.

Immediately I thought of Ian, the jazz violinist from the handful of talent shows I'd been in. I got his number two days later from the union and invited him down to the club. As soon as Jerry heard him play, he was in, and Atzel, who remembered Ian from the talent show, concurred. Ian then recommended another violinist and a cellist, friends of his from the Thornton School of Music in Los Angeles, and Jerry talked Ronel into dusting off the horsehair bow for his upright, and by the end of the week we had a genuine string section.

"Meet me at the first chorus," I said to the new band members. We were preparing to break out a new number at our first full rehearsal. It was one of my favorite lines from Bing, and I'd been waiting for the chance to use it. Plus, I was exercising my newfound confidence following the New Year's Eve show. I started singing a cappella and the strings came in right on cue at the chorus. The new layer of sound was transformative.

It was the first rehearsal Atzel ever sat all the way through. He told the musicians afterward he was going to let us play together at the Amethyst Club for a few weeks to jell and then bring us into the studio to cut the album. He also mentioned a road tour in the spring to promote it. "So keep your calendars open," he told everyone.

"Man alive," I said to Jerry before going home that night. "This is real showbiz."

Being the old pro he was, Jerry just smiled and closed the lid on the keys of his piano. "Rest those pipes, Shelstein," he said and went over to speak to Kiran.

When Atzel suggested a voice coach, given how much more singing I would be doing under the new contract, I immediately contacted the person he recommended. Up until then I hadn't realized how wrong much of my technique was, or how badly I was straining my vocal cords, even as I tried not to. The voice coach taught me to open my throat and form my mouth to enunciate the lyrics more fully. She taught me how to breathe evenly and pump my diaphragm. She showed me how to support the notes and had me practice scales, arpeggios, legato runs, and staccato runs until I was nearly ready to go all out bel canto. It was a lot of work, but after a few lessons my voice became stronger, my pitch improved, and my range increased.

We cut the album in early March. Atzel billed himself as producer, though it was Jerry who did the sound checks and mixing and taught Atzel how to operate the soundboard. It was a small studio in a former warehouse in Belltown, a few blocks from the club, which Atzel typically rented out to local bands wanting to make a CD on the cheap. Because we didn't have to pay hourly rates, the band and I spent three weeks there perfecting the fourteen songs (all Bing numbers) to be included on the album, which would be titled A Night to Go Dreaming.

Then in mid-April, with two cases of CDs in the luggage compartment on the tour bus along with our bags, The Jerry Parrington Orchestra—featuring yours truly—went on tour. We played Portland, Ashland, Sacramento, San Francisco, San Jose, Fresno, Los Angeles, and San Diego. Each gig was typically a two-night stand, which meant we were on the road for nearly four weeks. The venues ranged from sophisticated to seedy, with a couple of college campuses thrown in. We drew good audiences, and the CDs, with Tess peddling them at every stop, flew off the table. Plus, the band played consistently well. Jerry, Kirin, Ronel, and a few others were road tour veterans. They came in, did their jobs like the consummate professionals they were, and retired to their hotel rooms. But to me and Ian and his two friends from music school, it was a great big adventure. We went sightseeing through the big cities during the day and at night, after the show, hit a few more drinking establishments before they closed. At one college campus we played, we were invited to a fraternity party, which, after an hour of drinking beer from a red Solo cup and making small talk with ponytailed coeds, had me feeling more middle-aged than ever before.

By the time the bus rolled back into Seattle, we were exhausted—happy but exhausted. By every estimate, the tour was a success. People came out, the CDs sold, and local papers gave us glowing reviews. Two of the reviews mentioned the Bing Crosby connection: one positively ("He channels the voice and the spirit of America's greatest crooner"), which pleased me, and one negatively ("He lacks the sympathetic eyes and effortless charm of the original"), which stung. But even the negative review applauded my overall performance and gave special kudos to Jerry's orchestration.

My time away from home, however, was a strain on Lencie, especially in regard to taking care of Rory. She had to rely on help from parents of Rory's friends from school, which she didn't like having to do. Her studies sagged as well. So when I finally returned, she was relieved. As for myself, I felt lost hanging around the house again. I realized I might have been a little depressed coming down from the thrill of the album debut and road tour. I began to wonder again how long I could keep this up, what would become of it all, and whether it was all just a great big charade to showcase what a fraud I really was. Bing Crosby? Really? When was the novelty going to wear off? At what point would people say, *Okay, I get it*, and go back to listening to whatever vapid pop album they were used to? The doubts persisted no matter how hard I tried to shake them.

The band had an eight-day break before playing the Amethyst again, yet Atzel wanted us to develop new songs during the break so we could go into the studio again in a couple of months. He talked about doing an album of contemporary songs, mentioning a Tom Waits song and a Lucinda Williams song he thought would work. I wanted to tell him the songs were far too edgy—Bing didn't do edgy. Furthermore, I was dedicated to doing Bing and only Bing and didn't want to fool around with anything different. The Vince Gill song was an exception, and I wanted to keep it that way. Meanwhile, no doubt, Atzel pictured himself as another Rick Rubin, producing his own version of the American series with Johnny Cash. Yet, I had about as much enthusiasm for doing contemporary numbers as I did for singing the classic Christmas songs.

AFTER A WEEK OR SO, Lencie and I were back to our routine, which for me meant walking Rory to and from school. Feeling lazy one day (as well as perhaps a little sorry for myself, burdened as I was with this domestic duty), I decided to pick him up in the car after I'd been cruising about aimlessly for most of the afternoon. Once I had him strapped in, he asked if we could go feed the ducks at Green Lake and I said sure. First, though, I needed to get a coffee, so I pulled into the drive-thru espresso stand a few blocks from the lake, and as the woman inside was finishing up with a customer at the opposite window, I studied the rhinestone-studded back pockets of her skinny jeans. Then, when she turned and came to our window, I recognized her immediately. It was Shakira.

"Hi, Nicole," I said.

She leaned out the window to get a better look at me. Her hair was still blonde but not as blonde as it used to be. Otherwise she looked the same as when I saw her last, just not dressed so stunningly. Over her skinny jeans, she wore a Posies T-shirt with the elastic collar cut out.

"Hey," she said, seeming to only half-recognize me.

I reminded her of my name. "It's Chris," I said, and added, "The talent shows?"

"Oh, yeah. Hey, Chris," she said, brightening up. "It's good to see you."

"You still singing?" I asked.

She shrugged, and said, "No, not so much." Her face went kind of blank as she seemed to realize that instead of fulfilling her dream of being a singer—which I assumed was why she'd moved to Seattle from Idaho in the first place—she was a barista at a drive-thru espresso stand. "So what can I get you?"

"Let's see," I said and ordered a double latte for me and a hot chocolate for Rory.

As she made our drinks, I wondered if she would ask me what I'd been doing. Would I brag to her about the Amethyst Club, the album, the road tour? When she came back and handed the drinks to me, however, it was as if I was any other guy getting coffee. She didn't say a word as she gave me my change.

"Good to see you," I said and put a dollar in the tip jar.

"Thanks," she said, "you too." And then she pulled the sliding window closed.

At the lake, Rory ran ahead as I carried our drinks to a bench near the swing set. When I lifted the latte to take a sip, I could smell a distinctive fragrance—not espresso aroma, but perfume, ever so faint. Somehow it had gotten onto the lid of the cup or maybe the cup itself. Perhaps this was a barista trick, I thought, one of those subliminal things. A touch of Chanel, or whatever, to trigger guys' pheromones and keep them coming back. If so, I liked it. I took another sip, inhaled the fragrance, and pictured Nicole leaning out the window to take our orders. Then as I watched Rory push himself higher on the swing, an idea took hold of me.

"Rory," I called. "Let's walk." I handed him his hot chocolate and began walking down the paved pathway around the lake. It was a sunny day, daffodils in bloom, rhododendrons about to burst open. We walked a good ways around the lake before Rory asked if we were going to feed the ducks now.

"Later," I said. "We have to go now."

He said he wanted to stay and feed the ducks, but I told him no, not now, and headed toward the parking lot. As I strapped him into his safety seat, I told him I had something important to do and then drove straight back to the espresso stand. There were two cars ahead of me, but eventually I pulled up and the window slid open.

"Back so soon?" Nicole said. She didn't look very surprised at all.

"How would you like to sing some duets with me?" I asked her.

She looked up as a car pulled in behind me, and when she looked back at me, I gave her a short and fast account of what I'd been doing since the talent shows and explained how I'd been thinking of ways to develop the act and had always liked her voice. Then I wrote my cell phone number on a napkin and told her to call me.

"If you're interested," I said, "we'll see how it goes."

"Sure," she replied, appearing to catch on finally to what I was proposing. "I'll think about it."

And with that I pulled away from the espresso stand. As I drove home I congratulated myself on the idea of trying out Nicole as a singing partner. She could bring new energy to the act, the way the string section had. But at the same time I knew I was kidding myself. This wasn't the only reason I wanted to sing a duet or two with Nicole. I lifted my coffee cup and inhaled the perfume again, and then looked around to see if Rory was watching me. He'd fallen asleep in his safety seat, though, so I took another whiff of the perfume and started humming one of my favorites from Bing—"Fancy Meeting You Here"—his big hit with Rosemary Clooney.

DESPITE MY DOUBTS THAT Nicole would call me, she did so the very next day, and we agreed she would come down to the Amethyst for the next rehearsal. I said I would email her the lyrics of a few songs Bing and Rosemary Clooney had done, and added she could download them from iTunes. We'd try out the songs on Monday, I told her, and see how Jerry liked them.

"Do you think he'll mind?" she asked with understandable apprehension.

"I think he'll love it," I said. I knew I was taking more of a chance with Atzel than with Jerry since Atzel always liked to be the one to initiate any big changes to the act.

I was also taking a chance with Lencie, I knew quite well, so I didn't mention anything about Nicole to her just yet, having decided I would tell her after the duet was a done deal and Nicole was part of the act. I knew Lencie would be jealous—and she would have every right to be. I was jonesing for Nicole. I kept the empty paper cup and white plastic lid with the perfume on them in the car, still able to catch a faint scent off them now and then. At the same time, I kept telling myself it was nothing. Nicole wasn't interested in me. Why would she be? And if anything came of her audition and Nicole joined the act, I would tell Lencie about it pronto—end of story.

Naturally, Nicole rocked the audition. Jerry and Atzel looked skeptical at first when I introduced her to them, and even more so when I told them we were going to do a couple songs together. But when Nicole stepped up to the mic, they could see the kind of stage presence she had, especially in the sleeveless, open back cocktail dress she wore. Atzel said he wanted to hear her sing on her own first, so she did a Lauryn Hill song, a cappella, which got the whole band paying attention. Then she asked Jerry if he might accompany her on Cole Porter's "I Get a Kick Out of You," and by the end of the song she'd won everyone over.

"Thank you," she said with an embarrassed smile as she placed the mic back in the stand.

"Very nice," Atzel said. "You have a lovely voice, Nicole."

I could see Jerry behind the piano nodding his approval.

I then joined Nicole on stage.

"Is this thing on," I said, tapping the mesh of the mic. No one laughed, though Jerry had a smirk on his face "Are you ready?" I asked Nicole.

"Ready as you are," she said.

I snapped my fingers three times for the beat and started in on "Button Up Your Overcoat," a little ditty that involves a good bit of repartee between Bing and Rose. And Nicole was right there with it:

"Hey, Nicole, would you like to tiptoe through the tulips?"
"Not now, thank you."
"Well, would you care to hop a Chattanooga Choo-Choo?"
"I don't think so."
"Would you like to go out under the moon?"
"It's much too early for that kind of action."
"Then what do you want to do?"
"I just thought we might team up on a nice duet."

And we were off to the races. Under Nicole/Rosemary's energetic vocals and charming manner, I was thoroughly inhabiting the Bing persona. I'd sung the occasional quirky duet with my cousin Jennifer, of course, but that was nothing compared to this. This was pure magic.

After "Button Up Your Overcoat," we slid effortlessly into "Singin' in the Rain." For texture, I let her take the melody (higher) while I took the harmony (lower), and on the second verse, for variety, I whistled along to her vocals. On the third round of the chorus, Jerry joined in on the piano, and Nicole and I really got into it then. We even improvised on the kind of playful gestures Bing and Rosemary always made part of their act. Nicole put her palms out and looked up and shrugged, while I shook out the collar of my sport coat and pretended to open an umbrella—and we went on singing. When we finished, we gave each other an affectionate shoulder hug.

"Okay," said Atzel. "Work up two more numbers and we'll give it a try a week from this Thursday."

Nicole and I hopped off the stage and went smiling to the bar to toast our success. I complimented her on being so well prepared. She said it was easy. "And what fun," she exclaimed. She stayed around for the full rehearsal, and at break Joey, the guitarist, had a drink with her, which I tried to ignore. After the break Atzel sat down with her at a table with paperwork to sign.

When rehearsal ended around 10:30, I asked Nicole if she would like to go with me down the street to another bar for a nightcap and talk about the songs we wanted to do on Thursday.

"Just a Coke for me, though," she said. "I've had my limit already."

"Agreed," I said, and I took her jacket off the chair and held it out for her.

I SHOULD HAVE TOLD Lencie about Nicole when I got home, but I didn't. And I knew why. I was too attracted to Nicole to chance it. I knew that by telling Lencie, by putting everything out in the open, I risked negating my attraction for Nicole, and that's not what I wanted—not yet at least. I would tell Lencie about Nicole eventually, I figured. I would have to. But for now what Nicole and I shared on stage at the Amethyst Club—and whatever else we might share—was too enchanting. Telling Lencie about her would only break the spell.

Life for me and Lencie and Rory went on as usual. Lencie received a special honor for being in the top fifth percentile of her class. We went to an awards dinner at the college where she was presented with a carved hunk of glass with her name etched on it. All evening long she thanked me for everything I did to help her.

"I hope it's worth your while," she said over dessert, and then leaned over, placed her hand on my thigh, and inserted her tongue in my mouth while everyone else at our table listened to the keynote speaker.

"It is," I said. I meant it, but I also knew there was something of an untruth in the way I said it.

Later that night, after sending the babysitter home and putting Rory to bed, we had quite the romp in the bedroom. I couldn't remember the last time Lencie had been so into it, and so adventuresome, and afterward it occurred to me how ridiculous I had been to even think of starting something with Nicole.

The next week, though, Lencie began a new quarter at the college with a whole new slate of classes—two of which, she said emphatically, were crucial to her passing the state board exam at the end of the year—and just like that we were back to our routine and the low-grade exhaustion that accompanied it. During the same week, Nicole and I worked up a couple more numbers, both from Bing and Rose's album *That Travelin' Two-Beat*. The duet definitely added a playful element to the act without the songs getting too cute or corny.

I finally told Lencie about Nicole after the second rehearsal. "It was Atzel's idea," I said. We were in the kitchen making supper. "I'm not so keen on sharing the stage, but he thinks it's good for the act."

"You're not sleeping with her, are you?" Lencie asked without looking up from the potato she was scrubbing at the sink. I couldn't tell if she was joshing me or not. I suppose she was and wasn't.

"Not yet," I said and put my arms around her waist and nuzzled the back of her neck so she wouldn't see me blushing with guilt and embarrassment at her question.

"When can I hear this new duet?" she asked and turned the water off.

"Thursday, if you want," I said.

So on Thursday, Lencie found a way to put her studies aside for a night, and we dropped Rory off at the Keoghs'.

The show that night at the Amethyst went great. With advance notice, Atzel got our regular fans to come out in force and pack the club. The band and I opened with a set. We mostly did our favorites, and to appease Atzel, we added a version of Tom Waits's "Alice," a sweet, tender ballad rearranged by Jerry that made me realize Tom Waits was basically an old sentimental crooner himself. I was a little uncomfortable singing the song, just as I'd been when I first did the Vince Gill number, but I just kept picturing Bing in my mind's eye, his willingness to try new things—such as the duet he did with David Bowie on "Little Drummer Boy"—and soldiered through it.

Toward the middle of the second set, I announced to the house that I wished to invite a very special lady up to the stage to join me for a couple of songs. I watched then as Nicole, standing in the back near Atzel's office door, removed the shawl she was wearing and made her way to the stage in a brilliant white dress with a swooped-out neck and a long, sweeping hemline. It was as if she'd stepped straight out of the movies. She was no longer Shakira, as I used to think of her. She was Rosemary Clooney in all her hometown loveliness and poise.

I took her hand as she stepped onto the stage and into the lights.

The house applauded, mesmerized, it seemed, by the sight of her. We wasted no time.

"Well, how do, Nicole?"

"How do?" she said right back and tossed her hair over her shoulder.

"Don't you look lovely this evening."

"Thank you. It's a very special night."

"It is indeed."

"And look at all these fine people in the audience." She swept her arm out and there was more applause.

"Only the best for the Amethyst," I quipped. "So why don't we sing a song."

"I would like that."

We bounced right into "Button Up Your Overcoat" and then "Singin' in the Rain," and from there, to close the set out, we did our two new songs. When we finished, the applause and whistles from the audience were all we needed to know the duet was a success. The applause kept up so long that I had to promise the audience Nicole would be back next week.

"So be here," I said and gave a wink to the audience, "or be square."

Moments later, back in Atzel's office, Nicole giddily swirled about the room with her hands on her head. "That was amazing," she said. "Wasn't it?"

"You were great," I told her. She was great too! *We* were great!

"Thank you soooo much for asking me to sing with you." She could hardly contain herself as she paced about the room.

"Thank *you*," I said. "They really loved you." Then I remembered Lencie still out at the table sitting by herself. "Would you like to join me and Lencie for a drink out front?"

"Yes, yes," she said. "But let me calm down first." She took a deep breath to show she was trying to regain her composure. "You go ahead," she said, letting the breath out, "and I'll join you in a few minutes."

AFTER THE DEBUT WITH Nicole, things got crazy. Atzel changed the schedule and had us playing the Amethyst every Thursday and Saturday night. And even with this added night, there was no letup in the people coming out to see us. The Facebook and Twitter comments were glowing, and on a whim Atzel took us to Spokane and Vancouver, BC, for a couple of Tuesday night bookings where the response was just as positive.

The only letdown to all this excitement came a month into our shows in Seattle. A columnist for *The Stranger* penned a piece calling the act a throwback to a period of "genderist dualities" when women were "playful kittenettes" and men "knuckle-dragging sadists." It came out on a Wednesday, and the band had a good laugh reading it aloud before the show that Thursday. Kiran kept calling me a "knuckle-dragging sadist," and finally we agreed the writer of the piece didn't know what he was talking about, especially given he didn't say a word about the Bing Crosby–Rosemary Clooney connection. Three days later the TV show *Evening Magazine* came to the club and did a spot on us that aired the next week, and it was so flattering the stink from *The Stranger* review was quickly forgotten.

On the Monday following our debut, Nicole quit her job at the espresso stand. By then I'd been around her enough to know that the perfume on my latte cup had most certainly been hers. On top of the six-month exclusive contract she signed with Atzel, he dropped $1,000 on her to enhance her wardrobe. She told me she could hardly believe everything that was happening, and for the first few weeks she thanked me profusely every time I saw her. We worked up a few more songs, and before long our duet made up half the act. We even talked about her doing a couple of songs by herself, perhaps "Come On-a My House," Rosemary Clooney's biggest hit.

One morning after Lencie had already left to catch the bus and I'd walked Rory to school, I went to the café with my laptop and did some research on Rosemary Clooney. She'd had her share of troubles in life—drugs, mental health issues, a rocky marriage to José Ferrer, according to Wikipedia. But she eventually pulled through it all. She really did remind me of Nicole: pretty, blonde, an appealing smile and amazing voice. But more important than these features, there were two sides to Rosemary Clooney just as there were two sides to Nicole: the strong, determined side, and the sensitive, vulnerable side. I could see this in Nicole after each performance when she would let her guard down and, while sipping some wine at the bar, tell me about growing up near Boise, Idaho, in a small redneck farming town, which frankly sounded a lot like growing up in Shelton.

I also found websites for two Rosemary Clooney fan clubs, one in America and one in Japan. The Japanese loved Rose almost as much as they loved Bing. I clicked over to my email and sent a message to Atzel with links to the Japanese fan club for Clooney and the Japanese fan club for Bing, and at the bottom of the message I wrote, "We should go to Japan!"

I then logged off, went home, did my voice exercises, and took a nap. When I logged back onto the computer a few hours later, there was a message from Atzel that said simply, "Yes!" So I wrote back, asking, "Seriously?" and within seconds he replied, "I'm looking into clubs right now. Checking the schedule." So I looked on Google Translate for some Japanese phrases and replied, "*Hee, sore wa yokatta ne*," meaning "Wow, that's great!"

When I told Lencie that the band might go to Japan, I made the point of saying, "I'm sure we can work it out so you and Rory can come too." Dinner was over, the dishes done, and Rory was in bed.

"There's no way," she said, pulling three textbooks out of the roller suitcase she used for hauling her books to and from the college. She dropped all three onto the kitchen table with a thud.

"How come?"

She opened the dental terminology book and looked at me sternly. The director of Lencie's program at the college had recommended to her a specialist in strabismus, and in January she'd started doing more extensive physical therapy to strengthen her right eye's rectus muscles. Since then her cross-eye had become almost nonexistent, making her appear much more serious.

"Because it's not going to happen," she said. "That's why."

"I thought you might like going to Japan," I said. "What other chance will there be? All we'd have to do is pay for the plane tickets."

She calmed down some and said, rather plaintively, "I just can't ditch my classes for that long. I'm sorry."

At first I worried Lencie wouldn't want me to be alone with Nicole for such a long trip, an ocean away and free to romp around with her as much as I liked. But that wasn't her concern at all. She was more concerned about finding childcare for Rory while I was gone. Since I shouldered most of the childcare duties, even an overnight to Spokane put her in a pinch. If I went to Japan for two or three weeks, she wouldn't be able to study so hard and her grades might decline ever so slightly. She might even miss a class or two. I was annoyed and felt like telling her, *So what!* But I didn't. I didn't want to fight with Lencie. In fact, I wasn't so sure I even wanted her to come to Japan.

"You're such a great student," I said, trying to reassure her instead of quarrelling. "Your professors would understand."

She then started to cry and I walked around the table and put my hands on her shoulders. She rubbed her sleeve across her face, trying to laugh it off.

"I'm sorry," she said. "It's just very stressful."

"I know," I said and kissed the top of her head.

"I'm so close, and the state board exams…" And just the mention of the state board exams started her crying again.

"I don't even know if this trip is going to happen," I said. I did know that once Atzel set his mind to something, it got done. "And if it does, maybe your mother could come over and help with Rory."

"Yeah," she said flatly, "maybe." She scooted her chair closer to the table and leaned over the terminology textbook.

This response felt like a brush-off to me. "Don't make like I'm abandoning you," I said. "I have responsibilities too." I was already picturing me and Nicole between the crisp white sheets of a bed in a high-rise hotel in Tokyo, sipping sake and feeding each other sashimi.

"I know," she said and uncapped her pink highlighter.

CAN YOU CALL IT infidelity if you're not actually married? It's such a harsh word, *infidelity*, like something from the Old Testament, something a Canaanite or Hittite would be accused of, turning the person guilty of infidelity into an *infidel*. I prefer *unfaithful*, but even that has overtones of religious zealotry. My affair with Nicole hardly lives up to either label. *Betrayal* perhaps works better. Lencie trusted me, and I betrayed that trust. Point blank, I cheated on her.

The affair started in Portland. We did a Friday night show at The Polynesian, a club where they served mai tai drinks. The band members wore leis. I brought out my ukulele (which Lencie had given me for Christmas) and did a Hawaiian number with Nicole, who placed an orchid in her hair and did a swaying kind of hula dance beside me. The Portlanders ate it up.

But it was the mai tais that really got us. Before the show was even over, Nicole had exceeded her self-imposed two-drink limit, and after the show, I lost count of how many we downed together. The band all left after packing up, leaving Nicole and me to close the place down. We staggered out of The Polynesian and wandered about the Pearl District and down to the Chinese garden where I tried to climb the wall and tore my pants. Eventually we made our way back to the hotel just on the other side of Burnside, and once there, it was on. There was nothing discrete or reserved about what happened next. In the entryway, Nicole grabbed me and stuck her tongue down my throat. I ran my hand up under her coat and caught her ass and squeezed. When we got on the elevator, we kept at it, and after we stumbled into her room, we took a few swigs from a bottle of white wine she had in the small fridge and then tore one another's clothes off.

It was easy for me to justify what I was doing every time Lencie crossed my mind. Look at how much I did for her, how long I'd supported her and her kid! Look at what I'd accomplished in just a few short months! Bing had his share of affairs (though never with Rosemary Clooney). It came with the territory, I told myself. Bing wasn't perfect, and neither was I.

The next morning Nicole and I were both abashed. At 10:30 a.m. we dragged ourselves down to the lobby to catch the bus Atzel had chartered for us. We gave each other wan smiles, and she brushed her hand across my forearm in recognition of our adventuresome night, and then we rolled our luggage out to the curb and climbed onto the bus. As the other band members boarded, no one said much to either of us. Jerry paused between our two seats, looked from one to the other, and said, "That was a great show last night, guys."

"Thank you, Jerry," said Nicole.

"Yeah, thanks," I said, certain he knew about Nicole and me sleeping together, certain everyone in the band knew.

On the ride back to Seattle, I tried to sleep as much as my aching head and uneasy conscience would let me. Nicole and I kept quiet the whole ride, and when a band member—as a joke, no doubt—asked us to sing a song, we both grumbled and said absolutely not. Four hours later, outside the Amethyst, Nicole and I parted company with little more than a *See ya later*, which left me believing (and partly hoping) our fling had been just that—one night only, as they say in show business.

It wasn't, though. A week went by, long enough for me to pretend everything was normal at home and Lencie did not suspect any-thing—or at least wasn't going to voice her suspicions. But after the following Saturday night show, Nicole and I hung around the Amethyst sipping Pinot Gris, and at around 2:30 told Kyle, the bartender, we'd be glad to lock up for him if he'd let us hang out a while longer. Kyle wasn't keen on the idea, but he could see we weren't going to budge, and since he wanted to go home, he said he would lock the doors from the inside and all we needed to do was pull the front door hard so it locked when we left.

"It's a deal," I said and gave him a fist bump.

"Don't drink all my Pinot either," he said and tossed on his coat. "Also, I set the alarm, so don't try going out the back."

"So many rules," I whispered to Nicole as Kyle checked the cash register one last time.

Once he left, it was odd to be sitting in the club alone, just the two of us. The only lights were a small one over the bar, another over the stage, and the two exit signs in front and back.

"To us," Nicole said, and we clinked glasses.

"And to Bing and Rosemary," I tossed in.

We each took a sip and Nicole leaned over to kiss me.

"Well," she said.

"Well," I said back, and we both laughed. "I don't suppose you would like to sing?"

"Hmmmm," she hummed and looked at me quizzically. "Do you mean a duet?"

"No," I said. "A solo."

"Really?"

"Yes," I said. "Sing that Lauryn Hill song you did when you first came in." I remembered it as being quite lovely—and sexy.

"All right," she said and put her glass down on the bar and went up to the stage. The power to the microphone was off, but she held the mic anyway and started humming in a soft, sensuous way. The song was called "The Sweetest Thing," a hit for Lauryn Hill years ago. Nicole moved into it slowly, her voice becoming more soulful with each note. I glanced out the front window and saw a guy in a dark jacket and Seahawks cap on the sidewalk peering in. When he moved on, I looked back at Nicole. She came to the third verse and started humming again, becoming more sensuous, and when she resumed singing she'd segued effortlessly into "Killing Me Softly," the devastating Roberta Flack number. I was floored, all I could do was hang my head, and when I looked up, Nicole was smiling, knowing good and well what she was doing to me.

As she put the mic back on the stand and stepped down from the stage, I gave her a slow, lingering applause.

"Did you like it?" she asked.

"Yeah," I said, "I like it," and stood up and kissed her. I then took the bottle of wine from off the bar and led her back to Atzel's office and the leather couch he had there.

SEX WITH NICOLE BECAME part of my routine. Sometimes we'd go to her new apartment in the Cascade neighborhood, a short drive from the club. Sometimes we'd get a hotel room downtown. Sometimes we'd hook up before the show, sometimes after. The whole while, I still made sure Rory got to and from school and was fed and put to bed on time, giving Lencie plenty of time for studying.

It was at the end of May, while Atzel was still arranging the Japan tour, that he received a phone call that got everyone in the band buzzing. The call came from New Orleans, from Harry Connick Jr.'s manager. According to the manager, his man—"Mr. Connick"—had gotten hold of our CD and was blown away by it.

"I tell ya, man, I was just blown away by it," said Joey, our guitarist, doing his best Harry Connick Jr. imitation, presumably based on the singer's stint on *American Idol*. "Honest, it just *blew* me away. That's exactly what I told J-Lo and the skinny tattooed guy from Down Under, Keith something his name was, you know, married to the skinny chick from Down Under. I told 'em, I said, 'It *blew* me away.'"

It was Monday night, and we were all in the club, getting ready to rehearse.

"The gist of it," Atzel went on once the laughter settled down, "is that Harry Connick Jr. is flying up to Seattle next weekend to hear you play—and hear Bing here sing." He pointed to me. Lately he'd been calling me Bing a lot more, almost sarcastically, and I wasn't sure why.

"They're scouting us out," he added. "They might want us to open for him at the Paramount. He has a date there in September."

"How 'bout that," Joey said and gave Jerry a high five. "We've arrived."

Nicole smiled at me. It was a proud, congratulatory smile.

That evening everyone played with a little extra verve, and I went home after rehearsal feeling good. Harry Connick Jr. was coming to hear me. We were, after all, brethren in the fraternity of nightclub crooners. Who knew? Maybe he and I would become buddies, maybe he'd invite me down to New Orleans, maybe we'd do a duet together, like Bing Crosby and Frank Sinatra…*"Is that what you're sayin'? Well, did you evah! What a swell party this is!"* I could picture it clear as day.

When I got home, Rory was sick, throwing up badly. He couldn't stop and so Lencie and I called the emergency clinic. The doctor asked a few questions. When did it start? What was his temperature? Had he had any other illness recently? And so on. Then she said it was probably a stomach virus. She told us she would phone in a prescription for anti-nausea suppositories and also recommended an over-the-counter electrolyte fluid, and if these didn't work, we should bring him into the emergency room. So while Lencie kept a cool washrag on his forehead, I dashed out to the twenty-four-hour pharmacy. After the poor kid sipped some the grape-flavored fluid and his mother administered the suppository, he began to settle down and before long fell asleep. It was nearly 4:00 a.m. by the time Lencie and I got to bed.

Three hours later, I called Rory's school to let them know he'd be absent that day. I assured Lencie that I could take care of him when he woke up and let her take the car to the college, then made a pot of coffee and pondered the whole situation. I knew I couldn't keep going on like this forever. The duplicity was killing me. I wasn't cut out for leading a double life. I had to either leave Lencie or stop sleeping with Nicole—one or the other. Leaving Lencie would mean leaving Rory, though, and that was a thought I couldn't bear. Look how much the little guy needed me. And how much he meant to me. Besides, did I really want to leave Lencie? Was I in love with Nicole—as I knew I'd been, at least once upon a time, with Lencie? Was it Nicole I was attracted to or Rosemary Clooney? How delusional had I actually become in pursuing my Bing obsession? How much was I willing to sacrifice for it? What, I asked myself, would Bing do?

I knew I wasn't going to be able to sort it all out on just three hours of sleep. I suddenly felt paralyzed. I needed to get away, I told myself, to get some time to myself to sort out what I was going to do. So that afternoon I called Atzel and left a message that I had a family emergency in Shelton and wouldn't make it back for the Thursday show or maybe even the Saturday show. I knew it was a chancy thing to do to him, disappearing on him and everyone else for two shows like that, but I didn't know what else to do. I was desperate.

A short while later he called back and left me a message. "Let me know if there's anything I can do," he said neutrally, perhaps suspecting I was lying to him about the family emergency. "We'll just have to see how Nicole does on her own," he added.

The next day Rory was feeling well enough to go to school, and I arranged with the Keoghs to pick him up the following day. I also rented a Zipcar for Lencie and before she came home went to Whole Foods and bought several bags of groceries, including a bunch of ready-made meals, so the kitchen would be well stocked.

"I need to go home and talk to my uncle," I told Lencie that evening. "I should be back by Saturday."

"What about?" she asked, surprised by my sudden announcement that I was going to Shelton.

"He's making out his will"—a total lie—"and he wants to consult with me."

"It can't wait till the weekend? Can't you just call him?"

"It's kind of sensitive, I guess. I don't really know." I said this with some irritation in my voice to get her off my back. What I wanted to say was, *I need to get away so I can figure out how to end the affair I'm having with my beautiful duet partner—that is, if you want us to stay together. Maybe you'd understand if you weren't studying all the goddamn time. Maybe if you used me a little less like your nanny, you'd recognize that I have a life too and you wouldn't be so oblivious to the fact that I'm cheating on you.*

"Okay," she said finally. "I hope everything's okay. Tell Lillis and Sherrie hi for me."

IT WAS TOTAL FREEDOM to hit the road the next morning. I decided to take the scenic route and caught the ferry from the Seattle ferry terminal to Bremerton. I always loved riding the ferries, especially on a weekday morning when being on one seems like such an escape. You know you should be someplace else taking care of all your responsibilities or whatever, but instead you're standing at the deck railing, facing into the strong cold wind, and gazing up at the Olympics as the steel bow of the green-and-white behemoth plows through the entrancing waters of Puget Sound.

For the duration of the crossing, I tried not to think about either Lencie or Nicole. Instead I thought about Uncle Lillis. I felt bad about my lie to Lencie, which probably had the insinuation that he was terminally ill or something. Uncle Lillis had in fact, over Thanksgiving, indicated that he needed to revise his will. But he certainly was not dying. He wasn't even sick. He was planning, though, to retire eventually. So I began to wonder what would happen to the mill when he did. Would he put someone else in charge—certainly not Roger, the mean-spirited millwright—or would he just sell it? Uncle Lillis really was a great guy, far more like a father to me than an uncle. He had his own way of doing things, made his own decisions, and that's what I always liked about him. When a couple of guys a few years back tried to recruit him for the Tea Party chapter they were forming in Shelton, he told them he was a coffee drinker.

"That's not what it's about," one of them said, not picking up on his sarcasm. "It's about getting the goddamn government off our backs. You know better than anyone what all the government regulations do to business, Lille. It's about taking our liberty back, the way the founding fathers intended. It's about the Constitution, for christsake."

"I know what it's about," Uncle Lillis shot right back at them. "It's about a buncha old grouches trying to get out of paying their taxes. Well, I do my job and I pay my taxes, and I don't whine about it."

When he told me this story, I could hardly believe what I was hearing. Was this really my *Oorah*-shouting, NRA-dues-paying, Republican-voting uncle? Yes, it was. Because if there was one thing certain about Uncle Lillis, it was that he was his own man, and I admired that about him.

As I drove off the ferry into Bremerton, I laughed, wishing I could have been there to see the look on the faces of those Tea Party dudes. I'd left a message the night before to let Uncle Lillis and Aunt Sherrie know I was coming to Shelton, and when I reached Oak Bay I called the office at L&H to see if he would let me take him to lunch at the Pine Tree.

"Can't," he said. "We have an order to deliver by Monday. We're at full throttle."

"Put me to work," I said instantly, knowing that nothing would feel better than to throw on some work clothes and a hard hat and put in a day's work at the mill.

There was a pause at the other end, and I figured he was wondering whether I would be more help or hindrance. It had been ten months, after all, since I'd last worked at the mill.

"Okay," he said at last. "Come on by. I'm sure we can find a broom for you to push."

I knew I couldn't expect to swoop in and just climb onto the wheel loader or start scaling logs. I respected the guys at the mill too much to pull something like that. Sweeping sawdust suited me just fine.

When I walked into the front office, Carli, the office manager, was there. The place seemed awfully quiet, but only because everyone was hard at work, either out in the yard or in one of the sheds operating the saws.

"It's a big order all right," she said. "Everyone's working extra shifts. I don't know where your uncle is. You want me to call his cell?"

As she said this, Uncle Lillis charged into the front office. He clearly had a lot on his mind. "There's my favorite nephew," he bellowed. I was his only nephew, of course. "Did you hear about Jennifer?" he asked enthusiastically as we shook hands.

I hadn't, I said, and felt bad about being so out of touch with my own family. "Tell me."

"She's finishing up her master's degree at the UW in Tacoma as you know—"

"That's great," I said. I hadn't really thought much about my cousin since moving to Seattle and had forgotten all about her degree program.

"And she got a full scholarship to Stanford. To get her PhD. Can you believe it? In economics."

"That's crazy!" I said.

"We couldn't be prouder," said Uncle Lillis. "We're going to have to call her 'Doctor' from now on. Can you imagine?"

Now *there*, I thought, remembering my duets with my cousin, was someone who had their shit together. Why couldn't I be that together? I made a mental note to email her with my congratulations.

"So I bought this new side-by-side with a bucket attachment," Uncle Lillis went on, changing the subject. "It's kickass, which is why I got it. But it's also small and maneuverable. Gets into places the backhoe can't, like the planer shed. I want you to get on that thing, get a feel for it, and go through every inch of this place. We're buried in sawdust and mill ends around here. There's a mound back along the fence. Dump everything there for now. There're some overalls and gloves in the back. And don't forget your safety gear. I have to haul ass to Aberdeen to see about a trailer."

He ducked into his office, came out with his briefcase, and slapped me on the shoulder. "Now get to work," he said and was out the door.

Carli had a spreadsheet open on her computer, so she wasn't about to ask me for a song. I went to the back storage room and found the overalls and gloves, along with a pair of steel-toed work boots, a hard hat, and goggles, and went out into the yard to find the new side-by-side.

It was a sweet little ATV, and I got the hang of it right away. But contrary to what Uncle Lillis said, it didn't fit everywhere, and I ended up using a large scoop shovel and push broom in most of the sheds. Clearing out all the sawdust and mill ends took the rest of the afternoon, but I hardly thought about Lencie or Nicole, or even Bing, the whole while. I just did the job and felt good about it afterward. And that night, after a wonderful dinner of beef stroganoff and strawberry pie that Aunt Sherrie made, I slept better than I had in a good long while.

In the morning I called Lencie to make sure everything was all right, that Rory was feeling better and she was managing okay, and she said it was and thanked me for calling. We didn't have much else to say to one another after that, which felt kind of awkward, so we just hung up. Then I headed out with Uncle Lillis in his pickup truck to retrieve the trailer he'd bought the day before in Aberdeen. When I asked why he hadn't brought it back with him yesterday, he didn't answer, but instead asked me if I'd ever worked a boom and grapple.

"No," I said, answering honestly. The guys who delivered logs to the mill always unloaded their own trailers. Teamster rules. He knew that.

He then told me how for the past twenty years he'd been sitting on a two-thousand-acre parcel adjacent to Forest Service lands near the small town of Matlock and was now going to start harvesting on it, as well as on another two thousand acres he'd been able to lease on the cheap from the feds.

"Jennifer got us a grant from one of those environmental groups down in Portland that's all about selective harvesting and minimal scarification and riparian this and riparian that. It's their money that bought this trailer we're picking up. They're also going to find us buyers for the lumber we haul out of these two lots."

I was impressed. Uncle Lillis doing business with any kind of environmental group was not something I would have predicted. But then again...he was his own man. Plus, I figured my cousin Jennifer must have really worked to turn his head around on this deal.

"That's her whole thing," he said as we crossed the bridge over the Chehalis River into South Aberdeen. "Forestry economics." He glanced at me, and I just laughed.

"Word better not get out you're consorting with tree huggers," I told him.

"Or that my own daughter's one of 'em."

"Did this group help you buy that new ATV as well?"

Now he laughed. "No, no," he said. "That's just a little something I picked up for myself. The bucket makes it a business write-off. Unhitch it, though, and it's a great little vehicle for getting up to the deer camp come fall."

Just south of Aberdeen, there's a place called Cosmopolis, a company town built around the Weyerhaeuser pulp mill, which closed a number of years back. There isn't much town really, other than a few small houses and the equipment dealer where we were headed. The trailer that Uncle Lillis had bought was a twenty-three-footer, with a boom and grapple hook folded up and latched down to its front section. The dealer had to install a hitch plate in the bed of Uncle Lillis's pickup, but an hour later we were pulling the trailer off the lot.

We drove the backcountry roads most of the way to the Matlock property, where a week before, two guys from the mill, using the feller skidder that was now parked off to the side, had left a rack of logs in a landing area behind a screen of trees alongside the road. Uncle Lillis positioned the trailer into place for loading, and we donned our safety gear and got straight to work. He started off at the hydraulic controls, swinging the grapple hook about, grabbing a couple of logs, and positioning them onto the flatbed of the trailer. After he'd loaded a dozen or so of the big trees, he let me get behind the controls. I didn't have his light touch with the grapple hook, though, and nearly slammed my first log—a fir six feet in diameter—into the cab of his pickup.

"Easy there," he called out from a safe distance.

"I got it," I called back and tried again, really concentrating this time, until I was able to lay the log gently on top of the others stacked on the trailer.

It felt good to be in the woods again: the light slanting through the upper canopy, the rich scent of pitch and loam, the dense undergrowth of sword ferns, salal, ground moss, kinnikinnick, and Oregon grape. I missed it all. In the time we'd been living in Seattle, Lencie and Rory and I had gone to Discovery Park a few times. We'd strolled the well-trodden paths through the woods there, but it couldn't compare to being in the forest on the peninsula. These were real woods. Maybe it was just the knowledge of being surrounded by vast tracts of forest—and not city streets—that made the difference.

With the logs secured to the trailer, we headed back to Shelton. Pulling such a heavy load, Uncle Lillis drove the winding roads with great care. Everyone who's grown up on the peninsula has seen a log truck overturned and lying at the bottom of a gully or along an embankment after the driver took a curve too fast. So Uncle Lillis wasn't taking any chances.

As we made our way back to the mill, he explained these logs would have to be kept separate from the others. "They're certified," he said, sounding a bit snide about this fact. A few minutes later, though, taking a more serious tone, he said, "I'm going to need someone to manage this property. The deal is this grant involves a lot of monitoring. The harvest, the slash piles, everything. Jennifer needs good records so she can file her reports with the Portland people." He glanced at me to make sure I was listening, then added, "The job's yours if you want it."

I realized then that he'd been playing me this whole time. Bringing me along to pick up the trailer, going to Matlock to load the logs, having me work the boom and grapple, telling me all about Jennifer's grant...it had all been a setup. And I appreciated it, I truly did. But I was a bit stunned, too, and didn't know how to respond. I removed my cap and rubbed my brow.

"Does your head hurt?" he asked. "There's some Advil in the glove compartment."

I put my cap back on. "No, Uncle Lillis," I said. "My head's fine."

"Then what?"

I could almost feel myself tearing up, like I was on the brink of breaking down and bawling outright. He had always looked after me—the father I never had. Better than a father, really, because he didn't do what he did out of some heavy sense of parental responsibility or obligation. Rather he acted out of love, plain and simple.

"I appreciate everything you've always done for me, Uncle Lillis," I said, trying not to choke on my words. "God, I really do."

"So what's the deal?" he asked. "Is it the singing? I know your grandma would be proud of all you've done with your singing. She would be so proud."

His mentioning grandma did me in, and I let out a short gasp and quickly laughed and tried to wipe the tears from my face. "I guess that's part of it," I said and took a deep breath and looked out the passenger-side window at a marsh where two red-winged blackbirds clung to the stalk of a single cattail.

"It's more that my life is really screwed up right now," I said.

Uncle Lillis kept his eyes on the road and stayed quiet, guiding the truck slowly through the next set of curves, letting me take my time to say what I needed to say, to explain why my life was so screwed up. And that's what I did. I told him everything.

He listened, said things like "Well" or "Really," but mostly just listened. When I was finished, he let me sit there a bit while he pondered what I'd told him.

"I can't tell you what to do," he spoke up finally, "but you need to do something."

I didn't say anything, letting my silence be my consent.

"You need to do what you think's right," he went on, and after a pause added, "I can tell you this much...It's not right to keep sleeping with this Nicole and deceiving Lencie. Isn't fair to either one of them."

"I know," I said as we reached the outskirts of Shelton.

THAT EVENING I MET Stiles at the Harbor Tavern. He'd learned to moderate his gaming habit and was somewhat back to his old self, including responding to my text messages. He had a new look: he wore one of those black Norwegian seaman's caps, and his ponytail came out from under it in back. He'd also shaved off the soul patch. We got a pitcher of beer and shot a game of pool and then sat at the bar. He said he was still playing the Xbox he'd stolen from the ex's place—"Just not as much"—then remarked how the console's functionality was not up to date and he wanted to upgrade.

"I'm thinking of going back to see if the guy's got the newer version. Wanna come?"

"That's funny, Stiles," I said and refilled my glass from the pitcher. I caught him up on everything happening in Seattle, a shortened version of what I'd told my uncle a few hours earlier.

He wanted me to describe Nicole to him—"In detail," he made clear—but first we each downed a shot of Fireball whiskey.

When I was finished describing her, he said, "She sounds like the blonde chick in *The Wicker Man*. You ever seen that? I saw it the other night. It's this fucked up Brit flick from the '70s. The blonde's the innkeeper's daughter, drop-dead hot. She dances around buck naked in her bedroom singing this corny siren song, caressing all these phallic talismans she has on her dresser and windowsill, and driving the cop in the next room into a frenzy. They're all pagans on this island off of Scotland, and the cop shows up to solve a murder, and in the end they make a human sacrifice of him."

"Who's made a sacrifice?" I couldn't quite follow what he was talking about. It seemed Stiles was getting loopier every time I saw him.

"The cop, you idiot. This Nicole you're banging sounds like the blonde from this movie."

"Do you think Nicole's a pagan?" I was getting a bit drunk now.

"I didn't say that," he said. He refilled his glass from the pitcher. "But she could be. Didn't you say she was from Colombia?"

"No, I said she looked like Shakira."

"Fuck," he said, confused now as well. He took out his smartphone and started punching it with a forefinger, and an instant later declared, "Britt Ekland! That's the actress. God she was hot."

He had another shot of whiskey, yet when he offered to buy us a second pitcher, I told him I was done, I had to leave. He turned a little sullen at that and I felt bad, as if I were abandoning him. When I asked him if he'd seen the ex lately, he said no.

"But," he added, "I'm ready for him if I do."

I didn't ask him what he meant, and as I put my jacket on, he slumped over the bar. *Just don't shoot him, okay?* I wanted to say as a precaution, but I knew Stiles wasn't that crazy, not yet at least, so I told him instead to just steer clear of the guy.

"Hey," he said as I stood beside the bar and downed the rest of my beer. He looked at me a little sheepishly. "Listen, if you and Lencie break up over Britt Ekland, put a good word in for me, will ya? I might ask Lencie out."

I slapped him on the shoulder. "I don't think so," I said. The idea of him pursuing Lencie repulsed me. It wasn't just the idea of him, Stiles, being with her—gag me—but of Lencie being with anyone else other than me. I then asked him if he wanted a lift home.

He got up and said he had to use the can first and he'd meet me outside. I then left a few dollars on the bar and headed for the door.

It was a gentle spring night. There was the sour-sweet smell of wood pulp in the air—lignin and cellulose, the magical compounds in every piece of lumber ever produced. I filled my lungs with it, the smell of home, and looked up at the scattering of stars visible through the shifting clouds. My conversation with Stiles about my situation hadn't been very productive, but what did I expect? If I was counting on Stiles to be my Obi-Wan Kenobi, all the worse for me. I got a kick out of hanging out with him and that was good enough.

I stood outside the tavern waiting for him when a white pickup pulled up to the curb at a forty-five-degree angle like it might careen right into me, its high beams blinding me. I heard the truck door slam and then, "Hey asshole!"

I stepped out of the glare of the headlights and saw the ex coming toward me. "What's up," I got out before he shoved me with both hands hard against the front wall of the tavern. He was probably a head taller than me, and a lot heavier. He wasn't in his uniform either. He had a gray hoodie on underneath a canvas Carhartt vest and a camo cap on his head, and a stupid-ass goatee and mustache on his jowly face.

Bing Crosby was never a fighter—nor was I. Neither of us had the build for brawling, much less the inclination. Blood and bruises just weren't our style. In his movies, Bing would throw a punch from time to time, and as Father O'Malley in *The Bells of Saint Mary's*, he approves of fisticuffs among the inner-city ruffians at his school. But even then he's bested by Ingrid Bergman (Sister Mary Benedict), who proves to be the better cornerman. The point is, I wasn't going to fight Lencie's ex. So I tried to take Bing's tried-and-true approach—even though, admittedly, I was scared shitless of the guy—and play the mild-mannered peacemaker.

"Come on, dude," I said. "It's a big misunderstanding. Let me buy you a beer."

"Fuck that," he shouted back. He was now glaring hard at me, and I realized I wasn't just in a movie—that I was about to take a beating. "First you steal my shit. Now you try to steal my son from me. What do you even know about—"

And in the next instant he collapsed to the sidewalk, his limbs tensing and twitching, his eyes squeezing shut, and finally his whole body going limp and a low moan coming from deep inside him.

I looked over and saw Stiles standing there holding some kind of black and yellow device in his hand. It looked like a TV remote, and he was pointing it down at the ex. Then I saw the blue electric arch snapping between the electrodes and realized it was a stun gun.

"You've just been pwned, bitch," Stiles shouted down at the semi-conscious ex. "*Res judicata.*" He turned to me and said, "I got him right in the neck. He'll be down for a good ten minutes."

I didn't know what to say. It seemed to me the ex had been about to say something I might have needed to hear.

"Thanks, I guess," I said.

"You're welcome," Stiles replied, and we both stepped around the ex's lumpy body. "Remember what I said about Lencie," he said as we walked to my car.

I LEFT SHELTON THE next morning. The encounter with the ex had left me rattled. Stiles's intervention might have kept me from getting my ass kicked, yet I wished the whole scene could have turned out differently—though I wasn't sure how. Could the ex and I have talked it out somehow? Not likely. But then again, was tasing him the answer? Wouldn't the situation just escalate now? Once I passed

Olympia and had an entire inland sea between me and the incident, I stopped thinking about it, more or less. I turned my thoughts instead to Uncle Lillis's offer from the day before. After we'd gotten back to the mill and had stacked the logs in the corner of the yard designated for those trees, he said I could take a few weeks to make up my mind, and I told him I'd let him know as soon as I could. Why I didn't outright decline his offer and tell him, No, I didn't want the job. My star was rising in Seattle and I was going to ride it straight to heaven...I had no idea. Maybe I knew my star had ascended as high as it ever would. It might take me to Japan but not much further. And just maybe the thought of returning to work on the peninsula held some appeal for me. Just maybe.

As I drove I didn't weigh the pros and cons of Uncle Lillis's offer so much as try simply to talk myself into making a decision about it one way or the other. But I couldn't. I was a wuss, and thinking about what Bing would do, *WWBD*, didn't help me any. My whole act—from the baritone to the pomade—began to seem more and more like a joke. *What was I thinking?* I asked myself as I looked out the driver's side window at downtown Tacoma in the distance. *Grandma*, I thought. Was this all her fault? I pounded the steering wheel, angry at myself for even thinking such a thought. *It's my fault*, I knew. I was the joke. A total buffoon. Crooning sentimental songs from a bygone era had nothing on an honest day's work in the woods or at the mill. That's all there was to it. Bing Fucking Crosby! Who the fuck was I kidding? Maybe there was a reason he'd been forgotten—and maybe I needed to think about *that*.

Once past Tacoma, I pulled out my cell and called Lencie, just to hear her voice and tell her I would be home in about an hour. As her phone rang, I told myself I would give myself another week, that by this time next week I would make a decision and it would all be settled—one way or another—Shelton or Seattle, Lencie or Nicole, L&H or Amethyst. However, when Lencie answered, that anticipated week of deliberation instantly dissolved. I said hey and before another word could leave my mouth, she came right out and asked if I'd been sleeping with Nicole.

"Yes," I said.

I couldn't do otherwise, not after talking to Uncle Lillis, who had more integrity than anyone I knew, who made it clear that deceiving Lencie was as bad as the affair itself.

There was a long pause on the other end. The tedious stretch of freeway I was driving between Fife and Sea-Tac seemed like the perfect analogy for my life: neither here nor there, something to be gotten through, with the last-minute option of exiting at the airport and catching a flight the hell away from the entire mess.

Then I could hear Lencie crying.

"I should've known," she said through her sobs.

"I'm sorry," I uttered. It was a feeble thing to say, I knew, but it was all I had.

"I don't want you coming here," she said determinedly. I could hear her blowing her nose. "Ever."

What could I say? I couldn't argue with her. I had no defense. I couldn't even plea for understanding or forgiveness. I was a big chump, and I deserved whatever I got.

The highway topped the crest overlooking Kent Valley—Mount Rainier at one end, Southlake Mall at the other.

"Okay," was all I could say, and then nothing, silence from her end for five, ten, fifteen seconds, until finally I said, "Are you there?" and realized she'd either hung up or the call had been dropped. In either case, she wasn't going to call me back. So I hit redial, and when her voicemail picked up, I left a message saying how terribly sorry I was and that I hoped, maybe, at some point, we could talk.

I got off the highway in Tukwila and found a cheap roadside motel, bought a six-pack of tallboys at the gas station across the road, and in a total stupor drank all six on the bed in my room while flipping through channels. That's when I decided to reclaim my life, to stop kidding myself and man up, as Uncle Lillis might say. Sitting in that crummy hotel room—half-drunk, headachy, getting up to pee every half hour, debating whether to go back across the street for another six-pack or not—the property near Matlock appeared to me like a vision, my road to redemption. I would put up a wall tent, haul out a generator and Porta Potty, build a lean-to where I could set up a cookstove and portable sink. I would work sunup to sundown, being the best wood lot manager there ever was, mastering the art of selective harvesting, riparian setbacks, and whatever it took to secure certification for Jennifer and Uncle Lillis. And by these means I would earn back some measure of dignity for myself—if even just the smallest bit.

I would also ditch Bing. I had to realize Grandma, in her Bing Crosby fanaticism, was somewhat crazy. Some people might even say that as a surrogate parent she was even a bit abusive, not unlike Bing's abusive behavior toward his own boys, two of whom committed suicide as adults. I also had to realize that Bing's era—my grandma's era—was long gone and past. And good riddance. While he was a talented singer who soothed people's worried hearts during difficult times, he was also a sop, a golf-playing dandy who'd merchandized himself to absurd lengths. I could remember seeing a mousetrap in a display case in the Crosbyana Room in the Crosby Student Center at Gonzaga University with his smiling image on the box. A mousetrap! I felt like I was caught in that trap.

I woke up the next morning to knocking on the door of my room. "Housekeeping."

"I'll be out in an hour," I hollered back.

"Okay," a muffled voice said.

I lay in bed another half hour, trying to recover my resolve from the night before—*Go to woods. No more Bing.* Finally I picked up my phone and called Uncle Lillis to tell him I would accept his offer.

"But I need a couple weeks to get my life in order," I said. I didn't know what that meant exactly. I knew it involved Lencie and Rory, and Nicole I suppose, and also Atzel and Jerry and the rest of the band, but that's all I knew. Uncle Lillis offered to give me any help he could—more time, some cash, a truck, one of the guys from the mill to help with the move.

"Whatever you need," he said.

His tone made it clear he believed I would be moving back to Shelton with Lencie and Rory, and as I said goodbye, I didn't mention that I might never see them again. Then, after hanging up, it was *that* thought—how utterly heartbreaking it would be to never see them again—that totally crushed me. I started weeping. I saw Lencie's gentle face, her mild cross-eye, her soft hair. I remembered her sweet kisses, her laugh, and how genuine she was about everything she did. The thought of Rory gone from my life ravaged me as well. The night before I'd left for Shelton, he'd asked me to read to him after his bath. He was in his pajamas, his hair still wet, his skin flushed from the towel rubdown his mother had just given him, when he climbed onto my lap and snuggled against my chest. I would do anything, I realized, if it would mean having those two back in my life. I loved Bing and I loved my grandma, but I loved Lencie and Rory more.

Then the sheer lunacy of such an equation, that I could possibly weigh one against the other, disgusted me more than I could handle... and I reached for the wastebasket and retched out my guts until all I had left were dry heaves.

AFTER CHECKING OUT OF the hotel, I went to a restaurant on the Sea-Tac strip that I remembered stopping at with Lencie during one of our house-hunting trips to Seattle the year before. It was dark inside and had absurdly tall booths upholstered in padded brown vinyl. I considered ordering a Bloody Mary, knowing it's what Bing would have ordered, but I'd made up my mind I wasn't going to do what Bing would do any more. I was going to do what I would do. The problem was, once I discarded the Bing persona, I still needed to discover what it was I would do—as me, that is. Which essentially meant figuring out who the hell *I* was. So to start, I ordered a turkey club and chocolate milk-shake, both of which sounded really good to me in my hungover state.

When the waitress, a woman in her forties with full-sleeve tattoos on both arms, brought my shake, she looked me over and said, "Aren't you the singer I saw a couple of weeks ago? The guy who sounds like what's-his-name?"

I had my lips around the straw of my milkshake, yet the shake was so thick I couldn't get any into my mouth. "I could be," I said, giving up on the straw. "Which guy do you mean?"

"I don't know," she said. Her voice was light, with a buoyancy to it, though the rest of her was heavyset—her arms, chest, waist. "I went with my boyfriend. A club downtown."

"That was probably me," I said finally, giving in, feeling a touch of nausea return. Then I sat up, reached for her hand and started crooning. *"Would you like to swing on a star / Carry moonbeams home in a jar."*

"That's it," she said as I released her hand. "Who is that?"

"Bing Crosby."

"That's right. I remember my boyfriend telling me that. I enjoyed your show."

"Thank you."

She smiled sympathetically and asked, "You want me to bring you some Alka-Seltzer? You look kind of pale."

After the milkshake, Alka-Seltzer, and club sandwich, I began to feel better. I thanked the waitress, left a ten-dollar tip, and drove straight to the Amethyst Club.

Atzel was in his office. He looked different. He was clean-shaven and wearing a light-blue cardigan. I hardly recognized him. It was like he'd transformed from General Zod to Mister Rogers. Yet his manner hadn't changed. While typically the model of poise and composure, he'd always had a steely side to him, and right now it was coming through in the cold way he greeted me. He sat behind his desk and gave me a cutting glance that stopped me in the doorway. Maybe he was sore that I'd bailed on the Thursday and Saturday performances, which no doubt left him in a lurch and probably cost him a few bucks as well. I stood there awkwardly, said I was sorry about last week, and asked him how everything was going.

"We'll see," he answered. "How's everything back at the family farm?"

"It's a mill," I corrected him. "My family owns a lumber mill." I knew it didn't make a scrap of difference to him, and so I asked, "Are we rehearsing tonight?"

"Tonight," he said and typed something into his laptop while I stood there wondering if I should just turn and walk out, just not tell him I wouldn't be at tonight's rehearsal, that I was quitting the band, leaving Seattle, and moving back to Shelton to work at my family's goddamn *lumber mill*. But before I could do anything of the sort, he stopped typing, folded the screen down, and crossed his hands on top of his computer.

"Bad news," he said. "I spoke yesterday to Connick Jr.'s manager's associate assistant secretary, or some such butt-kisser, and they're opening with someone else, some nineteen-year-old guy from Moose Cock, Canada, or some such place. 'He's a cross between Pavarotti and Mel Tormé' is how this lady put it. Whatever the fuck that means."

I wasn't surprised. I never did like Harry Connick Jr. Too full of himself. Thinking he was some kind of national treasure. When I'd mentioned him to Stiles in the Harbor Tavern, Stiles said Harry Connick Sr. had been a hotshot prosecutor in New Orleans, also really full of himself.

"What about Japan?" I asked.

"I'm still working on it," Atzel said. "They're still dealing with all that tsunami shit and radiation and whatnot. It's hard to get people to respond. So don't rush out to learn any more Japanese."

In all the time I'd worked with Atzel—nearly a year at this point—I'd never heard him curse so freely or speak so cynically. Between his weird new look and this crude manner, I didn't know what to make of him. There was no way I could stand there and announce that I was quitting the act, effective immediately. I'd email him the news after I left.

"So I've been thinking," he went on, changing the topic. "Nicole did a great job when you weren't here. I'm going to give her a few solo numbers. Maybe have her open the second set." He looked at me in a way that said an executive decision had been made, end of discussion.

Yet, rather than protest, I was happy to go with this plan. It would make my departure that much easier. "That's a great idea," I replied. I now had my pretext for breaking our contract, which Atzel had failed to modify when he signed Nicole. "She deserves it," I said.

"Good," was all he said. He stood up and took his leather jacket off the coatrack in the corner. "I have to get somewhere. So you'll excuse me."

"Right," I said. "No problem."

I backed out of his office and he followed me to the bar. He told Kyle, who was polishing bottles, that he'd be back after a few hours and headed out the front door. I watched as he beeped his Audi, parked at the curb, and then got in and pulled out. I turned to Kyle and said, "I like Atzel's new look."

Like any good bartender, Kyle knew when to keep his mouth shut. He nodded and went about his business polishing bottles.

"Later," I said and left the club.

As I walked to my car, I started wondering…Why was Atzel giving Nicole such a big slice of the act? Had she really been that good singing solo, or had he come to the conclusion that my act was played out? This was, after all, the age of tenors and boy band altos. After the initial curiosity, baritones tended to creep people out. In fact, based on some of the comments on my Facebook page, Bing himself sometimes creeped people out.

I crossed the Aurora Bridge and made my way north to Nicole's newer, bigger apartment near Northgate, about twenty minutes from downtown and not too far from my own house—or what used to be my house until Lencie told me never to come back. I wanted to tell Nicole what Atzel had told me about giving her a steady solo portion of the act and then inform her I was quitting the act and leaving Seattle. If she wasn't home, I would just wait for her. Yet as I pulled into the parking lot of Nicole's apartment building, the first thing I saw was Atzel's Audi parked next to her Honda. As I looked at their two cars side by side, practically like catching them in bed together, it dawned on me that in changing his appearance, Atzel might very well be trying to Bingify himself. Of course, I couldn't say for sure whether they were sleeping with one another. But it didn't matter. It was clear to me that she was in it for her career, and that she and Atzel had something going on that didn't involve me.

So be it, I thought. Nicole and I were through. Atzel and I were through. Bing and I were through. The various elements of my so-called singing career were falling like dominoes. It was all very liberating. I pulled out of the parking lot, realizing that I was now free to haul myself back to Shelton.

But first I had to pick up a few things at the house and leave Lencie a note and perhaps write her a check so she wouldn't have to worry about money—and just pray that I could keep it together when I saw Rory's toys and socks strewn about the living room and walked into the bedroom Lencie and I had once shared.

SINCE IT WAS MONDAY, I knew Rory would be in pre-K and Lencie at the college. I let myself into the house and found it a mess. In taking on full childcare duties since the previous Friday, on top of her studying, Lencie hadn't had time to do dishes or fold laundry or tidy up—all the stuff I usually did—which made me feel terrible. I thought about cleaning up the house but decided that wouldn't be right. She might see it as a cheap ploy to try to get back into her good graces. Then I imagined her and Rory together in the messy house and him asking her where I was and when I was coming back, and Lencie not knowing how to answer and telling him they'd talk about it later, and then going to our bedroom and crying.

That's when I decided to walk over to Rory's school. It was the kind of move that, taking into account any number of factors, could get me into trouble. It hadn't been twenty-four hours since Lencie told me not to come back, however, so I figured the parental order was not in full effect yet. I also told myself I wanted to make sure he was all right and that someone was going to be there to pick him up and take him home. I was simply being a responsible adult.

The walk to and from Rory's school each weekday had become one of my favorite things. It was therapeutic, filling me with a sense of well-being and community, the kind of feeling I got from singing to people, from my grandma to the audiences at the Amethyst Club—and perhaps even more so. When I reached the school, I realized I was early. There was another forty-five minutes before the final bell, so I walked several blocks to the nearby café and got a latte to go. Then I hung about the front of the school drinking my coffee as the other parents began to arrive. I knew most of them by sight, a few by name, and we shared some small talk, as we usually did. It was clear to them, just as it was clear to me, that I belonged there.

The bell rang and kids poured out the door, and as soon as Rory saw me he rushed up to me and hugged my legs. I lifted him into my arms and said I missed him, and as I set him back down, I saw Lencie walking toward us. I knew she wouldn't want to make a scene, but nonetheless, the look she gave me was punishing and severe. I'd never seen her face so taut, as if she were clenching her jaw, or her eyes so unblinking. This was anger of another magnitude.

"Come on, Rory," she said, and as I put him down, she snatched his hand.

I still held his book bag. "Can I walk with you?" I asked as she led him down the sidewalk.

"Do whatever you want. Isn't that your MO?"

Rory glanced back at me, picking up on the tension between us. In all our time together, Lencie and I had had so few arguments, and never once did we have one in front of Rory.

To Lencie, I said, "I quit the club."

She just kept walking.

We must have looked like any perfectly normal young family, mom and dad walking their child home from school. Rory started telling me about what he and Stephen and Jared had been up to lately. It involved Hot Wheels, but otherwise I didn't hear him. My attention was on Lencie.

She then told him to be quiet. "Mommy's talking to Bing Crosby," she said.

We kept walking, though neither of us said anything more. I could see the tattoo on the underside of her right forearm—a toothbrush with a swirly dab of toothpaste on the bristles. Right after Christmas she'd mentioned wanting to get one, so on her birthday in March, I took her to a tattoo parlor in the U District and treated her to the toothbrush and toothpaste tattoo. On the same visit to the tattoo parlor, I thought about getting one of Bing in his hat, smoking his pipe. But I didn't, not wanting to steal attention from Lencie's birthday tattoo—and now I was glad for that decision.

"What else," she said to me.

"The other thing too," I said. "It's over."

Rory tugged at my hand. "What's over?" he wanted to know.

"That's between your mommy and me," I said. His head swiveled toward her as he tried to puzzle out what was going on.

"Uncle Lillis offered me a job," I went on. "I told him I'd take it."

This seemed to get Lencie's attention. She looked at me. Her cross-eye was effectively gone—just a trace, barely noticeable, yet still adorable, still part of the girl I loved. She kept looking at me, and she could see I was serious.

When we reached the house, I followed her and Rory inside without either of us saying anything. We ate graham crackers and Nutella at the kitchen table, and when Rory asked for some milk, Lencie asked me if I wanted some too and poured us each a glass. Then I said I should probably get going—to where, I didn't know, probably a cheap motel on Aurora—and she said okay.

The next night, though, after exchanging text messages in the morning, I was back at the house for dinner. Then afterward, after watching some TV with Rory and putting him to bed, Lencie and I sat on the couch and talked. We talked some about Nicole and the Amethyst, but not a whole lot. I made clear that both were done, and she seemed to accept that. So instead we talked about us. We considered where we—she and I—might possibly go from here if we were to stay together. I told her I loved her, and Rory of course, and she quietly said, "Me too." We agreed, however, that it wouldn't be easy. She said I would need to give her a lot of space to get over the hurt I'd inflicted on her. To begin with, she wanted at least a few more days, or maybe a week, before I came back to the house. I said I understood. We then agreed that my taking the job with Uncle Lillis was a good idea, but that I should ask if I could have a few months before starting. That would give her time to finish her program and take the state boards. She said she'd been in contact recently with a dental office in Olympia that was interested in hiring her. This came as news to me, but I didn't say anything. She had always said she wanted eventually to move back to Shelton, so it wasn't that big of a surprise really. Finally we agreed to use the remainder of my savings to get us through the next several months, and that I might even get a job at Home Depot or Lowe's—and then the three of us would pack up and leave Seattle.

"And you can still sing," she said and looked sympathetically at me. "Rory and I love your singing."

I just shrugged. At that moment, the thought of singing, even at home to my own loved ones, turned me off. "We'll see," I said.

Then Lencie and I kissed, tentatively, for the first time since Friday morning. As we sat on the couch, both dazed by everything but overall feeling good about our talk and our plans, I began to recognize how big the changes before us were. They were bigger even than our decision to move to Seattle in the first place.

DE-BINGING MYSELF WAS NOT easy. I went cold turkey for the three months before we returned to Shelton. I didn't listen to Bing, and I didn't sing Bing. When Rory asked me for a song, I gently told him I wasn't in the mood and offered to read to him instead. I stopped having my hair trimmed every other week and threw out the hair gel, and sometimes I went days on end without shaving. I also hauled a lot of the clothes I wore for my act, which now seemed more like a costume, down to the Goodwill. And when I wasn't working at Home Depot, having picked up a part-time job there, I threw myself into household chores with renewed vigor. I made beds, folded laundry, and mopped the kitchen floor once a week. I also cooked as never before. Lencie knew I was making up for my transgressions, but she was grateful just the same.

"What's in this chicken sauce?" she asked one evening as we ate a new recipe I was trying out.

"Tandoori spice, plain Greek yogurt, and a few other things," I said. "Do you like it?"

"It's delicious. Thank you, Chris."

"Yes, thank you, Chris," Rory chimed in.

Although Rory didn't know what had gone on between his mother and me, it was clear he sensed that something significant and possibly scary had transpired—and that things were okay now. On his birthday, a few weeks before we were to move, I made him a triple-layer chocolate cake, and we had a few of his school friends and their parents over for a small birthday party.

It was hard in some ways to leave Seattle, our little house, our cozy neighborhood, our routines. But we were also glad to be going home, as Lencie and I kept reminding ourselves. Only when we were actually back in Shelton, settling into a large bungalow house that rented for half of what the Seattle house had, did we finally breathe a giant sigh of relief over everything we'd been through while away. That's also when it occurred to me how much I'd been white-knuckling it in denying myself Bing for those final months in Seattle. So to ease the pressure, I started listening to him on my iPod while unpacking boxes in our new house. I also caught myself unconsciously singing scat under my breath, and that's when, realizing I was slipping, I decided to seek professional help.

Obsessions, it turns out, can be tricky things. Anyone who's ever had one knows what I'm talking about. When the obsession becomes out of control, like a runaway log truck that's lost its jake brake, is when the real trouble starts—and by definition an obsession is always out of control. That's what it means to have OCD, according to Dr. Ivanovic, the psychiatrist I began to see.

"It's like a musical scale," he said, using the analogy for my benefit. "Just as there's often a fine line between one note and another, there's often a fine line between enthusiasm and obsession, obsession and compulsion. It's all about the degree to which you're out of control."

Dr. Ivanovic put me on Anafranil, a kind of antidepressant specially designed to treat an obsessive-compulsive disorder—which he diagnosed me as having after a couple of sessions.

"A Bing disorder?" I asked facetiously.

"The object of the obsession is essentially irrelevant," he replied in his Serbian accent. He was tall and lanky and wore colorful ties designed by his abstract artist wife. They lived in Olympia, and he worked two days a week at the Mason County Behavioral Health Center in Shelton, where I would see him. "If the obsession interferes with your life, then it's a disorder. It's quite simple."

I've been taking the Anafranil since, and I've gotten better. The good doctor also had me do some cognitive behavioral therapy, beginning with writing down all my Bing-related behaviors—a list that, when completed, I found rather disturbing. We also talked about my grandmother. Before getting all this care, I could hardly go an hour without singing a Bing number in my head, but in time, with the medicine and the therapy, I could go a whole day, then a weekend, and then an entire week. Eventually—and quite miraculously, to my thinking—I started to lose interest in Bing altogether.

Which gave Lencie increased hope that we might have a real chance. She and Rory, after all, were the reason I went to Dr. Ivanovic in the first place. Once back in Shelton, I didn't want to risk losing them as I almost had in Seattle. Certainly not on account of some asinine obsession over a long-dead crooner that my crazy dead grandma had instilled in me. I needed to change for good, I realized. I needed to be Bing-free.

Lencie and I are now planning to get married. She loves being a dental hygienist, and my own teeth have never been cleaner. A couple of weeks ago, she told me that there's a new bachelor's degree in dental hygiene at Pierce College in Tacoma, indicating she might be interested in applying to it. She thinks she could commute there via the Tacoma Narrows Bridge without it being too hard. I told her that if that's what she wanted, we would make it work. Of course, it really helps to have her parents and my uncle and aunt to fill in now and then with childcare for Rory.

The ex, thank God, transferred to the state prison in Monroe and is now living over there. Lencie told me she'd heard through the grapevine that he's been seeing a woman there and that she's pregnant.

"How wonderful for them," I said, unable to check my sarcasm. I was just glad he was out of our lives, including Rory's. After the episode in front of the tavern, when he was zapped with 900,000 volts, the ex totally abandoned his efforts—pretty weak to begin with—at having any contact with his son. Thank you, Stiles.

As for me, I'm working for L&H Precision Lumber and wouldn't have it any other way. Maybe someday when Uncle Lillis retires, I'll take over the mill from him. It could happen. The grant for harvesting the lot near Matlock has another two years to go, and Uncle Lillis and Jennifer couldn't be happier with how I'm managing the property. I kid my uncle and cousin that I've become a regular silviculturist. When I'm on the job, I'm either in the woods or at the mill—two of my favorite places—and making solid union wages.

This past year I joined a group of carolers Aunt Sherrie organized to go from business to business in downtown Shelton on the Saturday before Christmas. We sang "White Christmas" and "Silent Night," of course, and the next time I saw Dr. Ivanovic, I asked him whether this was some kind of relapse on my part. He just laughed and said my obsession, in his estimation, wasn't an addiction. Total abstinence wasn't necessary, he told me. So it was fine if I wanted to sing now and then.

"Even Bing Crosby songs?" I asked him.

"Even Bing Crosby songs," he answered, and added, "In moderation."

So once a month now I go to senior centers and retirement homes across the Olympic Peninsula—from Shelton to Port Angeles to Aberdeen—and entertain the oldsters. They remind me of my grandma. They're tickled to hear me sing Bing, and we have a good time, and then I go home.

Books:

Morgan, Murray. *The Last Wilderness*. pp. 159 © 1976. Reprinted with permission of the University of Washington Press.

Steinbeck, John. *The Grapes of Wrath*. © 1939. Penguin Books. Reprinted with permission of the publisher.

Photos:

"Lighthouse," John Loo, 2013. Creative Commons License 2.0 (CC BY 2.0).

"Olympic Mountains 3," Ryan Quick, 2013. Creative Commons License 2.0 (CC BY 2.0).

"Ancient Groves," Alan Sandercock, 2017. Creative Commons Licence 2.0 (CC BY 2.0).

"Peter Donahue" © 2017 Craig Howard.

All other images are used under public domain.

Acknowledgments

Residencies at the University of Washington's Olympic Natural Resources Center in Forks, Washington, and the Icicle Creek Center for the Arts in Leavenworth, Washington, gave me valuable research and writing time. I also received help on this project from the Friends of Fort Worden, the Jefferson County Historical Society, and the Artists Trust's EDGE Professional Development Program, all in Port Townsend, Washington. The working manuscript benefited immensely from critical and editorial feedback from Alyssa Barrett of Third Draft Creative, poet and friend Ann Douglas, and Elizabeth Wales of Wales Literary Agency. I am forever indebted to the incredibly talented and hardworking team at Ooligan Press, including the irrepressible Julie Swearingen (initial Project Team Leader), structure and consistency guru Whitney Edmunds (Developmental Editing), eagle-eyed and judicious Lisa Hein (Line Editing), biblio-aesthetician Andrea McDonald (Design), and, of course, Michele Ford (main Project Team Leader), whose intelligence, steadfastness, and all-around book savvy saw this project through. Finally, I owe everything to my dear wife, Susan, whose unflagging faith and encouragement made this whole undertaking possible.

PETER DONAHUE IS THE author of the novels *Clara and Merritt* and *Madison House*, winner of the 2005 Langum Prize for American Historical Fiction, and the short story collection *The Cornelius Arms*. He is co-editor of the 2016 edition of the memoir *Seven Years on the Pacific Slope* and the anthologies *Reading Seattle* and *Reading Portland*. His Retrospective Review column on Northwest literature has appeared in *Columbia: The Magazine of Northwest History* since 2005. He teaches at Wenatchee Valley College at Omak and lives in Winthrop, Washington.

Ooligan Press

Ooligan Press is a student-run publishing house rooted in the rich literary culture of the Pacific Northwest. Founded in 2001 as part of Portland State University's Department of English, Ooligan is dedicated to the art and craft of publishing. Students pursuing master's degrees in book publishing staff the press in an apprenticeship program under the guidance of a core faculty of publishing professionals.

Project Managers:
Julie Swearingen
Michele Ford

Project Team:
Alison Cantrell
Emily Frantz
Marina Garcia
Lisa Hein
Des Hewson
Sydney Kiest
Jenny Kimura
Rachel Lulich
Karissa Mathae
Amanda Matteo
Meagan Nolan
Liz Pilcher
Peter Sanchez
Stephanie Sandmeyer
Alyssa Schaffer
Jenna Whitney
Desiree Wilson
Allyson Yenerall
Hanna Ziegler

Acquisitions:
Maeko Bradshaw
Vi La Bianca

Editorial:
J. Whitney Edmunds
Lisa Hein
Kaitlin Barnes
Alison Cantrell
Mackenzie Deater
Grace Evans
Michele Ford
Marina Garcia
Emily HagenBurger
Des Hewson
Jenny Kimura
Hilary Louth
Rachel Lulich
Karissa Mathae
Gloria Mulvihill
Scott MacDonald
Amanda Matteo
Stephanie Sandmeyer
Alyssa Schaffer
Thomas Spölhof
Julie Swearingen
Allyson Yenerall
Hanna Ziegler

Design:
Andrea McDonald
Michele Ford

Digital:
Stephanie Argy

Marketing:
Jordana Beh
Morgan Nicholson

Social Media:
Katie Fairchild